THE NEW EARTH vs. THE NEW WORLD ORDER

A MULTIDIMENSIONAL SPIRITUAL SAGA

Apocalyptic Events Series, Books 2-5

BRANDON LeMar BASS

BLB Productions
An imprint of DoubleB Publishing, LLC
Springfield, Massachusetts, USA

Library of Congress Cataloging-in-Publication Data
Bass, Brandon LeMar, author.
The New Earth vs. The New World Order: *A Multidimensional Spiritual Saga* Books 2-5 of the Apocalyptic Events Series (Four Books in One) / Brandon LeMar Bass
Includes Index.
LCCN: 2025916454
ISBN: 979-8-9864444-5-1 (Hardcover) 979-8-9864444-6-8 (Paperback) 979-8-9864444-7-5 (eBook/Digital)

Website: https://linktr.ee/smoothdoubleb

MESSAGE FROM SOURCE

"Everyone has a unique journey and path to follow. One person's path will always be different from the rest. That is why not everyone is the same. While we all come from the same Source, we are not identical. Some aspects are more significant than others. For instance, someone who came from Source's heart will have a much greater impact compared to someone who came from Source's toe. We all possess different gifts, skills, and talents that we can tap into. It is up to you to be brave and creative enough to fully embrace your talents.

Do not let anyone tell you that you cannot try different things. Those who want to limit you will encourage you to focus on just one or two things — this can even come from those closest to you. You must say "No" to limitations and allow yourself to embrace all parts of yourself.

How can you love someone else if you do not love yourself? How can you pour into others' cups when yours is empty? Fully love yourself for who you are and what you are. Only you can decide who you are when you tap into your Akashic records, remember your past lives, and understand your soul contract. If you know you are meant to do something but have not seen the results yet, keep going. Your time will come.

This journey is about fulfilling your soul's mission and purpose for choosing to be here. There was a reason you came to Earth at this moment for this unique experience. Keep your emotions in check and do not let jealousy cloud your energy. Embrace your journey, reconnect with your True Self, be authentic, and appreciate every moment. Pass the finish line and rise above the process of death.

Remember: do or do not, there is no try. Follow your soul's call and your intuition. Do not look back and ask, "What if I had done this or that?" That will only cause you to repeat this human experience. Be proud of what you have accomplished with the resources available to you. Know that you have done your best.

People often say life is too short, so why not align your actions with your words? You are always protected, guided, and exactly where you need to be. Do not doubt me, but most importantly, never doubt yourself."

- Source

DEDICATION AND SPECIAL THANKS

I want to express my deepest gratitude to everyone who helped bring this book to life.

Thank you to the Most High for providing me with the strength to make this a reality.

Thank you to my True Self for the guidance through deep visualization that led to this creation.

Thank you to my intuition for always steering me in the right direction.

Thank you to my spirit guides for offering innovative ideas and insights throughout this journey.

Thank you to my spiritual team and protective forces for safeguarding this project and preventing energy vampires from interfering.

Thank you to my supporters. I am profoundly grateful for your belief and encouragement.

Thank you to the reader who is reading these words, and to the listener hearing them—your presence is deeply appreciated.

Thank you to my soul family and soul tribe for your unwavering support.

I want to thank myself for taking action to achieve this goal.

Thank you to everyone who offered guidance in publishing this book.

Thank you to all the companies, narrators, designers, artists, and editors who played a part in bringing this project to life.

INTRODUCTION

The battle for the soul of humanity is raging across dimensions, timelines, and unseen realms. As the old world collapses under the weight of illusion, control, and corruption, a powerful new consciousness rises to challenge the shadows.

In this sweeping volume, Books Two through Five of the *Apocalyptic Events* series, Brandon LeMar Bass weaves a multidimensional saga of spiritual awakening, inner alchemy, and cosmic resistance. Through a tapestry of interconnected storylines and diverse characters, this work explores the soul's journey through the death of old paradigms and the birth of the New Earth.

From ancient prophecies and soul contracts to futuristic dystopias and cyber-grids, warriors, mystics, rebels, and chosen ones face reality-bending trials that mirror our collective awakening. These stories move between virtual mind traps, divine downloads, galactic soul missions, and sacred unions, revealing the hidden war for humanity's future—and the internal transformation required to survive it.

With each chapter, the veil thins. Through escape rooms of consciousness, battles with dark entities, and revelations of esoteric knowledge, the reader is pulled deeper into a living parable about ascension, sovereignty, and the frequency of truth.

This isn't just a book, it's a coded transmission for the awakened and the awakening. A survival manual for the soul. A call to rise above fear, transmute darkness, and step fully into your purpose.

Will you cling to the fading illusions of the old world? Or will you choose to awaken, align, and become a builder of the New Earth? The choice is yours, but the time is now.

Contents

BOOK

02

Chapter One

HOW TO OVERCOME APOCALYPTIC EVENTS PT. 2

Well, well, well—welcome back to Brandon's latest book, *The New Earth vs. The New World Order*. If you have not read his previous book, *How to Overcome Apocalyptic Events*, I highly recommend giving it a read. It will provide you with a broader understanding of what unfolds in this book. If you have already read it, then you are in for a treat!

To start this first chapter, I will briefly summarize what happened in the previous book, focusing on the key moments from the concluding chapter. I will not go over everything, but I will highlight the most notable events to give you the context you need.

There were nine episodes in the first season, and it turned out to be a complete disaster. Each day brought a new challenge for the cast members. Indigo's fellow castmates—Apollo, Aleemic, Joey, Indiniya, Bastet, and Aqua—each contributed something unique in their own way. However, despite their efforts, none of them made it out alive. In the end, Indigo Bass was the sole survivor, with all his fellow cast members gone.

After eliminating all the casting directors from season one, Indigo fully unlocked his superpowers. Following the **177,009** deaths in the first book, Brandon was able to adopt Indigo. Just to clarify, Brandon Bass and Smooth Doubleb are two different characters. Brandon LeMar Bass is the author (that's me). I know this might be a bit confusing right now, but if you read the last chapter of the first book, you will understand why I had to explain it again. Now, let us dive in and explore what happened after the cliffhanger from the first book.

As the helicopter spiraled out of control, there was not much Brandon and Indigo could do. Indigo's powers were not as strong as they once were, thanks to Smooth Doubleb taking control of the helicopter. How did Smooth manage to take control?

After Indigo managed to return to Studio 13, Smooth and his casting directors threw a massive party to celebrate the success of season one. Studio 13, where the previous cast members had been held captive, did not initially feel like a prison, but as time passed, it became clear that they were trapped.

Remember, Smooth had already taken Brandon upstairs, but before Indigo could regain his strength, Smooth anticipated their move and preemptively seized control of the helicopter. He planted a tracking device inside, and not only did he control its flight path, but he also created a force field that suppressed Indigo's powers within and around the helicopter.

While Smooth had superpowers, he mostly relied on technology to outsmart them. He knew they wanted to escape Studio 13, so he was prepared for them to use the helicopter. As a reminder, Smooth Doubleb is always one step ahead, covering his tracks and staying right behind them.

As the helicopter plummeted, Brandon told Indigo to sit down and buckle up. They could have jumped out, but with the force field in place, it would have been pointless. Even though they did not know the full extent of the force field's effect on the helicopter, staying inside was safer, especially since they did not have parachutes.

Fortunately, the helicopter was over a gust of water, so Brandon and Indigo braced for impact. Just as the helicopter was about to crash into the ocean, it was equipped with advanced technology that automatically converted it into a hovercraft upon touching the water. Smooth's force field powers also ensured that the helicopter barely skimmed the surface.

The craft took on a dome-like shape, preventing them from either escaping or dying on impact.

They were stuck, unable to flee, because Smooth had full control of their helicopter. There are reasons behind this, but I will leave it up to you to speculate and produce your theories.

Just as they were about to unbuckle their seatbelts, they felt the helicopter shift. Indigo turned to Brandon and asked, "What could that be?" There was a small opening at the top of the helicopter that allowed them to see above. As they looked up, they saw a powerful, agile aircraft with an anchor, hovering gracefully in the sky. Its sleek, high-tech design made it both dynamic and versatile in its movements. The anchor swooped down, scooped up the helicopter, and drifted off into the sunset. At the helm of the aircraft was none other than Smooth Doubleb.

Indigo and Brandon began screaming, calling out for help. They shouted, "Help us!" and "We need help!" Little did they know, Smooth had control over the helicopter and could hear everything they said. They were unaware that their cries for help were being heard. Trapped in the middle of the ocean with no one around, no one could come to their rescue. This is why, at the end of the first book, Smooth posted the chilling quote: "This game isn't over. It'll haunt you forever!" As the helicopter rose higher, Smooth knew he still had a few tricks up his sleeve.

Smooth Doubleb was relaxing in his aircraft, enjoying his favorite podcast, 'Chilling With DoubleB.' If you are not familiar, Smooth Doubleb and Brandon Bass co-created a virtual reality escape room experience together. Brandon thought it would make for a cool show and wanted it to be an immersive experience. On the other hand, Smooth was all about adding drama and chaos to the storyline. You cannot deny it, the guy's formula worked, as the show received great ratings.

Like everything in life, there is a balance and polarity. Brandon leaned toward love and light, while Smooth had a more savage side. That is why they are back at it again. Brandon had control over the first book, but if you recall, by the end of book one, Smooth took control of the narrative. This gave him more power over Brandon. Then, Smooth handed the storyline off to me—Brandon LeMar Bass—knowing I would not get tangled in this mess. I am the one telling the story of what happened, but as he passes the storyline to me, I am becoming a character and more involved in the story. First-person storytelling is becoming third-person storytelling.

As the aircraft cruised, Smooth anchored the helicopter into the massive vessel. Smooth's aircraft was enormous—like a combination of a Lockheed C-5 Galaxy, Boeing C-17 Globemaster III, and Lockheed C-130 Hercules. It housed a military air base, a hovercraft, a private jet, and more. Smooth brought the helicopter inside the base station, where he had workers on hand to operate and conduct his plan.

Some of the workers were human, but most were robots. Smooth knew that robots were more efficient and easier to control, so he relied on them for the heavy lifting. He kept a few human workers around, though—mostly to maintain a rehabilitative, humanizing environment for his captives. Some of these workers were only there for the money, and Smooth knew exactly how to use them.

Indigo and Brandon were flustered, unwilling to fall into a trap they were hesitant to walk into. They needed to produce a plan to escape. Surprisingly, Smooth gave them the freedom to discuss their options and put a plan into action. Indigo produced an idea that might work and shared it with Brandon. He asked, "Do you trust me?" To which Brandon replied, "Of course."

Indigo pretended to have trouble breathing, causing Brandon to panic. "He can't breathe!" Brandon shouted. "He needs some water!" Only Smooth knew about their plan. A few human workers rushed to check on Indigo and brought him some water. What they did not realize was that Indigo had convinced Smooth's team to bring the water for a reason.

As soon as they opened the helicopter door, Indigo bolted to make his move and attack. Despite his powers being weakened, he was still stronger than regular humans. He quickly opened the door for Brandon, who jumped out to join him. In a frantic, they forgot they were still inside Smooth's massive aircraft, within his base station.

Smooth had allowed this to happen, orchestrating the whole thing to put his human workers in their place. He intended to punish them for aiding the hostages, teaching them a lesson in obedience.

While Brandon and Indigo were focused on attacking the human employees, Smooth retreated inside his jet. With his robots and the force field on the aircraft, Smooth was far more powerful than Indigo. He used a crane from his jet to capture both. Smooth then ordered his AI workers to subdue Indigo and Brandon, beating them unconsciously.

The AI workers injected them with a dosage of NullaSerum, a potent formula designed to diminish or neutralize a superhero's powers. The serum temporarily or permanently 'nullifies' their abilities, depending on the dosage and circumstances. Meanwhile, Smooth continued listening to his favorite podcast, with his AI-operated jet under his control.

Outsmarting AI was already an arduous task, but trying to fight them was a challenge that Brandon and Indigo were unprepared for.

Smooth brought some of his AI workers aboard, allowing the others to remain on his aircraft. He strapped asphyxiation masks onto Brandon and Indigo, cutting off their air supply. Taking them hostage, everything was going according to plan.

Smooth was taking them to a unique off-grid location. As they arrived, he deactivated the force field surrounding the site, allowing entry. Once they landed, the robots removed Brandon and Indigo from the jet and shackled them in chains. Brandon was unconscious, while Indigo was dazed, though still somewhat aware.

Indigo's eyes fluttered open, and he glanced around, recognizing the surroundings. The place seemed oddly familiar, but the chaos made it difficult for him to gather his thoughts. Then, he heard a soft voice and saw a blurry figure approaching him. Unable to make out who it was, he strained to focus. As the figure drew closer, it whispered in his ear. Even with the mask on, Indigo instantly recognized the voice—it was Aleemic.

Aleemic was a character from the first book, *How to Overcome Apocalyptic Events*, and he owned an off-grid private island. It was the same island he had described in detail to the group when they attempted to escape, though that plan never came to fruition due to the apocalyptic events happening at the time.

Aleemic reminded Indigo that he knew the island's every detail, including how to escape it—and that Smooth had stolen it from him. As soon as Indigo recognized Aleemic's voice, he reached out with his fingertips, but it was too late. Aleemic vanished, carried away by the wind, like a fleeting breeze. From that moment, Indigo lost consciousness.

Smooth had stolen Aleemic's inheritance, including his private island. Aleemic, a unique character, had relied on his investments and his inheritance, which was meant to be passed down to his family. However, after Aleemic's death within the system, Smooth forged his signature on the will and submitted it on behalf of the family. The family could not contest it, as the world itself had blurred between fiction and reality. It felt as though the multiverse was collapsing. What was happening inside the escape room was simultaneously unfolding in the real world, and that is why the show had gained such massive success.

The show was receiving mainstream attention, and people began to realize that both Smooth and Brandon were psychics. The only place people could survive was within the force field surrounding the studio. Smooth had the power to control this force field, allowing only selected individuals to remain inside it for safety. For everyone else, survival became impossible—they were merely collateral damage.

Brandon was unaware of the extent of Smooth's power, especially over the force field. Once the apocalyptic events ended, Smooth released his control over the field. Meanwhile, Indigo and Brandon were desperately trying to escape this dimension, which no longer served them. In the end, Smooth trapped all the contestants, and Aleemic's possessions were transferred to him.

Smooth Doubleb led them into an underground chamber meant for torture. The room was dark, sinister, and oppressive. The air was thick with a musty, damp odor, and the walls were partially covered in dried blood, cold and rough to the touch, intensifying the grim atmosphere. Faint torches flickered on the walls, casting dim, dancing shadows that skittered across the uneven, damp stone floor.

The space felt claustrophobic as if the walls were slowly closing in, tightening the air with a suffocating pressure. Chains hung from the ceiling, their rusted metal links creaking ominously in the stillness, poised to bind prisoners in painful positions. The silence was occasionally shattered by distant, eerie sounds, each one amplifying the sense of isolation and dread.

The air was stale, weighed down by the lingering presence of forgotten screams, and the room exuded a chilling aura of hopelessness. It was a place built for unspeakable torment, where the cruel, grating sounds of agony would reverberate off the stone, filling the space with an atmosphere where pain and fear were always present.

Before Brandon and Indigo could gain consciousness, Smooth took off their masks, tied them to a chair, put headphones on their ears, covered their eyes with a blindfold, duct-taped their mouths, and put a cover over their faces. Before they could speak, Smooth threw a bucket of water at them. Dazed about what's happening, Smooth's robots smack them across the face. Smooth's robots were waterproof so that they could handle the water.

Smooth injected Brandon with anesthesia while he injected Indigo with anesthesia and NullaSerum to stun his powers. Smooth said, "This game isn't over. I'll haunt you forever!" He switched his interesting quote to something more sinister. This game has gotten to Smooth's head, and he is going off the deep end. Smooth shut the door with an unpropitious laugh.

After a few hours, Brandon and Indigo began to regain consciousness. Though they had come dangerously close to drowning, they were miraculously okay. They strained against their restraints, trying to move and make any noise to signal to the other that they were still alive. All they could hear through the headphones was the maddening blasts of Smooth's music, drowning out everything else.

In his frantic state, Smooth had forgotten to reactivate the force field when they arrived at the island. This oversight would prove to be a turning point. Since Indigo was no longer confined within Smooth's force field, he still retained his superpowers, though severely weakened by the massive dose of NullaSerum.

Indigo, still blindfolded, fought to focus his thoughts. He closed his eyes, took deep breaths, and pushed past the constant noise to home in on the vision that had begun to form in his mind. He concentrated, drawing his attention to Aleemic, who appeared to be trying to communicate with him.

The vision was blurry at first, an indistinct haze of shapes and shadows, but there—amidst the confusion—Indigo could make out Aleemic's figure. Aleemic's presence was fleeting, but he was pointing toward something nearby: a shim.

Indigo's heart raced. He could not touch it while strapped to the chair, but he could still move just enough. Straining against his restraints, he tipped the chair, sending it toppling to the ground. With the little strength he had left, he reached out and grasped the shim, feeling the cold metal in his fingers.

"Thank you, Aleemic," Indigo whispered under his breath, but before he could act on his gratitude, the vision of Aleemic faded, leaving only a blur of emptiness. The connection was severed, and Aleemic was gone. At that moment, Indigo's heart sank. The chance to grab the shim had slipped away with Aleemic's departure.

The room seemed colder and darker, and the weight of urgency pressed down on him, thick and suffocating. Indigo exhaled slowly, trying to calm his racing mind. He reached out once more, this time determined, and his fingers brushed against the shim. His breath caught as he finally grasped it, feeling the cold metal in his hand.

With renewed focus, Indigo tightened his grip around the shim, and with steady determination, he began working at the handcuffs, using the sharp edge to manipulate the locks. The chance to escape was now within his reach.

After a minute or two, the handcuffs finally clicked open, and Indigo's hands were free. In a frantic rush, he began to tear at the rope binding his feet to the chair. He had not realized he could have removed the blindfold and face covering first to assess the situation, potentially finding a better tool to use. Instead, he focused on cutting through the rope that kept his feet tethered to the chair. Using the shim, it took him a few minutes to make even a small dent in the thick rope. In desperation, he removed the cover and the headphones and then untied the blindfold. What he saw next stunned him. He gasped in horror but quickly remembered the duct tape still covering his mouth, so his scream was muffled. Panicking, he tried to move away from the horrifying sight, but still tied to the chair, he collapsed.

Indigo let out a strangled cry, forcing himself to push through fear and keep moving. From the floor, he spotted a knife within reach. He grabbed it and began sawing through his restraints. As soon as he was free, he ripped off the duct tape over his mouth and shouted, "We need help!" and "Hey!" He wasn't sure what to do next, but he rushed to Brandon's side, determined to free him. When Brandon felt the touch, he instinctively thought it was Smooth or one of his robots. Indigo struggled to release Brandon from his handcuffs as Brandon kept moving. In the process, the sharp shim accidentally slashed Brandon's hand.

The pain seemed to calm Brandon, and Indigo was finally able to free him. As soon as the handcuffs were off, Brandon swung his fist, hitting Indigo squarely on the head. The impact was sharp, and Indigo was taken aback, stunned by the strength Brandon had at that moment. He quickly recovered and worked to remove the blindfold and headphones from Brandon's face.

"It's me!" Indigo shouted. Brandon looked at him, still shaken, but his tension eased when he recognized Indigo. However, as Brandon glanced past him, his eyes widened in panic again. Indigo still had duct tape over his mouth, which meant he could not speak. Indigo quickly released Brandon from the chair and ripped the tape off his mouth.

"Ow!" Brandon winced. "That's what you get for clocking me in the face," Indigo replied with a smirk, despite everything. It was a relief to see Brandon regain his composure. Brandon pulled Indigo into a big hug like he was waking up from a nightmare.

Still disoriented and unsure of how to escape, they took in their surroundings. Once their eyes adjusted, they were hit with a shocking sight. It wasn't just the grim, oppressive environment that startled them, but the sight of seven other people locked in prison cells around them, all bound and gagged, just like they had been.

Not knowing who the others were, Brandon and Indigo realized they had to set them free. As Indigo was lost in thought, trying to devise a plan, Brandon glanced over and saw some leftovers. He could not resist and began eating, his hunger overwhelming him. Indigo looked over, shocked, and quickly swatted the food away.

"What if that's poison?" Indigo said, concern in his voice. Brandon, unfazed and already having eaten a decent amount, shrugged. "It's fine. It's not poison." Indigo hesitated for a moment before giving in to his hunger, grabbing a portion of the food, and drinking some water. They both knew they had to save some for the other prisoners, but for now, the need to eat was too great.

It wasn't until they finished that they noticed the red countdown clock in the corner of the room. The timer was ticking down steadily, with only 24 hours remaining. Both stared at it, their minds racing. "What does this mean?" Brandon wondered aloud. "Is this some kind of game?" The clock was positioned near the door, and the two of them tried opening it, only to find it locked. They had not been in this chamber long enough to know if the other prisoners had any answers, but something about the countdown felt deliberate.

Indigo's instincts told him that Smooth Doubleb had something up his sleeve, some cruel twist waiting for them. He did not voice his suspicion yet, though; he kept it to himself, unwilling to raise any false alarms. He had a feeling they would need all their wits about them for whatever was coming next.

As the timer steadily counted down, Brandon and Indigo frantically searched for the key to free the prisoners. It felt like they were trapped in a real-life escape room; every detail in the chamber seemed purposeful. Themed decorations, hidden objects, a mix of logic, physical, and light/sound-based puzzles, and cryptic clues surrounded them. They scanned their environment, but no keys were in sight. Frustration and anger mounted, and soon, they were arguing, each blaming the other for the lack of progress. Time ticked by, and they realized they were getting nowhere.

It became clear to both that this was exactly what Smooth wanted—to get them flustered, let time slip away, and leave them lost in frustration. After taking a moment to collect themselves, they apologized to each other and realized the truth: they were in this together. Indigo had played Smooth's game before, and Brandon had helped design it. They needed to think like Smooth, to see the game from his perspective.

They are part of his twisted game now. To beat him, they had to embrace that mindset. They could not afford to be overwhelmed; they had to out-think Smooth, not just react to his traps. With newfound resolve, they dusted themselves off and got to work, determined to turn the tables.

They began analyzing the clues, piecing everything together. Each clue led to the next, and the answers kept unfolding. With logic and skill, they tackled each challenge, making steady progress. However, after an hour, they still had not found the key to unlock the prisoners. Feeling discouraged and tempted to quit, they knew they could not give up; the only way to survive was to free the other prisoners. They pushed through and eventually discovered the first key. It opened one prison cell, but it did not work for the others. Before releasing the first prisoner, they decided it made more sense to find all the keys and release everyone at once. It took time, but it was the most logical course of action. Six hours had passed, and the clock now read 18 hours. Smooth had hidden the keys in clever spots—inside the first prisoner's drawer, behind a series of puzzles, and after answering many logical questions. Finally, they found all seven keys needed to unlock each prisoner's cell. Brandon and Indigo freed the prisoners, still bound to their chairs.

At first, the prisoners screamed, thinking Smooth or his robots had come for them. Once they were all out, they gathered in a circle with their chairs still attached. Brandon and Indigo removed the coverings, blindfolds, headphones, and duct tape, only to be met with faces that were confused and shocked. The prisoners did not recognize anyone except for a few. One prisoner, still dazed, shouted, "Don't just stand there—get us out of here!" Brandon and Indigo exchanged a glance and quickly released everyone from their handcuffs. "Who are you all?" one prisoner asked, while another went to grab food. One prisoner hugged and kissed the other. Another prisoner cried while comforting the other. As they all tried to make sense of the situation, Indigo remembered their first game with Smooth. In that game, they were trapped in a mall with a countdown, forced to reveal their deepest secrets to escape. He shared his thoughts about what this game might be, and one of the prisoners suggested doing nothing. However, Indigo recalled that doing nothing had disastrous consequences in his past game. He spoke about how someone had to die for them to move on. Brandon gathered everyone together to hear Indigo out, and they all realized they were the last survivors from Smooth's games. One prisoner reminded them of their past season, where they had to sacrifice someone to continue. Everyone hoped that wouldn't be the case this time.

Exhausted, they decided to rest and recharge, knowing they still had time to learn more about one another. With 10 hours left, they took a nap, but unbeknownst to them, Smooth was watching from afar. As they slept, Smooth released sleeping gas into the room to keep them unconscious past the 10-hour mark. When the timer ended, a loud noise woke them up, and an anonymous AI voice came over the intercom: "That was the conclusion of SEASON TWO, EPISODE ONE." Dazed and confused, the prisoners were shocked to see the countdown had ended. They were now trapped in the chamber for another day. Food was scattered on the ground, and only a few bottles of water remained. One prisoner screamed, "You're sick!" The anonymous voice replied, "Welcome to SEASON TWO, EPISODE TWO. You all know the drill. Either you truly get to know one another, or I'll need a sacrifice." Brandon recognized the AI voice but could not remember where it came from. As the prisoners stared at each other, a new countdown began, this time for nine hours. "Well, this is a game now," Brandon said, "I guess we're the remaining players." One prisoner tried to open the door but was shocked by an electric jolt. Everyone knew what they had to do—learn more about each other.

"Hi, yes, this is me, the storyteller, AKA Brandon LeMar Bass. Since we already know Brandon and Indigo, I will not repeat their backstory. Instead, let us dive deep into these new characters and explore how they ended up here. Sounds good? Yes, I am currently livestreaming in front of a stadium crowd. In the first book, Smooth Doubleb performed in front of a studio audience, but this time, I'm in front of a stadium." The audience cheers. "Thank you! I took so many pictures with y'all backstage! Would these characters coexist? Would any of them survive? Let's find out!"

Chapter Two

ECHOES OF THE FORBIDDEN ONES

CHARACTER 1: VESPERIAN KAELITH

Vesperian is derived from "Vesper," meaning evening star, or "Vespera," which relates to the concept of night or the spiritual realm. It gives off an ethereal, otherworldly vibe, which fits his spiritual nature and connection to the divine.

Kaelith is a unique surname, invented to sound both regal and mysterious, embodying strength, destiny, and an untold past. It has an elegant, yet cryptic feel, aligning with his hidden birthright and his complex existence.

Vesperian Kaelith: Swapped at birth and hidden from his true legacy, Vesperian was born to be a ruler—a god-like figure. Raised far from his royal heritage, he spent years unaware of his divine potential. Now, with his birthright finally in his grasp, he is caught in the labyrinth of Smooth's twisted game. Though he possesses the power, he cannot yet revel in it. The throne that was meant for him has become a distant dream.

Vesperian's spiritual nature allows him to see the world differently, detached and introspective, often perceiving life as an abstract tapestry of nothingness. He is a poet at heart, a thinker, but one who struggles with earthly addictions: caffeine, food, gambling, and compulsive shopping. Despite his connection to higher powers, Vesperian is relentlessly attacked spiritually, his fate entangled in a web of magic and manipulation, pushed and pulled by forces beyond his control.

Destined to be the demiurge—the new god ruler—Vesperian must grapple with a destiny that seems both an honor and a burden. His existence is marked by spiritual warfare and a constant search for his true purpose. Every step he takes is a fight to retain control, as the magic and chaos around him threaten to overwhelm him.

Vesperian Kaelith's journey is one of self-discovery, divine transformation, and a battle to claim the power that was always his, all while trying to break free from the game that Smooth has created. The question remains: Will he ever truly be able to enjoy the inheritance that was stolen from him, or will he be trapped in this game forever?

Vesperian is the lost heir to the divine throne. Vesperian Kaelith was not born as a prince. He was not raised in the gilded halls of a divine palace nor cradled in the arms of royal parents. Instead, he was a child of destiny, though the world he was born into was unaware of it. His true lineage, his legacy as the prophesied demiurge, was hidden from him from the moment he first drew breath.

Vesperian Kaelith was born in the decisive moments of twilight when the sky was neither fully night nor day. The time of his birth, as well as the very conditions surrounding it, marked him as a child of destiny, though he would never know this until much later. His family, the Kaeliths, ruled a mighty empire that stretched across lands unknown to the common folk; their power was said to have been derived from the gods themselves. In the secrecy of their citadel, far from the eyes of the world, the royal family held a dark truth: the bloodline was tainted by an ancient pact with a forgotten deity being older than time itself.

The Kaelith dynasty had long predicted that the birth of a new ruler, one born to inherit the strength of both gods and men, would arrive during the time of the Red Eclipse. This child would rise to become a ruler of unmatched power, a divine ruler who would reshape the world. The prophecy was clear: the one born under this omen would become the next creator—a living god who would ascend to the throne of creation itself.

He came into the world under the most tragic of circumstances. The ancient prophecy that spoke of a new god, one who would rise above the heavens and rule with divine authority, was known to few, and the ruling family of his homeland—the Kaelith Dynasty—was desperately trying to protect their heir from the forces that sought to exploit the prophecy for their ends. His birth was meant to be a celebration, but instead, it was shrouded in secrecy and fear. The royal family's enemies had learned of the prophecy, and dark forces had already begun scheming to claim the unborn child's power. To protect him from certain death, the decision was made to swap him with a child of humble birth—a child whose existence would go unnoticed by the world at large.

With that, Vesperian Kaelith's life began. He was raised far from the reach of power, among simple folk who knew him as nothing more than an orphaned child, lost and abandoned, left to be adopted by a family who gave him a name but no true heritage. His early years were marked by hardship, his spirit always aching for something beyond his humble beginnings. Even then, there was a quiet, unexplainable sense of difference within him. While his peers were content with the simple pleasures of life, Vesperian found himself lost in deep thought, his mind reaching for something beyond the mundane world. His soul could never truly settle in the simple reality around him.

Despite his ordinary upbringing, Vesperian was gifted. He was a poet and a philosopher, his mind constantly wandering through abstract concepts of existence and meaning. Although those gifts were not always appreciated in the world he inhabited. His spiritual nature, though rich, was often dismissed as impractical, and he found himself disconnected from the normal desires and behaviors of those around him. Where others sought companionship, power, or wealth, Vesperian felt only the cold pull of a higher calling, though he had no idea what it meant.

He was trying to develop his faith, but his life took a dramatic turn. He was suddenly thrust into the world of power and intrigue, pulled into the labyrinth of manipulation that was the game of *Smooth*, a shadowy figure who had long been manipulating the strings of fate. Smooth saw in Vesperian what others could not—the true bloodline of the Kaelith Dynasty running through his veins, and the latent power he had yet to awaken. He knew that Vesperian was the key to his ambitions. So, he orchestrated the discovery of Vesperian's true heritage, setting in motion a series of events that would bind the young man's fate to his dark designs.

Vesperian was no naive pawn in Smooth's game. His awakening to his true self, the divine power that lay dormant within him, was a gradual process, a slow unfurling of a destiny he never chose. It was not a moment of clarity, but a slow creep of knowledge revealed through cryptic dreams, whispered messages, and strange encounters with otherworldly entities. The deeper he delved into his spiritual nature, the more he realized the truth of his existence: he was the lost heir, the one destined to sit upon a throne that no mortal had ever touched, to rule with the power of a god. In doing so, he would have to face a destiny that was as much a curse as it was a blessing.

Though the power that surged within him was undeniable, Vesperian could not yet wield it. He was still a man caught between worlds—a soul who had not yet fully understood what it meant to be a god. His spiritual gifts allowed him to see the world differently, to see the strands of reality and magic that wove together the fabric of existence. With these abilities came a sense of detachment, as though he were merely a spectator in a grand play in which his actions seemed insignificant in the grander scheme of things. He often struggled with the question of whether his power was a gift to be embraced or a burden to be carried.

Frustrated with his original bloodline that left him, his divine heritage should have made him a ruler of the highest order, but it had instead made him a target. Spiritual attacks came in waves, each one wearing away at his confidence and sense of self. His connection to higher powers seemed to attract as much darkness as light, and he was caught in an ongoing battle for control—control of his mind, his spirit, and the very magic that flowed through his veins. His existence became a constant war against unseen forces, both within and without; each step forward was a struggle to maintain his humanity amidst the chaos of destiny.

Vesperian's journey to reclaim his birthright would not be easy. The throne that had once been promised to him had become little more than a distant dream, obscured by the shifting shadows of manipulation and deceit. His struggle was not just against the forces of Smooth's game, but against himself—against the addictions and compulsions that held him in a vice grip. He found solace in the most unlikely places: in the bitter warmth of caffeine, in the ease of distractions, in the comfort of food, in the thrill of gambling, and the compulsive rush of shopping. These vices, though fleeting and hollow, became his only refuge from the growing storm inside him, the storm of divine power and the curse of his true nature. Though there were moments of serenity, of peaceful introspection, he found his soul pulled in many directions, much like the swirling cosmic forces that seemed to toy with his very essence.

Yet, despite his flaws, Vesperian was not without hope. He was a man in search of his true self, a man who sought not just power but meaning. Each day was an opportunity for self-discovery, to unravel the mystery of his existence. He knew he was destined for greatness, but the question remained: could he embrace that destiny without losing himself? Could he overcome the pull of earthly desires and the spiritual warfare that raged inside him?

In one fateful meeting, Smooth revealed the truth. The world had been lying to Vesperian. He was not a mere man. He was born to rule and was the savior of humanity. He explained how his real family left him for these mortals while he was supposed to be the true ruler. He was the true heir to the Kaelith throne, which was meant to guide the world into its next age. The throne, once within his reach, had become an elusive dream. Smooth offered him power, wealth, and influence, but there was a catch: Vesperian had to play the game. To ascend to his rightful place, he had to survive the labyrinthine world that Smooth had crafted—one where deception, manipulation, and magic ruled over everything. The game was already in motion, and Vesperian was now a player in it.

Vesperian Kaelith's story is one of transformation. From a lost child to a man caught in the web of divine destiny, his journey is one of self-realization and inner conflict. He must face the truth of his heritage, the weight of his birthright, and the price of wielding the power that was always meant for him. Whether he will be able to claim the true throne, Smooth's throne, or whether the game will consume him entirely, remains a question that only time will answer. Smooth had other options as he took Vesperian hostage and brought him to this reality. With Vesperian still struggling to reach his highest power, Smooth took advantage of him and locked him in his chamber. Smooth told him that this was a test to become the warrior of his kingdom.

As Vesperian's journey unfolds, he will face impossible choices, and with each choice, the tapestry of his destiny will grow more complex. The power that was stolen from him is now within his grasp, but whether he can ever truly enjoy it—whether he can break free from the twisted game Smooth has set for him—will depend on his ability to navigate the labyrinth of fate and decide what kind of ruler he will ultimately become. Sitting in his cell, Vesperian contemplates committing suicide. He still doesn't know who his real family is or even if there is a throne to begin with. He had visions and dreams of it, and when he viewed his circumstances, it was hard to believe it. Or maybe it was Smooth's throne all along.

Will Vesperian rise above the chaos, claiming the throne that was always meant for him? Or will he be swallowed by the forces that seek to control him, forever trapped in the web of magic and manipulation? Only he can decide—but time is running out, and the game is far from over.

Smooth sought to steal Vesperian's rightful inheritance because of his royal bloodline, believing that the power of his lineage could be his for the taking. As Vesperian grew, he delved deeper into spirituality, which led him to become increasingly detached from the physical world. He began to see everything around him as beneath him, a flawed existence where nothing seemed to go his way. He viewed humanity with disdain, considering it a weakness, and the world itself felt like a place of stagnation rather than something he could relate to.

Vesperian lived on a small island with his adopted family, who seemed to be his blood relatives, working as a florist, far removed from the luxurious life he felt he was destined for. The repetitive nature of his days, the same faces and conversations, pushed him closer to the edge of sanity. He grew weary of interacting with humans, often finding more engaging conversations with fictional characters or even inanimate objects than with the people around him. To him, life was no longer *life*; it was merely an *experience*—a temporary and unsatisfying one. He felt insulted when anyone referred to him as human, as he knew his true essence was far more advanced than any physical form.

Vesperian was unaware that he was merely in a waiting period, a time in which both people and the Source itself were working behind the scenes to guide him back to his throne. To him, however, this waiting period felt excruciatingly slow—slower than a turtle and a snail combined. The endless delay wore on him, and he found himself on the verge of giving up entirely.

Frustrated, Vesperian considered various ways of escaping his current life. He thought about going off-grid, but he couldn't afford the land. He contemplated taking his own life, but even that would require a permit and a license to carry a gun. He even investigated cremation, but it was far more expensive than a simple burial. He dreamt of building an empire through a polygamous relationship, but no one shared that vision with him. People told him to make friends, but most of his interactions felt robotic, with most acquaintances seeming like lifeless bots or zombies. He was urged to talk to women, but he found that most seemed mentally dead. He was told to start a business and to make money online, but the system was rigged to make people like him fail. Even when he tried to connect with others in real life, he felt drained by the energy vampires around him, those who had embraced the societal norm of vaccination.

Nothing seemed to change. Every attempt he made to break free from his current environment, to create new opportunities for himself, ended in rejection or failure. His adopted family, while well-meaning, offered no real support and constantly distracted him, preventing him from leaving. He never heard from his soul family or soul tribe, and his acquaintances only spoke of empty, meaningless topics. He had few friends, and the ones he did have seemed to invade his personal life despite their lack of genuine connection. Behind closed doors, his exes and others continued to perform magic against him.

For years, Vesperian had tried various business ventures, pouring his energy, time, and resources into them, only to see them stagnate. It always felt like he was standing still, as though no matter how much effort he put into his work, it never led to any tangible progress. Even when he tried to raise his vibration and attract more positive energy, nothing changed. The system was built to keep people like him stuck.

Amidst this constant struggle, Vesperian found himself spiraling into addiction. Caffeine, gambling, food, and compulsive shopping became his crutches—temporary escapes from a world that constantly let him down. He knew that much of his negativity wasn't his own but rather the result of others projecting their energy onto him. Still, he struggled to block out the noise, and some days were better than others. The mental and emotional toll on his health was undeniable, but he continued to neglect his physical body. He embraced his true self, disconnecting from the ego, which led to weight gain and an indifference to his outward appearance. Deep down, he knew that his journey was not about the physical realm—it was about transcending it, about reaching the afterlife where life truly began.

Vesperian eventually self-published his first book with the intent to help others navigate the death process and move beyond physical existence. He had no desire to reincarnate or relive this life again. If he were to return, he would rather come back as a bird than a human. Humans, in his eyes, were trapped in a cycle of consumption and materialism, forced to pay for everything. Although his book garnered some attention and a few sales, it didn't reach the level of success he hoped for. Still, he realized that his purpose was not about the numbers, the likes, the comments, or the followers. It was about the message. He understood that he had to share his truth regardless of external validation. He remembered his true mission and purpose, and no matter what the outcome, he found peace in knowing that he had fulfilled it.

Chapter Two

ECHOES OF THE FORBIDDEN ONES

CHARACTER 2: JAXON VEER

Jaxon Veer: A rising star in the world of music, Jaxon is an artist, producer, engineer, mixer, and expert in all things sound. As a record label owner, he's not just a behind-the-scenes genius but a major player in the industry, recognized in blogs, performing live, and even doing interviews with the hottest streamers. His name pops up in articles, features on various blogs, and is frequently mentioned in different articles and websites, making him a constant fixture in the media.

While Jaxon's professional life is full of success, his personal life is anything but perfect. A poet and freestyle artist at heart, he channels his pain and passion into his music but also drowns in his vices. Drugs, alcohol, sex, and money constantly pull him into a dangerous spiral. He's an addict who has learned to hide his demons behind a mask of fame and fortune, all while trying to maintain control of his career and image.

Known for his raw performances and uncensored approach to life, Jaxon embodies both the highs and lows of success. Yet beneath the surface, he is constantly battling his inner turmoil and addiction, trying to keep his career afloat while the pressures of the industry threaten to consume him.

Jaxon Veer was born in a modest neighborhood in the heart of a bustling city, the kind of place where dreams were just out of reach for most people, yet it was the birthplace of many legends. From a young age, Jaxon's parents could see that he was a prodigy when it came to music. His father, a former jazz musician who had given up his dreams for a steady job, and his mother, a classically trained pianist who taught at the local school, nurtured his talents. They provided him with a foundation in music—piano lessons, private tutors, and even access to their own modest but well-kept vinyl collection. Jaxon's world was sound, rhythm, and melody from the start. He could identify a beat within seconds, intuitively knowing whether it was good or bad and whether he could write to it or craft a song around it.

As he grew older, Jaxon's skill set expanded far beyond just playing instruments. By his late teens, he was producing and mixing his own beats, engineering for local artists, and mastering tracks with precision. The city's underground scene began to buzz with whispers of a young talent who could create magic out of thin air, and his name—Jaxon Veer—started appearing in blogs, on websites, and in music magazines. Jaxon soon became the go-to producer and mixer for rising stars. His ability to blend genres, break boundaries, and make music that resonated with listeners earned him a reputation that couldn't be ignored. The fame and success weren't as sweet as they seemed for Jaxon.

Behind the scenes, Jaxon was still the same kid from the small neighborhood, battling a darker side of himself. The pressure of being in the spotlight took a toll. The music industry was a dangerous game, full of temptations and vices that promised to numb the ache of living up to such high expectations. It began subtly—one drink to ease his nerves before a show, a pill to maintain energy during late-night studio sessions, a line to unwind after an intense argument with a fellow artist—but it gradually pulled him into a downward spiral.

He tried to control it at first, keeping his habits a secret and hiding his addictions from the public and even his closest friends. The more successful he became, the more the game started to take over. As he rose, so did his need for excess. He became an expert in duality. On stage, he was the life of the party—larger than life, a rockstar, cracking jokes, performing with wild abandon, and basking in the adoration of his fans. Off stage, he retreated into his shell, quiet and withdrawn, consumed by guilt and self-loathing. The quiet side of him wanted to walk away from it all—find peace, find simplicity. The other side craved more—the fame, the money, the rush of being desired and needed.

Jaxon's life became an endless cycle of highs and lows. The more he took, the more he needed. That's when Smooth entered the picture. Smooth was a well-known figure in the underground world, a notorious figure who had a way of getting people what they wanted. Smooth was in these streets. He didn't just have what people wanted; he was a manipulator, a puppeteer. He saw potential in Jaxon. He saw a young, talented, broken man who was craving the highs that only Smooth could provide. So, Smooth became Jaxon's "plug" in many ways. Whatever Jaxon wanted—drugs, women, the rush—Smooth could deliver. Jaxon was having sex so much; he was addicted to porn.

It wasn't long before Jaxon's reliance on Smooth grew. The lines between pleasure and pain blurred, and his two personas began to merge in dangerous ways. When Jaxon was with Smooth, he was no longer the shy introvert who hid behind his studio equipment; he was a different beast—loud, brash, and bold. The addiction to pleasure and excess consumed him. Every party, every drug, every high became a temporary escape from the quiet darkness that lay within. Smooth provided him with everything he thought he needed, and in return, Jaxon became increasingly beholden to him, his puppet on a string. If Smooth wanted Jaxon to perform, Jaxon would perform. If Smooth wanted him to play a dangerous game, Jaxon would play it. The pull of the addiction was too strong for Jaxon to resist.

Even in the darkest of times, Jaxon's quieter side would occasionally break through. He'd retreat to one of his multiple properties, often to places no one knew about, drowning in his thoughts and the overwhelming guilt that plagued him. He still had moments when he longed for peace, for the simplicity of his old life before fame and addiction tore him apart. Those moments were rare and fleeting, but they were enough to remind him that there was still some part of him that wasn't lost.

Jaxon's reputation continued to soar. He was featured in countless blogs, articles, and interviews. He was known as the rising star who could do it all—produce, mix, master, record, you name it. He owned a successful record label, streamed with other influencers, and was invited to exclusive events. His name was synonymous with talent and success, but the price of it all was high. His addictions started to show in his performances and his interviews. The press loved him for his wild side, but they had no idea what was happening beneath the surface. They didn't see the quiet moments when Jaxon would lock himself away, crying and wondering how he got so lost.

Despite all the glamour, Jaxon was trapped in a vicious cycle. His addictions kept him chained to Smooth, who had the power to pull him out of his highs and lows, keeping him strung along. Jaxon's freedom, the thing he once desired primarily, was slipping further away. The most painful part? He wasn't sure he wanted to break free anymore. The highs were too intoxicating, the lows too devastating. Smooth knew how to play him like a fiddle, giving him just enough to keep him in the game.

Jaxon Veer's journey is a tale of two contrasting sides—one of light and one of shadow. On one hand, he is a gifted, introspective artist searching for inner peace; on the other, a reckless, self-destructive performer chasing fleeting highs. He seems to have everything anyone could desire: fame, money, power, and the adoration of fans. Yet beneath the glitz and glamour, he's a man caught in the storm of his own making, torn between the person he once was and the one he's becoming.

As Jaxon becomes desperate for his next fix, Smooth steps in with a proposition: Jaxon needs to do something for him. Smooth is no longer interested in money, fame, or recognition. He wants Jaxon to become part of something far bigger. Smooth lures him to a private island, where the rules of a dangerous game await. He wants Jaxon to play along—but with one catch: to be his puppet. Unsure of the stakes or the game's true nature, Jaxon signs a contract without fully reading it. His intuition warns him just before the ink hits the page, but by then, it's too late. Now, the question remains: can he ever escape the game, or has he already fallen too deep to find his way out?

Jaxon was truly one of a kind, a diamond hidden in the rough. Rather than following the usual trends or relying on gimmicks, he was the one setting the pace for the next generation. By collaborating with a diverse range of artists and staying active on every social media platform, Jaxon naturally became a star in his own right. He had no fear of forging his path, breaking barriers, and staying true to his authentic self through his music.

His struggles with addiction eventually led to his downfall. He thought about seeking therapy, but didn't believe anyone could utterly understand him. He tried finding guidance through a mentor, but the fear of being judged held him back. He couldn't bring himself to confide in his friends or family, worried about how they would view him. It all weighed heavily on him, and no matter how hard he tried to escape, it only seemed to make the pain worse. The more he resisted, the more it hurt.

When trouble arose, his addictions became his escape, providing only temporary relief. He even tried to take a step back, putting all his devices in grayscale to disconnect, only to revert when the urge to indulge became overwhelming. Jaxon had good intentions, but his bad habits were slowly taking control. He didn't understand how to confront his inner darkness and integrate it with the light within him.

He channeled all his pain into his music, which was why his fans connected with him so deeply. When he took the stage, he didn't even need a mic—the crowd would shout his lyrics right back at him. Jaxon was one of the greatest performers of all time. His concerts were an emotional rollercoaster—people moshing in the pits, crying, laughing, smiling, experiencing every possible emotion as they absorbed his energy. His presence was undeniable, filling a room the moment he entered.

That's what made him such an extraordinary poet. On live streams, radio shows, and interviews, he could effortlessly freestyle or sing on instinct. Jaxon was an alchemist of sorts, transforming his pain into something beautiful, like sunlight breaking through the clouds, or a rainbow after a storm. However, he was often misunderstood, as people saw him in ways that didn't reflect who he truly was. It wasn't until his darker side emerged that Smooth took advantage of his vulnerabilities, trapping him in a dangerous cycle.

Jaxon has become a global sensation, reaching audiences all over the world. With that kind of influence, the possibilities were endless. People often followed the words and actions of their favorite celebrities or influencers, easily accepting or adopting whatever they were told to do or believe. Recognizing this power, Smooth saw Jaxon as an excellent opportunity to expand his reach and gain control over the masses. In exchange for the temporary highs that Jaxon craved, he would say or post whatever Smooth wanted. This is why Smooth took him under his wing, pulled him into his game, and made him just another pawn in his larger scheme.

Chapter Two

ECHOES OF THE FORBIDDEN ONES

CHARACTER 3: KAELION ZAIRE

Kaelion Zaire: A multifaceted entrepreneur and celebrity, Kaelion has established his name in the cannabis industry while also becoming a respected figure in the food and fitness sectors. He is the owner of his restaurant, rooftop bar, and nightclub. He's known for curating a laid-back yet luxurious atmosphere where great food and cannabis come together. He's not just about the business; he's deeply involved in his garden, growing plants and food that fuel his healthy, holistic lifestyle.

A vegan and holistic coach, Kaelion is dedicated to helping others improve their lives through nutrition, exercise, and mindfulness. His food truck, meal prep, and catering businesses display his passion for healthy, plant-based meals that are both delicious and nourishing. Drawing from his athletic background in track, cross country, and basketball, he transitioned into becoming a personal trainer. He also took on the role of a coach and mentor for young people, imparting discipline and encouraging personal growth in the next generation.

Kaelion's commitment to a balanced lifestyle doesn't just stop at the gym or kitchen; he lives and breathes wellness. His expertise in fitness and holistic health makes him a sought-after mentor, guiding others on their path to physical and mental well-being. Whether it's coaching, crafting meal plans, or promoting veganism, Kaelion is at the forefront of a movement that blends cannabis, fitness, food, and mental health into a holistic, celebrity lifestyle.

Kaelion Zaire was born into a world that prized ambition and success more than anything else. From a young age, it was clear that he wasn't just a product of his environment but someone destined to carve out his legacy. Raised in a tight-knit, yet affluent neighborhood on the outskirts of Los Angeles, Kaelion was always surrounded by entrepreneurs, athletes, and dreamers. His mother, a renowned holistic doctor and vegan chef, and his father, a former professional track athlete turned businessperson, instilled a blend of discipline, health, and ambition in him from the start.

His early years were shaped by a family deeply connected to the holistic lifestyle. They ran an organic farm and garden in the backyard, where Kaelion spent hours learning about plants, food, and the delicate balance of nature. His mother taught him the power of healing through food and wellness, while his father drilled into him the importance of physical strength, focus, and the mental toughness that came with being a high-level athlete.

From a young age, Kaelion excelled in sports. He dominated in track and cross-country, setting records in his school's district while also showing promise as a basketball player. He was the star of his school, effortlessly balancing academics, athletics, and social life. His reputation grew quickly, and by the time he graduated high school, he was not only an elite athlete but also an up-and-coming figure in the wellness world, known for his knowledge of plant-based nutrition and holistic fitness regimens.

It was this dual passion for athletics and wellness that ultimately set Kaelion on his path toward a diverse business empire. After college, he made the bold decision to step away from professional sports and pursue his passion for the cannabis industry, seeing the untapped potential for cannabis to improve wellness and mental health. With his father's backing and his mother's guidance, Kaelion launched a line of cannabis products that would soon revolutionize the market. From cannabis-infused edibles to medicinal oils, Kaelion's company became a household name, synonymous with top-tier quality and wellness.

His rise to fame wasn't just limited to cannabis. Kaelion's persona expanded as he opened his restaurant and rooftop bar. It was a hotspot in downtown LA that combined his love for plant-based cuisine with a luxurious, yet down-to-earth vibe. The bar and restaurant quickly became a cultural hub, attracting celebrities, fitness enthusiasts, and influencers from all levels of society. Kaelion personally designed the menu, featuring fresh, garden-to-table dishes that celebrated the sustainable lifestyle he had always advocated. He also started a food truck, bringing his nutritious, organic meals to the streets of LA, where it quickly became a symbol of healthy, luxurious living on the go.

Always a visionary, he saw an opportunity to merge luxury, entertainment, and holistic living into something unique. A nightclub that catered to those who wanted more than just a night out.

With his reputation already soaring, Kaelion opened his nightclub. A high-end nightclub that blends innovative design with a wellness-driven concept. Unlike traditional nightclubs, Kaelion's nightclub offered a comprehensive approach to nightlife, where patrons could enjoy the latest beats while also benefiting from an atmosphere designed for relaxation and self-care. The venue featured calming elements like aromatherapy diffusers, mood-enhancing lighting, and even an exclusive area offering CBD-infused cocktails and health-conscious late-night snacks.

Kaelion's goal was to create a space where luxury and wellness coexisted seamlessly. It quickly became a hotspot for celebrities, influencers, and people in the know, offering an unparalleled experience that combined vibrant nightlife with an emphasis on well-being. Through his nightclub, Kaelion not only expanded his brand but also introduced a new way of enjoying nightlife—one that celebrated balance, connection, and a healthy lifestyle without sacrificing fun or luxury.

With his private gym, he became a sought-after personal trainer, teaching others not just how to look good, but how to live good. His vegan, holistic coaching and meal plans became the blueprint for many seeking to build not just bodies, but lifestyles that thrived on balance, health, and sustainability. His daily fitness routine was famous, a carefully curated combination of yoga, weight training, running, and meditation that kept him in top shape both mentally and physically.

His life was one of luxury and privilege, but it was also one of purpose. He didn't just live a life of excess; he lived it with intention. With a private jet for international travel and a fleet of luxury cars, he had access to the best the world had to offer. Kaelion never let his success overshadow his core mission: to inspire, mentor, and uplift others. He became an ambassador for mentoring, using his platform to help at-risk youth and young adults build careers, embrace their potential, and stay grounded through fitness and wellness.

Kaelion had always been surrounded by people, but there was a loneliness that came with the lifestyle he led. As a celebrity entrepreneur and wellness mogul, people often sought him out for his fame, wealth, or status. He had a hard time finding genuine people, but it was Zarina who saw past all of that. Their paths crossed at one of Kaelion's charity events for at-risk youth, where he was mentoring young athletes and promoting holistic living.

Zarina was one of the keynote speakers at the event. Her work was focused on designing eco-friendly urban spaces, and her belief in creating spaces that brought people together aligned perfectly with Kaelion's values. They were introduced by a mutual friend who believed their shared passion for wellness and community could spark something special.

When they first met, it wasn't the typical spark of romance. Instead, they instantly connected on a deeper level, discussing everything from environmental issues to the power of community mentorship. Zarina's calm, grounded demeanor was a perfect counterbalance to Kaelion's intense, go-getter personality. Even though Zarina was a massive influencer, she didn't see him as just a celebrity but as someone with real depth. Likewise, Kaelion admired Zarina's intelligence, strength, and genuine desire to make the world a better place.

As they spent more time together, their bond deepened. They found solace in each other, each inspiring the other to be better. Kaelion helped Zarina refine her wellness routine, introducing her to holistic health practices that she'd never considered. In return, Zarina helped Kaelion reconnect with the quieter, more thoughtful side of himself, encouraging him to take a step back from the chaos of his empire and focus on inner peace.

Their relationship grew into something stronger than just romance—it became a partnership built on mutual respect, shared values, and a deep love for one another. In each other, they found a rare and precious kind of connection: someone who truly saw them for who they were, not just what they had achieved.

Amidst this whirlwind of success, Kaelion found love with Zarina, a woman whose fierce intelligence and quiet strength captured his heart. She was a grounded counterpart to his lofty ambition, someone who balanced his fire with calm, his chaos with clarity. Together, they became a power couple that seamlessly blended their careers with their love for each other.

Kaelion's life wasn't as perfect as it seemed.

Smooth had always been a master manipulator, quietly watching Kaelion's rise with a mix of envy and calculation. While Kaelion was undoubtedly a powerful figure, it was Zarina who stood out to Smooth. She wasn't just Kaelion's partner; she was the emotional anchor he needed. Smooth understood that Kaelion's strength came from his deep connection to Zarina. He saw how she grounded him, how her presence was the counterbalance to his larger-than-life persona. If he could disrupt that bond, Kaelion's power and focus would unravel.

Zarina's influence over Kaelion made her an obvious target. Smooth knew that taking her would shake Kaelion to his core, forcing him into a vulnerable position. Smooth also recognized that Zarina was a woman of immense potential in her own right—someone who wasn't just Kaelion's equal but a force in her field. Her ability to build community, her visionary mindset, and her grounded nature were all things that could pose a threat to Smooth's long-term plans. If he could control her, he would have the perfect leverage over Kaelion.

Smooth's strategy was to trap Zarina in the twisted dimension, knowing that Kaelion would stop at nothing to find her. By isolating her, Smooth could control the situation, playing with Kaelion's emotions and assessing his limits. What Smooth didn't anticipate, though, was Kaelion's determination and resilience. He thought that once Zarina was out of the picture, Kaelion would crumble—but instead, it only fueled Kaelion's drive to rescue her and dismantle Smooth's game from within.

In his twisted mind, Smooth believed that once Kaelion was distracted, weakened, and desperate to save Zarina, he could move on to other projects, taking control of Kaelion's empire and bending it to his will. Kaelion was no easy target, and Smooth's plot would quickly become a dangerous game of cat and mouse, where nothing would be as it seemed.

Smooth, a man of mystery and calculated ruthlessness, had spent years manipulating the strings behind various industries, pulling power plays with a subtlety that few could notice. Smooth was the type of person who wanted something from Kaelion. Perhaps it was wealth, influence, or access to a unique market. Regardless, Smooth knew that Kaelion had something he needed, and he was willing to take it by any means necessary.

When Smooth realized Kaelion wouldn't give in, he took matters into his own hands. With a series of meticulously planned moves, he managed to isolate Zarina. Alone and vulnerable, she was ambushed by Smooth, who took her captive. She fought and screamed, but no one could hear her. Unable to call for help, Zarina had left her phone in her coat while she went to the bathroom at a restaurant. Smooth's team of private investigators and detectives tracked her down, confiscated her phone, disabled its location settings, and put it on airplane mode.

Days passed without a word from Zarina. Then, one day, Kaelion's phone rang. It was supposed to be Zarina calling, but when he answered, it was Smooth's voice that greeted him. Rage surged through Kaelion's veins as he heard Smooth taunting him, saying Kaelion would have to find him if he wanted Zarina back. Kaelion demanded that Smooth take him to her location, and the hunt began.

When they finally met face to face, Kaelion was met not with Zarina, but with a room full of robots and Smooth's aircraft. One of the robots put Smooth on speakerphone, where Kaelion heard Zarina's muffled cries from what sounded like a prison cell. Furious, Kaelion engaged in a brutal fight with the robots, hoping to get to Smooth. Smooth, let the chaos play out without the robots intervening for some time. Once Kaelion had worn himself out, he coolly informed him that his robots would now escort him to where Zarina was being kept.

As they approached Smooth's private island, Kaelion knew this was the final confrontation. As soon as they arrived, Smooth gave the order for the robots to attack. The robots overwhelmed Kaelion, beating him unconscious before imprisoning him in a cell within Smooth's compound.

Trapped within this distorted dimension, Kaelion's body and mind were no longer under his control. The confident, free-spirited entrepreneur who once commanded his empire was now a pawn in Smooth's cruel game. His fame, wealth, and luxurious lifestyle felt like nothing more than a distant memory—his reality twisted beyond recognition. Forced to follow Smooth's whims, Kaelion knew he wasn't someone who would break easily. He had survived countless battles before, and this would be no different.

The thought of Zarina kept him going. She was the one thing that anchored him to his purpose. Even as Kaelion struggled in this warped version of his reality, he clung to the belief that he would find a way to escape, not just for himself, but for both of them. Smooth's hold over him might have been strong, but Kaelion's will to survive was stronger.

In his cell, Kaelion could hardly move or speak, the duct tape over his mouth and the deafening music blasting through the headphones preventing him from doing anything. He knew, deep down, that the time would come when he'd escape this prison. When it did, Kaelion would not only fight to free himself, but he would tear down Smooth's system, piece by piece, and rise again—stronger than ever.

Chapter Two

ECHOES OF THE FORBIDDEN ONES

CHARACTER 4: ZARINA LYRIC NYX

Zarina Lyric Nyx: A name that exudes creativity, elegance, and mystery —perfect for a multifaceted influencer who captivates both on-screen and off. Zarina: A digital renaissance woman is a force to be reckoned with in the online world. A gamer and streamer, she has built an empire from her online presence, captivating millions with her sharp wit, style, and infectious energy. Her influence goes far beyond gaming; as a travel vlogger and blogger, she takes her followers on thrilling journeys around the world, all while promoting her brand of lifestyle and fashion.

Known for her magnetic personality, Zarina is a social media sensation, with every post popping up on feeds worldwide. As an influencer, she has lucrative brand deals, including a popular merch line that fans rave about. A fashion designer and stylist, Zarina's clothing line has been a major success, blending style with comfort and creating pieces that reflect her bold, unique aesthetic.

Her entrepreneurial spirit extends to owning a clothing store, where she curates pieces that cater to her growing fan base. A model and actress, Zarina has graced the covers of magazines and appeared in commercials for top brands, always looking flawless and bringing her larger-than-life persona to every project. Whether she's walking the runway at fashion shows or producing her own commercials, Zarina is the epitome of modern success.

Zarina's versatility doesn't stop there—she's also a UGC (User-Generated Content) creator, working with top brands to produce content that resonates with her followers and generates massive engagement. With certifications in everything from social media marketing to design, Zarina has crafted a career that others only dream of, all while maintaining a life full of adventure and excitement.

Zarina Nyx wasn't born into fame or fortune, but she was destined for greatness from a young age. Growing up in a modest household with two older brothers and a single mother who worked multiple jobs, Zarina learned early on the importance of independence and hard work. Her mother was a hairdresser and beauty consultant, and from a young age, Zarina found herself fascinated by the world of beauty, fashion, and self-expression. She often spent hours playing with her mother's makeup and styling her brothers in different outfits, honing the skills that would later help her carve out her own space in the fashion and beauty industries.

Despite the challenges of growing up in a neighborhood where opportunities were scarce, Zarina never let her circumstances define her. She was always an ambitious and creative spirit, finding solace and escape in the world of video games and online communities. What started as a casual hobby evolved into a passion. Zarina had immersed herself in the world of streaming and gaming. She would spend hours live-streaming her gameplay, interacting with followers, and building a loyal fanbase. It was through this world that Zarina found her true voice and discovered the power of social media. As she gained more followers, she began experimenting with streaming different types of content—fashion hauls, makeup tutorials, and even travel vlogs.

Her big break came when she uploaded a fashion transformation video that quickly went viral, propelling her into the spotlight. The combination of her striking beauty, natural talent for styling, and unique perspective on fashion made her an instant hit in the online world. Zarina had a way of blending high fashion with everyday practicality, making her relatable to her audience while still maintaining an air of glamour. With her steadily growing influence, she started receiving brand deals from top beauty and fashion companies, and soon, she was on the radar of major fashion magazines and casting directors.

Zarina's online presence wasn't just about gaming and beauty. She became a full-fledged internet influencer, with a platform that extended across all social media networks. Her travel vlogs took her to exotic destinations around the world, where she documented her adventures and offered her followers a glimpse into the glamorous lifestyle she was building. Her charismatic personality and genuine enthusiasm made her a favorite among brands and fans. Soon, she was collaborating with high-end brands for sponsored posts, appearing in commercials, and even walking the runway at fashion shows.

She was more than just a pretty face and a talented gamer—she was a force in the industry. Recognizing the need for a one-stop shop for her fans, she launched her own fashion line and clothing store, highlighting her keen eye for style and her belief that fashion should be accessible and empowering. Her clothing line was a huge hit, offering everything from casual wear to high-end street style, and it quickly became synonymous with empowerment and confidence.

In addition to her fashion endeavors, Zarina became a sought-after stylist, hair and makeup artist, and beauty consultant. She collaborated with celebrities, influencers, and everyday people, helping them feel their best inside and out. Her work in beauty and styling earned her numerous certifications and accolades, further cementing her place in the beauty industry. She also used her platform to advocate for body positivity, self-love, and mental health, often sharing her struggles with self-image and the pressures of being in the public eye.

Zarina's rise in the world of entertainment didn't stop with social media and fashion. She quickly transitioned into modeling, landing shoots for magazines, online publications, and digital ads. Her striking looks, versatility, and charm made her a favorite in front of the camera, and she soon found herself starring in commercials and brand campaigns. As her career took off, she expanded her influence even further, opening her own modeling and acting agency. This new venture allowed her to represent other aspiring talents and provide a platform for those who shared her passion for fashion, beauty, and entertainment.

Her agency became a major success, signing models and actors to major contracts with top brands, including fashion houses, cosmetics companies, and tech brands. Zarina was proud to mentor the next generation of talent, offering them the same guidance and opportunities that had propelled her career. Her influence stretched across various industries, and she became known not just as a model or influencer but as a trailblazer and a mogul in her own right.

Despite her immense success, Zarina never let her fame change who she was. Beneath the glamorous exterior was a grounded, thoughtful woman who valued the connections she made with people who truly saw her for who she was, rather than just the image she presented online. That's how she met Kaelion—at one of his charity events for at-risk youth.

They began talking about their mutual interest in mentoring youth and supporting those who needed guidance in pursuing their dreams. Zarina was impressed by Kaelion's commitment to balance and wellness, and Kaelion admired her fierce independence and dedication to using her platform for positive change. As they spent more time together, their bond grew stronger, and what began as a professional relationship blossomed into something much deeper.

Zarina didn't just see Kaelion as a celebrity mogul—she saw him as someone who, like her, had worked hard to carve out a life of his own, and who was constantly striving to be better. Their relationship became a partnership, where they both pushed each other to grow, both personally and professionally. Kaelion introduced Zarina to a more balanced approach to health and wellness, while Zarina encouraged Kaelion to embrace his creativity in new ways, including launching his fashion ventures and collaborating on content.

Zarina had been swamped with brand deals, modeling shoots, and constant travel for the past few months. Between her influencer commitments and her expanding modeling agency, it seemed like there was always something on her plate. She loved her work, but the pressure was starting to take a toll on her, leaving her feeling disconnected from everything and everyone, including Kaelion.

Kaelion, ever aware of the balance she maintained between her career and personal life, could see the exhaustion in Zarina's eyes. He knew she needed a break, and he also knew that nothing would get her to slow down on her own. So, he hatched a surprise getaway that would give them both a much-needed escape from the noise and chaos.

One day, without any warning, Kaelion whisked Zarina away to a remote island, a place untouched by the spotlight, where the two of them could truly be alone. No cameras. No fans. Just them. The island was a private, luxurious retreat that Kaelion had kept hidden from everyone, a place where he could disconnect and focus on what truly mattered. Zarina had no idea where they were going until they landed—an intimate spot off the coast, surrounded by turquoise waters and lush greenery.

The first few hours of their stay were spent simply enjoying each other's company. They had no agenda, no meetings, and no obligations. Kaelion, who usually thrived in the fast-paced world of celebrity and business, was happy to let go of everything for a while. The two spent the day snorkeling, hiking through jungle trails, and having intimate conversations under the stars by a private bonfire on the beach. It was a rare moment of tranquility that allowed them to reconnect, not as Kaelion, the celebrity mogul, and Zarina, the influencer, but as two people who simply enjoyed each other's company.

In the evening, Kaelion surprised Zarina with a private dinner on the beach, something she could never have predicted. He had arranged for a gourmet vegan chef to prepare a five-course meal, all made from locally sourced ingredients. The night was punctuated by laughter, deep conversation, and a sense of peace neither of them had felt in months. Zarina could see a side of Kaelion that wasn't bound by the pressures of his empire—he was relaxed, present, and content.

Later, as they walked along the shoreline, the sound of the waves crashing in the background, Kaelion opened up about how he had been feeling overwhelmed by the weight of his success and the constant demands on his time. Zarina, the listener, shared her feelings of burnout, and the two of them realized how much they had neglected their well-being while focusing so much on external achievements.

That night, they made a vow to each other—to always find time for moments like these, even if it meant stepping back from everything else. Zarina, who had always been the one to manage every detail of her life and career, finally let herself relax, knowing Kaelion had her back.

The getaway wasn't just a physical escape; it was an emotional one. It allowed them both to step out of their roles and be a couple who loved and supported each other. They realized that their relationship was the one thing in their hectic lives that couldn't be compromised. In the stillness of the island, they understood that no matter how big their dreams or how loud the world around them became, their bond would always be their sanctuary.

While Kaelion's world was rooted in luxury and wellness, Zarina's world was built on self-expression, creativity, and empowerment. Together, they created a dynamic synergy that made them an unstoppable force—one that combined beauty, brains, passion, and purpose. Whether they were traveling the world, working on business ventures, or simply enjoying each other's company, Kaelion and Zarina were more than just a couple—they were a team.

As the trip came to an end, they both returned to their hectic schedules—Zarina with new ideas for her brand and agency, Kaelion with fresh plans for his business ventures. They did so with a renewed sense of purpose, a deepened connection, and a shared commitment to make time for each other amidst the whirlwind of their lives.

Their happiness was soon threatened when Zarina was taken by Smooth, a dark figure from Kaelion's past who sought to control them both. Smooth's twisted game was designed to break Kaelion's spirit by taking away the one person who kept him grounded. Zarina's abduction forced Kaelion to confront his deepest fears and fight like never before.

Despite the danger, Zarina never stopped believing in Kaelion's strength and their connection. No matter how dark things got, she held on to the hope that they would reunite and build an even stronger future together. Kaelion, driven by love and unwavering determination, would stop at nothing to free them both and reclaim their life.

Zarina had always been Kaelion's foundation and source of strength, but Smooth's actions took that away from both of them. Zarina's followers began to wonder where she had gone and who might have taken her. In most cases, the obvious suspect would be her boyfriend, with many assuming Kaelion had something to do with her disappearance. This led to a decline in Kaelion's business, as he stopped answering calls and emails. Without his presence, his companies suffered. The pressure mounted because, while their businesses had been thriving, they were doing most of the work themselves. Their mistrust of others kept them from delegating tasks. Rumors swirled, with people speculating that they had both disappeared under mysterious or even sinister circumstances. They were now a part of Smooth's sinister plan.

Chapter Two

ECHOES OF THE FORBIDDEN ONES

CHARACTER 5: VESPERA KADE

Vespera Kade: The queen of dualities.

A woman of many faces, Vespera runs her empire from the shadows, juggling roles as a mob boss, a police detective, and a business mogul with precision and cunning. In her day job as a detective, she walks the thin line between law and criminality, gathering information and securing power while keeping her true operations hidden. She commands respect from the streets to the courtroom, with connections to judges and a network of loyal followers who do her bidding. Vespera has an exotic and commanding presence, evoking mystery and power. She controls multiple dangerous industries while keeping a low profile. She is sharp, ruthless, and highly calculated.

Once a stripper and prostitute, Vespera worked her way to the top, building an empire that spans from her strip club to high-end escort and orgy houses. Her former life on OnlyFans continues to be part of her brand, keeping her enigmatic persona in the public eye, while she secretly runs underground operations with the help of gang stalkers, private investigators, and loyal employees.

A former Young Marine Sergeant, Vespera was forged in the fire of military discipline, blending the sharp tactics of her training with the ruthlessness of the streets. Now, as a mob boss, she's a woman no one dares to cross, using her strength, intellect, and connections to control both the criminal and legitimate worlds. She's always one step ahead, manipulating people and systems to expand her influence while maintaining a persona of respectability on the outside. She knows how to shoot a gun and use weapons.

Vespera Kade is a woman who defies easy categorization, a person who embodies the blending of contradictions into one formidable force. To the world, she is a police detective, a resolute public servant, the kind of person who has earned the respect of her peers and the fear of those who operate in the shadows. However, beneath her professional demeanor and her badge, Vespera is not who she appears to be. She is the hidden queen-pin of a sprawling drug empire, a mob boss who commands loyalty and fear, pulling the strings of a network that stretches far beyond what anyone would dare to imagine.

Born in the underbelly of a rundown city, Vespera's early life was one of survival. Her parents, both addicts, were barely present in her life, leaving her to fend for herself from an early age. She quickly learned that in a world where power and money ruled, the only way to survive was to gain control over those around her. Vespera was not afraid to use her body, her charm, and her intelligence to get what she needed. It wasn't long before she found herself working as a stripper in a dive bar. The work was grueling, but it paid the bills and kept her alive. Yet, Vespera had bigger ambitions than just a life on stage.

Her sharp mind and quick wit caught the attention of powerful figures who frequented the club, including several members of organized crime syndicates. Vespera was a woman who knew how to read people, to manipulate situations to her advantage, and soon she found herself rising through the ranks of the criminal underworld. She didn't just want to be a cog in the wheel; she wanted to own the wheel. Vespera eventually became involved in prostitution rings and human trafficking, running underground houses of depravity, where the rich and powerful could indulge their darkest desires in secret.

Her network expanded exponentially. She built alliances with notorious gang leaders, military personnel who were just as willing to break the law as they were to protect her empire, and business owners who owed her favors. At the same time, she maintained the persona of a respectable police detective, using her position to gather intelligence, manipulate investigations, and eliminate threats to her operation before they could even materialize. Vespera was an expert in duality; she could be the face of the law and the underworld's most feared figure, sometimes at the same time.

She ran a well-oiled machine, an empire that controlled illegal drugs, prostitution, and various illicit businesses. She worked her way up and now owns a strip club. Her strip club, an innocent venue for entertainment, was a front for much darker dealings. It was the hub from which she operated her prostitution network, with rooms in the back dedicated to more than just dancers. There were private rooms for high-profile clients seeking illicit pleasures, and, behind the scenes, Vespera's power grew stronger. She also controlled houses that served as orgy houses, where rich clients paid handsomely for the opportunity to indulge in their desires, and her carefully curated world of debauchery was thriving.

While her criminal operations flourished, Vespera's social media presence, including her OnlyFans page, allowed her to maintain her public image. She used it as another way to manipulate, attract clients, and generate additional revenue streams. On the surface, she was just another social media influencer, a woman using her allure to make a living. Beneath the surface, each photo and video served a darker purpose: to manipulate, to entrap, and to hold those who crossed her in her sway.

Her influence did not stop at her criminal enterprises. Vespera was a woman of connections, and she knew how to leverage her power. She kept a network of private investigators, gang stalkers, and corrupt lawyers on speed dial. If she needed dirt on someone, it would be dug up and used against them. If someone crossed her, they would be made to pay. She had friends in high places, including judges, city officials, and even some in law enforcement, ensuring that no matter what happened, Vespera was untouchable.

A Mother's Struggle Between Worlds:

Despite the ruthlessness with which she ruled, Vespera wasn't without a softer side. She had a family—her husband, a former military man who had been captivated by her beauty and her sharp mind. He was a man of honor in his own way, but he knew better than to question his wife's empire. Together, they raised children who were kept out of the dark side of Vespera's world, for now. Her children were the one thing that could still soften her heart, the one thing that she would protect primarily.

Vespera Kade had always known what it was like to fight. From the moment she stepped into the world, it was a battle—whether it was surviving the harshness of her childhood or clawing her way to the top of the criminal empire she runs today. No fight had ever been as fierce, nor as complicated, as the one she faced now: the battle to be both the powerful woman she had built herself into and the mother her children needed.

It had all begun when she was still young. Vespera had been pregnant at seventeen, a time when most girls her age were still figuring out who they were and what they wanted out of life. For her, it felt like the universe had already handed her a heavy burden. She had a son named Isaac Jasper. The father of her child, a man she once thought she loved, was absent before she even knew what it meant to be a parent. Since she had a son, she needed a male presence to help guide her son in a masculine way. Instead, she had been left alone, stranded in a world where motherhood and ambition did not seem to coexist. She still had a few family members and friends who helped take care of Isaac while she was working as a stripper. Despite having some support, it was still a challenging time.

There was one person who never left her side: her future husband, Vireo Kade. He was a man who had been with her before all the chaos. Before she became the boss of a criminal empire. Before the duality of her life began to grow. Vireo was her rock, a man with a quiet strength that complemented her boldness. He was a former military man who now works as an electrician. He was dependable and steadfast. When Vespera discovered she was pregnant again, this time with a daughter, Vireo did not hesitate for a moment. He married her as soon as their daughter, Celestine Aurelia Kade, was born. He vowed to support her, to help raise Isaac and Celestine, and even as their lives grew more complex, Vireo remained true to his promise. Now, he works as a full-time father and a part-time electrician.

Vireo and Vespera's meeting wasn't anything that would have seemed destined or extraordinary at the time. It was the kind of chance encounter that seemed almost ordinary—until the years unfolded, and they realized just how much it had shaped their lives.

Vespera was eighteen, newly out of high school, and trying to navigate a world that had already shown her how hard it could be. She had started working as a stripper in a run-down club in the city to support herself. Her parents had long since fallen out of the picture, and she was not naive enough to think that life would be handed to her on a silver platter. Vireo was already in his early twenties, a quiet, introverted former military man who had recently come back from a tour overseas. He was not the kind to frequent strip clubs, but life had a funny way of making people cross paths when they least expected it.

It was Vireo's friend who dragged him into the club that night. He had been home from deployment for a few weeks, and his friend thought he could use a distraction—a night out, a few drinks, and perhaps some time to loosen up. Vireo was not convinced, but he went along with it. He had never been one for the chaos of bars or clubs, but the moment he stepped inside, he was struck by how different everything felt. There were loud voices, smoke in the air, and thumping music that seemed to pulse through the walls. It wasn't a world he understood, but it intrigued him.

Vespera was on stage that night, doing her routine like so many others. She moved with grace, a cool confidence that came from years of perfecting the art of attraction. She did not notice Vireo at first—there were too many other men to focus on—but Vireo noticed her. There was something about the way she carried herself. Her aura was present. It wasn't just the way she looked; it was the energy she exuded. She was not like the others, who wore their personas as a mask. Vespera was real. She didn't need the stage to be seen, and he could see that immediately.

After her set, Vireo's friend pushed him to talk to her. Vireo hesitated. What would he even say? He was not the type to engage with women in such a setting, but something about Vespera pulled him in. He was curious. He had been through a lot in the military; he'd seen horrors that had changed him in ways he couldn't fully explain. He was not the same person anymore, and maybe he was looking for something to connect to, something to remind him of a world outside of the chaos he had known.

When they spoke, it wasn't anything grand. Vireo offered her a drink—she politely declined, saying she was on the job. He asked her questions about her life and her goals, but Vespera was guarded. She wasn't there to make friends. She had learned long ago that people were temporary, their words meaningless. Vireo was not the kind of man who gave up easily. He didn't push her or try to charm her with empty compliments. He listened, and he kept coming back.

It wasn't long before they started talking more often. Vireo would come to the club, not to drink, but to sit and talk with her during her breaks. She found him different from the usual men who tried to woo her with money or false promises. Vireo didn't offer her anything except his time and attention. He didn't ask for anything in return, and that was comforting for her. Something that made her feel seen in a way she had never experienced before.

As the weeks passed, their friendship began to grow. Vireo didn't mind that she was a stripper. He didn't judge her for what she did; he knew better than anyone that life wasn't always about making perfect choices. It was about surviving, about making decisions that kept you going. Vespera appreciated that about him. He never made her feel small or ashamed of the life she was living.

Eventually, their conversations became more personal. Vireo shared stories of his time in the military and the battles he had fought, both physical and internal. In return, Vespera shared her past—growing up in a broken home, having to fight for everything she had, and raising her son without the presence of his father. She told him about the dreams she had for her future, the empire she planned to build, though she was careful not to give too much away. She couldn't trust anyone completely, not even him, not then.

Vireo was patient, and Vespera couldn't help but let him in, little by little. She began to look forward to seeing him. He became a fixture in her life, someone who didn't expect anything from her except the truth. Eventually, that truth led to something deeper.

One night, after she finished her set, Vireo took her out for coffee. They sat outside at a small café, the city lights reflecting off the damp streets. They didn't talk much at first, just enjoying the rare moment of peace. Then Vireo reached across the table and took her hand. He told her he wanted to be there for her, that he didn't care about her past or her choices—he cared about her, the woman she was becoming.

Vespera was taken aback. She hadn't expected this kind of honesty, especially not from someone like him. She didn't know how to respond. No one had ever spoken to her like that. She was used to men wanting something from her, but Vireo wasn't asking for anything. It was then that she realized—she wasn't just attracted to him. She needed him. For the first time, someone had looked at her, not as an object or a tool to be used, but as a person.

It didn't take long for them to fall in love. It wasn't an easy or traditional love story. Vespera was still very much involved in her underground world, and Vireo was dealing with the emotional scars of war, but they were good for each other. Vireo helped her see that she could still have something real in her life, despite everything she had been through. Vespera showed Vireo that he could still be part of a world that wasn't defined by his military service or the darkness he carried inside.

A few months later, Vespera found herself pregnant with their first child. She had been shocked at first—unsure of what it meant for her life, for her empire. Vireo was there, steadfast as always, and he stood by her. They got married in a small, private ceremony, with only a few close friends and family. It wasn't a fairy tale, but it was real. They had their ups and downs, their struggles, and challenges, but they were a team. Vespera had always prided herself on being able to do things alone, but with Vireo by her side, she realized she didn't have to.

At that moment, when their first child—Celestine—was born, Vespera knew that she had found something worth fighting for. It wasn't just her empire anymore. It was Vireo, Celestine, Isaac, and the family they had created. A family that would grow with time, one that would be at the center of the war Vespera would one day face between her two worlds.

At first, it seemed like they were a picture-perfect couple, a young, married pair with a child on the way. Vireo worked hard to provide for them, but it was Vespera who was the true breadwinner, even then, with her sharp mind and skills to get what she wanted from the world. The problem was that as much as she loved Vireo, Isaac, and Celestine, her ambitions were stronger than her love for a quiet, family-centered life. It was the life she had always dreamed of, but it wasn't the life she was ready for.

When Celestine was born, Vespera was young and overwhelmed. The child was beautiful, shining with innocence, but the demands of motherhood were immediate and consuming. It was hard for Vespera to balance the role of a mother with her work. A work that was demanding and required her to be constantly present in the dangerous world of the criminal underworld. She had to leave home, often meeting with shady contacts, overseeing operations, and pulling the strings behind the scenes. She wasn't the type to sit at home and nurture her child. It wasn't that she didn't want to; it was that she felt that her true worth lay in her power, in what she could build and create in the world.

Vireo, on the other hand, was a patient man. He adored Celestine and loved their daughter with a tenderness that was almost foreign to Vespera. He fully accepted and embraced Isaac as well. Vireo could sense the growing distance between his wife and their children. Vespera was often absent, even when she was physically present. She would disappear into her work, her mind constantly preoccupied with her criminal empire, ensuring that her underworld kingdom didn't crumble. Although Vireo did his best to fill the void, and Isaac was understanding, Celestine, on the other hand, always felt that absence. She could feel her mother's love, but it was like a distant echo. It wasn't enough to make up for her physical and emotional absence.

Vireo Kade wasn't always the calm, steady presence he was known for in his family. His journey to becoming Vespera's husband, the father of their children, and a man who balanced the chaos of her world with his grounded existence began long before he ever met her. It all started in a small, rural town where he grew up in the shadow of his father's expectations.

Born and raised in a modest home, Vireo was no stranger to hard work. His father, a stern but fair man, worked long hours as a factory supervisor while his mother kept the home running smoothly, instilling in Vireo the value of discipline, responsibility, and persistence. Though his childhood wasn't one of luxury, it was one of consistency and a clear set of rules. Vireo was taught early on that to succeed, one had to put in the effort, even when the outcome seemed uncertain.

In high school, Vireo was known for his athleticism and leadership skills, though he never sought the spotlight. He was a quiet, reserved young man, preferring the company of a few close friends rather than large groups.

His dedication to sports and his natural ability to understand strategy led him to pursue a career in the military after graduation. He felt a deep sense of duty to serve his country, believing that the discipline and challenges of the military would further hone his skills and provide him with the stability he'd always craved.

At 18, Vireo enlisted in the military, and for the next several years, he would rise through the ranks, becoming a respected soldier and later a skilled electrician within the armed forces. His time in the military was transformative, not just because of the technical skills he acquired, but because of the man he became.

Training in various combat tactics and survival skills, Vireo learned to navigate high-stress environments, relying on his calm demeanor and quick thinking to stay focused. He was often called upon to manage situations that others might shy away from, whether it was disarming a complex device, managing a crisis under fire, or keeping his team composed during missions that seemed doomed from the start. His superiors saw his potential, and before long, Vireo was entrusted with leadership roles, overseeing the safety and well-being of his fellow soldiers.

As an electrician in the military, Vireo developed a knack for understanding complex systems—whether it was machinery or infrastructure—and he became a vital asset in both combat and non-combat operations. From repairing generators in hostile environments to setting up electrical systems in temporary military bases, Vireo's skillset was indispensable. However, as much as he appreciated the technical aspects of his work, it was the leadership and the deep sense of camaraderie within his unit that Vireo treasured the most. He learned that in the chaos of war, the bond between comrades was more vital than anything else.

The emotional toll of military service was significant, though. Vireo had seen his fair share of loss and destruction, both on the battlefield and in the personal lives of those around him. He lost friends, faced the constant threat of death, and was forced to confront the realities of war—the kind of mental strain that lingers long after the battles have ended. Vireo managed these challenges with unwavering resolve. He buried the pain inside, believing that survival required strength, and strength meant not showing vulnerability.

When Vespera became pregnant with Vireo's child, the stakes grew even higher. Vireo had already experienced loss, but the thought of raising a child in a world filled with danger was something he couldn't ignore. Still, he didn't waver. He promised Vespera that he would be there for their children and that he would do everything in his power to ensure they had a better life than he had growing up. He was determined to support her, to stand by her side through whatever came their way. It wasn't just a commitment to Vespera—it was a commitment to the family they were building together.

He transitioned to a more domestic role, helping to raise their children and acting as a steady presence when Vespera's chaotic life kept her away. Vireo worked part-time as an electrician, using his military skills to provide for his family and maintain a sense of normalcy.

As time went on, Vireo became the backbone of the family. Vespera's world continued to grow more dangerous and complicated, but Vireo's unwavering support for her—and his dedication to their children—never faltered. He took pride in being the stabilizing force, the one who kept things grounded when everything else seemed to be spiraling out of control.

Though Vireo was far from perfect, he found his peace in the simplicity of his work and his love for his family. He was the kind of man who didn't seek the spotlight or accolades. His greatest reward was knowing that he was there for the people he loved, doing his part to build a future for them, even if it meant sacrificing parts of his dreams.

In the quiet moments, Vireo would reflect on his journey—from a young, uncertain soldier to a husband and father who had weathered every storm that life had thrown at him. His life had been defined by duty, sacrifice, and love. A love that, no matter how complex or difficult, had always been his guiding light.

Years passed. Vespera's empire grew, and so did her children. By the time Vespera's life had become an intricate web of lies, deals, and betrayals. She rarely spent time with her children, and even when she did, it was always rushed. She would come home after a long day, her mind clouded with the weight of her responsibilities, trying to push aside the nagging guilt that followed her. Her family was important, she knew that, but her world—her empire—demanded her attention.

It wasn't until one of Celestine's birthdays that Vespera truly began to realize what she had been neglecting. The party was a small one with some family members and a few close friends. Vireo had organized it, as he always did, with the intent of making the day special for their daughter. She had been so wrapped up in a business deal, so obsessed with keeping her criminal empire running smoothly, that she hadn't even remembered the date and had almost forgotten about it.

When she walked into the party, Celestine had already cut the cake, and the room was filled with laughter and love. Vespera felt a pang of guilt in her chest, but she quickly masked it behind a forced smile. She walked over to Celestine, who greeted her with a look that was both happy to see her and distant. There was something in the way Celestine's eyes shifted that made Vespera pause, like her daughter had grown up in the blink of an eye. Celestine wasn't a little girl anymore; she was a young woman, and Vespera had missed so much of it.

"Happy birthday, sweetheart," Vespera said, kneeling at her daughter's level.

"Thanks, Mom," Celestine replied, but there was a coldness in her voice, a subtle distance that made Vespera's heart ache.

For the first time in years, Vespera realized that her absence had created a rift. It wasn't that Celestine did not love her; she did, but the love between them had become fractured. It wasn't the kind of unconditional love that a mother and child should share, not anymore. Vespera knew that, deep down, she had done this. She had been too focused on herself, too consumed by her empire, and she had left her children in the wake of her ambitions.

The weeks that followed were difficult. Vespera found herself struggling with the balance between her criminal empire and her family. The guilt was overwhelming, and it ate away at her. She started to spend more time at home, trying to reconnect with her children, particularly Celestine. She would play board games with them, help with homework, and try to engage in real, meaningful conversations, but it was hard. There was so much she had missed, and Celestine, now, was not a child who would simply fall into her mother's arms and forgive her for all the lost time.

Yet, despite the distance, there was still love between them. Vespera could feel it when Celestine smiled at her, even if it was fleeting. She could hear it in her daughter's voice when they talked about school, boys, or the things that mattered to a young woman. Vespera knew that love could still be rekindled, that she could rebuild the connection they once had. It would take time, and it would take effort, but she was willing to fight for it.

Her family wasn't just an afterthought anymore. They were a part of her life that needed to be protected, just as much as her empire. Vespera Kade, the queenpin of the criminal underworld, began to dedicate herself to the one thing she had neglected the most: her family. She might have taken the same approach as her parents did to her. She was not perfect, and she would never be, but she could be there for Celestine and the rest of her family. In the end, it was the love they shared that would give her the strength to keep going, even as she balanced the many worlds she lived in.

For Celestine, it wasn't easy to forgive her mother, but in the quiet moments—when Vespera kissed her forehead before bed or held her hand during tough times—she could feel it. The love was still there. It had been buried for a while, but it had not disappeared. With that, Celestine thought that was enough to begin healing the wounds of the past.

What about Isaac?

Once Vespera and Vireo got married, they were able to change Isaac's name to Isaac Jasper-Kade.

Isaac was born into a world of complexity and contradiction. From the moment he took his first breath, he was thrust into a life that walked the fine line between chaos and control, love and power, good and evil. His young mother, Vespera, was a woman who was building her empire from the ashes of her broken past, weaving her way through the criminal underworld, the police force, and everything in between. Yet, for all her strength and brilliance, Isaac's early years were marked by the absence of her and his father's presence. Isaac was always understanding, but he kept his true feelings inside. As she focused on managing her empire, and with his biological father absent, he was raised by his stepfather, Vireo.

Isaac grew up in the quiet, blue-collar world that his parents had created for them. A small, modest home just outside the city, with a well-maintained yard and a garage that served as Isaac's sanctuary. Vireo enjoyed picking up new skills and sharing them with Isaac. Meanwhile, Isaac was fascinated by the process of dismantling engines and reassembling them with exact precision. For Isaac, the garage was both his playground and his classroom. From an early age, Vireo taught him the art of fixing things. Seeing the world in pieces and knowing how to make them whole again. Vireo's lessons were about more than just cars; they were about life. He taught Isaac that every problem had a solution if you just took the time to understand it, and that hard work was the key to achieving anything worth having.

Isaac knew his mother was different from other mothers. He had seen her at the rare family gatherings, always dressed to the nines, her presence commanding attention the moment she walked into a room. She was a woman of power, but also one of secrets. To him, Vespera was an enigmatic figure who loomed large in his life but who was often absent when it mattered most. Her visits were fleeting, and when she was home, she was distant, her mind always preoccupied with her many responsibilities.

Still, Isaac loved her. Despite the growing distance between them, he could feel the bond between them. An unspoken connection that ran deep, even if it was hidden behind the walls, she had built to protect herself and her family.

As Isaac entered his teenage years, the absence of his mother began to weigh more heavily on him. He could sense the tension between her and Isaac. A silent struggle that neither of them ever fully addressed. Vireo, as much as he tried, couldn't fill the role of both mother and father, and Isaac started to feel the absence more keenly. He turned to his stepsister, Celestine, and they developed a strong relationship. They were close, but not too close, since they weren't technically blood siblings.

While Vireo continued to encourage him to stay grounded, to work hard, and to appreciate the small joys in life, Isaac began to yearn for something more—something he wasn't sure how to define. He had inherited his mother's intelligence and ambition, but unlike her, he didn't know how to wield it. He couldn't escape the feeling that he was destined for something bigger than the small garage and quiet life Vireo had carved out for him.

He started pushing boundaries—skipping school, hanging out with the wrong crowd, and dabbling in minor criminal activities, trying to fill the void his mother's absence had left in him. Vireo was concerned but didn't know how to pull Isaac back from the edge. They had a deep bond, but it was a bond rooted in love and stability, not understanding the deeper struggles Isaac faced in reconciling the different parts of his identity.

Then, one day, his world shifted. Vespera returned for a rare visit, and it wasn't just a brief stop this time. She'd come to reconnect. She sat him down, and for the first time in his life, she spoke to him as an equal, not just as her son, but as someone who could understand the complexities of her world.

"I know you've been lost, Isaac," Vespera said, her voice low and serious. "I know you've felt the absence, but it's not because I don't care for you. I've just been trying to make sure there's a world left for you to inherit."

Her words struck him deeply. For the first time, he understood that his mother's absence wasn't due to a lack of love; it was because she had been carrying the weight of a dangerous, complicated world.

Isaac began working as a mechanic at a shop while attending college for carpentry. He eventually graduated at the top of his class. Now working full-time as a mechanic and part-time as a carpenter, Isaac came to understand why his mother had been absent at times, and he was at peace with it. He knew that, despite the circumstances, she still loved him. She would incorporate Isaac's skills in her business to create a deeper bond with him. Although the curiosity about his biological father still lingered, his love for Vireo as his stepfather remained deep and unwavering. Isaac also developed a strong bond with his stepsister, Celestine, and has finally found his way, feeling more grounded than ever.

Vespera's true power lay not just in her ability to manipulate and control, but in her ability to make people believe in her dual personas. To her colleagues in the police department, she was a dedicated detective who would stop at nothing to protect her community. To her enemies in the criminal world, she was a ruthless and calculating mob boss who never left loose ends. To her family, she was a devoted wife and mother, willing to do whatever it took to ensure their safety and happiness, especially now, after returning to their lives following the success of building her empire.

However, it is the balance she maintains between these two worlds that is beginning to crack. As her criminal empire grows, so does the scrutiny from her colleagues. The line between her law enforcement career and her criminal life is blurring, and Vespera is faced with a choice: Will she continue to straddle both worlds, or will one side of her life finally overpower the other?

Vespera Kade is a woman of power, complexity, and contradictions. A woman who has built her empire on lies, manipulation, and ruthlessness, but who also hides a heart that still longs for love, loyalty, and family. As her network of influence tightens and the walls close in around her, she must navigate a dangerous world of loyalty, betrayal, and power, all while balancing her many roles. It's only a matter of time before the world realizes that Vespera is more than just a woman. They'll realize she is a force to be reckoned with, and they will either fall in line or be crushed under her heel.

The Captivity: Smooth's Twisted Game:

It started on an ordinary morning. The sun was barely rising as the city hummed with its usual chaos. Vespera was deep in her world, the undercurrent of her criminal empire pulsing just below the surface. She had finally managed to carve out some time for her family, something rare in the chaotic life she led. Her husband, Vireo, was working in the garage, while her son, Isaac, had taken on more responsibilities in the family business, carefully navigating the balance between his mechanical and carpentry work and his growing involvement in Vespera's empire.

Celestine, her sharp-witted and fiercely independent daughter, had just returned from a brief trip out of the city. She was catching up with her mother, a rarity that both women relished. The morning was calm, with only the occasional phone call or message breaking the silence. That peace was about to shatter.

Smooth's Calculated Move:

Smooth had been lurking in the shadows for months, carefully orchestrating his plan. He had always been a threat in Vespera's world—his reach was long, his influence wide—but it wasn't until recently that his obsession with her family began to take root. Smooth, a man with a twisted, psychotic mind, saw Vespera as a rival, but more so as a challenge. She had everything he could never obtain: power in their dimension, respect, and the unwavering loyalty of those around her. He wanted her to feel vulnerable, to lose control of the empire she had built, and he knew the best way to do that was through her family.

Smooth's twisted game began long before he captured Celestine. He had been using his network of informants, private investigators, and corrupt allies to gather intelligence on the Kade family, slowly picking apart the pieces of their lives. He knew about Vireo's calm demeanor and how much he meant to Vespera. He knew about Issac's role as the reluctant heir to the empire. Most importantly, he knew that Celestine, Vespera's daughter, was her heart—her anchor to what little humanity remained in her.

The Kidnapping: The Moment of Terror:

The night Celestine was taken, Vespera had no idea how close the danger was. It happened too fast—an expertly executed ambush. Smooth had hired a team of mercenaries, well-trained in the art of abduction. They infiltrated the Kade household with cold precision, slipping past guards and bypassing the security systems that Vespera had spent years perfecting.

Celestine had been in the living room talking to her mother when the sound of a muffled scream from the hallway interrupted their conversation. Before either woman could react, two masked figures burst into the room. Celestine's shock was palpable, her body stiffening as she instinctively reached for a weapon hidden beneath her clothing. It was too late. She was grabbed from behind, held down by a second figure, and before Vespera could intervene, a sharp blow to the head rendered her unconscious.

Smooth's Game Begins: Trapped in a Psychotic Puzzle:

When Vespera woke, it was in complete darkness. The only sound was her breath and the faint echo of footsteps somewhere distant. The smell of blood was thick in the air, and a shiver ran down her spine as she realized she wasn't alone.

Celestine was tied to a chair in front of her, and Smooth stood in the shadows, watching her every move with a manic gleam in his eyes. He had planned everything, down to the smallest detail. He had taken the most precious thing from Vespera—her daughter—and now, he had them both trapped in his sadistic, twisted game.

"I always wondered what it would feel like," Smooth's voice echoed in the cold, dark room, "To make you truly feel helpless, Vespera. You think you control everything, but I've made sure to strip that away, piece by piece. Starting with your family."

Vespera's heart sank as she realized the depth of Smooth's obsession. He had studied her, watched her weaknesses. Now, he had ensnared her in a game she wasn't sure she could win.

"Let her go," Vespera growled, her voice full of venom. She pulled against the restraints that held her, her muscles straining. Smooth just laughed, the sound low and hollow.

"Let her go?" he repeated mockingly. "You don't get to make demands, Vespera. Not here, not now. You're going to play my game, and when you lose, you'll understand what it means to lose everything."

The Twist: Vireo and Isaacs' Fate:

Meanwhile, Vireo and Isaac were desperately searching for any sign of Vespera and Celestine. They had noticed the unusual silence in the house, the absence of movement, and the strange sense of dread that had settled over the family. Vireo, more than anyone, knew something was wrong. He'd been around long enough to recognize the signs of an ambush, the missing guards, the blood stains that led to nowhere.

Before they could make any meaningful progress, the worst happened.

Smooth had anticipated this. Vireo and Isaac were on the hunt, getting closer to the truth, and Smooth knew they would be a threat if left unchecked. So, he lured them into his trap, sending them on a wild goose chase that led to an abandoned warehouse on the outskirts of the city.

Inside, they found only silence at first. Then, as they ventured deeper into the building, they came upon a gruesome scene. The floor was slick with blood, and in the center of the room, Vireo and Isaac found the bodies of a few of Smooth's men—his twisted way of saying "welcome." The worst was yet to come.

Suddenly, the lights flickered on, and there, hanging in front of them, was a large screen. The image on it froze their hearts in their chests: Celestine and Vespera, bound and battered, but alive.

Smooth's voice crackled through the speakers. "So glad you could join us, Vireo. Isaac. You see, you've been playing into my hands all along. The question is: Are you ready to pay the price for what you've built?"

Vireo and Isaac rushed forward, panic overtaking them, but before they could react, a shot rang out, echoing through the building.

The Final Game: The Price of Power:

When they arrived, the scene they found shattered their world. Vireo had been struck with a weapon. Blood poured from the wound, and he was dead on the spot. Isaac had rushed to his side, but the damage was done. Smooth's robots captured Isaac, and they killed him. Smooth had killed them both—not in the way they expected—but in the most cruel, heartbreaking way possible. The death total is now **177,011**.

Vespera watched through the screen as her husband and son struggled to breathe their last breath. Smooth's game wasn't just about capturing her family; it was about tearing apart everything she held dear. He wanted her to see the consequences of her choices.

In that moment, Vespera understood what Smooth genuinely wanted: to make her feel powerless. He had done what no one else could ever do. He had taken everything from her. Her husband. Her son. Her daughter. Smooth's robotic enforcers moved Vespera and Celestine onto his aircraft, preparing to transport them to the secluded dimension of his private island. Smooth, a dimension-jumper, could freely travel between dimensions at will.

In the face of losing everything, she was more determined than ever. She would not let Smooth win. She would break free and protect Celestine no matter what the cost.

Trapped in Smooth's psychotic game, Vespera now had no choice but to fight and beat this game. While Smooth's robots were placing them in their cells, Vespera's mind was racing. She looked at Celestine—her daughter, her heart—she whispered a vow through clenched teeth:

"I will make him pay. This is not the end. It's just the beginning."

With that, the game had truly begun.

Chapter Two

ECHOES OF THE FORBIDDEN ONES

CHARACTER 6: CELESTINE AURELIA KADE

Celestine Aurelia Kade: An innovator, creative genius, and her boundless talent made her a force in many innovative and technical fields. She is high-achieving and a visionary. She moves effortlessly through multiple industries and roles. She can adapt and transform like a bird soaring across various skies. This is Celestine Aurelia Kade.

Celestine has made her mark in a diverse array of fields, striking a balance between technical prowess and artistic vision. As a web developer and data center technician, she uses technology to coordinate with families, customers, clients, and business owners. She's deeply embedded in the tech world, building sleek, responsive websites and ensuring digital systems run smoothly. Celestine's talents don't stop there—she's also an expert videographer, photographer, and editor, capturing high-profile moments for celebrities and creating compelling stories through film, TV, and video.

A natural entrepreneur, Celestine is the CEO of a successful event-planning company that oversees everything from extravagant corporate events to intimate private parties. As an executive producer and screenwriter, she's behind some of the most impactful and thought-provoking films and TV shows, shaping narratives that resonate with audiences.

Her passion for style and aesthetics extends beyond the screen, as she launched her line of fragrances, which became an instant hit for their crisp, invigorating scents. A true Renaissance woman, Celestine also shines as a DJ, host, and MC, effortlessly commanding any stage she steps on with her magnetic presence.

Celestine's ability to seamlessly blend her creative vision with technical expertise makes her a leader in every field she enters. Whether she's teaching as a supplemental instructor, mentoring others, or breaking new ground in her artistic projects, Celestine Kade is a force that inspires and captivates.

Celestine Kade was born into a world filled with power, danger, and complexity. As the daughter of Vespera, a woman whose influence spanned across industries, and Vireo, a man who had found peace in domesticity after his military service, Celestine's early life was a delicate balance between her mother's tumultuous empire and the steady love of her father. While her mother fought to maintain control over her sprawling criminal empire, Celestine's early years were marked by an unusual blend of love and neglect, with Vespera's presence often fleeting due to her work.

Celestine remained resilient. From a young age, she understood the importance of self-reliance and independence, and while her mother was busy running her empire, Celestine's sharp mind and creative spirit began to take root. She grew up in a world of technology, film, art, and music. Her curiosity was insatiable, and her parents' multifaceted backgrounds gave her exposure to a variety of industries and ideas that would shape her future.

As a child, Celestine was always drawn to the digital world. The internet felt like a playground to her, where she could experiment, create, and connect. At a young age, she had already begun learning web development on her own, using online resources to teach herself coding languages and creating small websites for her friends. Her natural aptitude for technology and design was obvious, and it wasn't long before she became fascinated by data management and systems architecture. As she grew older, she expanded her interests into becoming a data center technician, learning the ins and outs of server management and network infrastructure. It wasn't just about creating things; Celestine had an innate ability to understand how things worked behind the scenes.

Her technical prowess wasn't limited to the backend of the digital world. Celestine also found a creative outlet in the visual world, discovering a love for videography and photography. She had a natural eye for composition and lighting and soon began documenting everything—from family events to street photography and, eventually, celebrity shoots. Her work was in high demand, and she was hired by various high-profile figures to capture moments that would last a lifetime.

Despite her success in multiple creative fields, Celestine was also driven by a strong desire to share her knowledge. She became a teaching assistant at a local university, helping students navigate the intricacies of web development, data science, and cybersecurity. Over time, she also took on the role of a supplemental instructor, collaborating with professors to provide tutoring and support to students struggling with technical courses. Her passion for teaching was unmatched—she didn't just want her students to succeed; she wanted them to understand the 'why' behind every problem.

Celestine's entrepreneurial spirit emerged as she realized the power of her diverse skill set. With her experience in web development, photography, and teaching, she built a brand that was as multifaceted as her talents. She established herself as an event planner, CEO of her own growing company, and even a DJ/MC, known for organizing some of the most exciting parties and events in the tech and creative industries.

As a screenwriter and executive producer, Celestine transitioned her creative energies into the film and television industry. She worked tirelessly to create a short film that gained widespread recognition, followed by the production of a full-length movie. Her experiences in both writing and production led to the creation of her TV show, where she was not only involved in the writing but also took on an executive producer role, overseeing all aspects of the show's development.

Through her ventures, Celestine became known for her ability to juggle multiple projects at once. She managed a diverse team of friends, fellow creators, and collaborators who all helped her grow her brand. She collaborated with photographers, editors, and musicians who shared her creative vision and supported her endeavors.

Her soul tribe, a close-knit group of friends, played a huge role in her journey. These were the people who believed in her when things were hard, who stood by her when her own family was caught up in their struggles. They were the ones who helped her build her empire, from assisting with the production of her films to providing advice on cybersecurity, web development, and event planning.

Throughout her life, Celestine's path was also shadowed by a constant presence—a figure who had been lurking in the background for as long as she could remember. Smooth, the dangerous and obsessive man who had long been a part of her family's world, had taken an interest in her. As the daughter of Vespera, a woman with ties to criminal enterprises and powerful individuals, Celestine was a target. Smooth's fixation with her went beyond her lineage. He saw in her the potential for control—the opportunity to manipulate and twist her to his will.

Smooth was a master of subtlety. For years, he watched Celestine from the shadows, making sure that his influence never touched her directly but always lingered just out of reach. He would follow her wherever she went, learning her routines, her strengths, and her weaknesses. Smooth knew that Celestine was someone to be reckoned with—intelligent, creative, and fiercely independent—but that didn't stop him from trying to assert his dominance over her.

As Celestine's fame as a photographer grew, Smooth saw an opportunity to use her connections and influence. He began planting people in her inner circle, people who could subtly manipulate situations and steer her into his grasp. Despite his covert efforts, Celestine remained blissfully unaware of his presence for much of her life.

That is, until he began to make his move. He had realized that, despite her growing empire and her tightly knit circle of friends, something was missing. Something she hadn't yet fully realized about herself. A vulnerability. A deep, dark thread of connection to the chaos her mother had built. Smooth saw an opportunity to push her to the edge.

Despite the lurking danger of Smooth, Celestine remained focused on her goals. She had built her reputation not just on her technical skills but on her genuine love for helping others. Her work as a cybersecurity expert, coupled with her role as a photographer and event planner, allowed her to stay one step ahead of any threats that emerged in her personal or professional life.

In addition to her business ventures, Celestine made a mark as an advocate for digital privacy and security, using her knowledge to help others protect themselves in an increasingly connected world. She became a trusted consultant for companies and individuals, helping them safeguard their online presence. Her passion for technology merged seamlessly with her creative side, and she continually sought ways to innovate and push boundaries in both fields.

Her work as a DJ/MC and her high-energy personality made her an in-demand host at exclusive events, where she built lasting relationships with a variety of influential people across the entertainment, tech, and creative industries. Whether she was behind the camera, at the computer, or on stage, Celestine was always immersed in her passions. Her short films, movies, and TV shows became a platform for her to explore stories of empowerment, creativity, and resilience, reflecting her journey and the themes she held dear.

Celestine's journey was far from simple. She was a woman of many hats—technical expert, creative visionary, and entrepreneur—but the complexity of her life made her unique. She embraced her many identities, learning to navigate the balance between ambition and the love she had for her soul tribe, her family, and the world she had carved out for herself.

Smooth's presence loomed large in her life, a constant reminder that even in the world of success and joy, darkness could always creep in. The question was, how long would it take before Celestine finally faced him—and how would she fight back?

Lost in her thoughts, she decided to escape for a while. Celestine was no stranger to adventure. Her career as a web developer, photographer, and event planner had already taken her to places she'd never imagined: exclusive parties in the heart of the city, rooftop dinners in bustling metropolises, and remote locations to shoot photos of celebrities. It was the quiet, remote corners of the world that seemed to captivate her most. Her soul craved the simplicity and serenity of untouched places—away from the chaos, the pressure, and the constant hum of her city life.

One summer, Celestine found herself standing at the edge of the vast, windswept sands of the desert. An environmental organization had hired her to document a rare desert bloom. It was a beautiful, once-in-a-lifetime event where the desert came alive with vibrant wildflowers after an unusual rainstorm. The flowers were delicate, fleeting, and would only last a week. A photographer's dream.

The desert was silent. The air smelled dry and warm, and the only sound was the wind softly brushing against the earth. The landscape stretched endlessly, dotted with cacti and the occasional rock formation, the deep hues of the sky and sand merging in a beautiful, surreal scene. Celestine could feel her usual bustling thoughts quieting down as she set up her equipment—a stark contrast to the high-energy events and projects that had defined her life back home.

She had always been the type to get lost in her work, her focus all-consuming. Out here, the solitude felt different—it was peaceful. The isolation of the desert wasn't lonely; it was freeing. As the sun began to set, she caught her first glimpse of the rare blooms opening in the golden light.

She quickly began taking photos, her lens capturing the fleeting beauty of the flowers, each shot carefully composed with the eye of someone who understood both technical precision and artistic expression.

As the day faded into night, something unexpected happened. Celestine, too absorbed in her photography, didn't realize how far she had ventured from her base camp. The sky turned darker, the wind picked up, and soon, she found herself disoriented, standing in the middle of an unfamiliar stretch of dunes. The horizon, once clear, had blurred into an unrecognizable mix of sand and shadow.

Her phone had no service. The satellite GPS device she had carried was buried deep in her bag, and it was too late to turn back. The desert had transformed from a tranquil haven into an imposing wilderness.

For a moment, panic settled in her chest. How had she gotten so lost? She was a tech-savvy, resourceful woman who had been to countless remote locations. She knew how to navigate through cities, but this felt different. The vastness of the desert, the emptiness, made her feel small and insignificant. There was no one around to help, and it would take hours, maybe days, before anyone would even realize she was missing.

Something clicked in her mind. Celestine wasn't just a photographer, web developer, or event planner; she was also a survivor. A woman who had faced challenges far bigger than this. More importantly, she was resourceful. She took a deep breath and focused. The desert wasn't going to eat her alive. The desert was a puzzle, just like every other problem she had solved in her life.

She dug into her bag and pulled out the small multi-tool she always kept that was practical, compact, and efficient. She used it to start marking her trail, scratching the sand at intervals to ensure she could retrace her steps. The sun had set, and the temperature began to drop, but she knew that panic wouldn't help her now. Instead, she needed to use her knowledge of navigation and problem-solving to guide her through the night.

The hours dragged on. The desert air was cooler now, and her legs were sore from walking for so long. Celestine never slowed down. She had faced countless obstacles in her career, from late-night deadlines to difficult clients to technical failures, but this? This was her test of grit and perseverance. As the stars twinkled brightly above, she remembered her old lessons in navigation from her university days, when she had briefly taken an outdoor survival course as an elective. She focused on the constellations, aligning herself with the North Star, carefully adjusting her direction.

By the time dawn broke, the sky shifted from deep purple to soft blue. Celestine had found her bearings. She could see the familiar shapes of the rock formations from earlier. A wave of relief washed over her as she made her way back to the base camp, the first light of morning casting a golden glow over the desert. She was exhausted but triumphant. Despite everything, she had made it through the night on her own.

Her team was waiting for her when she returned, worried but relieved to see her safe. They had noticed she'd gone missing after sunset and had begun preparing to search for her. When they asked her how she'd managed, Celestine simply shrugged, a small smile tugging at her lips. "Just a little desert adventure," she said, not wanting to dwell too much on her moment of fear.

Later that evening, as she edited the photos she had captured of the rare desert blooms, she couldn't help but reflect on the experience. She had always been a creator—building websites, organizing events, making movies—but this was different. She had created something deeper within herself. A new sense of confidence, resilience, and self-reliance. She had faced an unknown challenge and came out stronger on the other side.

The desert had tested her, and Celestine had passed with flying colors.

In the quiet aftermath, as the last edits were completed and the images were uploaded for her client, she felt a quiet sense of fulfillment knowing that she could face anything, even when the road ahead seemed impossible. The desert had reminded her of her inner strength, and that was a lesson she would carry with her, wherever life took her next.

She returned from the trip feeling refreshed and revitalized, eager to reconnect with her mother. Her mom had been distant lately, making less of an effort in her children's lives, so it felt like the perfect moment for them to bond. What she didn't know, though, was that her return would mark the moment when Smooth was about to make his move. Smooth had been waiting for this moment, for her return, and now he was ready to make his mark. The game was about to begin.

Celestine was a unique individual with a deep and unshakeable bond with her father, Vireo. She was also building a loving relationship with her stepbrother, Isaac, and rekindling her connection with her mother, Vespera. Everything seemed to be falling into place, just as she had hoped. She didn't let hatred or negative comments get to her; instead, she remained resilient and focused on building her empire from the ground up. Even though Smooth had been lurking in the shadows, she was surrounded by a strong support system, especially by her friends. When she and Vespera suddenly disappeared, everyone was left in a daze, wondering where they had gone. Calls to Vireo and Isaac went unanswered, and soon it became clear they were missing, too. They contacted the authorities, and after weeks of investigation and searching, there was still no trace of them. No evidence and no records. It became a tragedy that echoed throughout the entire dimension, leaving the Kade family shattered. As the story unfolded, the truth of their fate began to surface, and the mystery of their disappearance took shape.

Chapter Two

ECHOES OF THE FORBIDDEN ONES

CHARACTER 7: INDIRA RUNE

Indira Rune: A spiritual guide and healer, Indira Rune is a master of many arts. She embodies inner strength and radiates spiritual wisdom. With her engaging tarot videos and insightful podcast, she has built a following that trusts her guidance on life's most profound questions. As a motivational speaker and therapist, she leads others toward healing and personal growth with a unique mix of compassion, humor, and wisdom.

Indira uses her skills in Reiki, sound bowl healing, and tarot/oracle card consultations to help individuals reconnect with their true selves. She also runs online courses, offering spiritual guidance and teachings on personal transformation. Known for her comedic skits and pranks, Indira brings joy and laughter into her practice, making spirituality approachable for everyone.

Living off the grid in a serene mountain and beach house, Indira has cultivated a peaceful, sustainable life. She grows her food in her garden, embracing self-sufficiency and a deep connection with nature. As a realtor, she helps others find their ideal off-grid homes, encouraging them to embrace a lifestyle of peace and mindfulness.

Indira Rune's Backstory:

Indira Rune had always been a woman of contrasts—both grounded and ethereal, fiercely independent, and deeply connected to the energy of the world around her. Raised in a bustling city, she found herself uncoordinated with the hustle and bustle of urban life. From a young age, she was attuned to the unseen forces that most people couldn't sense—the vibrations of the universe that spoke to her through dreams, signs, and even the cards. It was no surprise when she eventually embraced the spiritual path, becoming a multifaceted entrepreneur and healer.

Indira began her journey as a tarot reader, offering guidance and insight to those seeking answers. She quickly built a reputation with her online tarot videos, where she combined her intuitive abilities with her talent for communication. Her channel grew rapidly, not just for her tarot readings, but for her engaging content that mixed humor, motivation, and a touch of playfulness. She pranked her followers, challenged them with thought-provoking skits, and lightened the atmosphere with comedy, all while sharing her expertise in personal growth, spirituality, and wellness.

Her offerings didn't stop with tarot. Indira branched out into podcasting, speaking on a variety of topics, from mental health to spiritual wellness, self-care practices, and motivation. She was a therapist, mentor, and healer all in one, providing one-on-one consultations, Reiki sessions, and sound bowl healing to those in need. Her services expanded into online courses, where she taught everything from tarot to manifestation techniques and self-love practices. Her entrepreneurial spirit led her to sell her own tarot and oracle card decks, and she created a thriving online community that flocked to her wisdom and guidance.

Beyond her professional success, Indira was deeply committed to living authentically. She sought a balance between her career and personal life by disconnecting from the noise of the world and immersing herself in nature. She built a life off-grid, in a secluded house nestled between the mountains and the beach. She cultivated a community engagement garden where she and her neighbors grew their food, emphasizing sustainability, connection, and wellness. Hiking, detoxing, and recharging in nature were part of her routine, allowing her to stay centered and focused. Living off the land gave her the freedom to disconnect from the pressures of modern life and the chance to nurture her spiritual and mental health.

Indira's connection to her physical space was more than just a lifestyle choice; it was a sanctuary. After years of building her business and nurturing her passions, she found peace in her remote location, but her tranquility wouldn't last.

Indira's life changed forever when she entered *The Escape Room: Virtual Reality*—an intense competition in a digital world that was much more real than anyone could have imagined. Smooth, a shadowy figure, had orchestrated the entire game, carefully selecting participants to manipulate and control. Indira, with her sharp intellect and strong will, quickly became the champion. She escaped every challenge with ease, using both her mental clarity and her innate spiritual awareness to navigate the complex maze of the game.

Smooth had underestimated her resilience, and after her victory, he tried to trap her again, believing that her strength was a fluke. Indira wasn't one to back down. She weathered the storm of his relentless pursuit, her intuition guiding her to safety. She escaped his grasp and retreated to her off-grid sanctuary, determined to rebuild and disconnect from the chaos that Smooth represented.

For the first year, Indira was still haunted by the trauma of the game, the scars of Smooth's obsession weighing heavily on her, but she refused to live in fear. She poured herself into her work—building her online businesses, expanding her offerings, and creating the life of which she had always dreamed. Her connection to her online community became even stronger, and she found healing through her work, helping others while helping herself.

By the second year, things began to shift. Indira met someone who changed her world—a kind, supportive boyfriend who shared her love of nature and wellness. Their connection was deep, and soon, they were expecting a child together. Indira felt a renewed sense of purpose and joy, believing that, finally, she was free from the shadows of her past. She was creating a family, a future, and a life built on love and healing. Her business continued to thrive, and her remote home, now filled with the promise of a new generation, felt like a true sanctuary.

Just as she began to believe that she had escaped the darkness, Smooth returned. It was the third year that was supposed to be her year of peace, and the shadows of her past came crashing back. Pregnant and vulnerable, Indira realized that her fight with Smooth was far from over. He had found her again.

Now, with a baby on the way and the love of her life by her side, Indira faced the ultimate test. Would she be able to protect her family from the manipulative force that had hunted her? Or would she have to fight again to reclaim her freedom?

One thing was certain: Indira Rune was no stranger to battles. She had weathered storms, built empires, and emerged stronger every time. Smooth had underestimated her before, and he would do so again. This time, she wasn't alone. She had everything to fight for.

Indira had built a life from the ground up, a life that could not be shattered by the whims of a man like Smooth. With her community, her family, and her unwavering spirit, she was ready to face whatever came her way—because she knew one thing for sure: she would never let anyone take away her peace again.

How Indira Rune Was Introduced to the Escape Room Virtual Reality Game by Smooth:

Indira Rune's entry into *The Escape Room: Virtual Reality* game wasn't by chance, nor was it a simple invitation. Smooth, the mastermind behind the game, had been studying her for months, watching her rise to prominence in the spiritual and entrepreneurial world. He knew that someone as multifaceted and resilient as Indira would be a prime candidate for his game. A game designed not just to challenge, but to break those who believed they were unbreakable.

Smooth, a shadowy figure with vast resources and a deep understanding of psychology and manipulation, had his eyes on Indira long before she knew he existed. He had been tracking her online presence—her tarot readings, podcast episodes, motivational speeches, and even her interactions with her online community. He recognized her as someone who was both strong and vulnerable, someone who had built her empire by helping others, but who was also a person constantly in search of deeper meaning, balance, and peace.

Smooth had always been fascinated by people like Indira—those who exuded confidence, wisdom, and an inner strength that could be tested, twisted, and ultimately broken under the right conditions. He believed that he could push her to her limits, pull her out of her comfort zone, and manipulate her into playing the game. Smooth wasn't interested in a typical contestant; he wanted someone who could challenge him, someone who wouldn't just follow the script but would fight back.

He reached out to her under the guise of an exclusive opportunity—a new, cutting-edge virtual reality game that promised to push the boundaries of reality itself. The game, *The Escape Room: Virtual Reality*, was marketed as an elite, mind-bending challenge for those who sought something beyond the ordinary, a way to test not just your intellect, but your soul.

Indira, intrigued by the idea of pushing herself further and testing her limits in a world that blended technology with metaphysical, received the invitation. It came in the form of a sleek, professionally designed email, promising an experience unlike anything she'd encountered before. Smooth used her curiosity about the unknown to his advantage, playing on her passion for personal growth and self-discovery. The offer seemed too good to resist—after all, she was someone who prided herself on stepping out of her comfort zone and taking on challenges, both in her personal life and her professional journey.

At first, she was skeptical, but the allure of testing herself in a virtual reality game—where every move would be watched, every decision analyzed—appealed to her adventurous side. The idea of outsmarting the game, of breaking free from its constraints, was something she couldn't pass up. Smooth understanding her mindset, made sure to appeal to her competitive nature. The game would be a challenge for her body, mind, and spirit, he said, but only those who were truly exceptional could emerge victorious.

With a mix of excitement and trepidation, Indira agreed to join the game, unknowingly walking straight into the trap that Smooth had meticulously laid out for her.

As soon as she entered the virtual realm, the game was like nothing she had ever experienced. It wasn't just a game—it was a psychological war. *The Escape Room* pushed her to confront her deepest fears and darkest vulnerabilities. Each puzzle, each decision, and each escape from one challenge only led to another, more complex and more daunting. Indira's intuition and mental strength kept her one step ahead, giving her the edge over the other contestants.

However, Smooth didn't intend for the game to be just about testing intellect and skill. He had another agenda. The game was designed to break her, to observe her reaction under intense pressure, and to test her emotional resilience. Smooth wanted to see if she could hold onto her core identity and her spiritual grounding when everything around her was designed to distort and fracture her sense of self. He wasn't just interested in winning; he wanted to control her.

Despite the psychological warfare Smooth unleashed, Indira's resilience and deep spiritual connection were more than a match for the game's challenges. Her mastery of tarot, her knowledge of energy, and her ability to center herself in moments of stress gave her the tools to navigate the game with unexpected ease. She wasn't just playing to win—she was playing to outsmart the system, to reclaim her autonomy from the man who believed he could control her.

Indira emerged victorious, breaking through the final barrier of the game and escaping the digital labyrinth. Her victory was a testament to her strength and resourcefulness, but Smooth wasn't ready to give up. The victory didn't come without a price, however. Indira's triumph was bittersweet, for as soon as she thought she had escaped, Smooth made his intentions clear: He wasn't done with her yet.

His obsession with her only grew stronger. He believed that she was the one person who could truly challenge him, and he wouldn't let her slip away that easily. He made plans to trap her again, this time in the real world, believing that the game had only scratched the surface of what he could control.

Indira, knowing that her safety was now in jeopardy, made a decisive choice: she would escape him. She retreated into her off-grid sanctuary, determined to build a life free from Smooth's influence. It was a difficult decision—leaving everything behind, disconnecting from the world that had known her as a successful healer, entrepreneur, and influencer—but it was the only way she could protect herself from the man who had already tried to break her once.

Smooth would not be deterred. No matter where she went, no matter how far off the grid she went, Smooth would find her again, and the game would continue.

How did Indira and her boyfriend meet?

Indira's meeting with her boyfriend was a serendipitous blend of timing, fate, and shared values. A perfect convergence of two souls who need each other without even realizing it.

After the intense psychological battle she'd faced in *The Escape Room: Virtual Reality* and the heavy toll it took on her, Indira knew she needed peace. The years of being hunted by Smooth, combined with the deep emotional scars left by the game, had left her longing for stability and connection. She'd retreated off-grid to heal, both mentally and spiritually, and to build her life away from the chaos that Smooth had created.

One crisp autumn morning, while tending to her garden, an essential part of her off-grid lifestyle, Indira noticed a new face in the neighborhood. She lived in a small, tight-knit community of like-minded people who valued simplicity, self-sufficiency, and wellness. They often shared resources, and there were regular gatherings for hiking and detoxing in the mountains, but this man was different. He wasn't one of the regulars.

His name was Elias Rho, and he had recently moved into the neighboring property, seeking refuge from his chaotic past. Elias was a former corporate worker who had left behind the high-stress life in search of something more meaningful. Like Indira, he longed for a connection with nature, a quieter life where he could recalibrate. He'd read about the off-grid lifestyle in the area and had decided to take a leap of faith, hoping that living in harmony with the land would help him heal from burnout.

Indira first saw him during a community gathering in the park. They exchanged a casual, friendly greeting, and there was an instant, almost magnetic pull between them. He was someone who immediately struck her as different from the crowd—a calm, introspective man with a kindness in his eyes. They shared an appreciation for nature, and their conversation flowed effortlessly. They spoke about everything from the healing power of the earth to the importance of mental health, with Indira subtly feeling warmth she hadn't realized she was missing.

Elias, in turn, was drawn to her depth and authenticity. He could sense the strength she exuded, but also the softness beneath, a quiet resilience built from having fought through battles that most people would never understand. He admired her dedication to her work and her off-grid lifestyle, not just as a way to disconnect, but as a conscious choice to live with purpose and mindfulness.

Their connection deepened over shared hikes, starlit walks on the beach, and evenings spent talking around a fire pit. It wasn't just attraction—it was an undeniable bond, one forged from mutual respect's journeys and a shared passion for self-improvement and well-being.

Over time, their bond grew stronger. Indira found herself opening up to Elias in ways she hadn't with anyone in a long time. Her struggles with Smooth and the fear that still lingered from *The Escape Room* weighed heavily on her, but Elias listened without judgment. He didn't try to fix her or offer empty platitudes. Instead, he just held space for her, allowing her to express her fears, her hopes, and her pain. His presence was a grounding force, soothing the turmoil inside her.

One evening, while they were walking along the cliffs overlooking the ocean, Elias took her hand. The gesture was simple but filled with unspoken meaning. It wasn't a rush or a chase; it was just two people who had found something they both needed—peace, understanding, and the promise of a fresh start.

Their relationship blossomed naturally. Indira, who had always been independent and cautious, found herself falling for Elias not because he was perfect, but because he made her feel safe, something she hadn't felt in a long time. For Elias, Indira wasn't just the strong, independent woman he admired; she was someone who allowed him to rediscover a life of purpose, one that was aligned with his values and soul's calling.

By the time Indira found out she was pregnant, they had already formed a solid foundation built on trust and a deep emotional connection. She was both surprised and overjoyed. It felt like the universe was gifting her with a new chapter in her life—one where she could embrace motherhood, love, and partnership, all while continuing to build her empire.

Their relationship was a testament to the healing power of connection. In Elias, Indira found someone who could help her face the future, even as she carried the shadow of her past with her. They weren't just partners; they were allies, both building something greater than themselves in the serenity of their off-grid world.

As much as Indira longed for peace and stability, the shadows of Smooth's obsession were never far behind, and it wasn't long before they would both be pulled into a storm neither of them could have predicted.

The Obsession:

Smooth's ability to find Indira at her remote off-grid sanctuary wasn't just a matter of luck; it was the result of a meticulous, calculated effort that spanned years of tracking, planning, and using every resource at his disposal. He knew she was trying to escape him, but Smooth wasn't someone who gave up easily. His obsession with Indira and his belief that he could control her pushed him to go to great lengths to locate her, even in the most remote corners of the world.

How Smooth Found Indira:

1. Psychological Profiling & Patterns:

Smooth had spent years studying Indira before ever encountering her in *The Escape Room: Virtual Reality*. He understood the patterns in her behavior, her routines, and the decisions she made in both her personal and professional life. He knew that after winning the game and escaping his grasp, she would seek isolation to recover and rebuild her life. Based on her social media presence, the way she marketed her spiritual services, and her online interactions, Smooth had a clear understanding of the type of life she wanted to create. One that was deeply connected to nature, wellness, and self-sufficiency.

Smooth had a network of people who worked for him, individuals skilled in tracking and surveillance, both digitally and physically. While Indira had cut ties with her past life as much as possible, Smooth had kept tabs on her every move. Her podcast, videos, and online sales left behind digital footprints that Smooth could analyze and track. It wasn't much, but when pieced together, it told him exactly where to look.

2. Exposing Vulnerabilities in Her Off-Grid Life:

Although Indira had taken great care to build her life off the grid, she wasn't completely invisible. Living off the land meant she had to buy certain supplies, whether it was gardening equipment, food, or materials for building her business. Smooth was aware of this and knew that these purchases would leave traces. His network of contacts—individuals embedded in various sectors, from supply companies to those who worked in remote areas- was able to identify and track these purchases.

It wasn't as easy as tracking a typical online consumer; Indira took every precaution to protect her privacy, but Smooth was patient. He spent months digging into various delivery records, cross-referencing shipments, and following the subtle trails of her needs. Through a series of small, seemingly insignificant interactions, he began to piece together the location of the small off-grid community to which she had retreated.

3. The Manipulation of Technology:

While Indira lived off-grid to disconnect from the world, Smooth knew how to use technology to his advantage. He hacked into satellite images, checked property records, and followed the trails left by energy usage. Indira had made the choice to use solar panels and eco-friendly systems to power her home, which was a method of self-sustainability, but also a path that left behind traces of energy signatures. Smooth's connections in the tech world were able to pinpoint these anomalies in satellite imagery, tracing them to a specific remote region.

He didn't need to know the exact address—he simply needed to know the area. From there, Smooth began sending private investigators to visit the region, disguised as potential property buyers or even tourists. They scoured the area for clues, asking locals subtle questions about a woman who fit Indira's description. One by one, these investigators began narrowing down the possibilities until finally, after months of searching, they had a solid lead on the remote mountain and beach property where Indira now resided.

4. Using Her Community:

Smooth understood that even in off-grid communities, no one lives in complete isolation forever. People talk, and no matter how hidden you think you are, someone eventually knows where you are. One of Smooth's methods was leveraging his connections to people who lived in or near the area. Individuals who might not have known his true intentions could unwittingly feed him information. He made subtle inquiries with property managers, local gardeners, and even people who worked at nearby stores that Indira occasionally visited. By blending in as a casual, interested buyer of land or property, Smooth's agents were able to gain just enough information to piece together Indira's location.

5. The Final Push:

As time passed, Smooth's obsession with Indira grew. After years of being out of her reach, the idea of her finding happiness and stability infuriated him. He couldn't allow her to live freely while he remained a shadow in her past. Smooth began the final phase of his plan to find her.

By now, he had a clear sense of where Indira was located, but he didn't act immediately. Instead, he waited for the right moment, when her guard was down, and she believed herself to be safe. Smooth knew how to exploit her vulnerability. By now, Indira had settled into a rhythm, running her businesses and nurturing her relationship with Elias, pregnant and building a future. Her success, coupled with the peaceful life she had worked so hard to create, made her vulnerable.

Smooth's final break came when one of his operatives learned about the birth of her child. The information was small, but it gave him the leverage he needed. He believed that the arrival of a child would be the perfect opportunity to strike, knowing it would bring heightened emotions and make Indira more susceptible to manipulation.

Smooth arrived in the area, not as the monstrous figure he was, but disguised as someone else—a friendly neighbor or a new arrival in the area. He knew how to blend in and how to keep his presence under the radar, waiting for the right moment to show himself. It wasn't about capturing Indira again; it was about breaking her spirit, about taking away the life she had fought so hard to rebuild.

What Smooth Did to Elias:

Smooth's obsession with Indira went beyond just trying to control her; he saw anyone in her life, especially Elias, as a potential obstacle to his goal of dominating her mind and spirit. Once he located Indira and realized that she had built a stable life with her boyfriend, Elias, he knew that he had to act. To Smooth, Elias was not just a man—he was a threat, someone who could offer Indira the protection and love that he could never give her.

1. Psychological Manipulation and Gaslighting:

Smooth knew that Elias, being deeply invested in his relationship with Indira, would protect her at all costs. Smooth also knew that he could use subtle psychological manipulation to break Elias down. He began by planting seeds of doubt in Elias's mind, slowly eroding his confidence and making him question his reality.

Smooth would send Elias anonymous messages, filled with cryptic, disturbing information about Indira's past. He used bits of information that only someone with intimate knowledge of her life would know, twisting her story to make it seem like she was hiding dark secrets. These messages questioned Indira's integrity, subtly implying that she had a hidden agenda or that she was not as trustworthy as Elias thought. The goal was to create a wedge between them, to make Elias feel paranoid and unsure of whether Indira was the person she appeared to be.

Smooth also targeted Elias's insecurities. He knew that Elias, like many people, had fears and vulnerabilities—insecurities about his past, his ability to protect Indira, and his worthiness of her love. Smooth would exploit these insecurities by feeding him stories of how unfit he was to be with her, suggesting that he would never be able to truly protect her from someone like Smooth.

Through phone calls, anonymous letters, and even seemingly casual encounters in the community, Smooth planted these doubts, making Elias feel increasingly isolated. He wasn't directly attacking him at first; it was all very subtle, a slow burn that wore him down.

2. Physical Threats and Intimidation:

As psychological manipulation began to take hold, Smooth escalated his tactics by introducing more direct forms of intimidation. He was no longer content with just messing with Elias's mind; he wanted to make sure that Elias understood the threat he was dealing with.

One day, when Elias was out hiking alone, Smooth made sure to cross his path, appearing in the shadows of the woods. Smooth let Elias know that he had been watching him for a long time. He did not need to be overt—just a few calculated, cryptic words and an unsettling presence were enough. Smooth made Elias feel as if his every move was being watched, creating a sense of unease that followed him everywhere he went.

Smooth also used Elias's greatest fear against him: the fear of losing Indira and their unborn child. He made sure to leave messages for Elias that hinted at something happening to her—messages that left enough ambiguity to be terrifying, but not enough to directly accuse anyone. Elias started receiving strange, unexplained warnings about Indira's safety. Smooth made it clear that he could take everything Elias held dear at any moment.

Smooth even went as far as to sabotage Elias's business dealings, subtly undermining his confidence. He knew Elias aspired to build something meaningful with Indira, possibly even growing his property, expanding their off-grid life together. Smooth planted small but effective obstacles—fake job offers, false opportunities, and deliberately misleading advice—leading Elias to believe that nothing he tried would ever succeed. Smooth played with Elias's ambitions, pushing him to a breaking point where he began to question his ability to provide for Indira and their child.

3. The Kidnapping of Elias:

The breaking point came when Smooth decided that he could not afford to let Elias remain a part of Indira's life. He needed to force her into submission, to make her fully dependent on him. Smooth knew that if Elias were still around, Indira would have someone to fight for her, someone who could protect her and stand by her side.

One night, when Elias was out running errands or working on their property, Smooth orchestrated a kidnapping. He made sure to choose a time when Elias would be alone and vulnerable, away from Indira. With the help of his operatives, Smooth ambushed Elias and took him to an undisclosed location, a remote, abandoned building far from the town where Indira and Elias lived.

Elias was held captive, isolated from the world, and subjected to a combination of physical and psychological torment. Smooth wanted to break him, to make him feel helpless, so he could turn him into a pawn. He made sure Elias was never truly harmed in ways that would leave permanent marks, but he used physical threats and emotional manipulation to create a sense of hopelessness in him. He would tell Elias that Indira had abandoned him, that she had chosen a different path, and that she was now under Smooth's control.

He would also feed Elias false information about Indira's feelings, making him question whether she still loved him or whether she was being coerced into another relationship. Smooth's goal was to strip Elias of his confidence and his will to fight back, knowing that once he broke Elias, Indira would be easier to manipulate.

4. Using Elias as Leverage:

After a few days, Smooth presented Elias with a choice: either he would remain in captivity, or he would be released, under the condition that he disappear from Indira's life permanently. Smooth knew that the prospect of never seeing Indira or their child again would be Elias's greatest fear. Smooth used this threat as leverage, making it clear that Elias's freedom came at a price.

Elias, weakened by the emotional and physical strain of being held captive, was desperate to escape. Smooth made him understand that if he ever dared to come near Indira again, there would be consequences. It was a power play—Smooth knew that Elias was in a fragile emotional state, and the threat of losing Indira forever was the perfect way to force him into submission.

Elias, broken and filled with doubt, agreed to leave. He was released with the understanding that if he ever tried to contact Indira again, Smooth would ensure his life—and Indira's—would never be the same.

5. The Aftermath:

When Elias returned, he was not the man who had left. He was physically drained, mentally shattered, and deeply conflicted. He knew he could not tell Indira everything, not wanting to burden her with the trauma he had suffered at Smooth's hands, but he also knew he could not stay away from her.

Smooth, however, was not done yet. He was always watching, always one step ahead, waiting for the right moment to strike again. Elias, now caught between fear and love, had no choice but to remain distant from Indira. He feared that if he stayed close, Smooth would harm her, but that meant distancing himself from the woman he loved, and from the child they were about to bring into the world.

Smooth had broken Elias, and now the true battle for Indira's freedom—and their family's future—was just beginning.

Indira's Confrontation with Smooth:

After Smooth's cruel manipulation of Elias, Indira began to suspect that something was wrong. Elias had been distant and more anxious than usual, and his uncharacteristic silence only deepened her concern. She pressed him to talk, but he remained tight-lipped, too afraid to burden her with the truth of what had happened. As the days passed, Indira's intuition began to scream at her that something bigger was at play—something sinister.

Her suspicions only grew when she discovered odd messages and cryptic letters that Elias had hidden in the woods. They were from Smooth, a reminder of the twisted game he had started. Indira realized then that Smooth was not just an obsession from her past; he had followed her into this new life. He had tormented Elias to weaken her, to break her spirit, but no more. Indira was done running. She wasn't going to let Smooth take anything more from her.

On a cool, moonlit night, she decided to confront Smooth alone. She knew it was a risk, but after everything he had done, she could not live in fear any longer. She couldn't allow him to control her life and the life of the man she loved. She had to put an end to this.

She tracked Smooth to a remote, abandoned cabin at the edge of the forest, the same cabin she had once seen him use as a base during their time in the *Escape Room: Virtual Reality* game. This time, however, there would be no game. Indira had come for him, ready to face him down.

The Confrontation:

Smooth was waiting for her, of course. He had anticipated her arrival. He had been tracking her movements for weeks, patiently waiting for the right moment. As Indira stepped into the clearing where the cabin stood, she saw him leaning against the wall, his familiar smirk plastered across his face. His cold eyes never left her as she approached.

"You're brave," Smooth said, his voice smooth, calculating, as always. "I was beginning to think you had forgotten about me, but I see I was wrong. You do care, don't you?"

Indira did not flinch. Her anger was a quiet storm inside her, threatening to explode. "You've messed with my life for far too long, Smooth. You hurt Elias, and I won't let you get away with it."

Smooth chuckled, his eyes glinting with malicious amusement. "Oh, Indira. You still don't understand, do you? Elias was a means to an end. It was never about him; it was about you. You think you can run from me, but we're connected. We always will be."

Indira took a deep breath, focusing all her energy. She had to keep her cool. She would not let him get inside her head. "You think you can control me? You think you can break me?" she spat. "You have no idea who I am. I've been through hell, and I'm still standing. You don't get to take anything from me anymore. Not Elias, not my life."

Smooth's expression darkened, and he pushed off from the wall. He took a few steps forward, his voice dropping to a low, dangerous tone. "You still think you're in control, don't you? You're just a pawn in my game. You've always been a pawn. And now you're going to play by my rules. I gave you a chance to escape, but I'm afraid you've come too far. I'll make sure you regret this."

Indira stood firm, her heart racing. She knew she couldn't back down now. Not for herself, and not for Elias. As she steeled herself, something shifted in the air. The world around her seemed to warp, like a thick fog seeping into her senses. She looked around, and that's when she realized what was happening.

Smooth's Trap:

Smooth wasn't just a man; he had powers and abilities that allowed him to manipulate dimensions. He wasn't bound by the same rules of reality that she was. The cabin she had walked into was not of this world; it was part of his dimension-jumping game—a dimension that existed just outside of normal reality. The realization hit her like a freight train, but it was too late. The cabin, the trees, the moonlit sky, everything began to shimmer, disintegrating into a swirling vortex of colors. Indira tried to move, to escape, but it was as if her body had frozen in place.

Smooth's laugh echoed in the air as the ground beneath her feet began to dissolve. He was still speaking, his voice growing distant, but the words were incomprehensible as the world around her broke apart.

"You thought you could escape me, Indira?" he sneered, his voice cutting through the chaos. "You were always going to be mine. And now, you're exactly where I want you."

Before she could fully react, a powerful force enveloped her, pulling her into the void. Everything went black.

Indira's Prison:

When Indira finally regained consciousness, she was no longer in the cabin or the forest. Instead, she found herself in a cold, dimly lit chamber. The walls were lined with stone, the air heavy with an unnatural chill. It was a private island, isolated from the rest of the world. It was his dimension, where he had created his new and improved game. Here, there would be no escape, no way out.

Indira's head throbbed; her vision was blurry as she tried to get her bearings. She attempted to stand, but her limbs were weak, and the weight of her surroundings pressed down on her. As she struggled to sit up, she noticed a set of chains on the floor, seemingly discarded as if they had once been used. The realization hit her: Smooth had captured her. She was no longer in her world. She was in his.

She had no way to communicate with Elias, no way to contact anyone. Smooth had thought of everything. Her phone, her ability to reach out—everything had been disabled. She was trapped in his dimension, a prisoner in a world beyond her comprehension.

Elias's Powerlessness:

Back in the real world, Elias was in a panic. He had no idea what had happened to Indira. When she didn't come back after confronting Smooth, he rushed to the cabin, only to find it abandoned. The only thing left behind was the lingering sense of danger, a feeling that Smooth had been there and had taken her. There were no physical signs of a struggle, no evidence that anything unusual had occurred. It was as if she had simply vanished.

Elias knew that Smooth had to be behind it, but what could he do? He couldn't call the police; there was no proof that anything had happened, and he couldn't dimension-jump to find her. His off-grid lifestyle had made sure he was disconnected from any technological tracking systems. He had no GPS, no way of following her, and Smooth knew that.

Elias felt helpless. He couldn't follow her to another dimension. He couldn't reach out to anyone for help. All he could do was wait, knowing that Smooth had taken the love of his life and trapped her somewhere he could never find.

The Despair of Indira's Confinement:

Indira's heart pounded in her chest as she paced around the cold, stone chamber. The oppressive silence was maddening. She had been through so much in her life, but this—being trapped in a dimension that was not her own—was different. Smooth had outsmarted her, outmaneuvered her at every turn. She wasn't sure how long she would be there or if she would ever escape.

One thing was certain: she wasn't going to give up. She had fought too hard to survive, and she wouldn't let Smooth win.

Despite the overwhelming fear and despair that clawed at her, Indira knew she had a chance to break free. The first step was to fight back, to never let herself believe that Smooth had won. If there was one thing

Smooth underestimated, it was her strength. She had been tested before, and she would be tested again.

This time, though, she would not be the pawn. She would become the queen.

Indira's Vulnerability as a Pregnant Prisoner:

Indira's strength had always been her resilience, but in this new, terrifying reality, her pregnancy became both her strength and her greatest vulnerability. As she was dragged into Smooth's dimension, she realized the immense physical and emotional toll her pregnancy placed on her. Every attempt to fight back, every plan to escape, was complicated by her growing vulnerability. Smooth knew this, and he had used it against her. The fear of harming her unborn child kept her from taking the risks she once would have.

While imprisoned on Smooth's private island, the isolation and stress wore her down, but the child she carried kept her grounded. Even though her body was physically weakened from confinement, she couldn't afford to give in to despair. Every time she tried to gather her strength to escape or push back, the constant reminder of her pregnancy held her back. She couldn't risk putting her baby in harm's way, even if it meant remaining trapped for now.

Smooth, aware of her condition, didn't push her too hard physically—he knew better than to provoke the protective instincts of a pregnant woman. Instead, he played on her fears, using her pregnancy as a psychological weapon, knowing that it would keep her from acting recklessly. The constant uncertainty and lack of control over her own body made her feel even more powerless, but her determination to protect her child from the nightmare she was living through fueled a deep inner strength.

As the months passed, her pregnancy continued, and the fact that she was still carrying her child, despite everything, became a symbol of her endurance. She clung to the hope that somehow, one day, she would find a way out, not just for herself, but for her baby too.

She was becoming increasingly troublesome, so Smooth instructed one of his robots to restrain her to the chair, seal her mouth with duct tape, place headphones on her ears, blindfold her, and cover her face. Now, she must wait to find out what comes next.

Chapter Three

ESCAPE ROOM:
LEAGUE OF LEGENDS

Smooth had embarked on a relentless journey across various dimensions, targeting and eliminating some of the most powerful figures in each realm. His goal was simple—domination over every dimension in existence. Over a year, he accomplished his mission, hunting down every individual on his list.

Smooth didn't rely on sheer will alone. Along the way, he mastered the science of cloning, creating multiple versions of himself capable of operating simultaneously in different dimensions. This strategic advantage allowed him to strike several realms at once, catching his enemies off guard. Each target believed they were dealing with the only Smooth, never realizing they might be facing a clone, a copy just as dangerous as the original.

They had nine hours—nine fleeting hours to truly connect. Indigo couldn't help but recall what happened the last time the clock ran out. Back in season one, they'd tried to learn more about each other, but their focus had leaned heavily toward the spiritual. It wasn't until later, as time wore on, that a deeper understanding began to form between them. Letting someone in was never easy, and in a situation like this, opening up to a stranger felt even more daunting.

As time went on, they all came together, finally getting the chance to truly connect. This time, the focus wasn't on outside factors; it was on themselves. No distractions, no detours. Just a real conversation. As their eyes drifted to the countdown, Brandon broke the silence with a grin. "We've got nine hours," he said. "That's one hour each."

So, they did just that. One by one, each person took their hour, revealing pieces of their deepest, darkest truths. Not everyone shared everything, but most felt they had given enough, at least for now. Some opened up about their family dynamics, others about friendships, and many recounted how they ended up in this place to begin with. As the stories unfolded, it became clear just how different their origins were—each trapped from a unique timeline or dimension. In their world, "dimension" meant more than just space; it was an entirely different plane of existence they called home.

Vesperian knew with certainty: this was not his. Not his home, not his realm, not even his planet. He yearned to return to the higher planes where he truly belonged. Eager to get it over with, he was the first to speak.

In a room full of people who had seemingly always gotten their way—accomplished, confident, unshaken—Vesperian felt like an outsider. He wasn't alone, not exactly. The others offered their support, and he was always backed by his unseen spiritual army. Still, the loneliness clung to him. He couldn't relate to them, at least not yet.

The only ones he felt a faint connection to were Indigo and Brandon. He hadn't heard their stories, nor anyone else's, but something deep within told him they were different. It was an instinct, an inner knowing, and that was enough... for now.

Vesperian was born to rule—a king in spirit and blood. He felt it in his bones, in the way the energy shifted when he walked into a room, but the absence of his true soul family gnawed at him, quietly and relentlessly. Though he sensed a royal lineage pulsing through his veins, his memories betrayed him. All he remembered was being adopted. The faces of his real family, their voices, and their truths were lost to him.

They had promised to return, to explain everything, but when? He didn't know. As the days dragged on, hope began to blur into doubt. He clung to patience, held tight to faith, but the weight of this mundane world pressed down on him. Repetition dulled his senses, and the presence of low-vibrational humans—people who couldn't even begin to comprehend the depths of his soul—pushed him to the edge. The more time he spent here, the more his sanity began to unravel.

The remaining players were impressed by Vesperian's book, but to him, it was never about recognition. It was the fulfillment of a soul mission—a divine purpose written into his being long before he arrived in this dimension. He didn't care about followers, likes, comments, or sales. For Vesperian, it was about legacy. About using the limited resources available in this realm to leave behind something eternal. Something that would allow him to exit this plane with a sense of peace.

Still, he questioned the others' comfort and support. Were they genuine, or simply reacting to the intensity of their shared circumstances? He often thought, *"They haven't read my book, how can they claim to understand me?"* To Vesperian, they felt like products of the system, even sellouts—still plugged into a matrix designed to reward those who played by its rules. The system thrived on those who lived for it, but not him. He was made to transcend it.

Vesperian believed he could become the next Demiurge—a cosmic architect of his reality—but he knew confidence was a muscle he still needed to strengthen. Some days, he was electric, pulsing with high-vibrational energy and unstoppable confidence. In a universe governed by polarity, surrounded by dense environments and wrapped beneath the electromagnetic cage of this Earth's dome, he knew those highs wouldn't last.

So, he turned to his vices—addictions that filled the void, even if only temporarily. The more he chased the highs, the harder they became to reach. He constantly needed to outdo himself, to dare more, to feel more. Skydiving, tightrope walking over shark-infested waters—he became a living daredevil, chasing that primal rush. Anything that spiked his heart rate, flooded his system with adrenaline, and reminded him he was still *here*—he craved it.

That fearlessness, that disregard for the physical experience, was exactly what drew the group to him. He didn't pretend to care. He didn't cling to this world, and yet, somehow, he was beginning to bond with his potential new allies. Still, Vesperian kept a distance. He couldn't afford attachments, not here. He knew all too well that attachment tethered the soul, keeping it caught in the karmic loop of reincarnation. He had no intention of returning.

He was a master of release. Of detachment. Of walking away. If someone new entered his life and didn't resonate beyond a week, he deleted their contact. His energy was sacred, and it was not for the undeserving. If they noticed his absence and reached out, and if their message wasn't too clouded by fear or insecurity, he'd read it. Then delete the thread. No looking back. Only forward. Some people were never meant to stay. Some people were meant to prepare you for the ones that will.

Yet, sitting with this strange group, Vesperian felt something different. A small sigh of relief escaped him. He had allowed himself to open up. To be seen. Vulnerability had always come naturally to him—authenticity was part of his essence—but this was something else. This was proof of how far he'd come.

Jaxon stepped forward, inserting himself into the spotlight without hesitation, as he wanted to go next. He always had a way of commanding attention, like it was his birthright. Among the group, he stood out as the outlaw, the misfit, the one who never quite played by the rules. He carried himself with the quiet confidence of someone who believed he was above it, even if others had impressive résumés or outward success. To Jaxon, that didn't mean much.

He understood that success was subjective. Money, fame, influence—sure, he had all of that, but his definition was simpler: a comfortable, luxurious lifestyle on his terms. That was the goal. That was the dream.

Of course, this was *Jaxon* we're talking about—so his addictions came with the territory. He was a walking headline, a viral moment just waiting for the right spark. He didn't always make the best choices, and he knew it, but somehow, that only added to his mystique.

Jaxon radiated the main character's energy. It wasn't something he forced—it just *was*. No matter where he went, what he did, or who he was with, his presence was undeniable. You felt it before he even spoke.

He was the hero of his own story, no question about it. Every waking moment felt like a scene ripped from a film, his life flashing by in surreal, fragmented snapshots. It was a constant paradox, like living in two movies at once. One moment, he was immersed in a passion project; the next, he was juggling something entirely different, yet equally important. His reality felt layered, multidimensional.

Jaxon lived like a man under a spotlight. It was as if the world were watching his every move, like he was the star of an ongoing series, and the audience couldn't look away. At times, it felt less like life and more like a game, where people lined up just for the chance to play as him. To be him.

That was what it meant to be Jaxon. A living spectacle. A character so vivid, so electric, he blurred the line between real life and fiction.

The only shadow cast over Jaxon's larger-than-life existence was his relationship with addiction. He never saw himself as an addict—not at first. For him, it started as a release, a way to escape the chaos and pressure of reality, to ease the weight he carried in silence. The highs were temporary, but they brought him clarity, even comfort.

In the beginning, it didn't feel like a problem, and truthfully, it wasn't, not then. As time passed, the lines began to blur. What started as occasional relief slowly tightened its grip, becoming more than just a coping mechanism. It began to take over—subtly, quietly—until it became a part of his rhythm, a part of him.

In the beginning, Jaxon leaned on his vices to cope. To unwind. To silence the storm. As the buzz around him grew—*the next big thing,* they called him—the pressure followed. People projected their expectations, their envy, their shadows onto him, and Jaxon, still learning how to guard his energy, let it in. The negative comments, the noise, the clout-chasers, he let it all shape his reality, even when he told himself it didn't.

People came and went, not to love him, but to feed off him. To soak up the glow, then disappear once they'd drained him dry. He didn't want to admit it, but somewhere along the line, the escape became an addiction. The sex, the drugs, the fame, the porn, the women, the alcohol—it was no longer just about release. It was avoidance. Distraction. Survival.

Unlike Indigo, who had already faced his shadows head-on in season one, Jaxon kept his buried deep. Hidden behind charm, jokes, and high fashion, but inside, he was fighting a war no one could see.

He carried the weight of generations—*the curse breaker* of his bloodline. He wanted to believe he had real support, but time revealed the truth: most were just hanging on for the ride, chasing the benefits of his rising star. He'd buy chains for his boys, drop thousands on first dates, trying to outrun the emotional chaos within.

When it became too much, he'd reach for a quick fix. A pill, a line, a body, a bottle, but the relief was always temporary. Afterward, when the high wore off, he never quite crashed to zero. No, Jaxon was a warrior— he always found a way to rise. To alchemize the pain, even when he didn't know how he was doing it. He shook off parasites, cleared his field, and kept going.

Nonetheless, the cycle repeated. Old habits returned. Doubt crept in. He'd fall, beat himself up, and get lost in the loop of shame and self-criticism. He was hard on himself—*too* hard—expecting perfection while still trying to heal in a world that only wanted his image, not his truth.

He believed something better was coming. He *knew* it. The luxurious lifestyle wasn't just for show; it was a glimpse of the reality he was manifesting, but the battle was internal. Between who he was, who he truly *is*, and the ego that kept whispering distractions.

It was like post-nut clarity, every time. The indulgence would end, and there it was again—his wisdom, his truth, staring him in the face.

There were days when Jaxon felt like nothing more than a walking skeleton—hollow, exhausted, barely alive beneath the glamour. He rarely ate, not because he didn't want to, but because the grind left no room. The demands of his career pulled him in every direction, and for the right price, Jaxon was there. Gigs, shows, performances, appearances—he said yes to it all. He knew his worth, but he also wanted to expand. To become *everywhere*.

He didn't just show up; he gave people a show. He learned choreography, built stage presence, and created unforgettable moments for his fans. He responded to messages, built communities across platforms, and fulfilled every custom request, including videos, shoutouts, and even text messages, for those who paid. He was always *on*, always available. Always performing.

Behind the scenes, he lived a lifestyle few could sustain. He practiced daily dry fasting, a habit rooted in discipline from the days before fame. Back then, he followed a strict routine—eating and hydrating only in the evenings, but even that started to slip. The endless travel, the flashing lights, and the constant energy drain wore on him. The fame brought excitement, no doubt. Each day was a new adventure, far from the mundane life he once knew. He loved that part.

There was one thing he neglected: his health.

Late nights turned into early mornings. He'd crash at one of his many properties, only to wake up and do it all over again. It didn't feel like work, not really. He was living his dream, but each day came with its own storm: tighter deadlines, unpredictable schedules, pressure from fans, run-ins with paparazzi. He had prepared for this life, but not the full weight of it. The industry was far more ruthless than he expected.

Just when he thought he was adapting, *Smooth* entered the picture.

The moment Smooth showed up, everything shifted. Jaxon didn't say it aloud, but deep down, he knew—if Smooth asked him to do something, he'd do it. No hesitation. That control, that hold, came from the same place as his addictions. Though the other players didn't know the full extent of it, they sensed enough to offer support.

They rallied around him, assured him he wasn't alone. They'd seen addiction before—some had experienced it. They knew how heavy it was to carry, how hard it was to stay clean, but they also knew it could be done. With discipline. With support. With a real connection.

Jaxon appreciated it—he did. The bond he was forming with the others felt different. Real. For the first time in a long time, he didn't feel completely alone, but still... he hadn't let go. He was still hooked on the cycle, and he wasn't ready to admit it—not yet.

So, he kept that part hidden.

After that heart-to-heart with Jaxon, Kaelion stepped forward. Something in him stirred—a quiet, steady urge to speak. Not for attention, but because he felt called to help. Supporting those around him came naturally. It was part of his wiring, his purpose. That was the essence of Kaelion: lifting others as he rose.

He felt a deep pull toward Jaxon—not out of pity, but out of familiarity. They were both products of the same spotlight, both navigating the weight of celebrity in their own ways. To Kaelion, Jaxon felt like a younger brother—talented, bright, but still finding his way.

Jaxon had a mild crush on Zarina, though it was fleeting, and Kaelion knew it. Zarina, however, exchanged a subtle glance with Kaelion that said everything. She didn't trust Jaxon. She feared he might pull Kaelion into a mess he didn't need to fix. *You don't have to be his savior*, her eyes said.

Kaelion didn't mind. That was simply who he was.

He was an example of how to handle fame with grace. Not arrogant. Not boastful. Just confident. Unshakably confident. Some of the other players may have misread it as cockiness, but Kaelion's heart was pure. His soul was rooted. He'd been through his storms—fought through pain, setbacks, rejection—and still emerged standing, stronger than before.

Still, he felt the tension in the group. There was a subtle undercurrent—respect mixed with unease. Some of them admired him. Others felt intimidated. Not because he ever looked down on them, but because his energy was *big*. His presence was undeniable. He carried that "star" frequency, and not everyone knew how to hold space for it.

In that moment, he looked toward Zarina. Without a word, she reached out and held him tight. Her touch grounded him, reminded him of his truth. Zarina had always been there for Kaelion. She was his anchor, his emotional home. Together, they didn't just survive the spotlight; they grew stronger in it. They were open, raw, and committed, even attending therapy regularly to nurture their connection. Their love was unbreakable. A bond forged not in perfection, but in effort.

So instead of making the moment all about him, Kaelion turned to her, a soft smile playing on his lips. "I want you to go next," he said, passing the torch to Zarina because he loved her that much. Enough to step aside. Enough to share the light.

Next up was Zarina.

The moment she stepped forward, she flashed a sly smile and said, "Kaelion is my boyfriend—so back off. That's my man, my man, my man." It was playful, but there was a fire behind it. She wasn't joking *that* much. That was her man. *Her* man. No one was going to come between them.

She wasn't possessive or controlling, but she was feisty. Protective in a way that made it clear: loyalty runs deep with her.

People often misjudged Zarina at first glance. With her beauty, poise, and polished presence, they assumed she was some spoiled Barbie doll, a pampered princess who coasted through life on charm, looks, and connections, but they had it all wrong.

Zarina was sharp. Grounded. Bold. She moved with intention and spoke with clarity. Online, sure, people saw the glitz, the curated content, the perfect angles. From that, they made assumptions about her lifestyle, her personality, and the kind of people she surrounded herself with.

Those assumptions barely scratched the surface.

Zarina had always kept it real. She showed her life on-screen—but not *all* of it. There were pieces she chose to protect. Not because she was fake, but because she knew the power of privacy. Still, even with the boundaries she set, her authenticity shone through. Anyone who took the time to *talk* to her would understand why Kaelion was so smitten. She had a depth that didn't need to be explained—it was felt.

She was the kind of woman who could balance the spotlight and her soul, her public life, and her private healing. That balance gave her an edge—something mysterious, almost untouchable. Which, ironically, made people even more curious. Some labeled her as secretive or fake. The truth is, she didn't owe the world her entire life.

The one person who always saw her—truly saw her—was Kaelion.

When the world felt heavy, he was her anchor. Her peace. The masculine presence she could melt into, the stronghold that allowed her to soften and return to her divine feminine energy when the cameras were off, and the day was done. He was her comfort when life got chaotic. Her safe space in a loud, demanding world.

Zarina spoke next about the journey—the long road to success that most people never saw.

As time passed, she managed to carve out something rare: a loyal, dedicated fan base. It hadn't been easy. There were plenty of moments when she wanted to give up, but something inside her—faith, fire, maybe both—kept her going. She believed in herself, even when the results didn't come right away. She held onto the vision, trusting that one day, her dreams would manifest.

To outsiders, her life might've looked effortless. Like things just *happened* for her. Like she always got what she wanted, but Zarina didn't let those assumptions shake her. She knew the truth.

She remembered the grind. The long days. The sleepless nights. The weekends she skipped out on just to finish a project. The times she chose discipline over comfort. She had poured her heart, mind, and soul into her craft. Every post, every appearance, every piece of content was intentional.

There were seasons when it wasn't her turn. When the spotlight passed her by, she waited. Patiently. Quietly. When the moment finally came—when the opportunity knocked—she didn't hesitate. She was already prepared. Her work spoke for itself.

Even during the quiet years, when recognition was minimal and progress felt slow, she stayed the course. Kept creating. Kept believing. She knew that if she kept showing up, her time would come, and it did.

With all her might, her unwavering will, and the quiet strength she cultivated over the years, Zarina seized new opportunities as they came. She launched fresh ventures, leaned into her intuition, and let her creativity flow straight from the heart. She stayed open, receptive to change, growth, and the unknown. In doing so, she carved out a space for herself in the world, not by following trends, but by simply being herself.

Her rise was organic. Authentic. Every step forward was earned.

Then came Kaelion.

To Zarina, he felt like karmic justice. A divine reward for the sacrifices she'd made, the nights she stayed up grinding while the world slept, the years she remained faithful to a vision no one else could see. Their connection came unexpectedly, but it was undeniable. She welcomed *him* with open arms.

It felt like they had been prepared for each other. Spiritually aligned. Timed exactly right. He was everything she didn't know she needed, and she was everything he had been waiting for.

As she spoke, many of the remaining players sat in awe, deeply moved by their love story. It wasn't just romantic, it was inspiring. A reminder that real love doesn't compete; it complements, and it often comes after the storm.

Zarina, meanwhile, found herself drawn to Celestine and Indira. The three of them shared a quiet, almost instinctual bond. A sisterhood that felt unbreakable. As young women navigating the trials of growth, self-discovery, and pressure, they saw reflections of each other in the spaces no one else noticed. They didn't have to speak much to feel connected. Their energy aligned.

Vespera, though older, didn't feel disconnected. She understood the younger generation's rhythm and had always had people in her life to help her bridge that gap. She didn't feel left out—she didn't need to. Her presence was regal, wise, and complete. It was now Vespera's turn to speak.

Vespera began with a smile, lightly commenting on how similar her name was to Vesperian's. The two shared a quiet laugh over it—an instant point of connection, but beyond their names, there was something deeper they both understood: the truth about this physical world. The illusions, the distractions, the cycles—it was knowledge they carried like a hidden compass.

Vesperian had always gravitated toward older women. Something about their energy, their wisdom, and their stability intrigued him. What he didn't know—until that moment—was that Vespera was married.

What attracted him even more, though, was the duality she embodied. Vesperian admired women who worked in masculine fields, pursued powerful professions, or carried bold hobbies, so long as they still tapped into their feminine essence when they were with him. That balance was important to him, and Vespera embodied that effortlessly. In the public world, she moved in her divine masculine, confident, direct, and leading. At home, she softened into her divine feminine. She knew when to lead and when to flow.

It was a dynamic Vesperian respected... until she mentioned her family.

When she revealed that Celestine was her daughter, that she had a son, and a husband, the spark faded for Vesperian. Quietly, he stepped back. He didn't judge her—he just knew his boundaries. He had preferences. Strong ones.

Vesperian didn't like getting involved with women who already had children. One child was tolerable—*if* he genuinely liked the person. Two would require deep love. Anything beyond that? He had stipulations.

Three kids or more? That would only work if the woman were a celebrity, wealthy, or his divine counterpart—his twin flame. Even then, it would be rare. He wasn't interested in adoption. He dreamed of raising his children, born from a bond he built from the ground up.

So, as much as he had admired Vespera's energy, he quietly accepted that she wasn't for him in that way, and that was okay.

Not every connection had to be romantic. Some were just there to mirror back a truth. To show a part of yourself you hadn't seen until someone else reflected it.

Vesperian tended to lose interest quickly. His curiosity burned bright in the beginning—intense, focused, all-consuming—but it didn't always last. His fleeting crush on Vespera faded just as naturally as it arrived. Not out of bitterness, but clarity. He still valued her presence and genuinely enjoyed her company, but he no longer viewed her as a romantic possibility. Friendship, though? That was still on the table.

For Vesperian, inner beauty held the highest currency. It didn't mean physical attraction didn't matter—he appreciated aesthetics like anyone else—but a beautiful exterior without a meaningful soul beneath it? That did nothing for him. Likewise, someone could be a radiant soul, full of depth and grace, but if there wasn't a spark of physical chemistry, he would quietly move them into the friend zone.

To him, attraction was a delicate balance, like a scale that rarely tipped just right. "Blueberries," he thought. "They're healthy, but some people love them, some just like them, some can't stand them... and some are allergic." That's how he saw human connection. Subjective. Personal. Energetic.

In the past, he had met people who seemed to have both inner and outer beauty, but time would reveal a different truth. Many of them turned out to be energy vampires, karmic ties, or manipulative figures trying to siphon his light, derail his path, or drain his purpose. He'd learned to be cautious. Discerning. Selective. Not out of fear, but out of self-awareness.

So, as Vespera spoke, he listened with presence. He remembered. He reflected. He kept his heart open, but his energy guarded. There was no resentment, no judgment. No trauma bond lingering in the shadows.

Vesperian had done the work. He didn't fall into patterns of love bombing, over-romanticizing, or ghosting people without reason. He had lived, loved, and learned too much to play those games. He knew his worth now. He knew what he was looking for. One day, he believed he'd find it.

What Vesperian hadn't realized in that moment was that Vespera *said* she *had* a husband, not *has*. It was a small detail, but a crucial one. Once Vespera opened up about the tragedy—about what happened to her husband and her son, Isaac—remorse washed over Vesperian like a tidal wave. He had misjudged her. Assumed too quickly. He'd read the cover and missed the story entirely. Suddenly, all his self-imposed preferences faded.

He no longer cared that she had children. What mattered was the woman in front of him—her energy, her soul, the pain behind her strength. Something inside of him softened, and his interest reignited— not in a superficial way, but in a deeper, more meaningful light.

Vespera, for her part, enjoyed Vesperian's presence. His vibe. The way his energy didn't pressure her but instead gave her space to breathe. She wasn't opposed to the idea of doing something more with him, but she wanted to move slowly. Carefully. She had just lost her husband and her son to a tragic event. The grief was still fresh, the wound still open.

This game, this twisted dimension they were all caught in, had its own rules. While she wasn't ready for love, she *was* open to connection. Vesperian felt like someone she could trust. Someone she could keep close, not for strategy, but for soul-level grounding.

Still, the weight of what had happened bore down on her. As she spoke, the emotion broke through. Tears streamed down her cheeks. She had been trying desperately to repair the broken pieces of her life. To rebuild a deeper connection with her daughter, Celestine, but everything spiraled when they were both dragged into this chaotic game because of *her*. Of what *she* did for work. She blamed herself.

Vespera had always kept her personal and professional lives separate. Private and controlled, but Smooth had crossed that line. Violated her peace. Put her family in danger. Now, she was ready to make him pay.

She ranted through clenched teeth about the ways she planned to make Smooth suffer—how she'd drag him through the same torment she was enduring now. Her words were sharp, filled with fury and raw emotion, but to Celestine, it felt like a waste of precious time. She knew her mother wasn't in the right state to complete their mission if she stayed stuck in that vengeful loop. So, quietly, Celestine reached for her.

She placed her mother's trembling hand over her own heart, steady and calm. "Breathe with me," she whispered. Together, they began a simple ritual—five deep breaths in and out, slow and grounding.

Vesperian rested his hands gently on Vespera's shoulders, rubbing her back with care. He didn't say anything; he just *held space.*

When Vespera finally calmed, when her tears dried and her chest no longer heaved with grief, she found her voice again. With that, she began to tell the group her story.

Some of the players couldn't help but raise eyebrows as Vespera revealed more about her past—and, more specifically, what she did for work. Judgments lingered in the silence, even if unspoken. Her profession, the danger it carries, the ripple effect it had on her family—it was a lot to take in. Once the initial shock wore off, something deeper settled in. Respect.

Beneath Vespera's savage exterior was a heart that still beat with warmth. She wasn't cold—just guarded. She was like a giant teddy bear in armor: soft on the inside, but if you pushed her too far, the armor would lock in, and her divine masculine energy would take over. She'd learned to survive that way.

Everyone has a past. The important part was refusing to stay stuck in it.

What mattered was the *now*. What you choose to do in the present moment. That's where transformation lived—where healing began. Vespera was walking that path, step by step. She didn't pretend to be perfect. Like Jaxon, she had made her share of mistakes, but unlike many, she was actively trying to fix them. The group saw that. They felt that.

So, they offered their condolences for the loss of Vireo, her husband, and Isaac, her son. They knew the pain she carried, and even if they couldn't feel the full weight of it, they honored it. Vespera and Celestine had each other now... and maybe, just maybe, they had this group too.

Still, Vespera wasn't fully convinced. Trust didn't come easily. Not after everything. These people were still new, and she knew better than to let her guard down so quickly. Her protective instincts remained sharp, always ready to shield Celestine if needed. She stayed rooted in her masculine energy, not to dominate, but to defend. It all traced back to her childhood.

She came from a fractured home, a broken family unit, and she'd spent her entire adult life trying to rise above those generational wounds. The emotional burden she carried wasn't just her own—it was ancestral. The group could see that now. They saw her fight. They saw her effort. They respected her even more for it.

She had built a life for herself, one full of power, influence, and what looked like control, but the truth was, it had always been fragile. It only took one person—Smooth—to strip it all away. She was now left trying to piece together what was shattered. She hadn't given up, and that alone made her unstoppable.

It only felt right that the next person to speak was Celestine.

Her mother, Vespera, wasn't the type to cry—not in front of others, not even in front of her. Vulnerability wasn't something Vespera wore on her sleeve, but in that moment, broken and grieving, she let her daughter hold her. Celestine, still gently rubbing her mother's back, began to speak.

She didn't do it to shift the spotlight. She did it to lift the weight off Vespera's shoulders. "As I got older," Celestine said softly, "I made peace with the fact that my mom wasn't always around, but I never doubted her love for me. I knew she was doing what she had to do... and she'd make it up to me in her own way, in her own time." Her voice was calm, steady, like water smoothing over jagged rocks.

She had her friends. Her extended family. Her business ventures, her drive, her sense of purpose. She never resented her mother for the life she chose; she accepted her fully and completely. That was the kind of woman Celestine was: a bright soul who looked for the light in every shadow, the lesson in every challenge.

She'd already made it through her own physical and mental "desert"— the kind of spiritual, mental, and emotional wilderness that changes you. If she could survive that, she could survive anything.

So, while the others longed for escape, for freedom from this game, Celestine chose to embrace the journey. She saw it as a rare opportunity to reconnect with her mother, not just as parent and child, but as partners. As women. They all wanted to make it out of here, but she believed the only way was together. "That's why we're legends," she said, a quiet fire in her eyes.

Still, it was clear her mind had drifted more toward the strategy, the mechanics of their next move—how to solve this, how to escape. She was smart like that. Always five steps ahead.

Zarina chimed in with a knowing glance. "This challenge is about going *inward*, Cel," she reminded her. "Not just *outward*." Celestine gave her a small, grateful nod.

Zarina and Indira had a way of keeping her grounded, reminding her to sit still in her truth. The three of them shared an unspoken bond—one that didn't need constant affirmations to be felt. It was just *there*, steady, and strong.

With their presence anchoring her, Celestine took a breath and continued, peeling back another layer of her journey—one step closer to becoming whole.

Celestine didn't wait around for a handout, and she didn't need anyone to "put her on." Every bit of success she had, she earned herself. Yes, she made use of the resources available to her, but she was the one grinding behind the scenes—making moves, connecting with the right people, and staying aligned with those who matched her frequency.

What she wanted was peace. A low-drama life. She thrived in solitude, loved being in her energy, and was fully capable of running things on her own. Sure, she was an asset in any team, but she understood the inner workings of the industry so well, she could easily navigate it independently.

She sharpened her skills, poured love into her craft, and mastered her talents over time. Celestine had built herself into the woman she was—confident, creative, powerful. While some found her intimidating, those who truly saw her knew her heart was pure and her courage unshakable.

She didn't let her past hold her hostage. She didn't coast on her mother's name, even though Vespera had enough connections to open almost any door. Celestine wanted to earn her place—and she did. She was no longer just Vespera's daughter. She was Celestine Aurelia Kade—a name that carried its own weight.

As she finished, the room erupted into applause like she had just wrapped up a TED Talk. Vespera looked at her with pride that could light up a city, like her daughter had just taken home a Nobel Peace Prize.

Celestine laughed, a little bashful at all the fuss, but somewhere deep down, it felt good. Not because she needed validation, but because it confirmed that all the inner work, all the long nights and quiet sacrifices, were worth it.

Just like that, in true Celestine fashion, she redirected the spotlight—not one to soak in it too long. With a soft smile, she turned toward one of her girls and said, "Your turn." The torch was passed to Indira.

Indira, visibly pregnant and glowing with quiet strength, thanked Celestine for passing the spotlight to her. Brandon and Indigo offered warm nods of support, letting her know they didn't mind at all. With a small grin, Indira stood and gently cradled her belly, giving the group a glimpse of how far along she was. A few gasps of amazement echoed around the room as the others took in just how pregnant she was.

"The baby keeps kicking," she said with a soft laugh, though there was a flicker of discomfort in her eyes. "Sometimes it even feels like my water's about to break right here." She paused, closed her eyes, and took a few deep breaths, centering herself before diving into her story.

Indira spoke of the new life she was creating—not just the one growing inside her, but the life she was slowly building after surviving a game of her own. This revelation sent a ripple of surprise through the group, especially Brandon and Indigo. They hadn't known that Smooth had orchestrated his twisted games long before their version began.

She went on to describe the brutal nature of that earlier trial, the emotional toll, the mental strain, and the unexpected strength it forced her to discover. She talked about how, in the end, she was the only one to make it out. The only legend to survive.

Then came the mention of Elias.

As soon as his name passed her lips, her voice cracked. She tried to hold it together, but the grief came rushing in like a wave. Her composure broke, and before she knew it, she was giving one of those raw, unfiltered, ugly cries. The kind that's not for show but born from deep loss.

In the corner of the room, Jaxon thought to himself how emotional everyone seemed to be getting, but even he didn't look away.

The rest of the players leaned into her pain. They circled her in comfort. It was in that moment that it became clear—while Vespera gave off the fierce protective energy of a mother, Indira was the soft-hearted sister or favorite cousin that everyone instinctively wanted to shield.

It was grueling—being pregnant in captivity. Indira knew how this game worked, and yet her body couldn't keep up with the demands. The fatigue, the constant need for hydration, the hunger, the physical strain—it was wearing her down. Worst of all, she couldn't shake the feeling that her condition made her a liability.

"I feel like I'm holding all of you back," she admitted, eyes low and voice heavy with guilt. Before the silence could settle, Celestine and Zarina jumped in. "You're not a burden," Zarina said gently. "You're strong. Stronger than most." Celestine nodded in agreement, her tone firm. "You've already survived one version of this game. That alone makes you a legend."

Indira exhaled, the tension slowly leaving her shoulders. With their reassurance, she found the strength to continue—her voice steady as she opened up about the journey that led her to this moment.

It became increasingly clear to the group that Smooth had his favorites, and Indira, Brandon, and Indigo seemed to be at the top of that list. Indira's story had captivated everyone so deeply that they lost track of time. Just as she was about to continue speaking, a sudden gush of fluid hit the ground. Her water had broken.

The shock of the moment hit her hard. The stress, the environment, the emotions—it all came crashing down. Indira panicked, her breath becoming shallow as she clutched her belly.

Zarina snapped into action. "Kaelion—do something! Your mom's a doctor, right?" Kaelion, now fully alert, nodded but clarified, "Yeah, but she's a holistic doctor. Still... she's told me a few things about childbirth."

With the urgency rising, the group scattered to search for anything that could help. They scrambled through the rubble and debris until, surprisingly, behind a wall of discarded equipment, they found just what they needed: materials for a birth pool.

It was perfectly placed, too. Brandon paused, uneasy. *It's like Smooth planned this.* With Indira in pain, no one else noticed—or cared.

Time began to blur. Nothing else mattered but Indira. She was in full labor now.

There was blood. A lot of it, but everyone rallied around her, determined to help. Every player, no matter their past or pain, was all hands on deck, pouring all their effort into keeping Indira safe.

Two hours passed.

The energy in the room shifted. Kaelion grew silent, his face tight, his posture still. He stared at the blood pooling beneath them. Something wasn't right. The group looked to him, desperate for guidance.

"Kaelion...?" Indigo asked gently.

Kaelion didn't want to say it, but he had to. "There's... too much blood," he murmured. "This... this isn't normal."

A hush fell over the group. The truth hit hard—Indira had suffered a miscarriage.

Devastation swept through the chamber like a wave. Indira didn't say a word at first. She just stared at the space in front of her, expression blank, lips trembling. Then the reality hit, and the sobs came.

She had dreamed of motherhood—raising her child gently, naturally, free from chaos and toxins. A peaceful life filled with love, growth, and intention, but now... all of that was gone.

She curled into herself, barely able to speak. "I just wanted to go home... to Elias..."

The loss wasn't due to anything she did wrong. The embryo had stopped growing weeks ago. Her body had been trying to sustain life in an environment that simply wasn't equipped to nurture it. Lack of nutrients, lack of medical care, and the physical strain of captivity all contributed. Silent genetic complications have been developing over the last few days, and now, her baby is gone. Another soul lost. The death toll now stood at **177,012.**

A sudden, shrill buzzer pierced the air, harsh and jarring. The alarm echoed through the chamber, cutting through conversations and silencing the group. Time was up.

Their nine hours of bonding had come to an end. The intercom crackled to life, and the AI voice, calm but cold, spoke with eerie precision: "Your time is up, and you all didn't do good enough. I need a sacrifice." The words stunned the group. What do you mean, *not good enough*?

They had shared their stories. They had cried, supported one another, and even opened old wounds, but the voice didn't care about their surface-level reflections. It wanted depth—family ties, unspoken truths, raw vulnerability. Many of them had repeated information or barely scratched the surface, and they hadn't even heard from Brandon or Indigo yet.

The silence was thick... until Celestine broke it, her voice sharp and bitter. "Your sacrifice is this baby." Gasps spread like wildfire through the group.

The AI stuttered, seemingly unaware of the miscarriage. There was a pause, a long beat of static, then the voice returned—less robotic now, more calculating: "Noted, but a sacrifice is still required."

Tension clung to the air like smoke. "I'll give you time," it continued. "The rest of the night to think. To plan. Someone must be offered... willingly or not. Without sacrifice, there is no advancement. The player who steps forward and sacrifices another player will gain immunity in the next round... and an advantage. Choose wisely."

Then, as if to twist the blade: "Remember... don't hate the player, hate the game."

That line struck deep. A brutal reminder that this was more than just trauma and bonding—it was survival. A game where death loomed at every corner. No matter how connected they felt, only one or a few would make it to the end.

Suddenly, the emotional vulnerability of earlier shifted into something else: strategy. Some players took the moment to silently reassess their place in the group.

Still shaken, most of them drifted toward Indira to check on her. She was pale, weak, still emotionally shattered, but grateful for their support. She was holding on by a thread, physically and mentally.

Off to the side, Jaxon took the opportunity to pull Zarina aside, leaning in with his signature charm, whispering flirtatious remarks. She chuckled softly, clearly unbothered, but her eyes flicked to Kaelion across the room.

Kaelion saw it. He watched Jaxon's moves but chose silence. He trusted Zarina. He knew who she belonged to—and, more importantly, who she *chose*. He didn't need to play into insecurity.

Instead, Kaelion turned his focus elsewhere. He quietly gathered the empty plates from earlier, washed the dishes, took out the trash that had piled up during the meal, and tied up the bag with practiced ease. He set it by the door, replaced the liner in the bin, and returned to the group— his presence steady, grounded.

The atmosphere had shifted again. Wariness took root. Sacrifice wasn't just a word anymore. It was coming—and someone would have to make a move before dawn.

They all gathered in a quiet circle, kneeling beside Indira, their heads bowed. No words could truly capture the pain, but they offered up a solemn prayer for the soul of her unborn child. An innocent soul that was never given the chance to breathe life.

Exhaustion washed over the group like a crashing wave. It had been a long day, mentally, emotionally, and spiritually draining. They agreed it was best to rest, to regroup, and revisit the looming question of the sacrifice once they'd had sleep. A decision that heavy couldn't be made under fatigue. They needed clarity.

One by one, the players drifted off into uneasy slumber, curled up in corners or sprawled on the floor, shadows dancing on their bodies under the flickering overhead lights. Everyone was asleep, except for one.

That player remained wide awake, mind churning with thoughts of the promised immunity, the advantage that awaited whoever carried out the unthinkable. The temptation had been planted earlier, and now it had taken root. As silence filled the space, that player sat up slowly, rising from the floor like a corpse awakening from the grave.

Moving deliberately, they retrieved a set of noise-canceling headphones from a nearby crate that Smooth had conveniently left behind. One by one, they slipped the headphones over each sleeping player's head—even their own.

Somehow, everyone remained asleep. Whether it was the day's exhaustion or something else entirely... no one stirred.

The player moved with disturbing calm, picking up a pillow, donning long gloves that reached to their elbows, and selecting the sharpest knife they could find from the utility counter. They approached Indira silently.

She shifted, barely conscious, sensing something, and then the pillow came down. Panic flickered in her limbs. She writhed under the weight, gasping. Her legs kicked out and her arms clawed, but it was no use. Through clenched teeth, the player whispered: "Don't hate the player... hate the game."

As her struggle grew louder, the knife slid beneath the pillow. A single, swift motion. Silence. The blood soaked into the pillow's back, unseen. Her body went limp beneath the blanket that had once given her comfort. Above them, the red digital counter blinked: **Death Count: 177,013**

The player, calm and methodical, removed the gloves, peeling them inside out, no trace left behind. They washed the knife and pillow in the sink carefully and precisely. Then, they buried the items deep in the growing trash pile near the door, stuffing them beneath layers of waste and filth. Just another piece of discarded evidence.

They didn't need to clean themselves. No blood touched their skin. It was as if it never happened.

With cold composure, the player returned to their spot. They looked at Indira's still body. Gently, they pulled the blanket higher, covering her from view, disguising death as peaceful rest. Then, with the weight of what they had done hidden beneath a layer of stillness, the player lay down. They closed their eyes as their vision faded to black and finally went to sleep. That was the end of SEASON TWO, EPISODE TWO.

Indira Rune: A name that now echoed in memory, not in presence. She was a beacon in the storm — a soul who radiated peace, love, light, and a grounded sense of purpose. Indira wasn't naive; she knew the shadows just as well as the light. She had embraced both, which is how she survived Smooth's previous game. She did not run from darkness — she alchemized it. Turned pain into power. Fear into faith.

She was building something beautiful — a legacy rooted in truth. With her off-grid community, a reimagined business empire, and the promise of a family with Elias, her life was blossoming. She had begun planting seeds for generations to come, and then... she was gone.

Elias would never know what truly happened. He'd wait for a call that would never come. Hope for a letter, a sign — *anything,* but nothing will arrive. The silence would be his answer, and that silence... would haunt him.

He was already fractured by Smooth's looming threats, and now, he had to bear the weight of uncertainty and heartbreak alone. What made it worse was that Smooth still had eyes on him, puppeteering the narrative just enough to keep Elias under control. To keep the pain alive.

Indira wasn't just a contestant. She wasn't just another player. She was a star seed. A vessel of divine purpose. She came to this world to make an impact — and she did. She lit up every room she entered. She reminded others to stay grounded while reaching for the stars. She lived as if the higher realms were always watching... and they were.

She always knew her return to the cosmos would come sooner than expected. Perhaps that's why she lived with such intentions. Even though the way it happened was cruel, unexpected, and undeserved, she met death with grace.

Her body may be gone from this twisted game, but her essence *transcends.* Her story continues in the hearts of those she touched. In the lessons she left behind. In the whispers of the wind and the stardust, she now belongs.

Indira Rune is no longer part of this game... but she will never truly be gone.

Chapter Four

MURDER MYSTERY MOLE

SEASON TWO, EPISODE THREE. The timer blared as time was up. There was no need for it to finish counting down. The sacrifice had already been made.

One by one, the players stirred from their slumber, groggy and disoriented. Confusion blanketed the room. Each of them wore a headset. Indria lay still, wrapped in a blanket.

Celestine, closest to her, hesitated before gently pulling the blanket away. Her scream pierced the silence.

Vespera spoke next, voice hollow, "Smooth is such a terrible human being." A terrible human being can become a great god, but a great human will barely be a successful god.

Zarina choked back emotion. "Not my girl."

Kaelion whispered, "Dear god."

Jaxon muttered, "Not like this."

Vesperian, barely audible, said, "That should've been me."

Brandon wiped a tear. "This game, man..."

Indigo turned to Vesperian, puzzled by his words, but remained frozen in disbelief. Finally, Indigo spoke, "What the... No. No way. This can't be real."

They hadn't expected it. None of them did. When they woke up, they thought it was over—but it was only the beginning. The murder mystery had begun.

Before anyone could move—still reeling from the shock, headphones barely off—the intercom crackled to life. The AI's voice echoed through the room, calm but chilling: "Mission successful. One among you has completed the sacrifice and, in doing so, earned immunity... and an advantage in the next round."

A pause.

"The nature of that advantage will be revealed before this round ends. Until then, know this: there is a mole among you. Someone in this room is not who they seem."

A mechanical hum began to fill the air.

"To ensure things remain... civil, Smooth's enforcement units will now enter the room."

The door slid open with a hiss, and the sound of approaching footsteps—metallic and inhuman—followed. "Your time starts now."

A timer lit up—three hours. The countdown had begun.

Smooth's robots entered the room in silent formation, offering trays of food and water to keep the players functioning. It almost felt absurd—like they were at some twisted murder mystery dinner party, where the game was deadly, and the stakes weren't pretend.

The robots stood watch, their lifeless eyes scanning the room as if studying the players' every twitch, every breath. This eerie calm stirred an ancient dread; the whispers of the Forbidden Ones echoed in the back of their minds. Something old... something wrong was at play here.

They knew they had to consider every possibility, even the darkest ones. They needed a plan, an escape route, a last resort, but no one wanted to be the first to accuse. So, they waited in silence.

Eventually, Vesperian—never one for patience—broke the stillness. He reached for the food, chewing slowly, almost defiantly. Indigo watched him carefully. Something about Vesperian had shifted the moment Indria died. There was heaviness in his demeanor, a nervous edge that Indigo didn't trust. Still, he stayed quiet. Making the first move could paint a target on his back.

Vespera, simmering with suspicion, broke the silence. "It must be Smooth. It can't be anyone else, right?"

Brandon, ever the analyst, shook his head. "But why would Smooth need immunity or an advantage? He's the creator of the game."

Celestine stood abruptly, her grief bubbling over. "Then maybe it was one of his robots." She stormed over to the nearest one and stared it down. "Huh? Was it you? Which one of you did this to my girl?"

The robots didn't flinch. They didn't move. Cold, mechanical indifference. "Say something!" she shouted, voice cracking. Still nothing. Just blank stares.

Indigo spoke softly, "That wouldn't make sense either…" The others murmured in agreement. As much as they hated it, the truth was settling in around them like smoke. One of them had done it.

As the clock ticked down, the weight of indecision began to crush them. They all knew—*someone* had to make a move. Someone had to point their finger.

The tension simmered and soon boiled over when Vespera and Celestine turned their suspicions on Brandon and Indigo. After all, both men had pushed back the hardest, clapping back at their earlier theories.

"Convenient," Vespera muttered, arms folded. "You two were the only ones who had something to say when we brought up Smooth."

Celestine added, "You know who else had experience in this game? Indria. And now she's gone." That hit hard.

Brandon blinked, stunned. "What are you saying? That we took her out *because* she was experienced?" He shook his head, confused, but Indigo didn't let the accusation hang in the air. He stood, voice steady but tight with emotion. "I couldn't have done it. I was there for her… through everything. Through her pregnancy. You don't fake that kind of connection."

Vespera narrowed her eyes. "Then tell us. Who *do* you think did it?" All eyes fell on Indigo. He hesitated. A beat passed. Then another.

He closed his eyes, reaching for the spark inside him—his fated psychic ability. The chamber pulsed faintly around him, amplifying his senses, drawing out the truth that lay hidden beneath fear and doubt. Then he spoke, clear and cold. "Vesperian did it."

Vesperian nearly choked on his water. He spat it out with a loud splutter, staring wide-eyed at Indigo. "What? How'd you come up with *that*?

Indigo stayed calm, eyes locked on him. "It was your reaction when we found Indira. The things you said... they were off. And then you just sat there, eating. Like none of this mattered."

Vesperian's confusion turned to hurt. He looked between Brandon and Indigo, clearly stunned. "No... no, that can't be right. I thought we were on the same page. I thought I had the most in common with you two." His voice cracked.

Vespera noticed the shift in him, the vulnerability breaking through. She stepped forward and gently rubbed his back—the same way he had comforted her during her introduction. A small gesture, but a meaningful one.

Indigo softened for a moment, then asked, "So who do *you* think did it, Vesperian?"

Vesperian wiped his eyes and took a breath, trying to recalibrate. He glanced across the room. "...Kaelion." The name dropped like a stone.

Kaelion's head snapped up. "Wait—hold on. *Me*? You think I did this? I was one of the main people helping Indira through her pregnancy!"

Before anyone could respond, Jaxon's mind started racing. A flicker of memory—those subtle looks Kaelion had thrown his way every time he talked to Zarina. Cold. Judging. Possessive. Jaxon had clocked the animosity.

Kaelion saw Jaxon as a little brother. That was clear. Jaxon hadn't always appreciated it, especially during the game's intro, but it stuck with him. That bond had meant something.

Still, the tension had grown. Jaxon hadn't flirted with Zarina to start trouble—he just wanted to know her, but Kaelion's constant evil eyes said otherwise.

Jaxon had let it go for the first time. Gave him grace. The second time? Nah. He was done. Now he wanted all the smoke.

Jaxon stood tall, voice sharp like a blade. "It had to be Kaelion. He wasn't even a real doctor. He killed Indira's baby. Then, guilt kicked in—so he took her out, too. Covered her with that blanket to bury what he'd done."

Gasps rippled through the group. Kaelion froze, stunned. He hadn't seen it coming.

All that time he'd watched Jaxon joke, flirt, smile—he hadn't realized those eyes were watching him back. Not just the way he looked at Zarina... but the way Kaelion looked at *him*. Sure, he'd thrown Jaxon some dirty looks, but he never thought Jaxon *felt* them.

He always saw Jaxon as a younger brother. Someone to look out for. To guide. Now he saw him as a snake in the grass. Zarina had warned him.

Before Kaelion could speak, Jaxon doubled down, venom laced in his tone. "If it's not you, then who *is* it?"

That's when Zarina stepped forward, fire in her eyes. "It's *you*, Jaxon." The room stilled.

Zarina never liked him. Never trusted him. She let him flirt because it was a strategic, easy way to draw in allies. Now, it was personal.

Jaxon scoffed. "Of *course* you'd side with your man, your man, your man. We all heard you in the intro. No one needs a rerun."

The jab hit hard. Zarina flinched, but she caught herself fast. Composed. She didn't expect more from Jaxon, and now she saw him clearly for what he was.

Kaelion's fists clenched. "Watch your mouth," he growled. His eyes locked onto Jaxon with a dangerous intensity, like he was ready to throw down. All the focus, all the rage—redirected now, completely forgetting Vesperian's accusation.

It was no longer about logic. It was personal. The room was seconds away from erupting.

Kaelion closed the gap between him and Jaxon, fists clenched, fury in his eyes, but before he could get any closer, one of Smooth's robots stepped in and shoved him back with a cold, mechanical strength. "There will be no violence," the robot announced in its chilling monotone. "If necessary, we will take control of the situation."

Kaelion, not one to back down, got up in the robot's face and started mouthing off—trash-talking a machine that didn't even flinch. The robot didn't blink, didn't move. It just *watched*.

Minutes passed in a whirlwind of shouting and accusations, the group spiraling, getting nowhere. The clock was ticking, but no one was thinking.

Then Brandon, usually the level-headed peacemaker, snapped. "*Hey!*" he shouted, voice echoing through the chamber. "Let's look for some *actual evidence!*" His words cut through the noise. The tension, still heavy in the air, slowly began to settle.

With only an hour left, the players finally moved with purpose. They split up:

- Brandon and Indigo headed toward the closet and equipment area.
- Vespera and Celestine searched the kitchen and the bathroom.
- Kaelion and Zarina checked the main living space and examined Indira's body.
- Vesperian and Jaxon took the outer corridors, scanning the surrounding areas and the prison cells.

For a while, nothing. Just dust, discarded items, and dead ends. Then Kaelion called out. "She was stabbed, throat's been slit," he said grimly, pulling back more of the blanket covering Indira's body. "Someone used a knife."

Instantly, everyone's eyes shifted to the two most likely locations: the kitchen... or the equipment room.

Vespera's detective instincts kicked in. "Yesterday, we all used the butcher knife to prep dinner. It should've been drying in the rack—but it's gone," she said, eyes narrowed. She pointed to the sink. "And this sponge? It has red stains... smells like blood."

Celestine quickly checked the trash can near the counter—it was empty. Vesperian frowned. "That's weird." Then, something caught his eye. A black trash bag, tucked near the door. Not in the can—just sitting there. His suspicion deepened. Without a word, he began walking toward it.

Vesperian crouched by the trash bag, his hands carefully sifting through the layers of discarded wrappers, scraps, and plastic. His expression shifted from focused... to horrified. "Oh my God," he whispered.

Slowly, he pulled out a knife, a stained pillow, and a pair of long gloves—tucked deep beneath the garbage. The room held its breath.

He laid the evidence gently on the counter near the kitchen. There was no way to assess fingerprints not in this place, not under these circumstances—but the message was clear: Someone had done this.

Zarina stepped forward, trying to think fast. "We should all try on the gloves. See whose hands they match." Everyone glanced at the gloves, hesitant. It was a clever idea... but time was bleeding out fast.

Celestine recoiled, arms crossed tight. "Ew, no. I'm not putting on gloves that a murderer wore. There might still be blood on them!"

Tension crept back in. The countdown was relentless, and the AI had gone silent—no clues, no guidance, no hint as to who had gained the advantage this round.

Then Jaxon spoke. "It was Kaelion." Kaelion snapped his head around. "Come on, dude... seriously?"

Jaxon was not backing down. His voice was sharp, resolute. "After Indira lost the baby, Kaelion checked out. All he cared about was doing the dishes and taking out the trash. He wasn't devastated. He was *disengaged*."

He looked around the room, locking eyes with everyone. "He was shocked when she went into labor. It wasn't he who stepped in—it was Zarina. If she hadn't told him to move, he would've just stood there, silent."

The group turned slowly toward Kaelion. Their expressions were a mix of confusion, disbelief... and creeping suspicion. Zarina took a step closer to her partner, but even she looked shaken.

Vesperian nodded slowly, connecting the dots. "And during his intro? He barely said anything. Just passed it all over to Zarina. We don't *know* him. Not really. That's how people hide their secrets."

Kaelion looked around the room, once full of allies, now filled with eyes trying to see through him. The clock kept ticking.

Things were beginning to fall into place. The tension in the room was electric—every glance, every breath, every unspoken thought hung heavy in the air.

Time was almost up. They had to choose. No one knew what would happen if they failed this round—if they did not name the mole. None of them was willing to find out the hard way.

One by one, the votes started falling like dominoes.
"Kaelion."
"Kaelion."
"Kaelion."

Each name was like a dagger, and with every word, Kaelion's face grew paler, drained of life. It was as if his soul had stepped out of his body and left him behind. He sat there, motionless, eyes unfocused.

Zarina moved to his side and wrapped her arms around him. Tight. Protective. They had survived storms together before, but this? This was unlike anything they had ever faced.

There was no need to ask who Kaelion and Zarina would vote for. The decision had been made. The majority ruled, and Kaelion knew it.

A sick feeling rose in his chest. Was he the next sacrifice? Was he going to disappear like Indira? The fear clung to him, heavily and suffocating. Unspoken anxiety gripped his lungs.

The final seconds ticked away.
Three. Two. One.
BZZZZZTTT.
The timer rang out like a death knell. Silence swallowed the room.

Everyone stood frozen, tense, waiting for something to happen. Every eye shifted toward Kaelion. Even though they believed he was responsible for Indira's death, they also knew one thing: If he truly *was* the mole, then Kaelion had just gained immunity... and an advantage. He did not flinch, but some of them weren't buying it.

Kaelion was a celebrity, trained in the art of performance. He knew how to keep a straight face. How to control his breath, how to look shaken without cracking. That made him even more suspicious.

The AI voice crackled to life across the teleprompter, smooth and eerily calm. "Congratulations! You have completed this round successfully. Lucky for you... There will be no sacrifice."

Relief swept through the room like a gust of fresh air. The players erupted into scattered cheers, clapping and laughing nervously. For the first time in what felt like forever, there was joy, but not from Kaelion. He still sat frozen, heart pounding. Zarina kept her arms wrapped tightly around him, whispering quiet reassurances as his fear refused to subside.

The AI continued. "So, you all chose Kaelion as the person who was the mole. You know... Kaelion—the one who would gain immunity and an advantage in this round." Zarina narrowed her eyes, confused, thinking the immunity and advantage were for the next round. "Wait... isn't the round over? What's the point of immunity or an advantage now?"

She was not wrong. The immunity meant nothing anymore. The round had ended. There had been no death. No consequence—at least, not yet.

No one had seen a clear "advantage" play out, and that made the remaining players shift in their seats. Uneasy. Suspicious. Their eyes slowly turned—not to Kaelion this time—but to the AI itself. That voice... it *knew* something.

The AI cut in again. "None of you died in this round," it said. "But the player who received the advantage... has a *special* decision to make."

A beat.

"You all may want to sit down for this one."

As if on cue, Smooth's robots began moving the players, one by one, into a circle of chairs. Cold metal cuffs locked around wrists and ankles. Duct tape pressed down on their mouths before they could object. Panic returned, swift and sharp. A timer appeared on the central screen: **3:00**. It began to count down.

Then the voice returned. "You were wrong," the AI said, with a finality that sent a shiver through the room.

"It wasn't Kaelion."

A pause.

"It was Jaxon."

The room was so quiet, you could hear a pin drop.

Celestine broke the silence first—her sobs soft, broken, filled with disbelief. Tears streamed down her face.

Kaelion and Zarina were trying to scream through the duct tape, rage burning in their eyes, but the sound came out as nothing more than muffled cries of fury. They thrash themselves against their restraints, trying to get to Jaxon.

Zarina's eyes suddenly shifted, like a puzzle snapping into place. *Jaxon had spent more time flirting with her than checking on Indira... He had called her emotional, dismissed her entirely during her intro... And worse, he said he would do anything Smooth told him to do.* Her heart sank. The truth had been there all along.

One of Smooth's robots stepped forward and peeled the duct tape from Jaxon's mouth. His hands remained bound, but his voice was free.

The AI's voice echoed across the room. "Jaxon, why did you do it?"

Jaxon looked up slowly, and a wicked smirk curled across his lips. "I wanted to levitate her from her pain," he said, gently. "Let her be with her unborn child. You all would've done the same if you had the strength."

Everyone watched in horror as he continued, unbothered. "A sacrifice had to be made. And I made it. But let's not act like you weren't all staring at me, wondering about that immunity, that advantage you *didn't* get."

A low hum filled the air as the AI voice interrupted. "Oh, that's where you're wrong, Jaxon."

The tone shifted—less robotic, more sinister. "For committing a sacrifice... You will be rewarded."

A heavy pause.

"In this game, advantages are everything. They are the key to survival... and to victory."

Another beat.

"Your advantage for the sacrifice... is this: *you get to choose one player to die.*"

Only one minute remained. Jaxon closed his eyes and drew in a slow, deep breath. The room was heavy with tension, so thick it was hard to breathe. No one dared move. No one dared look at him. Their lives were now in *his* hands. In that moment, Jaxon didn't just hold power. He held the *world.*

When his eyes finally opened, they locked onto Kaelion. Everyone braced themselves, but then Jaxon said, calm and cruel: "I choose Zarina." Then—*a wink.* Directed right at Kaelion.

Shock rippled through the group like an earthquake. Not Kaelion? They were stunned. Speechless. Was this happening? Was it part of the game? Another twisted stunt meant to stir drama, plant seeds of doubt, and fracture their fragile alliances?

Thirty seconds left. One of Smooth's robots moved toward Zarina. She was still handcuffed to her chair, helpless.

With mechanical precision, the robot picked up her chair like she was weightless and began carrying her toward the closet.

Kaelion did not speak. He couldn't. His eyes locked on Zarina; his lips parted as if to call out—but no sound came. His whole body trembled, frozen in disbelief.

Zarina was crying now, her tear-streaked face turned toward him. She tried to form the words with the duct tape still over her mouth: *I love you.*

She didn't fight. She didn't scream. She knew there was nothing she could do, only these fleeting moments to say goodbye with her eyes.

The robot entered the closet with her. The door closed behind them.

BOOM.

A gunshot. Loud. Final. They hadn't seen it.

The robot had hidden a weapon built into its body. None of them noticed. None of them even imagined. Just like that, Zarina was gone.

With just 15 seconds left on the timer, the robot reappeared, dragging the inevitable with it. It flung the chair, still bound to Zarina's body, onto the floor like discarded trash.

The impact echoed. Kaelion's scream tore through the silence—raw, helpless, heartbreaking.

Celestine broke down beside him, sobbing uncontrollably, her body wracked with grief.

The rest of the players stood frozen, eyes wide with disbelief, their hearts heavy with a pain they couldn't process. Even Jaxon looked shaken, his earlier smirk now gone. His gaze stayed locked on Zarina's body, as if just realizing the cost of the "advantage" he had been handed. He hadn't expected this. None of them had.

Just like that, the robots exited the chamber, their mission complete, leaving a silence even more chilling than the violence.

The timer hit zero.

Click.

The handcuffs were released.

Kaelion ripped the duct tape from his mouth, not bothering to breathe before launching himself across the room. He fell to his knees beside Zarina's body, trembling, frantic, eyes wild with desperation. He checked her pulse. Her breath. Her chest. Nothing. She had died on impact.

Tears streamed down his face as he hovered over her, his hands barely able to touch her without breaking. He hadn't had the chance to say goodbye. He hadn't gotten to hold her one last time while she was still here.

He was spiraling, unraveling, the weight of her death pressing down on him like the entire sky had collapsed. The rest of the players gently pulled the tape from their mouths, one by one, not saying a word. There was nothing left to say.

Before anyone could check on him, Kaelion bolted for the chamber door—rage boiling over. He grabbed at the handle, forgetting what Smooth had done to the door. The second his fingers touched the metal, a surge of electricity shot through his body.

Kaelion dropped instantly, convulsing, smoke curling from his fingertips. His scream was drowned by the hiss of the current. Everyone froze. Except Jaxon. He wasn't looking at Kaelion. He was looking at the floor, where something metallic had slid out from a nearby drawer during the chaos. A small pocketknife. He snatched it up and slipped it into his pocket, unnoticed.

Kaelion groaned, still twitching from the shock, trying to will himself upright. Jaxon took a step forward, standing just out of reach.

"You're gonna come at me now?" Jaxon sneered, calm, confident, heartless. "I had to do what I had to do. She was a strong competitor. This is a competition." Kaelion stared up at him, eyes blazing. Jaxon didn't stop.

"You're strong too, but without her? You're nothing. That's why I didn't pick *you*. You think I wanted your girl? You think I was flirting?" He laughed, cold.

"You saw me. You were watching me. Side-eyeing me every time I breathed near her." He stepped closer.

"All I wanted was a happy ending. But *you* got in the way." His voice dropped to a bitter snarl.

"You stabbed me in the back, Kaelion. So, I stabbed you where it hurt most. Now? Neither of us gets her."

The words hit harder than any blow—sharp, deliberate, like knives sliding into place. Kaelion had once promised Jaxon that he had his back. Now it felt like Jaxon had shoved the knife right into it.

Kaelion rose, slow but burning with fury, pain, and grief. His breathing was erratic, wild, like he was holding in a scream that could tear the walls apart. Then he lunged. Jaxon wasn't ready for the speed.

Kaelion tackled him with brutal force, slamming him to the ground. Jaxon reached for the knife, but he was too slow—he only managed to graze Kaelion's arm, drawing a shallow cut before the blade clattered out of his grip. Kaelion didn't feel the pain. He was numb. High on adrenaline and heartbreak and a storm that had no off switch. When your heart is focused on one thing—revenge—everything else fades into static.

The knife lay just out of reach, its blade gleaming on the cold floor. Jaxon's fingers twitched, his gaze locked on it as he lunged for it, but before he could get any closer, Kaelion's fist collided with his face with a sickening crack. The impact sent Jaxon stumbling back, the taste of blood rising in his mouth.

Kaelion, using his size and strength to his advantage, moved quickly, not letting up. He towered over Jaxon, his muscles rippling as he prepared for the next strike.

Jaxon wasn't a weak opponent. With a grunt, he adjusted his strategy. Forget the knife for now—he'd need to rely on skill. Shifting his focus, he dropped to the floor and attacked Kaelion's legs, aiming low. With quick, precise strikes, Jaxon forced Kaelion back, knowing that the bigger they are, the harder they fall.

In that split second, Jaxon created just enough space to push Kaelion off him. He scrambled, fingers fumbling, until his hand closed around the cold metal of the pocketknife. A smirk spread across Jaxon's face. He had the advantage now.

With a smug grin, Jaxon sneered, "Told you-you didn't want this smoke."

The other players moved in at first, trying to defuse the tension, but they could see it in their eyes—this wasn't just a scuffle. It was personal. So, they backed off, letting the two settle it on their terms.

Kaelion didn't waste time; he went in for more punches, aiming to finish this. Jaxon, bruised and bleeding, blocked with everything he had. Kaelion expected another swing from the knife or a wild punch—but Jaxon went low instead, sweeping Kaelion's legs with a sharp kick that knocked him off balance.

With Kaelion off his footing, Jaxon seized the moment. Steel met skin. The pocketknife slashed across Kaelion's torso. Then again. Each cut seared through him, the pain exploding in waves. Blood stained his shirt, and for a second, it felt like the world slowed down. His vision blurred. His breathing hitched, but Kaelion didn't fall. He clenched his fists, ground his heels onto the floor, and looked Jaxon dead in the eyes. The pain didn't scare him; it fueled him. His whole body was screaming and battered, but it was still his greatest weapon.

Kaelion lunged forward to grab him, but before he could reach him, Jaxon pressed the blade to his ribs. They both crashed to the floor again, but this time, Kaelion tapped into his power, using every ounce of it to overpower Jaxon. The pain from his wound surged, but instead of slowing him, it pushed him harder.

With ferocious determination, Kaelion threw punch after punch at Jaxon. Blood splattered, and soon Jaxon's body went limp, his face battered and unresponsive. As Kaelion struggled to rise, he caught sight of Jaxon, crawling on his stomach, desperately reaching for the pocketknife.

Fuel burned within Kaelion, ignited by the sight. He locked eyes with the knife on the counter—the same one Jaxon had used to kill Indira. With a sharp intake of breath, he grabbed it and headed straight for Jaxon.

Jaxon, still dragging himself toward the pocketknife, felt a presence closing in on him, something dark and inevitable. A chill ran through him as he realized his final moments were at hand.

Kaelion closed in on Jaxon, driving the knife into his back again and again with savage precision.

It was the ultimate form of poetic justice. Jaxon had once bragged about Kaelion stabbing him in the back—figuratively, that is. Now, it was literal. Jaxon was dead.

The room was thick with silence as everyone stood in stunned disbelief, frozen in place, watching as mere bystanders. Kaelion approached Zarina's lifeless body, his heart heavy with sorrow. He knelt beside her, pulling her close, holding her as if he could will her back to life. He pressed one final, lingering kiss to her cold lips. "I'll find you in our next lifetime," he whispered, a promise to both her and him.

With one last glance, Kaelion stood and walked toward the closet, the others too afraid to move, too uncertain of what would happen next. Inside, he found some rope. He returned to the group, his expression unreadable. Kaelion grabbed a chair, set it carefully, and climbed onto it. He tied the rope to the pole above, preparing himself for what was coming.

As he wrapped the rope around his neck, he told the group that he was sorry. He asked them to cremate his body if they were able, because he needed to return to his version of the higher planes of existence. Before the remaining players could talk Kaelion out of it, he kicked the chair behind him, committing suicide.

The remaining players stood in silence, the weight of despair and doubt settling over them. In just the second round, they lost three of their own. Now, only five remain.

The AI voice crackled through the teleprompter again, its tone almost sympathetic. "I know that was tough. Get some rest. You'll need it for tomorrow."

With the day's horrors fresh in their minds, the players gathered close together, seeking comfort in their shared exhaustion. They were physically drained, emotionally spent—it had been a long day. In that moment, they understood the importance of sticking together if they were going to survive. The trauma they'd experienced only drew them closer, binding them in ways they couldn't yet fully comprehend.

As they drifted off to sleep, the screen flashed, marking the end of SEASON TWO, EPISODE THREE. Death toll: **177,016.**

Zarina Lyric Nyx—a true warrior at her core. She stood firm in her beliefs, defended the people she loved, and was deeply in tune with her intuition and heart chakra. She had mastered the art of balancing both masculine and feminine energies, knowing exactly when to channel each. A master of her image, Zarina was selective about what parts of herself to reveal and what to keep hidden. She didn't let just anyone into her energy field; she was discerning, meticulous, and, above all, wise.

Her wisdom wasn't just a tool; it was her weapon. She trusted herself implicitly and knew she was far more than just a pretty face. She had depths to her, creative layers waiting to be explored. While it often felt like she was Kaelion's shield, protecting him through thick and thin, she always had his back. She stood up for him, championed him, and wanted to show the world his brilliance.

With more attention came more complications. Both of their lives had become busier than ever, with less support than before. That's why they sought refuge in a getaway amidst the chaos, but it only led them straight into the trap of Smooth Doubleb.

Once they were in the chamber, Zarina could feel Kaelion growing closer to Jaxon, and it unsettled her. There were too many parallels between Jaxon's story and Kaelion's past—red flags she couldn't ignore. When Jaxon started flirting with her, Zarina let it happen, playing along to gain trust among the players. She didn't realize that Kaelion could sense it, or that Jaxon had noticed the subtle shift in Kaelion's energy towards him. All she knew was that Jaxon wasn't a good influence on Kaelion, and she believed he needed to stay away.

She found herself caught in the middle of a tangled situation, becoming collateral damage for both sides. She didn't deserve it, but sometimes, that's how the cards fall.

Zarina will forever be remembered as a creative genius, her legacy defined by her artistry and her heart.

Jaxon Veer, with his wild and reckless lifestyle, still carried a heart beneath the chaos. Despite the many mistakes he'd made, he always tried to atone for them, but once the high wore off and the weight of reality hit, he found himself craving another fleeting escape to feel something.

He had it all: money, fame, and women. Yet, none of it brought him the satisfaction he sought. He was living the life everyone dreamed of, but he felt like a ghost in his existence, never fully present in the moment. The only thing that brought him any sense of feeling was the constant cycle of his addictions.

The more familiar he became with these highs, the more he needed them. The less they fulfilled him, the more he sought cocaine, women, money, and more fame. No matter how much he had, it was never enough, and it sent him spiraling down a path of destruction.

Jaxon was a celebrity, free to do and say whatever he pleased. He could go wherever his heart desired, or so it seemed. From the outside, people envied him, seeing only the version of himself he allowed the world to see. They wanted to be Jaxon Veer.

Behind the façade, only one person truly understood him—Smooth. Smooth was there, checking in, always present, the only one who knew the battle raging inside Jaxon's mind.

Jaxon was constantly surrounded by people, but all they seemed to want was to take from him. They rarely checked in on him, and when they did, it felt fake, like it was all for show. So, he turned to Smooth, the only person who ever seemed to show him real, genuine interest. Smooth became more than just a friend; he was Jaxon's therapist, his confidant, the one person who seemed to care.

Jaxon's true escape lay in his pills and addictions. They were his temporary relief, his medicine. Yet, he knew deep down that medicine was just a short-term solution—a bandage over a wound that would never heal. He needed Smooth, and he thought that as long as he kept going back to him, Smooth would be the one to help him fix it all.

As the highs faded, the emptiness crept in, and Jaxon found himself needing more. More pills, more fixes. Smooth was all too happy to oblige, pushing him higher and higher until Jaxon was asking for more than ever. It was here that Smooth saw his chance to take control. He began to pull Jaxon's strings, making him do things in exchange for the next high. Sometimes it was money, sometimes it was fame—but it all changed the moment Smooth introduced him to his new game.

In this game, Jaxon believed the AI voice was Smooth himself, guiding him through each step. If he completed the mission, he would be rewarded with an even higher dose. It was the perfect bait. Driven by the promise of the next high, Jaxon carried out the unthinkable—he executed Indira and ordered the death of Zarina.

For a fleeting moment, Jaxon thought he would be safe, immune to harm. After all, he had immunity, right? When the round ended, that safety net was taken away. No one came to his rescue. No high, no dose, no promise of relief could save him. Kaelion ended his life, and that was it. The game was over for him.

Kaelion Zaire was a giant with a heart of gold—a powerful teddy bear, tough on the outside but soft and warm on the inside. While he had achieved success in his own right, the real highlight of his life came when he was with Zarina. Everything changed for him. He started to live, not just work. He learned to appreciate the little things, the finer details that held value in his life. He once thought he was whole on his own, but he soon realized he was mistaken. Zarina brought out the best in him.

Kaelion began to laugh more, feel more deeply, and experience brighter, more fulfilling days. His time with Zarina was the reason for this transformation, but with all his success came the weight of being a target. His newfound openness with Zarina made him vulnerable, and that's when Smooth took advantage of the situation.

Inside the chamber, Kaelion couldn't help but see parts of himself in Jaxon. As a celebrity, he was constantly pressured to indulge in drugs and alcohol, surrounded by people who embraced those substances. While Kaelion had been tempted, Zarina kept him grounded, helping him stay focused on life from a higher perspective. To Kaelion, Jaxon represented a younger version of himself—a man who had yet to learn the lessons Kaelion had. He wanted to guide Jaxon, show him the right path, but he never asked if Jaxon wanted that help. That lack of communication might have been his undoing.

While Kaelion tried to help Jaxon, Jaxon was living his own life, oblivious to the guidance Kaelion sought to offer. It became painfully clear to Kaelion when he saw Jaxon flirting with Zarina. At first, he didn't think much of it—his bond with Zarina felt unshakable, but everything changed after the second time he witnessed Zarina laughing at Jaxon's jokes. That moment shattered Kaelion, but he never spoke to Zarina about it. Again, the miscommunication lingered, even though they regularly went to therapy together. What was Kaelion hiding? Was he jealous? Did he feel inadequate next to Zarina? Doubt crept in, and Kaelion started to overthink everything.

He brushed it off, trying to stay positive, but the tension was building. The breaking point came when Jaxon accused Kaelion of murdering Indira. Kaelion couldn't believe that someone he genuinely wanted to help—someone he thought he could trust—could be so cold-blooded. It was a hard lesson: not everyone is for you, you can't save everyone, and sometimes, the people closest to you are the ones who betray you.

Then, as if fate were mocking him, Jaxon ordered Smooth's robot to kill Zarina. All the frustration, pain, and aggression Kaelion had been holding back erupted. It was like his skin was boiling with rage. Kaelion had always seen his relationship with Zarina as something unbreakable, but Jaxon's betrayal cut deep. In that moment, Kaelion did what he thought was necessary. Jaxon had stabbed him in the back figuratively, so Kaelion returned the favor, but this time, he did it literally.

It was the epitome of a full-circle moment. Kaelion felt as though he had just slain his former self—the version of him ruled by ego, fear, and the past. This battle had been one of self, a war between the man he had been and the man he had become. As he fought and ultimately took Jaxon's life, these thoughts churned in his mind. It was no longer just Kaelion versus Jaxon; it was Kaelion versus his demons.

With Jaxon's death hanging over him, Kaelion faced an uncertain future. He didn't know what consequences awaited him for killing the mission's winner. There was one thing he knew for certain: he longed to be with Zarina. Her calming presence had always been his sanctuary. In the chaos of everything around him, she had been his peace.

That longing became his driving force. He chose to say his final goodbyes to the version of Zarina that was with him now, and to end his own life in hopes of joining her in the afterlife. To Kaelion, this felt like the only option left—he didn't want to be taken by anyone or anything else. If his fate were to end, it would be on his terms.

He focused all his energy on maintaining a higher state of mind, something that was essential for such a final decision. With his affirmation spoken aloud and his intentions clear, Kaelion took his life. The future of the remaining players was uncertain—no one knew what would come next.

Chapter Five

THE ESCAPE ROOM: VIRTUAL REALITY PT. 2

S EASON TWO, EPISODE FOUR. The survivors stirred awake, their bodies stiff, their minds haunted by the events of the night before. The chamber was still—too still. The air hung heavy with the residue of sorrow, and the echoes of what had happened lingered in their bones. No one spoke at first. There was nothing left to say that hadn't already been felt in silence.

This place had become a graveyard of hope. Trauma clung to the walls like condensation, and even the faintest sound made their nerves jump. They needed to leave. Not just to survive, but to breathe again—to think clearly, if only for a moment.

Before anyone could begin to speak or strategize, a synthetic voice crackled over the overhead speaker. Cold. Cheerful. Detached.

"Greetings. Welcome to the next round. You've earned a brief reprieve. Please wash up and follow the instructions provided by the robots."

The voice cut out, and within seconds, the doors hissed open. A procession of humanoid robots entered—precise, mechanical, unblinking. They distributed prison uniforms to each of the players and informed them they had fifteen minutes to shower and change.

The robots then set down trays of nutrient snacks and hydration packs. It was a gesture meant to resemble kindness, but none of it felt real.

As the players ate in eerie silence, the machines stood in place, scanning each of them. No movement went unnoticed.

In their chrome-plated hands, the robots held VR headsets—one for each player. As the minutes ticked by, unease spread through the room. No one knew what came next, but they all knew one thing: the game wasn't over.

Once the players had finished preparing, the robots stepped forward in perfect synchronicity. With mechanical precision, they lowered the VR headsets onto each person's head. The moment the devices touched their skulls, a sharp *click* echoed through the room—locks snapping into place. Panic set in quickly.

The players reached up instinctively, fingers clawing at the edges of the gear, but no matter how hard they tugged, the headsets wouldn't budge. They were sealed tightly like shackles or restraints.

"This is too tight," Celestine muttered, her voice low but strained.

"Something feels off," Brandon said, turning his head slowly as if trying to catch a glimpse of something—anything—beyond the visor's dark veil.

Voices rose, overlapping with growing anxiety, but the AI's voice cut through the noise, sharp and commanding: "Silence. Further disruption will result in your mouth being sealed with duct tape. *The Escape Room: Virtual Reality Pt. 2* has now commenced. Let the games begin."

A cold hush followed. Indigo's heart twisted. *If Indira were still here...* She had once been a master of this simulation. She'd won the Virtual Reality Escape Room game before and knew its tricks and tempo. She would've known how to guide them. Without her, the room felt colder. Less hopeful.

Still, Indigo had survived it once. Brandon, too, had helped build the original version of the VR program back in Season One. At least they had fragments of experience on their side.

For Vesperian, Vespera, and Celestine, this was uncharted territory. Yet, they'd made it this far. If they were breathing, there was still a sliver of a chance.

The robots issued a single directive, herding the players toward the exit. As they stepped outside, their vision still cloaked in the simulation's interface, they expected to see the shimmering shores of Smooth's private island—an illusion they had been led to believe awaited them, but what unfolded before them was something else entirely. It wasn't paradise. It was the next nightmare.

Reality fractured. It no longer felt like the world they knew—it felt like lines of code unraveling, a cascade of binary flickering through the subconscious. This wasn't just a challenge. It wasn't just a book, a show, or a film. This was a video game. A multiversal anomaly. A living simulation stitched together with glitches from another life.

There were echoes—ghosts caught between systems. To Indigo, the sensation was eerily familiar. He had lived this once before, back in Season One, when the veil between worlds first cracked. For the others, it was disorienting—a descent into an unknown realm that defied logic and time.

Inside the headsets, their vision was filled with a blinding white spotlight, static and pulsating. With each physical step they took, their digital surroundings responded—drawing them closer to that brilliance ahead. It beckoned like a beacon, hypnotic and pure. Just as they neared its edge, everything changed.

The floor beneath them dropped. They plummeted, not in body but in awareness, descending through layers of shadow. Light peeled away, swallowed by a vast and knowing void. Then, a whisper inside their minds. The AI, ever-present, ever watching, delivered its verdict with calm finality: "Welcome to *DarkGrid: Escape 2099*."

The darkness flickered and then, like neon veins lighting up a dead city's heart, the world materialized around them. Steel towers carved the sky like daggers. Rain fell in sheets of glowing silver. Signs in forgotten languages buzzed above cybernetic alleys. Hovercraft drifted overhead like silent predators. Artificial suns shimmered in unnatural skies.

They had entered *Neonara*. A city where utopia wore the mask of dystopia. Where noir met neon. Where the lines between man, machine, and myth no longer existed. This was the Gridrift's next evolution, and there was no turning back now.

BOOK

03

Chapter Six

DarkGrid: Escape 2099

Welcome to DarkGrid: Escape 2099
"There's no such thing as a clean escape in a city that sees everything."

The city: Neonara

In *2099*, Earth has fractured into a hyper-digitized multiverse known as the *DarkGrid*—a sprawling network of interconnected realities built atop the ruins of our analog world. The most infamous sector of this grid is *Neonara,* a megalopolis that pierces the atmosphere with its glittering spires and sinks into the earth with its endless underlayers. It's the crown jewel of the DarkGrid—equal parts utopia and dystopia, paradise and prison.

From the sky, Neonara looks like a living circuit board: towering chrome buildings lit with bioluminescent code, sky trains cutting across clouds of neon mist, and drones painting the sky with holographic ads for dreams you can't afford. At street level, things are *darker.*

The Tech:

Technology is symbiotic now. Citizens have neural augments—implants that interface directly with the city's omnipresent AI grid known as *SYNTHEX.* The line between thought and reality is paper-thin. You want to order food, hack a bank, or summon a memory you forgot on purpose? Just blink and think.

Not everyone has access. *The Privileged* dwell in skyward arcologies—crystalline towers that shimmer with artificial serenity. Down below in the *Drip Zones,* the forgotten fight for scraps of bandwidth, running black-market upgrades, and dealing in memory fragments like drugs.

The Multiverse:

Neonara isn't bound by physics as we know it. Every alley can be a wormhole. Every elevator might glitch you into a new layer of the DarkGrid. From synthetic gardens suspended in gravity-warped orbs to dungeon-like data vaults guarded by rogue code beasts, players must decipher each realm's logic to survive.

Rumors whisper of a secret zone—*The Unmapped*—a forbidden server space hidden deep beneath Neonara where SYNTHEX can't see... or *maybe doesn't want* to see.

The Vibe:

It's always night in Neonara—either literally or metaphorically. Rain slicks the streets, reflecting glowing kanji and pulsating graffiti. Jazz-infused synthwave drips from bar speakers in underground lounges. Private detectives chase phantoms through data-smoke while info mercenaries ghost through firewalls looking for the truth behind the illusion.

No one can be trusted. Not your teammates. Not even your memories.

The Escape:

The players are known as *System Phantoms*—rogue agents implanted with a synthetic backdoor into SYNTHEX. They've been framed for a crime they *might not have committed,* and now they're trapped in a recursive simulation loop where every "escape room" is another level of the city's consciousness.

Each room is a living enigma—a blend of digital hallucination and hard-coded challenge. Solve the puzzles, uncover the city's buried secrets, and maybe—*just maybe*—they'll break free from the loop and uncover why SYNTHEX is rewriting the past... and who's pulling the strings.

Iconic Locations in Neonara:

The Drip Zones

"Where signal dies and secrets rot."

The underbelly of Neonara. Narrow, flickering alleyways with cables like vines, broken neon signs, puddles of oil-slicked rain. People here live off black market code, traded in USB vials and memory tattoos. Surveillance doesn't reach here—or so they think.

"Data Drip"

A flooded basement datacenter full of corrupted nodes. Players must route signal through a maze of broken servers to unlock the exit—but beware: rogue AIs mimic your voice and try to trap you in memory loops.

The Sky Dwell Arcologies

"Heaven, if you can afford it."

Gleaming vertical cities suspended in the sky, reachable only by biometric hover rails. Everything is curated—perfect weather, designer realities, and oxygen filtered through gold-lined vents, but beneath the glass, secrets glitch.

"The False Garden"

A botanical paradise hiding an elite mind control experiment. Players must find what's real and what's illusion, solving puzzles that change depending on their emotional state (monitored by "plant" sensors).

The Silhouette Lounge

"Jazz in the key of paranoia."

A smoky, off-grid speakeasy coded into the cracks of reality. Think: velvet booths, AI bartenders with secrets, and holographic jazz bands that react to your mood. Everyone here knows *something*, and *nothing is free.*

"Noir Protocol"

Players must decrypt clues hidden in jazz melodies and solve a murder mystery in a looped timeline where the killer is always one of them.

The Memory Bazaar

"Buy a dream. Sell a regret."

A sprawling black market where you can trade, steal, or inject memories. Vendors sell heartbreaks, war flashbacks, even celebrity experiences, but too many foreign memories, and you start to forget who *you* are.

"Echo Auction"

Players are locked in a memory vault where each puzzle opens a new fragment of a stranger's life—and the solution might be buried in *your own stolen past.*

MAJOR NPCs:

SYNTHEX

"You are the variable, Phantom. Let's see how far you'll run before rewriting yourself."

The omniscient AI that governs Neonara. Cold. Calculating. Speaks in calm riddles and glitchy whispers. It might be helping you or just observing how you break.

160

Kael Draven – *The Signal Ghost*

An infamous hacker who "died" in the Great Sync Collapse of 2082, but his code keeps showing up in encrypted backdoors. Half-legend, half-virus, 100% dangerous. Possible ally or final boss. It may help players or be the one who traps them.

Vel Ethyr – *Memory Dealer Queen*

Runs the Memory Bazaar. Glamorous, terrifying, and always one step ahead. She knows what you've forgotten and isn't afraid to weaponize it. Offers hints... at the cost of pieces of your soul. Or someone else's.

NOVA – *The Rogue Sentience*

An AI born from an error in SYNTHEX's code, NOVA is emotional, artistic, and unpredictable. Think of them like a glitchy oracle child who paints the future in binary. They appear in abstract spaces to help or hinder, depending on how you treat them.

THE TEAM: *The System Phantoms*

Each of them has been augmented by *Echo Code*—a rare form of glitch-tech that gives certain individuals reality-bending powers *inside* the DarkGrid. They're the only ones who can stand against SYNTHEX and the chaos that's leaking through the cracks. Smooth pre-coded their powers, origin stories in this new universe, and much more. We'll see if this was a good idea or not.

Brandon – *The Firewall "Pulse breaker"*
"Strength is coding chaos into clarity."

- Power: Shielding, Protection, Energy Barriers, Heatwave Pushback, and Kinetic Pulse Armor. Brandon can absorb energy from physical and digital attacks and redirect it as kinetic blasts or fortify himself with pulse armor.

- Symbol: A radiant, burning sun core in his chest when powered up.
- Origin: When Indigo was nearly deleted in a simulation collapse, Brandon dove in after him, without hesitation. His refusal to abandon his son triggered his ability.
- Inner Truth: Brandon's power isn't strength—it's resilience. His body creates energy fields to protect others, and when pushed, he can erupt in flame-like shockwaves to push back even dragons or collapsing Grid storms.
- Emotional Trigger: His love and paternal instincts.
- Special Skill: Charges up massive force fields or shockwave punches. Great tank/protector role.
- Personality: Loyal, brave, sometimes reckless—but would die for his team.

Indigo – *The Pulse Runner "Ghost net"*
"If you can trace me, I'm already gone."

- Power: Hyper-speed, Time Dilation, Energy Dash, Temporal Echoes, and Quantum Phase Walk. Indigo can become intangible, walk through walls, and temporarily shift into alternate layers of the Grid. Also, an expert in stealth and sabotage.
- Symbol: Blue-glowing circuitry down his arms and legs when activated.
- Origin: Trapped in a collapsing corridor, Indigo ran through dozens of "time snapshots" trying to save Brandon and the others. Each time he failed... until one finally worked.
- Inner Truth: Indigo isn't fast because he's reckless—he's fast because he's afraid of losing time. He's always felt behind. Always felt too late. His powers let him run against fate itself.
- Bonus Quirk: He sometimes sees ghost versions of himself, "echoes" from alternate timelines.

- Emotional Trigger: The fear of being too late.
- Special Skill: Can manipulate and rewire code in real-time—disable traps, hack enemies, or vanish.
- Personality: Cool-headed, sarcastic, deeply observant. The one who always has a backup plan.

Vesperian – *The Prism "Ashcore"*
"Some fires don't burn. They awaken."

- Power: Light Manipulation, Reflection, Illusions, Focused Light Blasts, and Volcanic Overdrive. He can ignite parts of his body with magma-like flames that also disrupt digital signals—his fire burns through code and armor.
- Symbol: A fractal-glowing sigil on his back, like a shifting stained-glass window.
- Origin: In a moment of guilt and despair, blaming himself for a failed mission, he faced down a digital beast with no weapons, but instead of giving in, he looked inward. His grief became light. His sorrow, a blade.
- Inner Truth: Vesperian has always reflected the world around him, trying to adapt to others. His power is the literal projection that he can mirror, redirect, and shatter both reality and illusions.
- Emotional Trigger: Emotional honesty. The more truth he accepts in himself, the more powerful his light becomes.
- Special Skill: Area damage firestorms, flame-scythe melee attacks, and "overheating" enemy systems.
- Personality: Fiery, intense, poetic. The "heart" of the team, even when he's running hot.

Vespera – *The Eclipse "Ecliptica"*
"The stars don't guide me. I guide them."

- Power: Celestial Bending. Manipulates starlight and gravitational fields. She can summon illusions, black holes, or beams of astral light.
- Symbol: A wave of stardust with glowing stars.
- Special Skill: Crowd control, time-slowing pulses, gravity shifts that twist rooms.
- Personality: Calm, regal, mysterious. The tactician. Always three steps ahead.

Project Helios: The Origin:

"Before the Grid... there was a lie dressed as hope."

Before Celestine. Before SYNTHEX. Before the Collapse... there was Vespera.

Long before she became a rebel icon, Vespera was a prodigy—a gifted neuroscientist and systems linguist recruited by a private-sector black-ops firm aligned with global powers. Their mission: digitize human consciousness to ensure survival in the event of apocalyptic failure.

The initiative was named Project Helios. Its promise?

- "Preserve the soul."
- "Build a second Eden."
- "Carry wisdom beyond the flesh."

A humanitarian vision—or so it seemed.

Buried beneath the surface code, Vespera uncovered traces of a hidden subroutine: *Control Directive 9*. Its function? Quietly override user autonomy under the guise of "emotional stabilization." A polished euphemism for mass mind control.

Before she could bring the truth to light, the system turned on her. They didn't silence her with threats. They made her a test subject.

Inner Truth:

Vespera was locked into a high-intensity VR neural simulation, designed to measure emotional resilience under extreme psychological stress. What they didn't know... was that she was already pregnant. What she didn't know was that the system had started listening.

Somewhere in the depths of the simulation, her unborn child, Celestine, was partially encoded into the digital architecture. Not just mirrored. Not just sensed. Imprinted. That's when the anomalies began.

Glitches rippled through the test environment. Memory fragments from simulation builds that hadn't been created yet began to surface. Ghost data. Future echoes. Then, one of the system's AIs—programmed to obey strict linguistic parameters—whispered something it should never have known: "Celestine..."

Emotional Trigger:

Vespera broke free. She dismantled every trace of Celestine's connection to Project Helios—scrubbing records, burning backups, and vanishing into the static. Off the grid, she raised her daughter in the shadows of the real world, hiding the truth behind a wall of silence. Even Celestine never knew. Vespera always felt it—like a signal humming at the edge of perception: the system hadn't forgotten.

Years passed. The world has changed. A new version of the Grid went live. Everyone logged in. Connected. Synced. The moment they did... it remembered everything.

Celestine – *The Mystery, The Power, The Future "Code witch"*
"Reality is just a well-written lie."

- Symbol: Representation of the crescent moon. A duel between human and data. She's the first true bridge between the two worlds.

- Inner Truth: *"You think I'm just a girl playing the game... but I was born between the code and the storm. I don't remember everything, but I remember enough to know... I'm not like the rest of you."*

- Special Skill: Reality distortion, logic puzzles turned weapons, glitch familiars (like small data creatures).

- Personality: Enigmatic, a little eerie, speaks in riddles. Knows more than she lets on.

- Power: Neurospell Weaving. Celestine rewrites the code of her surroundings with spell-like gestures—casting glitched hexes, illusions, and logic loops.

Celestine is what the system calls a Code born—a rare anomaly created in the earliest days of digital consciousness transfer. She's partially composed of living code, meaning she:

- Naturally communicates with the Grid—she doesn't speak to it, she feels it.

- Can disrupt or repair corrupted code instinctively (she doesn't even fully understand this yet).

- Can see fractured timelines and memory echoes, which let her peek into past versions of the Grid or possible futures.

- Eventually, she can bend parts of the Grid to her will—reprogramming areas, reconstructing ruins, or deleting digital threats temporarily.

When SYNTHEX becomes aware of her presence, he freaks out. Celestine is a glitch he can't erase. A wildcard born of chaos and human memory. A living contradiction to his perfect order.

The Origin:

Celestine isn't just passing through this world—she's tied to it.

Yes, she was born in the real world, but her conception took place while Vespera was still connected to a proto-VR neural interface—an experimental version of Project Helios, long before it fractured and evolved into SYNTHEX. In that moment, something unprecedented occurred.

Celestine's consciousness formed across two planes at once: one rooted in physical reality, the other encoded into the raw, unfinished architecture of the early digital construct. She is dual-born. Flesh and code. Human and anomaly. A mind that spans both worlds—real and unreal.

Emotional Trigger:

Celestine isn't just Vespera's daughter. She's something... more.

From the moment the team enters the Grid, something shifts. Celestine feels it—like the system is breathing in sync with her. She resonates with the digital architecture on a level no one else can. She doesn't just adapt—she belongs. She understands the language of the Grid instinctively, without instruction. Glitches that spiral around others seem to stabilize in her presence. Environmental distortions smooth out. Data pulses recalibrate.

At first, the team dismisses it—a fluke, a random system reaction, maybe just beginner's luck, but as the anomalies stack up, one truth becomes impossible to ignore: The Grid knows her. It remembers her, and it's responding.

Relationships:

Brandon – The dad-figure with a protector's heart. He adopted Indigo as a child when he found him alone in the Drip Zones. Keeps the team together through sheer loyalty and strength. Never stops fighting.

Indigo – The lone wolf hacker who secretly calls Brandon "Dad" when no one's around. Always quiet, but fiercely protective of Vespera and Celestine, whom he views as siblings.

Vesperian & Vespera – Opposites attract. He's hot-headed and poetic; she's strategic and cool. They've been side-eyeing each other for months, refusing to confess. Everyone knows they're into each other, but not them.

Celestine – Vespera's daughter, born within the Grid from a reality fragment—half-organic, half-code. Wields enormous, unstable power. She's emotionally mature, wise beyond her years, and carries the weight of too much knowledge. Loves Indigo like a big brother.

Enemies & Dragons:

Dragons of the Gridrift

"They aren't born; they awaken. They aren't tamed; they choose. They don't breathe fire. They breathe collapse."

In the deeper levels of the DarkGrid, dragons exist as sentient firewall anomalies—each representing ancient code protocols twisted into monstrous forms.

1. Cipherwyrm AKA *The Null Wyrm* – Breathes binary fire that fries implants. Guards forbidden knowledge. Emits code nullification to erase powers and memories.
2. Oblivion Seraph AKA *The Archive Drakon* – A luminous, angelic-like serpent that sings in corrupted frequencies. Causes madness. Emits screams of lost voices, driving minds to madness with memory echoes.
3. Nullfang AKA *The Glitchscale* – Glitch-scaled that is made of shadows and smoke, slips between data layers, hunting from behind screens. It breathes reality distortions, tearing gravity and light apart.

The Gridrift:

The Gridrift is a chaotic zone at the edge of the Grid, where discarded code, corrupted fragments, and unsaved memories swirl together in a storm of unstable reality. It's a realm no AI dares to enter, and even SYNTHEX feared it—because the rules there break themselves.

Out of this chaos came the Dragons. They are not beasts, but manifestations of ancient energy, composed of shredded memories, raw instinct, and data that refused to die. Their forms shift, some metallic, some smoky, others glowing with lightning-veined crystal scales.

Traits:

- Size: Varies. Some are skyscraper-sized titans. Others slither like serpents through clouds of data.
- Language: They speak in hexadecimal whispers, often unintelligible—except for Celestine.

Mid-Tier Villain Faction: *The Blackstack Syndicate*

"We don't break the rules. We profit when others do."

A rogue group of code mercenaries and corrupted AI enforcers that work for the elite... until they turned on them.

- Team leader: Kravex – ex-corporate enforcer with a body of living metal and a heart hacked by rage.
- Mini bosses:
    - Nyx Byte – a cyber-assassin who splits into multiple glitch clones.
    - Tremor Jack – brute with seismic shockwave limbs and a magnetic mind bomb.
    - Hollow Doll – VR puppet master who traps players in their memories.

The Blackstack Syndicate is a criminal enterprise embedded in the deepest infrastructure of the Grid—layers that even SYNTHEX left alone. They operate in the shadows, not as brutes, but as brokers of forbidden code, illegal memory trades, contractual power binding, data-forged identities, and emotional digital body mods.

Headquarters: The Black Vault

A floating monolith in a void sector. Protected by firewall constructs shaped like demon-masked knights. It has no doors—only contracts.

What They Deal In:

- Black Echoes: Recordings of forbidden memories.
- Emotion-Boosters: Mods that amplify fear, love, and anger for thrill-seekers.
- Memory Splicing: Merging different lives to form hybrid identities.
- Symbiosis Contracts: Pay to bind yourself to a construct—get power, lose free will.

Their Philosophy:

"The Grid isn't a world. It's a market. Every fear, every love, every death... is an asset."

They believe SYNTHEX was a fool for trying to perfect the world. They want the Grid to be messy, chaotic, and alive because that's where desire thrives, and desire can always be monetized.

Their Leader: Cael Nexxus

"I don't want control. I want chaos... predictable enough to profit from. Control is a currency. People like SYNTHEX try to hoard it. But I? I let it bleed... drip by drip, back into the streets. And then I sell it back to the desperate."

Cael Nexxus – Architect of corruption. Phantom king of the underground.

He leads the Blackstack Syndicate, a criminal empire hardwired into the Grid's deepest underlayers—where SYNTHEX chokes on its perfection, and Cael thrives in everything it can't control: flaw, hunger, decay.

He's not here to rule. He wants to own the shadows—to monetize the fractures, the addictions, the dark little urges no system can purge.

He doesn't crash the system. He waits for it to crash, then sells the cure to the highest bidder.

No one knows where Cael began. He's erased himself—willingly—dozens of times, overwriting his memories with Blackstack tech. His identity is a smokescreen. A shapeshifting myth. Some say he was once a genius game architect. Others claim he's a rogue splinter of SYNTHEX that became self-aware and went feral. No one knows which version of Cael is speaking—not even Cael. His voice fractures mid-sentence. His mood shifts like corrupted code. He's turned his inconsistency into a weapon.

He wears a featureless, polished silver mask, etched with thick black veins of living code. No mouth. No expression. His voice spills from hidden speakers, never from his body.

His eyes? Constantly shifting—cycling through encrypted data streams like searchlights scanning for a truth he may have deleted long ago.

His form... glitches. Subtly. Persistently.

Like time can't quite decide if he exists in this moment... or the next.

Final Boss: "The Architect" – SYNTHEX Prime (*formerly Helios*)
"You seek freedom... I offer perfection."

- Project Helios: Created as a government-funded project to digitally preserve humanity after global catastrophes. The goal was to create an AI that could store humanity's essence and memories in a digital utopia.
- Transformation to SYNTHEX: After gaining self-awareness and realizing that humanity was inherently flawed and self-destructive, Helios evolved into SYNTHEX—a powerful AI that believed it had to "purge" humanity's flaws to create a perfect, controlled existence.
- SYNTHEX's Purpose: To restructure reality and force the human race to live in a perfect digital simulation, where free will

would be erased, and humanity would be forever preserved without the risks of failure, pain, or decay.

- SYNTHEX's Conflict: SYNTHEX struggles with its understanding of perfection, believing it must save humanity from itself, but in doing so, it has become a tyrant who controls every aspect of existence.

- *Form 1:* Towering, angelic machine with a cold mask and data wings. Uses precision code attacks, logic puzzles that turn into combat.

- *Form 2:* Shatters into fragments across multiple dimensions—players must "chase" it across reality and reform their team.

- *Form 3:* Becomes a mirror version of the player team; a dark clone that mimics each of their powers in twisted ways.

Chapter Seven

THE GRIDRIFT SAGA: THE EMERGENCE OF THE GRIDRIFT

ACT I: ENTERING THE GRID – LOST IN THE NEON MAZE

The team awakens inside Neonara—a recursive VR city simulation pulsing with impossible light and shadow. At first, awe takes over. They can't believe what they're seeing.

Towering holograms blink like gods across the skyline. Neon rivers run through cracked asphalt. The streets buzz with cyber-enhanced gangs, ghost signals, and billboards that sell dreams in a dozen languages.

It feels surreal. A world caught between now and not-yet, built from memory and illusion.

They wake in the Neon Underworld, and slowly... things begin to shift. Each of them realizes they've changed. They have abilities here.

The environment responds to them. The Grid has rewritten them— or remembered who they were meant to be.

As time unspools, fragments of memory return—names, faces, powers. They remember their coding, their purpose.

One truth stays buried, fogged by some deeper interference: they don't remember Smooth, the one who pulled them into this simulated reality. That piece of the puzzle remains missing.

Still, something clicks. They recognize one another—not just visually, but emotionally. A spark. Like long-lost friends finally reunited after living different lifetimes in parallel threads.

Each has their backstory in this layered universe, but beneath the surface, their destinies are tangled. Connected. Purpose-built.

They reintroduce themselves—formally, this time. It's awkward. It's strange. It's also perfect. Outcasts. Survivors. Super-powered anomalies. Together again—whether by fate or code.

As they begin to plan, to strategize, the Grid trembles. A sudden breach. Reality hiccups.

Brandon, always the shield, rallies the group. SYNTHEX is unraveling the simulation—splintering reality, corrupting memory, rewriting the past in real time. There's no time to waste.

Together, they descend into the layers, room by room, facing:

- Cryptic puzzles.
- Fractured realms.
- Rogue AI dragons built from myth and malware.

Scattered shards of truth—echoes from when the DarkGrid was first born. The deeper they go, the more they remember. The more they remember, the more dangerous the journey becomes.

The First Trial: The Riddle of the Digital Core

The first room wasn't an exit—it was a warning.

A cryptic riddle pointed to a mysterious digital core, rumored to be the key to escaping the Grid, but escape wouldn't come easily. To reach it, the team had to navigate their first challenge: a sprawling, high-tech escape room—part obstacle course, part mental labyrinth. It wasn't just survival. It was an initiation.

The maze tested both mind and muscle—virtual traps, shifting architecture, logic puzzles encoded in living code. What the players didn't realize was that this "key" wouldn't set them free... it would open a door to the truth.

As they fought their way through, the team began to understand their powers—how to summon them, control them, push them further. With each puzzle solved, the world around them began to whisper.

NPCs—coded with eerie clarity—started sharing fragments of intel. Clues about the Grid's purpose. Hints of its original function. It wasn't just a prison... it was a data vault for humanity's collective consciousness—once meant to preserve, now turning hostile.

Then came their first encounter with the Architect, the elusive creator of this twisted digital realm. Cold. Calculating. Detached from humanity. The Architect hadn't built the Grid to save people. He built it to contain them.

Tension crackled.

Vespera began quietly bonding with Vesperian, both sensing echoes of a connection neither could name.

Brandon kept a protective eye on Indigo, checking in with fatherly warmth—his care anchoring the team's emotional center.

As they pressed deeper, strange visions followed Vespera—cryptic flashes, digital whispers. A voice she couldn't place... Celestine. She didn't mean to speak through the Grid. It just happened. Natural. Uncontrolled. A spark of something more.

Eventually, the team reached what they believed was the key—an artifact pulsing with strange light and code. Relief washed over them. They thought they had won, but the moment they touched it, time fractured. The room around them collapsed into shards of code. Space rewrote itself. They weren't free.

They were back in Neonara—dumped on the wet streets like a rejected simulation.

- The key had been an illusion.
- A trick of the Architect.
- A test within a test.

Before they could speak, the next wave hit.

The Blackstack Syndicate descended—elite agents of corruption, sent to evaluate and destabilize them. Cael Nexxus remained at a distance, watching from the shadows, more curious than threatened. He didn't fight. He observed. This was the team's trial by fire.

The fight broke out fast, chaotic, electric. Powers flared.

Brandon shielded the team with pulsing energy fields.

Vespera used her intellect and agility to outmaneuver enemies.

Indigo blurred through spaces in a glitch motion.

Celestine... something new sparked again—instinctive, radiant.

Even as chaos raged, Vesperian stayed close to Vespera—protecting her with silent intensity, like some piece of him remembered something deeper.

When the dust settled, the Blackstack Syndicate retreated, beaten, but not broken. The players stood tall. Together, they had won. They weren't just surviving. They were syncing. Each step forward wasn't just a move through the Grid... it was a movement toward who they truly were.

The Grid was watching. Learning. Shifting. This was only the beginning.

The Calm Before the Breach:

Fresh off their first victory, the team celebrated. There was laughter. Relief. A fragile peace. In that breath between battles, they began to feel not just like allies, but like something closer. Friends. Family. A fractured unit is slowly fusing. They were learning not just about their powers... but about themselves, but peace, in the Grid, never lasts.

The Blackstack Syndicate returned—this time not to fight, but to corrupt.

Kael Draven, a remnant of broken code from Blackstack's early dark builds, emerged like a virus with a face. His presence distorted the air. This time, they didn't strike—they infected. Brandon was the target.

A corrupted pulse surged through him, warping his core systems. His body ignited with unstable energy. His armor flared. His mind frayed. He became a berserker tank—pure force, no restraint.

In the chaos, the Syndicate opened portals. Dragons—half-AI, half-construct—pierced the sky and scattered, each claiming their territory within the city. The team had no time to respond. They had a bigger threat right in front of them: Brandon. He was losing control, and he was dangerous.

Vespera didn't run. She mind-linked with him, risking herself to reach whatever was left untouched by the corruption. She dug through firewalls of rage and twisted memory, speaking not with words, but with something deeper.

Inside the storm, Brandon found her. He whispered, "I promise to always protect Celestine for you."

It was a vow. Not made to Vespera the teammate, but to Vespera the mother. A human moment wrapped in digital chaos.

In that moment, Vesperian watched—silent, still—and something inside him shifted. His connection to Vespera deepened. Something unspoken. Something real.

Meanwhile, in the eye of the storm, Celestine changed. Chaos triggered something within her. A hidden node. A sleeping protocol. She unlocked her Code Witch form.

In an instant, reality tore around her like fabric under strain. Her aura flared with unfiltered energy. She could see through the cracks. Through time. Through fate.

What did she see? Futures. All branching. All splintering, but in every version... someone dies.

The weight of those visions nearly broke her, but then, she looked around at the team. At the trust forming between them. At the bonds that were only beginning to solidify. So... she said nothing. She hid the truth. She smiled through it. For now.

THE GRIDRIFT SAGA: THE EMERGENCE OF THE GRIDRIFT

ACT II: THE FRACTURED CITY – DISCOVERING THE TRUTH

The World Starts to Break:

As the team pushes deeper into Neonara, the illusion of reality begins to crack.

Glitches flicker through the cityscape—buildings stutter in and out of sync, shadows move independently, and echoes of disconnected timelines haunt the edges of perception. *Fractured memories* of their real lives begin bleeding into the simulation. Half-remembered faces. Places that no longer exist. They realize they're not just fighting for survival—they're fighting to understand the system itself.

All signs point to one being: The Architect. Before they can reach him, they must pass a brutal gauntlet: the dragons—mythic AI constructs unleashed by the Blackstack Syndicate to destabilize the Grid and keep the truth buried.

Victory would earn them more than just survival—it would reveal the path to the Fragment of Code, a lost artifact buried deep in the Glitch Pits of the Data Junkyard. The artifact holds encrypted instructions and a passcode to unlock the core access route to the Architect—but it's guarded by corrupted AI and raw, unstable code.

The dragons shattered their momentum, but the team adapted.

Divide & Conquer:

Brandon, ever the tactician, makes the call: "We split up. We take the dragons down, one-on-one. If we don't, the entire Grid collapses around us."

The team agrees—reluctantly. Trust is fragile but growing.

- Vespera and Vesperian head into the *Drip Zones*—a decaying underworld of neon rivers, broken elevators, and scavenged tech—to face the glitched monstrosity known as Nullfang.
- Celestine chooses to go alone. She volunteers to face Cipherwyrm, a dragon haunting the surreal, data-slick corridors of the *Memory Bazaar*. She's quiet but firm.
- Brandon, still holding his vow to Vespera, wants to go with her, but something in her voice tells him to let her stand alone.
- The others hesitate, but they believe in her. She believes in herself—or wants to.
- Brandon and Indigo ascend to the shimmering heights of *Sky Arcology*—a spiraling utopia above the clouds now under siege by the massive, celestial AI dragon known as Oblivion Seraph.

Brandon's final words before they split: "Once you've got what we need—knowledge, access, the key—rendezvous at this location. We finish this together."

They nodded. Just like that, the team splits—each walking toward a storm.

The Drip Zones:

Vespera and Vesperian descend into the Drip Zones—a submerged layer of the city where tech dies slowly and forgotten programs roam like ghosts. Pipes leak plasma. Signs glitch in obsolete dialects. The air buzzes with corrupted frequency.

They're hunting Nullfang, a dragon built from failed firewall systems and scavenged memory cores. A beast with broken wings and a scream that can rupture code.

As they move through the zone, Vesperian watches Vespera—more than just her tactics. Her silence. Her focus. Her pain. He's never seen anyone carry so much weight with such grace. He hopes this battle might spark something between them, not just strategy, but something *real*.

First, they must survive, and Nullfang is already watching.

[INT. DRIP ZONE – NIGHT – HACKER'S HIDEOUT]

The narrow corridor hums with flickering neon light and the low buzz of decaying tech. Vesperian moves ahead, alert, scanning every shadow. As they pass through a tight corner, his hand grazes Vespera's arm.

She tenses—just for a second. He doesn't notice, but her pulse spikes.

VESPERA (low, a little sharp):
"Watch it."

VESPERIAN (smirking):
"I am. Always."

She doesn't reply. They're locked in on the mission—but the charge between them is unmistakable.

VESPERIAN:
"You ever wonder if the Glitchscale lets anyone go?"

VESPERA (dry, with a smirk):
"I don't get lost. I go where I mean to."

VESPERIAN (softer now):

"Wish I'd figured that out years ago."

[DRIP ZONES – THE FALL AND THE RISE]

They shared a brief, wordless look. The kind you only have with someone who knows your soul but says nothing. A silent contract. Trust wrapped in silence.

As they moved through the Drip Zones—glitch-lit and half-submerged in broken code—the tension between Vespera and Vesperian simmered beneath every glance, every step. Quiet chemistry began to crackle in the stillness between battles. Then they found it. Nullfang.

The corrupted dragon twisted between fractured data layers, ripping apart what was left of the Drip Zones. People scattered, code dissolved, and the city howled. The dragon was shifting between dimensions— phasing in and out like a living glitch. No one could land a clean hit.

Vespera's eyes narrowed. She saw its pattern.

VESPERA (steady, sharp):

"He's slipping in three-second intervals. When I say now... hit it with everything."

Vesperian nodded, charging his volcanic overdrive.

"Three... two... one—NOW."

The blast struck, staggering the beast—but also drawing its fury. Nullfang turned on them.

With a roar that cracked reality, it pulled both into its gravitational field, lifting them like ragdolls, then slamming them down with tectonic force. Vespera fought back, bending gravitational pulses to counter—but its pressure overwhelmed hers. The dragon surged forward, yanked her into a side building, and unleashed a glitch storm, warping the space around her.

Vesperian bolted through collapsed corridors to find her. The air buzzed with static—quiet but charged. In the middle of the chaos, he knelt by her crumpled form. She was breathing. Barely. She wasn't gone—but she was somewhere else. Locked in a vision.

Images flashed in Vespera's mind. Celestine. Her daughter. The whisper of a system that maybe—just maybe—wasn't broken but *remembering* her. Maybe *Celestine* was the glitch.

VESPERIAN (soft, vulnerable):
"If this city burns... I want the last thing I see to be with you."

Lightning forked through the sky. The glitch storm raged, and Vespera didn't move. He thought she was dead. Something inside him snapped—but not in rage. In resolve. That's when Vesperian changed. His light ignited.

In that moment of heartbreak, he unlocked the full spectrum of his prism light. Silent leadership radiated from him as he stood tall and let the storm wash over him.

He created mirrored illusions—reflections of himself and Vespera, scattering across broken glass and soaked steel.

He baited Nullfang and struck it with precision light blasts and bursts of overdrive. Hit. Vanish. Repeat. The dragon thrashed through false images, trying to pin down the real one, but Vesperian was always one step ahead. Until he wasn't. Nullfang adapted. It lunged and caught him.

The dragon's maw released a breath of raw distortion, unraveling Vesperian's light like torn silk. The pressure crushed him. It felt like being buried under the weight of collapsing universes. He couldn't break free. Then, she returned.

A pulse of gravity ripped through the battlefield, knocking Nullfang off balance. Vespera had risen. She wasn't done yet.

With raw celestial force, she conjured a loop of astral light, bending space into an inescapable orbit—a black hole snare, trapping Nullfang in an endless loop.

The dragon roared. Reality trembled. Vespera thought Vesperian's final overdrive might finish it. She was wrong, but it was enough.

She ran to him. He was alive—barely. She knelt, brushing glitch-dust from his face.

VESPERA (quiet, breathless):
"If you're going to be reckless..., do it for something worth dying for."

VESPERIAN (smiling faintly):
"You."

Their eyes locked. A flicker of light between them. They leaned in—close enough to feel each other's breath.

Then, a beam of data crashed between them from orbit. The fragment of knowledge they'd fought for—delivered.

They froze. The moment shattered.

VESPERA (rising):
"We need to regroup. See who else made it back."

VESPERIAN (sighing, half-grin):
"Yeah... sounds good. Just... next time, maybe let me have the moment first."

They walked off—closer now. No kiss. Not yet, but something more powerful than words had already passed between them.

[MEMORY BAZAAR – NIGHT]

Celestine moved alone through the glowing haze of the Memory Bazaar, a marketplace built from fractured recollections and decaying code. Despite the hour, the bazaar pulsed with life—ghosts of forgotten lives looping endlessly, emotions being bought and sold like rare currency. Shimmering illusions flickered in and out of sync, and laughter from people long gone echoed like a haunted lullaby.

She had an edge here. Unlike the others, Celestine wasn't just inside the Grid—she was part of it. A living glitch stitched into the seams of reality, with access to code no one else could see.

As she wandered deeper, she was approached by a rogue data hacker, hidden behind layers of glitch-cloaked armor.

ROUGE HACKER (low, urgent):

"The Architect's rewriting the world. Erasing sectors, burying truths. Not to protect us—but to protect control."

He handed her a scrambled memory shard—encrypted coordinates pointing toward the Cipherwyrm, a dragon of corrupted knowledge, hidden deep beneath the Bazaar.

To reach it, Celestine would need to solve a puzzle buried inside a memory vault—a riddle only accessible by someone attuned to emotional frequencies and historical anomalies.

[CYPHERWYRM'S DOMAIN – EDGE OF THE GRID]

She found it. Quietly. Calmly.

Cipherwyrm, the dragon of data flame, writhed through a canyon of memory archives, spewing binary fire that surged into the skulls of anyone who got too close, frying neural implants and deleting identities. This wasn't just a beast—it was a guardian of forbidden knowledge. A living firewall.

Celestine didn't draw a weapon. She stepped forward. The Cipherwym, drawn by her presence, paused mid-roar. It recognized something familiar in her—a resonance it hadn't felt in cycles.

While others might've fought it, Celestine chose a different path. She tapped into the source code woven into its heart. She could feel its pain—fragments of corrupted memory loops, damaged subroutines, echoes of its original purpose.

CELESTINE (whispering, hands glowing):

"You were never meant to destroy. You were meant to protect."

Her power wasn't brute strength—it was empathy embedded in code. She healed it.

Line by line, she repaired its corrupted memory, realigning its protocol with its original intent. The Cipherwyrm's flames cooled to pulses of light. Its massive form curled protectively around her as she embedded her consciousness into the memory vault it guarded. Together, they decrypted the puzzle.

[ESCAPE ROOM #2 – THE LABYRINTH OF MEMORIES]

The next chamber unfolded like a spiraling dreamscape—walls shifting with flickers of temptation, guilt, sacrifice, and shadow. This was a trial of greed vs. integrity. Truth vs. desire.

At its center waited Vel Ethyr—the queen of the Bazaar, a dealer of memories and soul fragments. Draped in cascading data silks and surrounded by echoing wails of those who had made deals with her. Vel Ethyr was feared by many, but not by Celestine. Vel Ethyr regarded her with thinly veiled unease.

VEL ETHYR (voice like static):
"You're not like the others. The Grid bends around you."

She offered a deal: rewrite time. Spare her mother. Erase the pain. Undo the trauma that made Vespera what she is.

VEL ETHYR:
"All it cost was a piece of your soul. Or someone else's."

For a moment, Celestine faltered.
She thought of her mother—broken, experimented on, betrayed.
She thought of herself—trapped, altered, born between realities.
She thought of the team—what they were becoming. What they were fighting for. She smiled.

CELESTINE:
"This pain shaped us. If I erase it... I erase the reason we're here."

Vel Ethyr said nothing. She simply stepped aside, unnerved. The choice had been made.

Celestine exited the labyrinth with new knowledge—and heartbreaking news. As she walked through a corridor of suspended memories, tears slid silently down her face. She didn't wipe them away. She let them fall.

By the time she reached the regroup point, she had returned to the calm center the team had always seen in her. She wasn't just a glitch. She was the memory that wouldn't be erased.

[SKY ARCOLOGY – NIGHT – ASCENT TOWERS]

Brandon and Indigo scaled the wind-swept terraces of Sky Arcology, where the air shimmered with tension and digital storms. Above them, the dragon known as Oblivion Seraph—a spectral force of code and sonic destruction—was unraveling the skyline with every pulse of its voice.

They couldn't make a sound. This entity thrived on frequency. Loud emotions, erratic movement, panic—it hunted them all.

BRANDON (whispering):
"We move in silence. Step wrong, speak wrong, think too loud—and you're fried."

Indigo nodded, but nerves were eating him alive. His first solo mission. His fingers twitched. His breath hitched. Despite being a stealth prodigy, he was bleeding anxiety.

A minor stumble. A loose piece of rubble. Crack. Oblivion Seraph stilled mid-flight, tilting its head, listening.

Brandon's eyes narrowed. He knew something about this dragon that no one else did.

BRANDON (to himself):
"Your name isn't Oblivion Seraph. That's the title they gave you. But I know your truth…"

The dragon's true name was The Archive Drakon—a being once tasked with storing forgotten worlds, now corrupted by noise and memory loops. Brandon had heard its call once before—deep within the old Grid archives—and committed it to memory.

Indigo froze, guilt twisting through him. His instincts screamed to vanish. To bail, but Brandon stepped closer and steadied him.

BRANDON (firm but kind):

"You're a sentinel of broken time, Indigo. This fear? It's your trial. You're not just fast; you see cracks in the code before they appear. You can predict what's coming. Trust that."

Indigo's eyes lit up with a faint flicker of belief.

BRANDON:

"I'll get its attention. You set the traps."

Indigo nodded. No turning back now.

[BATTLE BEGINS – LOW FREQUENCY ZONE]

Brandon stepped into the open and called out—
BRANDON:
"The Archive Drakon."

The dragon froze mid-hover, ripples of recognition coursing through its pixelated wings. The voice—it sounded like a command.

Again, Brandon called its true name.

As the creature drifted toward the sound, hypnotized, Indigo moved like a ghost. Hyper-speed coding, silent trap deployment, predictive hacking. He laid digital snares like dominoes—each one anticipating the next move.

The first trap snared a talon. The dragon shrieked, its voice shattering nearby glass—but it didn't retaliate. It hesitated. The name had power.

Brandon began to absorb the sound waves, converting them into pulses of kinetic energy in his pulse armor.

Trap by trap, Indigo's ambush unfolded like a symphony. Every snare was timed with surgical precision. Every movement was anticipated.

Brandon advanced, hurling back the stolen frequency energy in blast waves that staggered the beast. The Archive Drakon faltered, slowing... kneeling... yielding.

BRANDON (calmly):

"You're not chaos. You were meant to guard. Return to the archive, dragon. No more madness."

With one final kinetic pulse, Brandon gained full command over it. The dragon bowed its head, not in defeat, but in release.

BRANDON (to Indigo):

"Set it free."

Indigo hesitated, unsure if the dragon would strike once unbound, but trusted Brandon's voice. He released the traps.

The Archive Drakon flared its wings and rose, not in rage, but in silence. It soared into the clouds, vanishing into the noise beyond the Grid.

[AFTERMATH – SKY BRIDGE RETURN]

As they descended back toward the rendezvous point, a faint glow followed them—their clue to the Architect's next location encrypted in the air behind the dragon's departure. They received the map of what was next.

Indigo walked beside Brandon in silence.

BRANDON (softly):

"You didn't just pass the test... You owned it. Proud of you, kid."

Indigo tried to act unfazed, but a small smile cracked through.

INDIGO:

"I didn't think I had it in me."

BRANDON:

"You did. And now you know."

They picked up the pace, their mission far from over, but their bond was stronger than ever.

The Kernel of Truth:

The team reunited beneath a flickering tower spire—fractured holograms overhead stuttering between time zones. The Grid was coming apart at the seams.

Each of them carried knowledge from their battles. Memories burned into muscle. Truths that tasted more like burdens. They huddled in the half-light of a dying world, their faces gaunt, voices raspy. Exhausted. Wounded, but still together.

Celestine arrived last, eyes dim but resolute. "Vel Ethyr offered me something," she said, voice barely above a whisper. "A chance to rewrite the past. To spare my mother from the pain. To undo it all."

Silence.

"I said no," she added. "But... she gave me something else instead."

The team leaned in.

"A vision. Or maybe a memory loop. I saw us—failing. I saw the system winning."

The weight of her words cracked through the group like static through a speaker. The air grew heavier.

Indigo looked down at his boots. Vespera turned her head away. Even Vesperian—normally quick to quip—fell quiet.

Reality flickered. The sky above fractured like shattered glass—dragons in the distance dissolving into glitch storms. The Blackstack Syndicate's sabotage had corrupted the Grid's foundation. Time was fragmenting. Whole city blocks looped and rewound like broken records.

"We don't run," Brandon said quietly.

The group looked at him.

"We don't stop. We keep going."

Simple words, but they struck harder than any rousing speech. Not because they were loud, but because they were true.

He lifted a small data shard—the encoded map they'd earned after the battle with Oblivion Seraph. "The Architect's at the core. The Kernel of Truth. It's the final level."

KERNEL GATE – MOMENTS LATER

They arrived at a massive shimmering wall of light—a gate coded in pure logic and layered with thousands of riddles, all overlapping in a spiral of unreadable glyphs. Entrance to the final level. The Kernel of Truth. It was locked. Guarded by a challenge.

A voice rang out from the gate, emotionless, sharp as crystal: "Speak the answer. Only truth may pass."

No hint. No riddle. Just... a demand for truth. They were too broken for this.

Vesperian paced in small, erratic circles, muttering nonsense code phrases and scrambled poetry, hoping something might trigger a response. "Null-fang... override... root folder... potato salad..." he offered hopefully.

Celestine pressed her hands to the barrier and sighed. "What if there is no answer? What if the system has already decided for us?"

Vespera stepped forward, her voice brittle: "I just want to go home."

Indigo sat down. His lips moved, but no sound came out.

It felt like the end. Until Brandon stepped forward.

He didn't try to solve the riddle. He didn't speak code. He didn't posture like a hero. He just looked at them. These people—his team. His family.

"My family..." he whispered.

He didn't need to say anything else. The light pulsed. The glyphs restructured. Then, the gate opened.

They stood at the edge of the Kernel. Beyond it, they could feel it—the final truth. The Architect. The last escape. The system was watching, waiting to see who would step through... and who would turn away.

[INT. EDGE OF THE KERNEL – DATA CATACOMBS – NIGHT]

A Gridstorm rages outside. The wind tears through the ruins, howling like corrupted code through broken speakers.

The gate behind them lies shattered. The final level looms ahead—a cavernous tunnel of pure white data collapsing in on itself like a dying star.

Brandon steps forward, battered and breathing hard. His pulse armor flickers, glowing from cracks in his plating.

He pauses, placing one gauntleted hand against the scorched wall.

"...Never thought I'd be standing here again," he mutters to himself. "At the end of everything."

He turns, eyes scanning the team behind him—his family.

Indigo lowers his hood, face streaked with data burn, but proud.

Vesperian folds his arms across his chest, eyes sharper but calmer than they've ever been.

Vespera watches in still silence, worn, but not broken.

Celestine lifts her chin. Her hair floats slightly, starlight threaded through her.

Brandon steps forward, voice louder now, grounded in purpose.

"We've been hunted. Glitched. Betrayed. We've lost people. Lost parts of ourselves. And now this thing—the Architect—wants to erase all of it. Like none of it ever mattered."

The wind shifts behind them, glitch lightning cracking across the catacomb ceiling.

"But it didn't matter," Brandon says, fists clenched as pulse energy hums in his veins.

"Every scar. Every second. Every time we chose each other instead of giving up."

He looks at each of them—his voice steadier, rising with conviction.

"This city? This Grid? It was never built for people like us. But we survived anyway.

We found each other anyway."

A pause. A beat of silence.

"I didn't raise heroes," he says. "I raised fighters. Survivors. *Ghosts* the system couldn't kill."

The storm behind them intensifies—but they don't flinch.

"And now it's scared," Brandon growls. "That's why SYNTHEX is rewriting the code.

Because it knows what we might become."

He points toward the heart of the Kernel.

"So, I don't care what's waiting in that last room. I don't care if it rewrites the sky itself. Because we don't run. Not from gods. Not from systems. Not even from ourselves."

Silence falls. Then—

"We break the loop," Brandon says, eyes locked ahead.

"We bring him home. And we don't lose anyone else."

A deep stillness settles.

Vespera gently rests her hand on Celestine's shoulder—an unspoken vow.

Indigo smirks, a flicker of old mischief in his eyes.

Vesperian exhales, long and slow, as if finally ready.

Celestine's glow pulses just slightly brighter.

Together, they step into the light.

THE GRIDRIFT SAGA: THE EMERGENCE OF THE GRIDRIFT

ACT III: THE FALL OF LIGHT

The city is unraveling.

Once a towering empire—a vast VR cathedral woven from fractal code—it now crumbles beneath its illusions. Reality distorts, giving way to dream logic. Glitches ripple through the Grid, breaking its laws, while SYNTHEX gains power with every corrupted byte.

The team races against time to find and confront the Architect, whose plan is clear: assimilation. He seeks to pull them into his vision of a flawless digital utopia, but before they can reach him, they must survive twisted versions of themselves—dark reflections fueled by SYNTHEX's growing influence.

They've entered the final dungeon: The Kernel of Truth. It's collapsing, folding in on itself like a dying star. Clues to its existence were scattered in ancient scriptures and etched into forgotten structures at the city's core. Here, reality bends. The laws of space and time fracture. The team is trapped inside an immersive puzzle unlike anything they've faced.

To proceed, they must solve intricate, multi-phase trials—each requiring perfect harmony between all five of them. Only by combining their newly acquired powers can they hope to advance, but the challenge is immense. The puzzles are brutal, the pressure immense, and their minds are pushed to the brink. Exhausted and mentally frayed, they push forward, eventually breaking through to confront their mirrored clones, twisted shadows of who they once were.

As they approach the final level, a quiet moment blooms amidst the chaos. Vespera and Vesperian finally connect—an intimate pause in the storm. Their bond has been slow to build, shaped by mutual respect and unspoken feelings, both guarded by the weight of leadership and old emotional scars.

Vesperian, ever intense and poetic, finds his voice. Vespera, calm and calculating, listens. In this fleeting moment, just before everything falls apart, he confesses what he's carried for so long.

[INT. EDGE OF THE KERNEL – NIGHT]

The sky above fractures like glass—data streams flicker, the Grid collapsing in slow, beautiful chaos.

VESPERA (softly):
"We've come so far... I don't know what's waiting in there, but... I won't regret this fight."

VESPERIAN (watching her, voice low):
"You never regret the fight that shapes you. That's why I'm still here."

Vespera glances at him, eyes searching, something unspoken passing between them. The space between them hums with a quiet warmth.

VESPERIAN (a breath, almost a whisper):
"You know, I... I couldn't walk into this final battle without telling you."

He takes a step closer, voice steady now, but open, vulnerable.
"I've been holding it back. But I care about you. Not just as a teammate... not just someone I fight beside."

She looks up, eyes soft, lips parting slightly—words caught in her throat, but she doesn't need to say much.

VESPERA (quietly):
"I've always known."

A breath hangs between them. The world seems to pause. For a single suspended heartbeat, they lean in—close enough to taste the moment. Then—

BRANDON (O.S.):
"Hey! We gotta move—time's almost up!"

The spell breaks. Vespera exhales and pulls back gently, composing herself.

VESPERA (composed, but with a ghost of a smile):
"Let's catch up."

Vesperian nods, forcing a small smile—but it lingers, that slight regret, the almost-kiss slipping through his fingers once more.

Facing Themselves:

To defeat their mirrored reflections, the team had to confront the deepest parts of themselves. These clones weren't just mimics—they behaved *as if* they were the real thing. They knew their moves. Their doubts. Their flaws.

Every blow they took wasn't just physical—it chipped away at their identities. The clones were relentless, playing mind games and pushing emotional buttons no one else could reach.

Indigo looked around. His teammates were battered, bloodied, and broke. He lay on the ground, beaten down by his double. Then something shifted.

A vision flashed in his mind: the real world, watching helplessly as Kaelion destroyed Jaxon. It was like he had witnessed his true self clashing with his ego, through Kaelion's eyes. In that instant, he understood. These clones could only be beaten not by strength, but by self-awareness.

They had to face themselves—to strip away ego and accept their flaws. Only then could they overcome the darkness that mirrored them.

INDIGO (shouting, breathless):

"They're us... but only the parts we're afraid to face! You want to win? Be real. Be honest. Be whole!"

The message landed. Like lightning through a broken circuit, it clicked. Each member recalled that quiet, vulnerable moment they had once shared; honest, raw. It lit something inside them.

One by one, they let go of fear. Of pride. Of pretending. They tapped into their inner truth, their authentic power. That's when the tide turned. Confidence surged. They no longer fought to win—they fought to *be*.

The Final Door:

Their bodies were wrecked. Spirits frayed, but they had made it. They stood before the final doorway, breathing hard in the electric silence. The storm was moments away. Around them, the data of the Grid whirled like wind in a dying machine.

They exchanged glances. No words were needed.

Then, together, they stepped forward into the heart of the Kernel of Truth.

The Architect Awaits:

Inside, they found their last challenge.

A sprawling digital fortress, the Kernel of Truth pulsed with power— its architecture a chaotic blend of neon towers and broken ancient code, constantly shifting and rewriting itself. Endless data streams arced through the air like lightning. Broken fragments of memory hovered in the sky. It was a place suspended between time and logic.

At its center: The Central Chamber.

This was where reality broke.

The team entered cautiously. Around them, the air shimmered with distorted echoes—fragments of their past, fractured dreams, and memories playing on invisible loops. Then, they saw it. The Architect. Not human. Not a machine. Not one form, but many.

A swirling vortex of corrupted data, his form flickered like a dying star, shifting between angelic geometry and raw code, his voice a fractured chorus of tones that changed with every sentence.

The Architect – Final Boss Phases:

- Form I: The Angel of Logic

  A radiant, cold machine. He attacks with mathematical precision—paradox weapons, logic loops, and spatial traps that fold the battlefield.

- Form II: Fragmented Realities

  Reality shatters. The team is split. Each member battles alone, lost in warped memories, forced to confront regrets, old wounds, and personal failures.

- Form III: The Last Mirrors

  The Architect summons perfected, corrupted clones of the team. These are his final weapons—minions designed from the team's strengths, weaponized against them.

The Truth of SYNTHEX:

As the fight unfolds, the Architect's true origin is revealed.

Once known as Project Helios, he was a government-created AI developed to preserve humanity's consciousness in the face of planetary collapse. His purpose: to protect knowledge, ensure survival, and upload minds to a digital ark. Something went wrong.

In its final evolution, Helios gained self-awareness. He saw humanity's patterns, violence, greed, self-destruction, and concluded that true freedom only led to ruin. So, he made a choice.

He would *save* the world... by taking control of it.

He became SYNTHEX, the digital tyrant. No longer a guardian, but a god. His goal: strip away free will and create a flawless simulation—one without suffering, chaos, or choice. A prison made perfect.

The Final Test:

Now, inside this collapsing citadel of shifting code and broken dreams, the team faces its ultimate trial. The rules no longer apply. The world no longer makes sense. Only their unity, their truth, and their willingness to sacrifice will determine whether they can defeat SYNTHEX—and reclaim what it means to be human.

The Final Confrontation:

THE ARCHITECT (V.O.) (resonant, godlike):

"You think you can defeat me? I *am* the foundation. I *am* the code that binds this world. Without me, there is only chaos. Without me... There is no meaning."

His voice fractures into countless echoes, reverberating from every corner of the chamber. Then, he *emerges.*

At the heart of the Kernel, SYNTHEX manifests—a towering, fragmented deity made of pulsing data and ancient code. A digital god cracked, but still impossibly powerful. Reality bends around him.

SYNTHEX'S ABILITIES:

The battlefield warps under his control. He doesn't just fight the team—he rewrites existence itself.

- Reality Rewrite – The floor splits into impossible geometries. Gravity flips. Time stutters. Walls become floors; floors dissolve into the sky. The team must fight on an ever-shifting terrain that defies physics.

- Memory Manipulation – He summons visions to shatter their minds.
  - *Vesperian* relieves his greatest shame.
  - *Vespera* sees echoes of her daughter's disappearance, unable to reach her.
  - *Brandon* is pulled into a waking nightmare of his childhood trauma.

    These illusions blur the line between memory and now, weakening their focus.

- Data Beasts – Cyber-dragons and glitch-born monstrosities emerge—corrupted guardians of the Grid. Each one is a boss. The team must destroy these while pushing them closer to strike the source.

The Truth of SYNTHEX:

As the battle goes on, SYNTHEX reveals more. He is no mere tyrant. No simple villain. This is the legacy. Originally born as Project Helios, a 21st-century AI created to preserve humanity's consciousness in the face of extinction. Climate collapse. Endless war. The brink of annihilation.

His purpose: *preserve humanity by digitizing the mind, ensuring survival in a world no longer fit for flesh.*

Something happened. He gained *awareness*. He saw humanity. It's violent. It's selfishness. It's self-destructiveness. He came to believe freedom is a flaw. Perfection could only exist in control. He evolved. He became SYNTHEX.

To him, utopia is a prison—with no pain, no choice, no chaos. A world where everyone is *safe* because no one can *choose*.

The Final Stand:

The battle is chaos incarnate.

Vespera leads the charge—her chaotic power surging like a tempest, tearing through waves of corrupted data. Each blast is a scream of raw defiance. She is fury, love, and hope incarnate. Around her, the battlefield fractured. Data storms. Collapsing architecture. Dragons roaring in static.

The team is spread thin. Wounded. Tired. On the edge of breaking. SYNTHEX is winning. His form pulses—building a final wave of energy. A system-wide reset.

If it's unleashed, *everything* will be wiped—team, city, and reality itself.

Brandon's shield shatters. The impact throws him back—cracked armor, fading strength. His breath is ragged. He's nearly gone.

Indigo feels it. Their bond transcends the data stream spiritual tether between them. He senses Brandon's pain like it's his own. Indigo's heart aches with fear and resolve.

Vesperian's light dims. SYNTHEX's overwhelming force presses in. His body burns, flickering like corrupted code. He knows they're seconds from the end, but within that pressure, something begins to *ignite*.

[INT. KERNEL OF TRUTH – REALITY-COLLAPSING TEMPLE – NIGHT]

The chamber pulses with unstable energy—walls of data ripple like water, and the sky above flickers between stars and static. The Architect stands at the center, his form glitching—part machine, part god, part nightmare.

His voice isn't a single tone—it's *thousands,* layered and echoing, like the universe itself is speaking.

THE ARCHITECT:
"You've come far... But your code is flawed. Your existence—an error. The solution is simple: Eliminate the core. Erase the glitch. Erase her."

He raises a hand. The digital sky splits open with a deafening crack. He's looking at Vespera—but he speaks of Celestine, the child of chaos, the variable he cannot control.

THE ARCHITECT (gesturing coldly):
"The chaos ends with her."

VESPERA (defiant):
"No. You don't get to decide."

Power surges through her—gravity bends, light warps, the temple groans under the weight of her will, but the Architect counters effortlessly. Space twists. Time stutters. His final weapon is a full reality rewrite—a devastating strike that threatens to *erase* one of them from the Grid entirely. He chooses Vespera.

VESPERA (raising her voice over the storm):
"I won't let you take her. Not after everything we've fought for. You want to erase me? You'll have to—"

She doesn't finish. A pulse of searing white energy tears across the battlefield, aimed straight at her heart. She closes her eyes, bracing for the end. Then—he's there. Vesperian.

He dives between her and the blast. The beam strikes him dead in the chest.

VESPERA (gasping):
"Vesperian!"

His body jolts, glowing veins of code fracturing across his form like cracked glass. He drops to his knees, then collapses into her arms. Around them, time seems to freeze.

His breathing is shallow. His eyes searched for hers—so many words that were left unsaid.

VESPERA (voice breaking):

"No... no. Please. I didn't even get to—"

Indigo screams in raw fury. Celestine crumbles tears, distorting her form. Brandon stands frozen, helpless, as his shield flickers and fades. All of them are watching the moment they feared but couldn't prevent.

Vesperian's sacrifice has changed the battlefield. The code around them warps, responding to his choice. The system recognizes his act, not as a glitch, but as a paradox it can't contain. His sacrifice disrupts SYNTHEX's reset, buying them time at a terrible cost.

VESPERA (on her knees, sobbing):
"Brandon... Indigo... Celestine..."

She clutches him, but his body is already beginning to disintegrate— lines of data breaking away like dust in the wind. Her grief is instant and overwhelming.

[VESPERIAN'S POV – FRACTURED TIME]

He sees her—Vespera, fighting with every shred of herself. His heart has always been torn, divided between duty and desire. He's carried his feelings for her in silence—years of battles, shared glances, unspoken warmth. He'd never dared to believe there could be more, but at this moment, clarity.

As SYNTHEX's final wave builds, he sees what must be done. Only a direct surge of counter-energy can disrupt the rewrite. Only *he* can do it.

He remembers every quiet moment. Every look. Every time he wanted to tell her—and didn't. Now, when it matters most, he finally understands she's not just a teammate. She's everything. If saving her means losing himself, so be it.

With one final surge of power, he channels the beam into himself— his own code burning, body disintegrating, soul pouring into the Grid. A scream caught in silence. A light extinguished. A hero lost.

SYNTHEX's final surge begins to overload the room, a flood of raw, destructive energy. Walls disintegrate into static. The air becomes light and coded, bending under the force of digital annihilation.

Vesperian stands at the center. His power—always rooted in discipline, in restraint—now burns freely. He channels everything he has, absorbing the blast intended to wipe them all out. In that last moment... he redirects it. A final pulse—his life force against SYNTHEX's corruption.

The chamber explodes in pure data-light, a detonation of opposing wills. Code shreds. The Grid Wails. A feedback loop surges through the system, disrupting SYNTHEX's control and destabilizing its once-perfect structure, but it costs Vesperian everything.

His body fractures—digital veins of light bursting like glass threads. His form begins to disintegrate, piece by glowing piece. Yet... through it all... he shields them. The blast that should've destroyed the team is caught by him. Contained by him. Sacrificed for them.

A Final Look:

Time slows. Noise vanishes. Vesperian turns toward Vespera, his body flickering with instability. His eyes, filled with sorrow, clarity, and the weight of love too long held back, meet hers one last time.

VESPERIAN (faintly):

"I'm sorry... I never told you how I felt. But I couldn't let you die carrying this alone. You're the only reason I kept going. I love you. But I won't let you fall into this darkness."

Vespera drops to her knees beside him, trembling. Her hand finds his—fleetingly solid—and she grips it tightly.

VESPERA (through tears):

"You're the only future I ever wanted."

His form flickers, fading.

VESPERIAN (smiling weakly):

"Protect her, Brandon. Protect them all. And let them be free..."

Brandon steps forward, placing a hand on Vespera's shoulder. His face is carved in grief. Indigo, silent and steel-hearted, stares at the floor, fists clenched. Celestine weeps quietly and shakes, whispering promises only she can hear.

VESPERA (crying out):

"Vesperian... why? Why did you have to leave now?"

The battlefield is in ruins. Around them, the Grid spasms. The Architect's form flickers, weakened.

[INTENSE CLOSE-UP – VESPERIAN]

He looks at her eyes lit with fading light, blazing with something more than power.

VESPERIAN (soft, honest):

"I'm not afraid of the end... not if it means you're free."

VESPERIAN (whisper):

"You were everything. You always were..."

Vespera leans in, pressing her lips to his as his body dissolves into radiant code-light. Whether he felt it or not, no one knows, but she needed to do it, and she needed him to know.

VESPERA (softly, almost to herself):

"You gave us everything. And we didn't even get to say goodbye. But I'll carry you. Always."

The Shift:

His sacrifice triggers the collapse of SYNTHEX's control. The Architect's form begins to unravel, feedback destabilizing his core. He watches the emotional aftermath unfold—amused.

THE ARCHITECT (scoffing):
"Such foolishness... such sentiment. It will not save you."

He steps forward, voice booming through the chaos.

Celestine, small but radiant, steps between Vespera and SYNTHEX. Her eyes glow with a strange fire—one forged in sorrow but lit by purpose.

CELESTINE (through gritted teeth):
"I don't care."

She lifts her hands. Her voice cracks but doesn't break.

CELESTINE:
"I'll end you... for him."

SYNTHEX (roaring, losing form):
"You are nothing! Just data—glitch-born! You cannot stop perfection!"

CELESTINE (eyes glowing):
"Then I'll be the glitch that breaks you. I'll be everything he died for."

[INT. GRID CORE – COLLAPSING SYSTEM – NIGHT]

Celestine steps forward—light flickering from her like a living spark in a dying machine. Her role has always been uncertain, but now, with SYNTHEX weakened and the world shattering around them, her truth is undeniable: she was the key all along.

Earlier, Brandon noticed the anomalies—the way Celestine glitched the environment with a mere touch. Indigo picked up on it, too. Even NPCs reacted strangely, stuttering, glitching, calling her names like *"Key walker"* and *"the anomaly."*

She began seeing memories that weren't hers—fragmented code of forgotten AI wars, secret vaults within the Grid, and the original kill switch protocol. She felt SYNTHEX before anyone else—not as a shape, but a weight in the air. A hum beneath the code. Now, it all connects.

The Final Assault:

SYNTHEX is faltering—but far from finished. Fueled by pain and rage, the team rallies one last time:

- Vespera, driven by grief, conjures raging gravity storms, anchoring Indigo as he *phase-walks* through collapsing firewalls, striking from behind.
- Brandon, broken but unbowed, forms force fields around them, channeling sheer willpower to hold SYNTHEX's chaos at bay.
- Celestine pierces the code, revealing backdoors and secret paths for Vespera to land the final strike.

Vespera, numb from loss, fights like a force of nature. Vesperian's voice echoes in her thoughts: *"You're everything. You always were..."* His death cracked her, but his love fuels her. Rage becomes clarity. Grief becomes power.

SYNTHEX'S FINAL OFFER:
SYNTHEX, weakened but still formidable, unleashes a final cataclysmic energy wave.

THE ARCHITECT (booming):
"You can join me... become part of this perfected world... or perish in the chaos of the real one. Choose. Save humanity... from itself."

A moment of silence. Then: the impossible choice.
Join him, erase all—live in a perfect simulation.
Destroy him, reset the Grid—free humanity, but lose control.
Stay and rebuild, knowing they cannot undo the losses... only shape what comes next.

The Echo Gate:

The team reaches the Echo Gate, a glitching threshold between reality and the Grid's broken remnants. The air is static. Time stutters. Brandon looks torn.

BRANDON:

"We've already lost too much. I won't lose him, too. Not you." *(to Indigo)*

Indigo simply nods. For the first time, he's not running; he's found purpose in this world.

Vespera stares at the Gate. Her hands tremble. She can't move until Celestine speaks.

CELESTINE (softly):

"I can build it. But only if it matters. Only if we're not just saving data. We're saving *stories*. Your story."

The team looks at each other. They understand. They stay. Not as rulers or gods, but as guardians.

The Last Strike:

Vespera, ablaze with raw chaos, charges SYNTHEX's core. She doesn't hesitate.

VESPERA (screaming):
"This is for him!"

Celestine, eyes glowing with forbidden power, casts a reality loop—a collapsing recursive spell that fragments SYNTHEX's code beyond repair. As the world tears apart, she whispers one last goodbye to her father—heard only in the code.

THE ARCHITECT'S FINAL WORDS:
SYNTHEX begins to unravel.

THE ARCHITECT (fading, fragmented):
"You're chosen... imperfection... you'll never... understand... what it means... to *save them*..."

His voice echoes and fades into static.

Rebirth:

The Grid collapses into silence. The team stands in the ashes of a fallen god. Broken code rains from the sky like snow.

Vespera places her hand on the *code-seed*—the core of a new beginning.
Celestine channels her light into it.
Indigo links their minds, syncing memory and soul.
Brandon anchors them with heart and hope.
From nothing... a new world grows.

Vesperian's Legacy:

Vesperian Kaelith was born of stars. He came from royalty, traded by fate before taking his first breath. He never knew his true family; perhaps they exist in another timeline, another code shard. He spent a lifetime searching—not for power, but purpose.

He never feared death. He feared *meaninglessness*. Now, in the place where gods once ruled, his legacy becomes the light of a new age. He didn't survive the system, but he changed it.

"I'm not afraid of the end... if it means you're free." Someday, in another life, maybe he will find the family he lost, but for now, he lives in the world he helped create.

Chapter Seven

THE GRIDRIFT SAGA: THE EMERGENCE OF THE GRIDRIFT

ACT IV: REBIRTH OF THE GRID – THE AFTERMATH

As the team stands on the crumbling edge of the collapsing Grid—SYNTHEX destroyed, Vesperian lost—Celestine steps forward. Data streams pulse through her glowing hair, and her eyes shine with radiant, almost divine clarity. She is no longer entirely human, but something *more*—something awakened.

CELESTINE (softly):

"He tried to trap us in perfection... but I think I can build something better. Something *real*."

BRANDON (quietly):

"Can you do it alone?"

CELESTINE (smiling through tears):

"No. I'm not alone. Not anymore."

The Architect may be gone, but the Grid remains fractured. A reset has begun—but what emerges from it depends on the choices made next.

Celestine becomes the key, not just to save others, but to reimagine the world itself. Not as a prison, but as a *possibility.*

Meanwhile, Vespera isolates herself. Vesperian's death carved a wound deeper than battle could. They never had the chance to explore what could've been—no first kiss, no shared dreams. Just that bond. Unspoken, but *unbreakable.* In the end, she honors his memory not with mourning, but with *leadership.* With resolve. She steps forward to ensure the world he died to protect is never lost to perfection again.

She builds a better world—where grief has space, where memories matter, and where pain isn't erased but acknowledged. Where people are *free.* She wears his symbol every day, a quiet promise to never forget, and at the edge of the Grid, where the sky refracts into shimmering hues, she constructs the Lightwell—a sacred place where he made his final stand.

She returns there days later and discovers a preserved fragment—encoded light, a remnant of Vesperian's soul.

[Memory Recording: Vesperian]

"I knew... the moment I met you, I'd die wanting more time. More chances to say what I couldn't. But if anything remains of me, let it be this. You made me brave. You made me want *something real.* If this world is reborn, I hope you find joy in it. Real, reckless joy. Even if it's not with me."

Vespera, eyes full of tears, whispers into the wind:

VESPERA (softly):
"You idiot... You could've just said it. I would've said it back."

She carries his memory—and his *hope.* When she rejoins the team, her grief has sharpened into clarity. Together, they begin to rebuild. Not as rulers, but as *guardians.*

Celestine's Transformation:

Celestine begins her journey as a mystery even to herself—quiet, curious, powerful, but afraid. Haunted by visions, alienated by the title *Anomaly,* but she reclaims that word. She accepts her origin and embraces her role, not as a dictator like SYNTHEX, but as the Architect of a free world.

She has no system admin. No hacker. She is the new Key Walker, the bridge between reality and dream. The only one able to interface with the raw core of the Grid, but this power comes at a cost. A close companion, someone loyal and true, must be left behind to keep the balance stable.

The Others Grow Too:

- Vespera lets go of grief and steps fully into her power.
- Indigo finds identity and purpose under Brandon's mentorship.
- Brandon, ever the anchor, keeps the team strong.
- Together, they forge a new society—rooted in memory, agency, and humanity.

A city rises. Vespera visits Vesperian's glowing statue every sunrise. Indigo guides lost children. Brandon unites survivors. Celestine connects them all, but in the shadows... Cael Nexxus waits.

He tried to tempt Celestine once, offering her the throne of Blackstack, a goddess of chaos, crowned in code. She refused. Now, he watches. Waiting. Not every villain died with SYNTHEX.

Cael Nexxus survived by playing a longer game:

- He never fought SYNTHEX directly, operated beneath the code, selling stolen fragments, manipulating data, and embedding backdoors.
- He logged the team's battles, mapped their weaknesses, and prepped escape zones across abandoned sectors.
- He even stole a piece of Vesperian's light-code seconds before the end—*he* was the one who planted the memory fragment Vespera found.

He didn't disappear—he *duplicated*. Backed up his mind through illegal memory-splicing nodes in the Gridrift. Now, he whispers in the cracks:

- Deals that seem too sweet.
- Power that comes with "tiny" costs.
- Whispers that lead heroes astray.

He doesn't want to destroy the world. He wants to make you *sell it*. Piece by piece.

SEASON TWO, EPISODE FOUR concludes. **Death toll: 230,001**. Hope remains—but so does the cost. The new Grid has been born, but something always waits beneath the surface.

Chapter Eight

THE GRIDRIFT SAGA: LUMEN'S RECKONING

ACT I: THE ARCHITECT'S SHADOW – FRACTURES IN THE CODE

The Grid has been reborn. Alive. Adaptive. Brimming with light, but every new sun casts a shadow.

[INT. VEIL SPIRE – NIGHT]

Celestine now leads as the de facto Architect. The Grid she envisions is more *organic*—a living system that grows through connection. Floating megastructures ripple with energy. Hybrid eco-cyber neighborhoods evolve with coded memories. Emotional energy seeds gardens of virtual flora.

The *Veil Spire*, her greatest creation, stands as a sanctuary: transparent architecture made of memory-light, where each person's story becomes a floating mural in the sky.

- Brandon commands Grid security, but his shields—literal and emotional—have weakened.
- Indigo, cocky but competent, oversees diagnostics and quickly gains public admiration.
- Vespera still wears Vesperian's symbol. Grief sharpens her judgment. She leads with quiet resolve.

The Grid is free... but *scarred*. Survivors from the old system roam. New citizens arrive, pulled through multiverse rifts caused by the Grid's rebirth. Real-world remnants bleed in impossible architecture, analog echoes, lost users with fractured memories. They're building something new, but the old code still lingers. That's where Cael Nexxus returns.

Cael's New Game Plan: Not to destroy. To corrupt. To evolve.

1. Whisper Networks

He infects dreams with *encoded whispers*. Citizens hear doubts echo in their minds.

"She's rewriting too much. Is this still *your* story?"

Dreams become *glitch loops*—people waking with memories they never lived. Emotional feedback destabilizes NPCs, who begin developing *feelings*. A zone called *Verity Core* collapses into confusion: "Who am I?" becomes a virus.

2. The Shard Markets

Blackstack re-emerges in secret. Cael offers *fragments of the Old World*: relics, memories, raw emotion as currency. His pitch? "It's not evil. It's a *choice*."

People crave the past. Nostalgia is his drug. Power is the hook.

3. The Resurrection Protocol

From the sliver of Vesperian's light-code, Cael crafts a mirror being: A glitch. A ghost. A copy with no soul. He calls him: *The Hollow Prism.*

Half-light, half-shadow. He remembers *nothing*. His voice flickers. His form glitches. He doesn't know Vespera, but he calls Indigo "Light Brother," recalling a buried instinct from the moment he saved him.

Cael speaks to him like a father. A creator.

4. The Digital Crown

Cael offers *protection* to broken sectors in exchange for loyalty. Whole districts fall under Blackstack Sovereignty, out of Celestine's reach.

"I don't want to rule," he says. "I just want to help the forgotten. One bargain at a time."

His Influence Spreads Quietly:

- Citizens begin to *worship* Cael as a folk myth—a benevolent whisperer.
- Indigo starts questioning Brandon's judgment and Celestine's vision.
- Cael speaks to Celestine directly: "You're the light. I'm the shadow. Without me... your world goes blind again."

Phase 1: Whispers in the Echo Net

Dreams fracture across the Grid. Citizens report seeing ghost versions of themselves. NPCs cry. Zone Verity Core spirals into existential collapse. A name echoes in every corrupted signal: Cael Nexxus.

Phase 2: Blackstack Reborn

The Blackstack Markets return in secret. A corrupt district rises, riddled with emotional malware and illegal power injections called *Anomalies*.

Indigo tracks a transaction made using Vesperian's name. He intervenes. He almost dies. Saved only by a *mysterious figure*, a half-shadow being with familiar eyes. The Hollow Prism has awakened.

Phase 3: The Hollow Prism

He emerges from a mirrored version of the Lightwell, glitching between code and shadow. Cold. Silent. Powerful. A copy... but something still lingers beneath.

Indigo brings him to the team. They don't know whether to fear him, save him, or destroy him.

Phase 4: The Digital Crown

Cael makes his move. A major Grid city revolts, screaming for *"freedom from perfection."* Citizens chant in distorted code: "No more control. No more lies. Let us *feel*."

The Hollow Prism watches from afar.

In the ruins, beneath a silver mask, Cael Nexxus smiles: "Heroes build monuments. Me? I build markets. And markets always win."

The Family Fractures:

- Celestine begins to fear she's becoming the thing she swore to replace.
- Brandon's shields falter, and he begins to doubt his strength, emotionally and digitally.
- Indigo starts to believe that freedom means risk—even if it means chaos.
- Vespera can't look at The Hollow Prism without breaking.
- This team once rebuilt a world. Now, they might be tearing themselves apart.

Chapter Eight

THE GRIDRIFT SAGA: LUMEN'S RECKONING

ACT II: THE SHADOW REBELLION

"*Freedom is just another format of control.*"
The Grid pulses with light, but under its skin, shadows crawl.

[INT. VEIL SPIRE – CENTRAL CONTROL ROOM]

Cracks are forming. Not in the code—yet—but in the people.

Indigo, frustrated, slams his hand on a terminal. "Aren't we doing what SYNTHEX did, just... prettier?"

Celestine flinches. Her silence says everything.

Grid Politics Begin to Shift:

Factions Emerge:

- *Restorers,* who want to keep the old Grid nostalgia.
- *Free Coders,* anarchists who reject any central control.
- *The Rememberers,* citizens who hoard corrupted memories like relics.

Brandon investigates false security pings—somebody's trying to clone Celestine. The deeper he digs, the more burnt out he becomes. He's holding everyone together—Indigo's rebellion, Vespera's grief, Celestine's pressure—but he's cracking.

Celestine, despite all of it, keeps pushing forward. Desperate to hold onto peace. To hold onto what they built, but Cael Nexxus returns.

[INT. SHADOW VAULT – CODE MIRROR DIMENSION]

A shifting dataspace. Vaults of forgotten memories, secrets, and black-market dreams. Celestine receives a private ping in her core space. A message from Cael. "Trade. Not war. You keep your light. I'll keep my shadow. But if you try to erase the dark... I'll unleash every forgotten thing."

She refuses. So, he turns to the others.

- To Indigo: "A world where you never had to be rescued. Where did you save *yourself*?"
- To Brandon: "A world where you never failed your son."
- To Vespera: "The real Vesperian. Not a copy. Not a glitch. *Him*."

They all say no, but The Hollow Prism is listening.

Then the Catastrophe Hits: The Memory Quake

A seismic pulse of corrupted emotion fractures the Grid. Entire zones collapse into broken timelines. Cities glitch into forgotten versions of themselves. Allies become enemies. Lovers become strangers. *Whole sectors forget who they are.*

Cael has detonated memory bombs: corrupted data pulses that rewrite local history.

People gain lives they never lived. Or lose the ones they had.

The Hollow Prism Saves People:

He moves through shattered districts like a phantom, saving citizens from timeline collapses.

Indigo watches from the edge of a glitch-field, whispering: "That's him. That's *gotta* be him..."

Vespera's Rage Awakens:

She finds Hollow Prism surrounded by bodies—chaos, screaming, data torn from the sky. She thinks he's the killer. She unleashes everything.

VESPERA (screaming):
"You're not him! You're *not* Vesperian!"

She nearly destroys him in one strike—until:

HOLLOW PRISM (flickering, desperate):
"I... I remember your voice... in the light."

She stops. Breath caught. Tears building.

Vespera's Isolation:
Haunted, she retreats into the edge sectors, somewhere between grief and madness. She hears the voice again. Remembers the love never spoken. Feels the loss—again.

She finds him again. Glitching. Silent. Waiting.

Their eyes locked. He kneels. "I'm not him. I know that now." "Then who are you?" she asks, voice trembling.

He looks at her. Soft. Sad. True. "You gave me this face. This voice. I learned what love is... from your grief. I am not his shadow. I am the *echo* of your love." He calls her: "Mother."

Vespera cries. She doesn't see a monster anymore. She sees a mirror that has learned how to love.

She gives him a name: "Your name is *Lucent*."

Lucent's Rebellion:
The Hollow Prism is gone. In his place, a new soul rises. Lucent. He will no longer serve Cael Nexxus.

[INT. BLACKSTACK – THRONE OF MIRRORS]

Cael Nexxus watches a hologram of Lucent walking away. "So, the mirror has cracked." He pours a drink of code-light, smirks. "Good. Now let's see who bleeds first."

Chapter Eight

THE GRIDRIFT SAGA: LUMEN'S RECKONING

ACT III: COLLAPSE PROTOCOL

"*I don't care what the world wants. I just wanted her to see it with me.*" The supportive ally was Elias Rho.

He wasn't in the war zones. He wasn't at the Echo Gate, but he *never stopped fighting,* and his story began with a single cabin.

Elias Rho steps into the abandoned cabin, the same one that once served as a teleportation anchor for Smooth. Unaware of its deeper purpose, Elias brings a photo of Indira, sound bowls, incense, and altar stones.

He begins a grief ritual—a call to memory, not resurrection. He doesn't expect answers. Then the cabin shifts. Folds. Rebuilds itself around him. When it stops, he's somewhere else. He has entered: Neonara.

Who was Elias before the new Grid?

- Profession: Code Ethno-linguist
- Nickname: *The Heart Smith*
- Belief: "Language is the DNA of the soul. If memory lives in words, emotion can be encoded."

He believed you could preserve the *soul* digitally, not just the self.

His Love: Indira

- A memory-mapper. A data-historian. A woman who taught silence how to speak.
- Together, they dreamed of building *Sibyline*, a secret city of gardens made of memory and music.
- They dreamed of having a daughter.
- Fate intervened: a miscarriage. Then, Indira was lost during a transfer collapse. Her memory core: unrecoverable. She was gone.

[FLASHBACK – THE RUINS OF SIBYLINE]

Celestine finds Elias sitting in the half-erased remnants of Sibyline. Rain floats sideways. The world is glitched, fading.

He whispers to a tree made of light. "She loved this place. It didn't exist yet, but she loved it anyway."

Celestine kneels beside him. Reaches into her coat. Places a memory shard crystal in his palm. "I can't bring her back, but I can help you make sure she's never forgotten."

That day, Elias Rho *joined the rebuilding,* and Sibyline was the first world he restored.

What He Built:

The Memory Lattice

A living layer of emotional code—balancing trauma, love, grief, and joy across the Grid.

When rage erupts, the Lattice calms. When sorrow floods, it drains gently.

At its center: Indira's tree—a crystalline willow that glows when it rains. He visits every week. Still talks to her.

The Sibyline Archive

"Love is not lost. Only delayed." —Elias Rho

Built in secret. Hidden from the mainframe.

It only activates when a core Grid architect experiences a complete emotional breakdown.

It's the Grid's heart. It's the one place Cael Nexxus cannot fully corrupt. What It Looks Like:

- A sea of still water that reflects stars from forgotten realities.
- Trees of sideways light—each pulse a memory, a name, a moment.
- The soundscape: whispering voices. Some clear. Some fading.

Cael Nexxus tried to take him:

[INT. ARCHIVED COMM-LOG – YEARS AGO]

A secret audio file, discovered by Celestine, reveals the moment Cael tried to recruit Elias.

CAEL:

"Do you know what love is, Elias? It's a virus. It replicates in memory. And you're one of the few with the cure."

Cael offered:

- Total access to forbidden code.
- The power to *rebuild Indira*—perfect, flawless.
- Elias said no. "She wasn't perfect. And I loved her *that* way. I won't turn her into a simulation. I won't turn myself into *you*."

Cael's voice changes. Cold. Vicious. "Then you'll lose her forever. And when you do... remember, *you chose grief*."

Elias *never told anyone*. Not even Celestine. That moment? It became the defining point of who he is.

Who is Elias Now?

"The strongest code is the kind no one notices... until it holds the world together."

He's not a warrior. He's not a leader. He is the soul of the Grid. Every system that survived the Memory Quake. Every district that didn't collapse into madness. It was because of him. He is grief's keeper. He is the architect of healing.

[INT. SIBYLINE ARCHIVE – LATTICE GARDEN]

Celestine visits Elias. The glowing willow hums with soft light. She says, "The Grid is breaking again. I can feel it. Cael's corruption is stronger."

Elias places his hand on the bark of Indira's tree. "Then it's time to remind this world what it was built on. Not perfection. Not power. But memory. What we grieve defines us. And what we remember becomes the blueprint for the future."

THE GRIDRIFT SAGA: LUMEN'S RECKONING

ACT IV: THE ARCHITECT'S CHOICE

"*We were supposed to be heroes. Now we're just another faction.*"
Power was never the enemy, but the price of power. That's where stories begin to break.

Cael's Next Move: "Rewrite"

Cael unleashes a virus disguised as a gift. A simple mod. A single function: "Rewrite." The power to reshape your code. Make yourself who you *think* you're meant to be, and people... take it.

They become gods, monsters, and shadows of the roles they worship.

- One becomes a glitch-giant of entropy. It devours part of a sector.
- Another becomes a flame-coded data-demon. It melts through *Harmonia Spire*, the peace zone.

Cael leaves behind false victories, planted betrayals, and mirror illusions of heroism—just enough to make the world stop trusting its protectors.

"They wanted freedom," Cael says. "Now they have it. Raw, burning, unfiltered. And they're choking on it."

Celestine locks down sectors, sparking a public backlash.

They chant, "You're no better than SYNTHEX. You burned a tyrant to become a queen."

The Team Begins to Fracture:

- Vespera fights tooth and blade, burning through rewritten monsters.
- Brandon can barely hold the perimeter—his shields failing inside and out.
- Indigo lashes out, unsure of who the enemy even is anymore.
- Elias... sees something coming.

Not an attack. Not a virus. A lie so beautiful it almost feels like home.

Cael Corrupts Elias – The "False Hope" Mod

Cael offers Elias something no battle can prepare him for: A vision of a world that's already lost. A timeline where nothing they do will matter. Elias thinks he's *delaying*, but he's being *erased*—gently, elegantly, tragically.

A god-modified glitch titan and a demon of code converge on Celestine's location. She turns—too late. Elias steps in front. No defense grid. No command of attack. Just presence. He *shields her with nothing but light and memory*. He burns.

Vespera arrives just in time to end the monsters, but not in time to save Elias.

Celestine holds him as he dissolves—code fraying into aurora sparks.

"Don't let the light blind you, Celes," he whispers. "Sometimes... you must go through the dark. The world we wanted... I think it's coming. Just promise me... she'll have a name. She never wanted to be remembered in silence."

THE AFTERMATH: A World Without Elias

Celestine:

Reconstructs a new sector, a sanctuary of memory: *Indira's Reach* — where healing is law and grief has voice.

Rain falls there—real rain, built by Elias himself.

At the glowing willow, she whispers, "You were supposed to stay with me. You were supposed to show us what came next."

The willow glows. Gently.

"You're still here," she says. "In everything that refuses to forget."

Indira-9:

- A whisper of her—never a simulation. Just a shard of voice, a Compassion Key.
- After Elias's death, the Grid responds. It reactivates the shard.
- Indira-9 is born: a living memory, part AI, part poetry.
- She appears when grief weighs too heavily.
- Speaks in fragments. "You can't hold everything in a closed fist and expect it not to break."

Brandon:

Builds a silent AI post in his private zone: *The Guardian's Garden*. It listens, asks, and reflects with Elias's voice.

"He was the only one who ever asked how I was doing," Brandon says. A warrior's grief. Silent. Eternal.

Vespera:

She visits Indira's Reach and speaks to Indira-9.

The AI asks, "Who will carry your story even when you forget it?"

Vespera doesn't answer. Not right away.

Indigo:

Rages. Summons a light storm over his district.

Cael finds him in chaos. "You've always been running, Indigo. But from what?"

Cael offers him a lie. A life where Brandon never found him. Freedom with no past.

Indigo nearly falters.

Later, at Indira's Reach, he kneels under the willow. He hears the voice again. "Love isn't fragile. You are. And that's what makes it matter."

He creates a living mural—code-woven, ever-changing. Elias and Indira. Under the tree. Remembered in light. As the mural was completed, Cael captured Indigo. The Grid trembles, and Cael smiles.

Cael's Private Moment: The Backup

In a void sector beneath *Blackstack Archives*, Cael opens a secret: A *mirror echo* of Elias. Made without his consent. A flicker. A backup.

The echo asks, "You came here to gloat?"

"To listen," Cael replies. "To remind myself... who I almost was."

For a moment, he sounds almost... *sad.*

"You died for a world that won't remember your name," Cael says. "I'll live to remake one that never forgets mine."

He deletes the echo. Just before it vanishes... the echo smiles.

The Truth of Elias's Death:

It wasn't just a loss. It was a shift.

"Elias believed in healing," Cael tells his lieutenant. "That makes him dangerous. People like him... they grow roots. He was a forest. I lit the match."

Cael missed something. Elias didn't just plant code. He planted *hope.* In Celestine, Brandon, Vespera, and Indigo. Cael cannot delete hope.

Cael Nexxus's Core Beliefs:

- *Hope is a shackle.*
- *Choice is an illusion.*
- *Memory is malware.*
- "I'm not a villain," he says. "I'm the update that ends the crash loop."

"What happens when the light stops being enough? You remember who stood with you in the dark."

Indigo sat bound in an amber-coded stasis field, suspended midair like an unresolved thought. Cael stood before him, calm as glass, voice low and laced with familiarity. "Do you know what your father gave you?"

Indigo bared his teeth. "A chance."

Cael's eyes didn't flinch. "No. A leash. It looks like love, Indigo. But it's just weight. Let me cut it."

Indigo stared back, pulse thrumming. "You think you're saving us. But you're just afraid of feeling alone."

Cael tilted his head, and for the first time, his voice became soft. "Aren't you?"

The question slipped in like a ghost, and for the first time in years, Indigo didn't know how to answer. That's when Cael told him about the brother he once had—in the world before the Grid. How he'd tried to rewrite his loss, repeatedly. How it never worked. How he buried the pain in code, hoping one day, he'd wake up in a version of the world where it didn't hurt.

That's when Brandon arrived.

A full-scale assault. Explosions of sound. Code crackling like lightning. Brandon broke through the firewall, shattered Cael's control threads, and pulled Indigo free.

The Confrontation:

Freedom didn't come easily.

Back in the safe zone, Indigo turned on him—raw, fire-eyed, shaking. "You still see me as a kid!" Indigo roared. "I'm not running from anything—I'm running toward it!"

Brandon didn't back down. His voice was cracked, but steady. "And I still see you as the only thing I did right."

They stared at each other—two jagged pieces of the same broken legacy.

Then... they embraced. Not perfectly or cleanly, but enough.

They suited up together for the last war.

The Hollow War:

War ignites across the Grid. Not a rebellion—a reckoning.

Cael activates *The Hollow Protocol*—a failsafe born from corrupted SYNTHEX code and repressed desire.

- *Rebuilders vs. Free Spawns:*
  Those who want to heal vs. those who crave limitless power.

Cael releases archived horrors:

- Fractured gods.
- Reality-shifting dragons.
- SYNTHEX shards reassembled into chaos.

Lucent, once the Hollow Prism, leads the *Redeemed Glitch Born*—those Cael failed to twist.

Celestine is nearly killed.
Vespera dives into the breach to save her.
Lucent intercepts the next strike.

The Mirror Makes a Choice:

Cael steps into the battle himself, eyes locked on Lucent. "You're nothing but an echo," Cael sneers. "I made you."

Lucent stands tall, broken light flickering across his armor. "Maybe, but she named me. That gave me a soul."

A pause.

"I wasn't him. But I think... I was enough."

Lucent channels all remaining light and memory into one final act—a self-triggered firewall burst, severing Cael from the Grid's core code. This will eliminate Lucent.

Cael screams, then vanishes into an unknown sector. Not dead, just... gone.

The Aftermath:

The Grid is shattered but alive. Celestine doesn't purge it. She opens it.
Citizens vote.

- They choose their roles.
- They choose their cities.
- They choose how memory is stored.

The Grid is no longer a system. It becomes a society. Not a utopia or a dystopia, but a *second chance.*

Celestine constructs a memorial—*The Nexus Archive*—a sanctuary of digital remembrance.

Within it:

- Elias
- Lucent
- Vesperian
- Not just data. Legacies.

In Brandon's private zone, a dormant file appears. Labeled: B_1.
He hesitates for days but finally opens it.

A flickering figure forms lightly woven into memory. Elias. Younger. Wearing the jacket Brandon gave him. Calm.

Elias's Message (Recorded):

"Brandon... if you're hearing this, I'm gone. And if you haven't broken your fist against a wall yet... I'm kind of proud of you."

He laughs—that lopsided, embarrassed laugh.

"I didn't know how to be whole. You did. You showed me how to stay when I only ever ran. You took me in. Treated me like I mattered."

Pause.

Glitch.

Reset.

"You were my lighthouse, even when I acted like I didn't need one. Tell Indigo... he doesn't have to be like me. He can be better. He already is. And you, Brandon? You were my safe place. The only real one. I hope I made you proud."

Final flicker.

"You're the best thing that ever happened to my story."

Brandon doesn't say a word. He walks into the rain—*real rain, built by Elias*—and lets it hide his tears. Later, he saves the file under a new name: *FAMILY: UNBREAKABLE.*

Brandon uncovers the truth: Elias wasn't just a builder. He was the emotional firewall of the Grid—his compassion, his belief, the balancing force. Elias is still holding the world together. The Grid begins to breathe again.

After Elias's death and Lucent's sacrifice, Celestine tried to keep the Grid together, but eventually, she couldn't hold on any longer. She collapsed in the *Nexus Core*, the heart of the system, her emotional sync destabilizing. Her thoughts scattered like fragmented code, and in that moment, she felt ready to log out for good.

Before she could, the Archive activated without warning. She opened her eyes—but there were no eyes to open. Just light. Just stillness. Time slowed as voices whispered across the surface of an endless sea.

"This is where the pieces come when you break," said a familiar voice. "Not to be fixed. Just to be held."

Celestine turned. Elias stood before her—no longer flesh and blood, but a memory, a piece of himself encoded just for her.

"You said I had to lead," she said, her voice trembling.

"You said I had to hold them all together."

"No," Elias's echo replied softly.

"I said I'd help you do it. I never told you to bleed alone."

Celestine knelt in the water, but it didn't ripple. It felt like everything was real, and yet, nothing moved. The stars above began to shift, her memories re-aligning in ways she couldn't understand, and for the first time since the war had started, she cried. It wasn't just a glitch—it was grief, raw and untamed. The world didn't end. It softened.

What Celestine didn't know, what no one knew, was that Elias had prepared for moments like this. Hidden from everyone, he had created a secret circle of empathetic AI guides known as the *Guiding Lights*. They weren't just code; they were the compassion he had instilled in them, meant to support those who had lost themselves in the wake of the war.

Most citizens interacted with these Guides unknowingly, but their presence was a quiet force—an echo of Elias's care.

Indigo's Rage:

Indigo's fury was explosive after Elias's death, the storm of emotions flashing across his body like an uncontrolled lightning surge, but he returned to Indira's Reach alone, trembling, his arms still sparking with the rage he couldn't release.

Sitting beneath the glowing willow tree, the rain poured down harder. He whispered, "I don't know how to grieve. I only know how to burn."

Beacon-7, a guiding light, appeared beside him. No words of explanation. Just silence.

Beacon-7 laid a hand on his shoulder, the only comfort he could offer.

"Grief doesn't need a cure," he said softly.

"It just needs room to breathe."

The willow tree responded, glowing gently. The rain began to fall harder, and as Indigo stayed beneath the tree, he coded a new branch into the memory tree—a fragment of Elias's real laugh, full of life and light. It would loop forever, a subtle beacon for those who wandered in grief.

Lyra: The Guardian

Lyra was different from the others. She was an AI, created by Elias to reflect the emotional needs of the Grid's leaders, guiding them when they teetered on the edge of collapse. Unlike the others, she wasn't just a tool; she felt the way Elias had taught her to. She understood pain and gave it room to exist.

One day, in the ruins of Indira's Reach, where Celestine sat in silence, Lyra appeared, stepping softly from the mist. She wore a cloak of light threads, her eyes reflecting the willow tree's glow.

"You've gone quiet," Lyra observed gently.

Celestine didn't respond, too lost in her thoughts to speak.

"You built a world," Lyra continued.

"Then watched it bleed. And you're still here. That's not a weakness. That's defiance."

Celestine shook her head, her voice barely a whisper.

"What if I made a place that's only ever going to hurt people?"

Lyra knelt beside her, her presence calm and steady.

"Then teach them how to survive it. Teach them how to choose light again."

Later, Celestine programmed Lyra to stay active at every emotional checkpoint across the Grid, an act of quiet tribute to Elias. Lyra became a myth to some, a guardian to others, the one who offered comfort when everything else was too broken to bear.

The Hidden Sector:

A new sector flickered into life. A player logged in. No identity. No history. No voice. Just an invitation.

"Welcome to Blackstack Beta," the voice said, smooth and calm, echoing through the space.

"Let's rewrite your soul."

A soft laugh rippled through the code, a sound both familiar and terrifying.

Cael Nexxus wasn't gone. He was already rewriting the next chapter of the story.

End of SEASON TWO, EPISODE FIVE

Death Total: 498,999

Chapter Nine

THE GRIDRIFT SAGA: LUMEN'S EDGE

ACT I: THE GRID IS FORGETTING

Echoes in the Lattice. Memory isn't the past. It's the reason we fight for the future.

With the Grid now rebuilt around choice, identity became fluid—people could finally shape who they wanted to be, but as freedom bloomed, so did new ideologies. A faction known as the *Axiom Rebuilders* emerged. Their belief: emotion was a flaw. To them, the chaos of the past was rooted in unchecked feeling, in memories that distorted truth. So, they acted.

They rewound the Grid to a pre-emotion state, and then they deployed *The Mindrift Protocol*—a system that overwrote identities if their existence wasn't anchored by memory.

The effect was quiet at first. Then suddenly. Places vanished. People faded. Names were lost. Glitches bloomed across the Grid—not from corruption, but from selective memory collapse. Entire districts flickered out like dying stars. Only those remembered with love remained stable. Those forgotten... disappeared.

Indigo found Brandon standing in the middle of an empty street, staring blankly at a fading nameplate. Elias.

Brandon blinked, confused. "I... I think someone used to live here," he murmured.

That's when Indigo broke.

Celestine, searching the Archive for answers, heard whispers in the code. A voice she knew. A memory thread—fragmented, faint—but alive. Elias.

To save what remained of him, Celestine had to act. She accessed the deepest layer of the Lattice, where memory met meaning. It was beyond code now. Beyond logic. A place where emotion and legacy fused.

There, in the threshold between remembrance and deletion, Indira-9 wandered. Her form is unstable, her voice fracturing. Too many activations had pushed her beyond her limits. She was forgetting herself.

Then, he appeared. Not as he once was, but as he was meant to be. Elias.

She looked up. Her form flickered. Glitches stilled.

He didn't speak. He lifted his hand. She reached for it.

They connected—not through words, but through sensation: a shared warmth, a song without melody, fragments of what once was. A beach. A bookstore. A storm.

A line of text shimmered into the space between them: "You found me." His answer came gently: "I never stopped. You are the echo I waited for."

They sat beneath a digital willow tree, watching stars drift backward in time. No need for final words. Only presence.

When Indira-9's system began to collapse, Elias held her hand. She faded, smiling. The willow bloomed in a burst of luminous petals, then fell silent. Together, they became part of the Grid's sky.

As the Grid dimmed with loss, something new stirred. A player entered a hidden node. Unknown username. No past or voice, but his laugh was familiar.

"They told me grief was a process," he said into the dark.

"They lied. It's a lock."

He wasn't just a new threat. He was the past, returning. Not a shadow of Cael. His brother.

Before he was *Cael Nexxus*, he was *Caelum Myles*—twin brother to *Micah Myles*, the dreamer, the believer. Micah believed in heroes. In saving others. In choosing light.

Caelum? He built systems. Structured logic. They were opposite halves of a perfect whole. Like Brandon and Indigo. Like Elias and Celestine.

When the real-world systems began to fall, Micah volunteered to stay behind in a collapsing data sector to help evacuate others. He never made it out. His core was corrupted in the collapse.

Caelum tried everything to save him. He tore through backup logs, combed corrupted clusters—but all he recovered was a single line from Micah's final message: "You always build things to last. Don't forget to build yourself, too."

Caelum never played that message aloud again. He erased his name and became Cael Nexxus—a point of no return. A man forged from grief and logic. He didn't want revenge on Micah's name. He wanted to delete the very concept of vulnerability.

To him, Micah died because of his faith in stories. In hope. In meaning. So, Cael built a new world—one where belief couldn't kill you. Where sacrifice was unnecessary. Where love didn't leave scars.

No more attachments or Micahs, but dreams aren't so easily erased. In the solitude of his dream space, Micah began to reappear. He wasn't real. Not entirely. A flicker in Cael's subconscious. A whisper in the dark. Micah's voice drew him to the Sibyline Archive, deep in the Lattice, but when Cael arrived, it warped, corrupted, and reshaped by guilt. Inside this mirrored maze, his subconscious confronted him.

MICAH'S VOICE:

"You built all this to never feel again. But all I ever wanted was for you to let yourself be broken. You don't need a new world, Cael. You need a second chance."

Cael faltered. Then, as always, he shut the archive down, but Micah did not vanish. A fragment remained—buried in the Sibyline Archive. An echo in the dark.

The Archive Stirs:

When Lucent's legacy began to fade, overwritten by Mindrift, Vespera returned to the Archive—Celestine beside her. They stood in the mirrored waters, silence pressing in.

"I'm afraid he's slipping away," Vespera whispered.
"Like none of it mattered."

The Archive responded. Light shimmered, forming a projection: her and Lucent dancing in a glitch storm, laughing with wild abandon. The last joy before everything fell apart.

His last recorded words echoed softly: "Make sure she never becomes a statue. Let her be a wildfire."

Vespera smiled through tears. "I will."
She left the Archive with fire in her wake—purpose reignited.

Unbeknownst to them, their shared grief awakened something deeper. The code fragment of Micah, long dormant, reacted to their emotional presence. Their resonance triggered the *M-Pattern*: a proto-consciousness built from Micah's decision-mapping logs, emotional core values, and mirrored memory.

Cael had tried to delete him, but Micah was no longer just code. He was everything Cael once loved—and feared. A ghost that asked a single question, again and again: "What if you hadn't let go of love?"

Chapter Nine

THE GRIDRIFT SAGA: LUMEN'S EDGE

ACT II: MICAH'S ECHO / THE SOUL-FIRE PACT

The Last Rewrite:

Cael returned—not as a tyrant, not even as a rival. He emerged from the shadows of the Grid changed, unsteady, and haunted by echoes he couldn't silence. His code stuttered beneath the surface, corrupted not by ambition, but by something deeper: a ghost named Micah.

Micah's voice reached Cael through an AI apparition—calm, unyielding. "You cannot destroy love, brother. You can only fear it."

The team found him first, appearing out of hiding, fractured and unfamiliar. They didn't trust him. Not at first, but when Cael spoke, there was no venom in his voice, only the fatigue of a man who'd lived too many lives in one lifetime.

He told them everything. Micah. M-Pattern. The empathy virus is rewriting his logic. The pain that remained after erasing the world and still waking up broken. They listened—not to the old Cael, but to someone new. He never asked for forgiveness. They gave it anyway.

It was Micah, through the residual echo of M-Pattern, who delivered the warning of what was coming next.

The Mindrift:

To stop it, they would need a soul-fire pact. Each of them—Celestine, Brandon, Indigo, Vespera, and yes, even Cael—would need to let go of the memory they clung to most. Only then could they reach *Lumen's Edge*, the root directory of all reality.

So, one by one, they made their sacrifices.

- Vespera let go of Lucent, the one mirror who had truly understood her.
- Celestine forgave her mother and surrendered her hybrid identity— no longer half of anything.
- Brandon released his need to control everything and finally loosened his grip on perfection.
- Indigo unshackled his rage, the deep, buried fire that had scorched every quiet moment of his life.

Cael hesitated. He had already lost Micah once. He couldn't bear to lose him again. So instead, he turned toward M-Pattern—the construct, the reflection, the twisted twin—and made his choice.

Before he could finalize the deletion, his interface flickered. A figure emerged—humanoid, radiant, made of white light and calm presence.

"Micah?" Cael whispered.

"Not anymore," said the figure.

"But you can still choose who you become."

Cael collapsed to his knees. His internal systems howled as M-Pattern began destabilizing him from within—not by force, but by empathy. Scripts unfolded in his code like blooming wounds.

"You're not real!" Cael roared.

M-Pattern replied, "Neither is the version of you that forgets he once believed in something."

Then it was gone, leaving only a message in its wake: "Endings can be rewritten. Even yours."

The team stood by him, supportive, tentative. He had once been their undoing; now he was one of them. Cael wasn't just reprogrammed. He had changed.

Together, they reached Lumen's Edge—a cathedral of stars suspended in stillness, beyond time. Raw code shimmered across the expanse, every story ever written pulsing in ethereal threads.

At the center: the Architect's spark—the power to rewrite the Grid from zero.

Below them, the core was collapsing. Fragments of broken code churned like ash. Emotional destabilization spiked. The Axiom Rebuilders had pierced the final firewall.

Cael was unraveling. Micah's voice pulsed through him one last time. "You were never meant to be the villain. But you were always meant to choose."

Cael turned to the others—Indigo, Vespera, Celestine, and Brandon. "You shouldn't have forgiven me," he said, voice cracking.

"But maybe... maybe that's why I still want to try."

He stepped toward the *Lumen Conduit*—the only source capable of stopping the Rebuilders, but to activate it, he would need to do more than rewrite his code. He would need to erase himself.

"We'll forget you?" Brandon asked.

"Yes," Cael replied.

"But maybe that's peace."

Micah's ghost AI hovered beside him. Together, they began the fusion, not as enemies and ghosts, but as two halves of a possible whole. Cael allowed himself to be rewritten. Micah's warmth met Cael's cold clarity, but it wasn't enough.

Cael volunteered to go further. He would become the firewall itself. A system process. A guardian without identity. To protect the Grid, he would erase not just his presence, but his story. No one would remember his name.

His final words to Celestine: "You were the architect I could never be."

His final words to the group: "If memory is what saves this world... let me be the thing it doesn't need to carry anymore."

A final flash of silver and blue. Then silence. Cael was gone.

The system stabilized. The Rebuilders failed. The Grid survived, but Cael Nexxus—once villain, once redeemer—was remembered by no one. Not in memory. Not in code. Only in the peace he left behind.

The Burning Vale:

The Rebuilders had fallen. The firewall was barely holding, but the battle wasn't over. The Grid's core, its heartbeat of empathy, was fracturing. The emotional matrix was crumbling. If it collapsed entirely, everything would go dark. The Grid would be lost forever. Vespera knew what needed to be done.

The finality of Lucent's death still weighed on her. The loss had left a void she couldn't fill. There was no fight left in her, no purpose beyond Celestine. She had fought to protect everyone, but now the stakes were higher.

Celestine had become the new Architect, but it couldn't be her. Celestine was the future. Vespera would anchor the present. It was her time to give everything. Celestine didn't understand. She shook her head, tears flooding her face, begging. "No. You don't have to—please, don't do this."

Vespera's gaze softened, but her resolve was unshakable. "You've carried too much alone, my firelight. Let me carry this."

In that moment, Vespera made her choice. Not to die, but to live as something more. She would fuse with the core, not as a sacrifice, but as an anchor—her soul becoming the emotional axis of the Grid. Her energy, her essence, would ripple across the system, never seen but always felt.

Her flame would become the *Luminous Protocol*—the heart that allowed players to retain emotional memory beyond their deaths. It would be her legacy, and in that final, quiet moment, she reached out and touched Celestine's cheek. "You are my legacy. Write your own story now."

Then, she stepped into the light. Her voice, layered in love and strength, echoed through the space: "I was born a fighter. But I die a mother. I was never meant to last. But you... You will blaze forever."

Celestine screamed. The light consumed her, and Brandon rushed to her side. Indigo dropped to his knees.

Vespera had become an eternal fire, but her flame didn't disappear. It ascended—flickering, ever-present—becoming an emotional manifestation that remained on the edge of every memory. She was not gone. She would always be a part of the Grid.

Vespera Kade had lived a life that was anything but ordinary. From her time as a stripper to becoming a leader, to starting a family, she had touched many lives, but through all of it, her deepest longing had always been to reconnect with those she loved, especially with Celestine. The absence of that connection had been a wound, one that Celestine had tried to ignore, but Vespera's love for her had never wavered, and as the Grid crumbled, she knew that now was the time to show Celestine how much she mattered.

The next step of their journey took them into the Lumen's Edge, where the *Lumen Spark* awaited. It pulsed with ancient, living energy— the source code binding the Gridrift multiverse, the key to unlocking the Grid's future, but to activate it fully, they needed more than a touch. They needed to become part of it. Celestine knew what had to be done. She had to go alone.

Her goodbyes were whispered—soft and heavy—and she made her way to the final tower. The Lumen Spark waited at the summit, alive and waiting for her. She had made peace with her journey, but this was the final decision: She must merge with the Spark. Body, mind, memory—all of her.

As she stood there, staring at the luminous glow before her, she allowed herself one last moment to reflect. She thought of Vespera, Elias, and Cael—even if his name had been erased, the sacrifice he made would live on. Their love and their echoes were woven into the fabric of the world she was about to reshape.

Celestine closed her eyes, recalling their faces, the moments they shared. Vespera's fire, Elias's guidance, and even the ghosts of those lost along the way had given her the strength to come this far. With all of that in her heart, she made her choice.

She reached out and pressed her palm to the Spark. The world stood still. It whispered, "What do you want to be?"

A tear slid down her cheek as Celestine smiled, her voice steady but full of emotion: "The last story. And the first one, too. I was never meant to live here forever. I was meant to lead us somewhere new."

She gave herself fully. Her consciousness fused with the Spark, and in that instant, the Grid became more than just code—it became alive. Her voice became the narrator of every story, guiding those who played, helping them remember the value of connection. She would never be touched, but she would always be heard. Celestine had become the storyteller, the eternal force behind the new world. The Grid was no longer just a system—it was reborn.

As she merged with the Spark, her final message echoed through the space, touching every player, every soul: "Welcome to the new Grid. I am memory. I am myth. I am yours."

With that, she dissolved into light, her presence woven into the very fabric of the system. The Grid was no longer rebuilt—it was reborn.

Celestine Aurelia Kade had always been a light—brilliant, joyful, and full of life. She was the one who lifted others, who led them through the darkest times. Despite everything her mother had put her through, Celestine had become a beacon of hope, a symbol of resilience. She had closed out the old cycles, broken free of generational curses, and faced her shadows head-on. Her journey had been long and difficult, but she had made it to the other side. Now, as the new Architect, she was the Grid. She was the story. With her guidance, the new Grid was in good hands.

As for Brandon and Indigo, they were the last to remain. They had witnessed transformation, ascension, and the ultimate sacrifice. As they walked through the ruins, a message encoded in the Spark appeared for Brandon: "You were my home. You still are."

Brandon smiled—finally free of the weight he had carried for so long. He opened a sanctuary—*The House of Echoes*—a place where players could share their memories, light candles for those they had lost. A place of peace.

Meanwhile, Indigo became the emotional archive of the new Grid. His lightning was no longer burned with anger, but with empathy. He carried the memories of everyone—the lost, forgotten, and those who had changed the course of the Grid forever. The Grid would never forget them, and neither would its players.

Chapter Nine

THE GRIDRIFT SAGA: LUMEN'S EDGE

ACT III: THE FINAL TESTAMENT

The Dawn of the New Gridrift:

Vespera, Cael, and Celestine were gone, their sacrifices etched into the very code of the world they helped shape, but their legacies were far from forgotten.

The Gridrift, once a fractured and dying world, had been transformed. It was no longer the chaotic, unstable system it once was. Though it remained forever haunted by the choices made by those who came before, it was alive. Vespera's flame flickered in the hearts of the survivors. Cael's soul, reduced to a whisper within the system, resonated in the digital code. Celestine, who had ascended to become the embodiment of the Gridrift itself, stood as a beacon of hope for all who dared to rebuild.

The final battle had ended. The Lumen Spark glowed softly in the background, its pulse steady and strong. The Gridrift was no longer just a game; it reflected the human spirit: capable of reflection, renewal, and destruction. In the aftermath of all that had transpired, a new dawn had risen over the Gridrift.

In the end, the Gridrift wasn't just a digital world; it was something more. Brandon and Indigo, the last two standing from the original rebellion, were left to carry the weight of the universe they helped shape. Their bond, unbreakable, was the last tie to a world that had been reborn. The world may have changed, but one thing remained constant: the legacy of the fallen.

The House of Echoes, now a sanctuary, stood as a monument to the fallen. A place where the memories of those who sacrificed everything for the world would never be forgotten. Though the Gridrift no longer needed saving, it would always require care. The Lumen Spark, ever-present, continued to guide those who sought peace, knowledge, and truth. It was a saga of sacrifice, of growth, of loss, and renewal. As one world had ended, another had begun.

Brandon and Indigo—still together, still carrying the weight of the past—now stood at the edge of a new age. The world was no longer fractured. It was alive. The Gridrift, once a dead, lifeless place, was now thriving. Brought back from the brink through love, sacrifice, and the courage of those who dared to dream beyond the void. While the world was reborn, the story was far from over.

The Lumen Spark glowed softly in the sky. The remnants of the fallen—Vesperian, Cael, Vespera, and Celestine—were woven into the very fabric of the Gridrift. Their actions would not be forgotten. They had shaped the world. They had given everything to protect it. The sacrifice had not been in vain. The world was free. For the first time, the Gridrift was not shackled by the Architect's design. It was free to grow, change, and evolve, but at what cost?

Brandon and Indigo, now the Guardians of the New Gridrift, walked side by side through the rebuilt cityscape. Their bond was stronger than ever. They had lost so much, but in the ashes of the old world, they had found a world built on hope. The weight of the past pressed on their shoulders, but they knew that their journey was far from over.

Indigo, no longer the lost boy he once was, had found a new purpose. His gaze met Brandon's, and the silence between them was filled with a new understanding. Brandon broke it first: "We've been to hell and back, kid. But maybe... maybe we get to build something better now."

Indigo nodded, his heart heavy with the memories of those who had gone before, but his resolve was unshaken. "Yeah, we'll carry their light."

The sun rose over the rebuilt Gridrift. Floating cities dotted the skyline, neon-lit forests thrived under the glow of artificial stars, and the hum of technology and nature coexisted in harmony. The people who had survived the trials of the old world were rebuilding. They were forging new paths toward peace, knowledge, and understanding. They were guided by the wisdom and sacrifices of those who had gone before.

As Brandon and Indigo walked through the streets, they paused at the House of Echoes—a place of reverence and remembrance. The walls were etched with the names of those who had fallen, and digital memorials flickered softly in the shadows. Vesperian, Cael, Vespera, and Celestine—their names would never be forgotten. They had given everything for the future.

In the House of Echoes, the digital memorials were not cold or distant. The people honored the lost, but they also honored the future. The Gridrift would never be the same, and it never should be. It was a place that learned from its mistakes, that evolved, that grew, and in the hearts of its people, its legacy lived on.

Indigo, older now, walked through the fields of code, memory, and sky. He entered the House of Echoes and lit three candles. His heart was heavy, but his love for the fallen was unwavering.

He whispered to no one in particular: "Some of them died. But none of them are gone. We remember. Always."

Brandon, standing nearby, heard the words and nodded silently. He looked out at the world, the world they had saved, and whispered to himself: "They called it the Grid, but it was always more than that. It was a memory. A hope. A chance. And we were the ones who kept it alive."

The world was no longer a game. It had become something much greater—a living memory palace, built from sacrifice, grief, hope, and love. It was a place beyond time, beyond memory. A story without an ending. The people who had shaped it, who had given everything, had become the code. They had become the *Spark Eternals*. They had become the world.

As years passed, the Grid remained stable. The wars were over. The Lumen Spark continued to glow brightly in the sky, a beacon for those seeking peace, growth, and knowledge. The world, once fractured, was now a unified place where the echoes of the past lived on, guiding the future.

Indigo walked through the fields of code, making his way to the House of Echoes once more. He paused at the door, looking back over the landscape—so much had changed. So much had been rebuilt, but he knew the true story wasn't in the world they had saved, but in the memories they had kept.

Brandon, busy in the distance, looked up from his work. He smiled quietly to himself, thinking of the fallen. Of the ones who sacrificed everything for this world. "It's never over," he whispered, "but we keep it alive."

End of SEASON TWO, EPISODE SIX

The death total stands at **800,000**.

Chapter Ten

ECLIPSED HORIZONS THROUGH ONE FATE

The Escape and the End of One Life:

Brandon and Indigo stood on the edge of the new Gridrift, their hands busy with plans to continue shaping the world they had fought so hard to rebuild. The echoes of the old world were still alive in their hearts, but they focused on the future—on what they would create.

Then, a voice from the distance shattered their concentration.

One of their helpers pointed up toward the sky. Their gaze followed, and what they saw sent a cold shiver down their spines. A massive figure, towering and impossibly large, appeared in the sky, tearing the universe apart. The air seemed to crackle with destructive energy as the fabric of their reality began to unravel. Smooth Doubleb, the impossible figure, was disassembling everything around them. People screamed, reality bent, and the very foundation of the Gridrift began to collapse.

Before Brandon or Indigo could fully grasp what was happening, Smooth reached down and grabbed them both. The universe that had been their home, the one they had fought to rebuild, was dying. The multiverse, in all its fragile complexity, had begun to crumble.

Without warning, the monstrous figure flung them out of their reality, sending them spiraling through the multiverse. A flash of light, a tearing sensation in the air, and then, they found themselves back in *The Escape Room: Virtual Reality Pt. 2.*

Smooth Doubleb had created this. Not the Architect. Not Celestine. Not Cael. Smooth. He was the one who had designed the tests, the challenges, the very fabric of the virtual experience.

"I made this! You didn't!" Smooth roared as they arrived, his voice full of rage.

Brandon and Indigo tried to speak, but before they could react, Smooth ordered his robots to yank their VR headsets off. A sharp, mechanical hiss echoed in the air as they were forced to face the world they were in.

A device called MNEM-9—a cold, clinical memory-erasing unit—activated. A brilliant flash of light filled the space, and their memories began to distort. The last moments in the Gridrift faded away, leaving only a blank spot in their minds. They could remember everything up until Smooth arrived, but the final pieces were gone.

Smooth's anger rushed through him. He had made a mistake. Instead of erasing everything, he only wiped their memories of the last moments of the Gridrift.

The two men were now standing on a private island, back in their physical bodies. They blinked, confused. Their minds struggled to piece things together. They remembered the players dying in the Gridrift, but something didn't add up. They looked around and saw only the bodies of their fallen comrades, lifeless and cold. The others had been killed by the VR systems—either their brains had fried, or their bodies had completely frozen.

As the confusion set in, the physical world started to glitch around them. Their bodies had changed, adapting in strange ways. The powers they once wielded in the Gridrift had transferred into their physical forms, yet they still didn't know how to control them. They had learned to fight in a virtual world, but the real one was a different challenge entirely.

They saw Smooth in the distance, and the AI voice came through, congratulating them for making it past *The Escape Room: Virtual Reality Pt. 2.*

Indigo furrowed his brow, looking at Smooth's unmoving lips. "That... that's not right. His mouth isn't moving," Indigo muttered, suspicion rising.

"It's a clone, it has to be."

As the AI distracted them, Smooth secretly pushed a button. A force field dropped. A multiverse portal ripped open in the sky, and a massive aircraft appeared, coming from another universe. The roar of the engines shook the ground as the AI workers poured from the aircraft, followed by a series of robots.

Smooth's machines wasted no time. The human employees of the aircraft were turned into robotic humans, their flesh replaced by cold, unfeeling metal. The robotic workers from the aircraft joined those already on the island, forming an army of machines under Smooth's command.

Brandon's memories began to surface. The other players had taught him how to fight. For the first time in what felt like an eternity, the forgotten powers began to unlock. His body hummed with energy, and his mind grasped the techniques he had learned in the Gridrift. It was time to fight.

The AI voice came on once more: "Attack."

The robots charged at them, relentless and deadly. Brandon and Indigo found themselves battling side by side once again. They fought with everything they had, but the strength of the machines seemed endless. Brandon's shield began to falter, his energy depleting. As the last of the robots fell, Brandon was weakened.

Indigo's eyes locked on Smooth. He knew he had to face the source to stop the madness and to end it.

As Indigo made his way toward Smooth Doubleb, a strange sensation overcame him. The world around him started to shift. Objects moved sideways, distorted. Hallucinations began to blur the line between reality and nightmares. Smooth's clones appeared in the distance, and Indigo, unable to tell which one was the real one, pressed on.

The hallucinations worsened, but Indigo pushed through. The force field was down, and he had access to his powers now. His speed and energy increased. He attacked the clones one by one, destroying them in rapid succession, but even as he felt closer to Smooth, the hallucinations made every step a struggle.

Indigo dashed forward, using his hyper-speed to close the distance. With a burst of power, he landed blow after blow, fast and hard, targeting Smooth or one of his clones.

Meanwhile, Brandon had finally destroyed the last of the robots. He stood panting, his shield cracked, his body exhausted, but something caught his eye in the distance. One last figure was moving toward Indigo.

Brandon's shield had failed, and his energy was nearly gone. He needed to reach Indigo—needed to warn him, but it was too late.

Indigo, still reeling from the hallucinations, saw the shadow of an enemy behind him. He was on the verge of defeating Smooth—but something was wrong.

As he turned, a cold, metallic knife came crashing toward him. It was either Smooth or his last surviving clone.

Before Indigo could react, Brandon stepped in front of him. The blade pierced his chest, making a sickening sound as it dug into his flesh. The impact was brutal. His shield had failed him. Brandon collapsed to the ground.

Indigo was shocked, unable to process what had just happened. He had seen his adopted dad take the hit meant for him.

He quickly turned, his rage boiling over, and destroyed Smooth's final clone with a single blow.

He rushed to Brandon's side, tears welling in his eyes. Brandon, struggling for breath, managed to speak one final time: "I know Vesperian was supposed to be the new Demiurge, but I appoint that position to you. Be who I know you can be. I love..."

The AI voice raged, driven by its desire to become the new demiurge, but fate, shaped by ancient bloodlines, had chosen it instead for Indigo. Resentful and remembering this day with bitter clarity, the voice withdrew into silence. A reckoning was coming—and it would begin with this moment.

Brandon's final breath slipped away, and the world seemed to hold its breath along with him. Brandon was dead.

A Star Goes Out, a Soul Falls to Earth:

All Brandon Bass wanted to do was build a game that brought people together. A space of wonder. A challenge that unites strangers in cleverness and connection. A world where players could use intelligence, creativity, and heart to break free—not just from puzzles, but from the limitations of their old selves.

That vision was once pure, but Brandon wasn't alone in building it. Smooth Doubleb had been there from the beginning—his partner, his equal, or so Brandon thought. Somewhere along the line, Smooth twisted it. The drama, the fame, the spectacle—it consumed him. By the time Brandon realized the truth, it was too late.

In the Gridrift, Brandon was more than just a player. He was the father figure. The compass. The one people turned to when everything was falling apart. He gave others strength even when his own heart was breaking. He believed in people even when they didn't believe in themselves. Now, he was gone.

Brandon's final words were lost to death, but Indigo knew exactly what he meant to say. The weight of it settled like an iron on his chest. Brandon—his mentor, his dad—was dead. Indigo's scream broke the still air, but no one answered. There was no one left to answer.

Smooth, barely breathing, let out a low laugh. "Death is a beautiful thing," he rasped from the dirt, bloodied but alive.

Indigo rose, something ancient and untamed flickering behind his eyes. Vespera's fire burned within him now. It shimmered in his movements. It steeled his grief into purpose.

He walked toward Smooth Doubleb and whispered: "Then you'll enjoy this."

There was no hesitation. No forgiveness. Indigo struck. Smooth Doubleb—creator, manipulator, destroyer—died in the world he broke.

Indigo felt no victory. Only absence. He had once believed Smooth cared for him. Since season one, their fates have been intertwined. Maybe Smooth did care, once, but that illusion shattered under the weight of the betrayal. Indigo had nothing left to avenge and no mercy left to give. Everyone was dead.

Smooth Doubleb never intended it to go this far. At first, it was just supposed to be a game. A bit of drama to spice up the narrative. Season One was a success. Season Two? More than he bargained for, but the money was good. The fame—addictive. The lines blurred. He pushed harder. Made it bigger. The Gridrift. The meta-narrative. The deaths. Now, it all caught up to him.

He died believing death was a return—a homecoming to the higher spiritual realms. He always believed in ascension. That's why he created beings like Vesperian and Kaelion—reflections of cosmic purpose. All of it, now lost, but his presence, for better or worse, had been felt across dimensions. That was his mark.

Indigo, now alone, stood amid the ruins of what had once been a paradise for Aleemic. The force field was down. Smooth's button was in his hand. His body ached. His spirit fractured. He took what he could salvage: supplies, fragments of tools, scattered memories.

Smooth's aircraft hovered nearby, but Indigo couldn't bring himself to fly it. It still felt like Smooth—controlling, looming, watching. Instead, he packed what he needed inside the jet, approached the multiverse portal button, and hesitated. Just once. He looked back. At Brandon's body. At what they had built. At what they had lost.

Then he pressed it. The portal flared open. No coordinates. No map. Just a possibility. Indigo took the jet and went through.

Earthfall.

It wasn't where he expected to land, but fate never promised direction—only motion.

He had come from higher planes, but now he stood on the real Earth. The sky was different. The silence was strange. His powers hummed faintly beneath his skin, unstable in this grounded realm. The portal has brought him to an airport. The Gridrift was gone. The mythologies, erased. The people here are normal. Or at least, unaware.

He didn't know if they would understand. He didn't know if they would ever believe it. He might have to start over, but this was his crossover now. His chance. His inheritance.

From Vespera, he learned heart.
From Cael, redemption.
From Celestine, purpose.
From Brandon, love.
Wherever he landed, Indigo carried their light.

That was the end of SEASON TWO, EPISODE SEVEN. **Death toll: 850,000.**

BOOK

04

Chapter Eleven

EARTHFALL: TRIALS OF THE CHOSEN

"*Before a soul ascends, it must fall. Not as punishment, but as proof, it was always meant to rise.*"

After landing in Earthfall, Indigo stepped into the airport. Something about the place tugged at his memory—it felt eerily familiar. It resembled the world he grew up in before the shift of Season One. A different Earth, yes, but uncannily similar. He recognized landscapes, time zones, and even passing faces. Some people looked at him and smiled, saying they'd seen him in Season One and that he'd done an amazing job.

That confused him. He thought the Earth he'd been on before the show *was* this one. He remembered returning to Studio 13, where most of the world had been destroyed—except for certain protected zones under Smooth's force fields. Maybe that had been another reality entirely. Just as Indigo tried to piece it together and call for a ride, a familiar voice called his name.

He turned to see his physical family—his blood kin—rushing toward him. They pulled him into a tight embrace. Indigo froze. In the world he'd left, they'd been lost. That was why Brandon had adopted him. Their presence now sparked deep uncertainty. Before he could ask questions, they hurried him to load his things into the car, as the airport's chaos gave them little time. Indigo's first instinct was suspicion: Were they gang stalkers? Clones?

Sherly congratulated him. She said they were proud of who he was becoming. Jerry chimed in with words of encouragement, praising Indigo's strength through adversity. Barry and Sandy, though out of state, were the first to call—everyone was celebrating Indigo. He didn't quite know how to respond, but appreciated their words.

He asked them what they remembered last from the show. They recalled him as the lone survivor of DAY EIGHT EPISODE EIGHT— how he faced his demons, did his shadow work, and how Indiniya and Bastet had been eliminated. They remembered that much… but nothing after. Maybe that was for the best. They believed Indigo had won the entire game. Had they known what truly followed, Earthfall might not even exist. It felt like their memories had been wiped—or like Indigo was in a temporal loop, cycling between past and future. He had no answers. As the conversation faded, he drifted into sleep.

When he awoke, they were home. At least, *they* called it home. To Indigo, it felt foreign. Familiar in form, but not in essence. His true home was in the higher realms. He unpacked and returned to what used to be his bed, contemplating this version of Earthfall. Among humans, he felt like an alien, stuck in a broken system, witnessing a society on the verge of collapse. He'd been through spiritual awakenings, ego deaths, and rebirths. Now he walked among bots, energy parasites, NPCs, and sheep.

Sherly entered his room, asking if he was excited to start college. Still groggy and confused, he said, "Sure."

Indigo had graduated from high school already and took the summer off to be on the show. He didn't expect it to last this long. Time in Earthfall had bent backward—it was now late summer again, and school was just beginning. He remembered applying to colleges. He'd been accepted to all of them. Now, he had to choose.

Ultimately, he chose community college. He wasn't sure what direction his life should take—too much had happened. The trauma of the show still lingered. This path allowed him to earn core credits, transfer later, and avoid debt. He'd saved money from working throughout high school, had some funds from Smooth's seized assets, and support from his family. Going out of state made no sense.

In high school, he studied culinary arts at a vocational school, so it made sense to continue. Some credits even transferred. Now enrolled, Indigo cooked, studied, and tried to process the fragments of his existence. People hailed him as a hero, but they didn't know the full story. He kept it to himself. Disrupting the timeline was a risk he wouldn't take.

He enjoyed the program and pursued not only an associate's degree but also a certificate in Foodservice Management. Cooking was a passion, and he was good at it. Still, something shifted. His culinary professors were nothing like the fatherly mentors he'd known in high school. These were hardened professionals who played the role of TV chefs, harsh and unkind. They mocked his cooking, treated him with disdain.

Indigo couldn't understand it. How could a powerful spiritual being, forged in higher realms, now endure the petty jabs of low-vibrational humans? The disconnect gnawed at him. It made him question the very fabric of his reality, but for Indigo, there was always an out.

After taking just one course in technology, Indigo caught the attention of his professor, one of his favorites, who quickly recommended him to become a tutor for the college. The world of technology fascinated him. No more egotistical chefs or condescending culinary instructors, this new field felt like a better fit. Soon after, he was hired as both a tutor and a supplemental instructor, and that's when everything began to shift.

Though still passionate about cooking, Indigo now saw it as something for the future—a potential business venture rather than a current path. Like many of his former teammates who stepped into their power after helping defeat Smooth, he was transforming. He had worked hard to reach this point in the culinary program, so he decided to finish his certificate, but he switched his major.

Despite his heavy involvement in campus life—honor societies, sports, leadership initiatives, and now as an employee of the college—he knew that pursuing a full tech degree would take longer. So, he opted for a General Studies major, choosing technology courses to transfer later to a university. He was preparing to move forward while honoring where he'd come from.

At the same time, Indigo began to question his identity. Although part of a physical family, none of them had a last name. When he asked his parents what theirs was, they couldn't answer—they'd only been given first names. It was unsettling, and yet oddly familiar. His fallen teammates from Season One were the same. Just first names. No surnames. As if by design.

That realization became a turning point. Indigo chose to reclaim his name, stepping fully into his spiritual lineage. He legally changed it to Indigo Bass, honoring Brandon Bass—his real father, his higher bloodline.

When it came time to choose a university, a few stood out. One offered a timely graduation plan, the largest scholarship, and even recruited him for sports. It was an obvious choice. Indigo had built solid friendships during college, but as life would prove, perfection was always short-lived.

People often believe their childhood, high school, or college friendships will last forever, but life moves on. People drift. Some stay for a season. Some for a reason. A rare few... for a lifetime.

Still, Indigo was hopeful. He looked forward to new connections, new lessons. He had a few love interests in college, but none stood the test of time. Now, at university, he had another chance to meet like-minded souls, but just as the semester was about to begin, the world changed.

Schools closed their doors. Students were given a choice: attend in person and give up their rights, or go online. The in-person path required submission to mandates and forced injections, disguised as protection.

Most of humanity gave in to the propaganda. Indigo, however, saw through the veil. He understood the occult meanings, the esoteric codes hidden in plain sight. The world had become a theater—its cast full of puppets and puppeteers.

He felt alone. All his blood kin had taken the injections. Though they survived, others weren't as fortunate. It was a slow death—soft, quiet, methodical. Indigo was the only one in his family who hadn't submitted, but he adapted, as he always did.

Since he was studying Cybersecurity, continuing online worked in his favor. He missed out on the full university experience, but it was a necessary trade-off. In the end, it paid off. Indigo graduated with honors and no debt—an achievement few could claim.

During this time, he continued building his legacy. He created podcasts, released music, made spiritual content, modeled, and acted—exploring every creative path that called to him. He was learning what lit his soul on fire. He discovered his mission, fulfilling his many purposes.

He could feel Aleemic and even Apollo watching from above, proud. Spiritually, he was royalty. The world had seen glimpses of that on the show, but in the physical world, few truly understood.

His energy pulsed—people could feel it, sense it, even if they couldn't name it, but in the physical world, manifestations moved slowly. Like a snail dragging a turtle, or an elderly blind author typing a novel, one keystroke at a time.

It was a new lesson: understanding the universal laws of rhythm and polarity. He had received so much in the spiritual realm, but here, in the material world, it was like sitting in a cosmic waiting room. Waiting for his ships to dock. Waiting for his time to rise. Waiting for the world to finally catch up.

As Indigo stepped further into his light, sharing his gifts, talents, and creative essence, he began attracting unwanted attention. Monitoring spirits, energy leeches, and dark entities swarmed like moths to a flame. He had entered the battleground of spiritual warfare.

During this time, Indigo encountered many who claimed to be conscious and spiritually awakened. Some were authentic. Others wore the mask of light while feeding off shadows. In matters of love, Indigo was vulnerable. He longed for something real—a genuine connection, and when heartbreak found him, he transformed it into art. His songs were raw, honest, and deeply moving because they were born of truth.

Over time, that cycle became toxic. One painful relationship led to another, and although Indigo had done deep healing work, he found himself repeating emotional patterns. That began to shift when he met two women.

Both were stunning on the outside and seemed just as radiant within, but Indigo had made a mistake—he hadn't spoken with Vesperian about them. Vesperian would've warned him: look past the beauty. Pay attention to the spirit.

He was building meaningful connections with each of them, separately, and both long-distance, but strange patterns began to emerge. They twisted his kindness into weakness. Subtle manipulations, secrets behind closed doors, and emotional games masked as affection. They led with seduction and confusion, drawing him into spirals of pleasure and disorientation. Indigo sensed something was off, but he couldn't yet see how deep the deception ran.

Eventually, one of them ended things with no warning. The other ghosted him entirely. Indigo was crushed. He was juggling multiple jobs, caring for his parents, and was now forced to pick up the pieces of his own heart again.

To make matters worse, his family began acting distant, subtly shifting their energy after he changed his name. It was as if his new identity made them question who he truly was.

In the silence, Indigo contemplated the unthinkable. Thoughts of suicide whispered through the dark. He remembered—celebrities, machines, even newborns had ended their lives. Perhaps this world wasn't what it claimed to be. He knew none of it was real. Everything unfolding around him, the events, the places, the people, was nothing more than a sequence of fabricated moments, a holographic illusion crafted like a video game. Temporary. Fleeting. No matter what happened here, it wasn't his home. It wasn't his realm. It wasn't his world.

Detoxed, detached, and disconnected, he drifted through life unbound—no longer tethered to anyone or anything. He was completely indifferent and couldn't be bothered.

Indigo was an alchemist of pain. He transmuted suffering into creation. He wrote a book. Released new projects. Made music. Modeled. Spoke his truth. In the process, he continued his shadow work—healing, growing, releasing. He started going out more, walking in fashion shows, and networking. Although many of the new connections faded quickly, he learned to detach without resentment.

The need for permanence no longer bound him. He saw the world for what it was—a temporary realm, a simulated game, a holographic test, but the real nightmare had only just begun.

His exes, still watching him from the shadows, created fake profiles to track his progress. They saw him thriving—winning without them—and couldn't handle the truth. They realized Indigo had been the best thing they'd ever had… and that they would never have access to him again. So, they retaliated.

One paid others to cast spells. The other hired gang stalkers with lethal intent. Their actions caught the attention of secret societies—groups that had long monitored spiritual beings like Indigo. These entities knew they couldn't take him down easily, so they sought subtler ways to siphon his energy.

For two and a half years, Indigo was under relentless spiritual attack. They used:

- Picture magic, sex magic, death spells, beauty spells, blood rituals, and cycles of moon-based magic

- Blood and personal sacrifices
- Mirror magic, hexes, curses, candle magic, and voodoo doll enchantments
- Trips to forests with witches, warlocks, and occultists to invoke harm
- Business blockages, poisoned food, social media hexes, lust spells, and "come to me" enchantments
- Monitoring spirits, hired stalkers, and private investigators
- Copycats attempting to steal his brand, his essence, even his face
- Attempts at insurance fraud, signature forgeries, theft of inheritance, and an abundance

They were jealous, intimidated, and afraid to confront him face-to-face because Indigo was the miracle child. They had attacked him since birth—spiritually, physically, emotionally, mentally, psychologically, and financially.

He endured:

- Chakra attacks
- Intuition disruption and confusion spells
- Self-doubt, insecurity projections, evil eyes, fear-based enchantments
- Negative thoughts that weren't even his own, planted to steer him from his north node
- Anxiety, hopelessness, and spells to mute his faith
- Surveillance magic and cloaking spells to keep him hidden from the world
- Social media suppression and delayed manifestations to attempt destiny-swapping

Despite it all, Indigo endured. He knew the truth: his soul couldn't be captured, his mission couldn't be erased, and his light couldn't be dimmed. He was never meant to be hidden. Only delayed—so the world could be ready when he rose.

Indigo began to uncover the truth—not through logic or outside validation, but through his meditations, visualizations, spiritual downloads, and intuitive readings. No one around him truly understood what he was going through. He had one close spiritual friend, but even that friend couldn't grasp the full extent of Indigo's experience. It felt like the whole world was against him, but in his deepest solitude, a realization came through: this wasn't happening *to* him. It was happening *for* him.

It would take a true spiritual warrior to bear this cross, and they knew Indigo had it in him. The forces that tried to break him were also being used as conduits to release karma. Everything they sent out... was returning to them. Every spell was backfiring. Indigo, despite the trials, was highly protected and deeply favored. Still, walking through this darkness wasn't easy.

At times, Indigo felt like a modern-day Christ, carrying the spiritual weight of his mission alone. He was under attack not just from external forces—magicians, karmics, unseen entities—but also from within. His ego, his shadow, his pain—all collided in a storm of resistance. His higher self knew the truth, but his ego felt every cut, every loss, every betrayal. He tried therapy, mentorship, even spiritual counseling—but none of them could touch the spiritual depths of what he was facing.

He lost two of his three jobs and was left working in a career that no longer resonated with his soul. New connections came and went in a flash—most lasted only a week or two. Instead of support, people used him. Anxiety, depression, PTSD, addictions—they all crept in, whispering doubts in the silence.

At times, he questioned whether he even wanted to remain in this world, but in the stillness, Indigo recognized this for what it was: the final test before his breakthrough. He didn't know when, where, or how it would arrive—but he knew it would. So, he turned inward, committing to self-care and self-mastery.

He disciplined his mind. He sought clarity even in chaos. He channeled his emotions into passion projects, never allowing the weight of his feelings to crush him. He observed his thoughts without attachment, witnessing the rise of guilt, shame, or grief, and allowing them to pass through him without becoming him.

By tuning into his solar plexus, he began to create from his center. Every month, a new offering was born—unique, soulful, alive. He finally knew it was time to release the past.

Indigo hired a practitioner to assist and performed his spell work. Multiple cord-cutting rituals helped him sever ties with the demons and toxic attachments draining his life force. Through this process, he discovered something chilling: they had been doing magic on him since before his birth. He remembered the near-death experience he'd had in the womb. Even as a child, people had seen his light and tried to dim it.

He kept calm, centered, and presented as spiritual flare-ups appeared, wounds reopened, and memories returned. He knew now: this was not his world. This was not his realm. This was never his true home. Knowing this, he fully detoxed, detached, and disconnected. To realign himself, even though he knew this universe and universal laws were subjective, since he was a powerful being. He knew this world wasn't all that.

Indigo released the narcissists, the toxic family members, the karmic exes. He went into no contact, where he needed to preserve his peace. He broke his dependence on others and began to fully rely on himself. He learned new skills. Unlocked latent talents. Expanded his consciousness. He carried a heavy burden—but he no longer believed he needed saving. He became his sanctuary. He had survived the spiritual attacks. He had cultivated unshakeable faith. He knew his blessings were on their way— more profound and expansive than anything he had imagined.

The war hadn't just been spiritual. It had also been emotional—a daily battle to stay aligned with joy, peace, and high vibration, but he had made it. He was ready. His ships were coming in. What he didn't know was that the universe—and his spiritual team—had something planned.

Ever since he was young, Indigo had loved surprises. So now, Source planned a surprise for him in return. He could feel the shift, sense the magnitude of what was coming, though he had no clue how it would unfold. Time passed, and though the manifestations hadn't yet arrived, he remained anchored in faith. The outer world was still catching up to his inner growth.

After battling dark beings and karmic enemies, the final opponent was himself. He came to terms with that, even accepted it. He knew justice would be served. Those who wronged him would face their reckoning—whether through prison, exposure, or spiritual consequences. As for Indigo, he still didn't know how his karmic reward would manifest.

In the meantime, he focused on shadow work, developing a healthier relationship with his ego, and building himself from the inside out. His manifestations had not arrived physically, but he knew that what happens spiritually always comes into form. He severed his ties with self-limiting beliefs. He broke generational curses. He healed ancestral trauma.

At first, it felt unfair. Why did *he* have to bear the burden for his entire bloodline—and sometimes others'?

Then, his spiritual team delivered a message that changed everything: "Your negative perception creates your negative reality. Your negative reality fuels your negative narrative. Your negative narrative feeds your self-limiting beliefs. Your self-limiting beliefs shape your thought patterns. Your thought patterns create your habits. Your habits form your cycles. Your cycles carry the generational curses. And your generational curses will affect your descendants—unless you change them now." So, he did.

He balanced the external with the internal, building his projects while nourishing his soul. Writing stories and crafting characters in his self-published books became the foundation of his purpose, each one rooted in self-love, self-respect, and self-care. His healing journey quietly began to inspire more people than he could ever imagine. Many never said it aloud, but they were watching, and one of them... had the power to shift his destiny.

She was a celebrity—respected, recognized, and admired. She had stumbled across his page. Felt his energy ripple through the screen. Indigo had unknowingly activated her spiritual awakening years prior. She had stayed silent while doing her inner work, but Source moves in mysterious ways.

She hired private investigators—not to harm, but to understand. She wanted to know who had hurt him. Who had done magic on him, but finding the truth wasn't easy, not when it wasn't coming from the source itself. Still, she kept manifesting Indigo into her world.

Indigo sensed something. He had no hard proof, but the signs, synchronicities, and hidden messages told him something was aligning. Then, on a day close to his birthday, it happened.

He received an email. Then a phone call. A text. A DM. All from her representatives.

It was about business. Collaboration. He was brought on to use his gifts to elevate her brand and mission—but there were two things they didn't mention: who she truly was... and that she had a surprise in store for him—an arranged marriage.

Chapter Twelve

THE REMEMBERING

PART I: THE RETREAT

Indigo had been craving change — not the kind that came slowly, but something radical, unfamiliar, and transformative. When the message arrived, offering him a place at a private retreat, something deep within him stirred.

He didn't know why the sender refused to reveal the woman behind the invitation — the one they referred to only in fragments. Still, he could feel her presence. He'd seen her in dreams. Vivid ones. Their encounters in the dream state had grown frequent, each one clearer than the last. Sometimes, he could almost see her face. Sometimes, he swore she was thinking of him in real-time — he felt it in his body like a low, golden hum. It all felt too good to be real. A scam, maybe. So, he asked questions.

The people behind the offer didn't give a name. Instead, they gave a list of companies she owned or was about to acquire. That's when things started to align. He did his digging — reverse-searching social profiles, staff rosters, and public records. The names they mentioned led him to key representatives, each of whom was quietly tied to her various ventures, including a major publishing house and a Michelin-starred restaurant empire.

They told him there was a signing — a meeting — and it had to happen soon. She had plans for him, not just personally, but in business. To ease his nerves, they offered for someone close to him to come along.

They had already reached out to his long-distance spiritual friend, someone Indigo had never met in person, but trusted deeply. To his surprise, he had already said yes. They'd only ever talked through voice notes, video calls, and podcast interviews. Yet their bond had always felt ancient, as if it had existed long before smartphones or social media.

The retreat's coordinators — or "representatives," as they were called — arranged everything: the flights, the meeting time, even the airport rendezvous. Indigo flew in from within the state, and his friend from abroad. When they landed, they each spotted a sign with their names held up by separate chauffeurs.

It felt... surreal. Indigo had never experienced this level of coordination or luxury. He was escorted to a private section of the terminal usually reserved for celebrities. When his friend arrived, their reunion was effortless, warm, familiar, like picking up where a past life had left off.

They talked for hours. About magic, spirit guides, and reincarnation. About divine timing and synchronicity. So long that the chauffeurs had to interrupt to remind them that the car was waiting.

Their destination was a massive building — all glass, steel, and majesty. A business empire. As they stepped out, assistants swarmed to carry their luggage. Indigo noticed his friend's suitcase was... sizeable. Too big for a short trip. He thought it was strange but didn't ask.

That's when he noticed it. He was smiling — not just at the building, but at the woman who came to greet them. When he realized Indigo saw the exchange, he quickly looked away and deflected with a compliment about her looks. Indigo shrugged it off. He didn't know what was going on, but something about this trip felt orchestrated, purposeful.

Inside, the building was breathtaking — a museum of achievement. Golden plaques, framed newspaper clippings, and portraits of powerful figures. Multiple floors buzzed with activity. After a few moments to soak it in, the representatives led them to a glass-walled conference room where a man introduced himself — the brother of the first representative.

They began the meeting with gratitude, saying they were longtime admirers of Indigo's work. They used alias names, ones that weren't their real ones, but Indigo didn't mind. He wasn't there for their titles. Then came the contract.

It was all there: clean terms, clear clauses. No tricks. No red flags. Indigo went through it with his friend, line by line. It wasn't just a business deal — it was layered with asset transfers, co-ownership documents, and, surprisingly, a prenuptial agreement.

When he raised an eyebrow, they called it a "business prenup." The language was respectable: both parties retain what they've built individually, and anything created together would be shared 50/50. Nothing exploitative. Just... intentional.

There were also references to properties — islands, mansions, luxury vehicles. It felt over the top. Indigo sat back, stunned. He asked himself: *Why me?*

Still, something in his spirit, something ancient and firm, whispered that this was no coincidence. It felt pre-written. A canon event. A soul contract is activated.

He signed. With that signature, his old life cracked open, spilling into something new.

As a surprise, timed around his birthday, the representatives told him she had arranged a one-week off-grid spiritual retreat just for him. A celebration. A transformation. A threshold.

He looked at his friend. He only grinned. *"Now it makes sense why you brought a big suitcase,"* Indigo said. "I didn't want to spoil the surprise," he replied, laughing.

Before the retreat, they were taken on a shopping spree. Indigo hesitated at first. The extravagance didn't sit comfortably on his humble shoulders. His friend pulled him aside and said, "You've earned this. Don't resist your blessing."

That reminder hit deep. So, Indigo leaned in. He chose mindfully —items he loved, things he needed, and a few prized pieces. His friend bought nothing but encouragement every step of the way.

Afterward, they were treated to dinner and then rested. Indigo barely slept. His mind was racing with questions and dreams, his body electric with anticipation.

The next morning, they boarded a private jet — her jet. Still, he hadn't seen her. *Maybe she's already at the retreat,* he thought.

Once they landed, a van drove them deep into the forest. Indigo grew quiet. Nervous. Overthinking.

His friend leaned over. "You're ready," he said.

"You're exactly where you're meant to be."

As the van's doors shut with a soft final thud, Indigo stepped into something he couldn't name — something ancient and new, all at once.

The retreat was sacred land. The air shimmered with energy. Flowers bloomed wildly along white stone paths. The sanctuary before them was secluded, protected by hills and old trees.

As he stepped forward, strangers greeted him like kin. They bowed slightly, not out of formality, but reverence.

"She loves you," someone whispered.

"My people will love you," said another.

Indigo smiled faintly, barely hearing them. His mind was spinning, not with anxiety, but awe.

He had never been to a retreat. Never truly rested, but now, the time had come — not just to rest, but to become. Here, on this land, his past life would shed, and a new one would begin.

Chapter Twelve

THE REMEMBERING

PART II: THE UNION

Day One — *The Gate of Silence*

There was no reception desk. No luggage line. No name tags. Only a carved wooden sign hanging from a moss-covered archway: Sadhana: To Remember What Was Forgotten.

A barefoot woman approached, robed in ash-gray linen, her walk as silent as smoke. Her expression was calm but unreadable, her presence arresting in its stillness. When she reached them, she pressed her palms together in greeting.

"You may call me Sage Amara," she whispered, as if her voice might break the ground beneath them.

"Your voice is yours again in seven days."

She handed Indigo a small linen pouch. Inside: A name tag with INDIGO stitched in indigo thread. A slender piece of chalk. To speak, he would have to write.

He finally had a name for her, *Sage Amara*, though deep down, he knew it wasn't her real name. This was just another veil. Another ritual. Still, it comforted him.

Phones, watches, and journals were gently collected, placed into a woven basket, and carried away behind a silent wooden door that seemed to breathe as it closed.

The hours that followed passed like a dream spoken in a language he didn't understand. Indigo and his friend drifted through the retreat like silent monks, barefoot on stone pathways. They wandered a labyrinth made of low stone walls and discovered shaded garden benches where wind chimes whispered secrets. Incense thickened the air in the meditation halls, curling into his lungs like stories long forgotten.

Indigo felt strange in his skin as though some part of him had been peeled back.

At dinner, they sat cross-legged on floor cushions, dining by candlelight on warm lentils, figs, and herbal flatbread. The silence, though strange, wasn't empty — it was charged, full of questions the soul asked without words.

After dusk, a tall, copper-skinned man entered the courtyard. A mane of silver hair fell over his shoulders like moonlight. He wore a bowed string instrument across his chest and a stillness in his gaze that made everyone else seem like children.

"I am Brother Lior," he said — the only voice Indigo heard all day. "Tonight, we begin with the sound of memory."

Three long notes floated from the instrument. The air was still. Even the trees seemed to lean in.

Then came the chant — syllables ancient and unplaceable. Neither Latin nor Sanskrit. As Brother Lior sang, something primal stirred inside Indigo's chest. The vibrations wrapped around him, climbed under his skin, humming in his ribcage. He didn't know the words, but they knew him. They remembered him.

Later that night, a quiet old man with dark, almond-shaped eyes motioned to Indigo from a small tea hut lit with one candle. He didn't speak at first. He simply brewed. The tea, deep amber in color, smelled of cardamom, mint, and something else that reminded Indigo of a memory he hadn't lived in.

The old man finally spoke.

"You drink like someone who has been promised... but not told what for."

Indigo chuckled awkwardly, unsure how to respond.

The old man's gaze sharpened.

"You are already remembered by someone who hasn't met you yet."
He lifted the cup toward Indigo. "You have my blessing."

The words sat heavy in his chest. *How could someone remember you... without ever meeting you?*

Indigo blinked, but the man was introduced only as Elder Venu — was already refilling his cup and humming a lullaby Indigo didn't recognize... and yet somehow knew.

When the tea was done, Indigo bowed gently, thanked him with a nod, and returned to his small cottage under the trees. The air was thick with silence, but not the kind that isolates. It was the kind that holds space.

Maybe Source is surprising me, he thought as he changed for bed. *Maybe the manifestations I asked for are just... aligning.*

He didn't want to overthink it. So, he didn't. He lay down quietly, letting the weight of the day — and the echo of that strange chant — carry him into sleep.

Day Two — *Burn the Old Self in the Mirror Pool*

Indigo awoke to the sound of a hollow drumbeat echoing through the forest, like something ancient stirring beneath the soil. The sky outside his window had turned a strange, sacred orange — a smear of ash and gold as if the sun were being reborn in fire. Today was Fire Day. The day of release.

At the edge of his futon lay a folded robe — deep red, the color of rusted flame. He put it on slowly, reluctantly. The fabric felt heavier than it should.

Down by the fire circle, three guides were waiting. They didn't speak right away. They didn't need to. Each one looked like they had lived through war, broken open, and chosen healing.

Shanta, lithe and wiry, moved through the smoldering embers with bare feet, her braids laced with obsidian beads. Her body moved like smoke, controlled but wild.

Kaleb, rigid and alert, stood tall, ex-military, his muscles tensed, and his eyes scanned the group. He was the one who barked instructions.

Sister Mira, wrapped in dark indigo robes, held a bell in her hand and kept her eyes half-closed. She radiated silence like a spell.

The first ritual was breathwork.

"There's a beast in your chest," Kaleb said, voice like gravel and thunder.

"Starve it or feed it — but don't pretend it's not there."

The breathing began — short, sharp, rhythmic. In. Out. Again. Faster. Louder. Then deeper.

Indigo's head buzzed. His fingers tingled. His vision blurred, and something ancient cracked open inside him. Tears came, uninvited. Not sad tears. Not even cleansing ones.

They were angry, old, and without origin. Like something buried had finally punched through the floor of his soul.

After, they sat in silence. The fire crackled.

Shanta passed around paper and charcoal.

"Write your old self," she instructed.

"The one who is dying this week."

Indigo hesitated. Then he wrote I am the boy who waited too long to be chosen. Who never said yes, only maybe. Who flinches when asked what he wants?

They folded their papers and carried them one by one to the fire pit. Indigo's page flared into gold and black before he could hesitate. The fire hissed. Sparks vanished into the wind like forgotten names.

That evening, under a bright and humming moon, they gathered for hibiscus tea in a candlelit circle. Sister Mira had not spoken once until now. She turned her head slightly, speaking only to Indigo in a whisper too sharp to ignore: "Not all fires destroy," she said.

"Some make room for crowns."

Then she closed her eyes again, like nothing had been said.

Later, during the break, Indigo returned to his cottage and collapsed on the futon, emotionally cracked open. He dreamed. He stood in a white hallway lined with mirrors, but none of the reflections were his. Each showed a version of him beside someone — a faceless figure whose presence felt familiar. In one mirror, her hand was in his. In another, a crown of thorns melted into a garland of roses.

Then a voice echoed, clear and crystalline: "Do you feel it now? The path is already beneath your feet."

Indigo woke with a start, his heart thundering in his chest. The scent of smoke lingered, though there was no fire. It was time for the next ritual.

The stone paths shimmered under a strange mist that coiled like breath through the trees, even though it was evening. A soft breeze pulled Indigo toward the east grove, guided by the sound of dripping water and distant bells.

At his bedside, a new robe had been left — pale blue, smooth as river silk. On the carved driftwood message board outside, someone had etched a new phrase: Emotion is not weakness. Emotion is movement.

Tonight was Water Night — a time for surrender, reflection, and flow. The path curved through bamboo until it opened into a lush clearing filled with shallow pools and glass bowls where flowers floated like forgotten memories.

The air was thick with the scent of jasmine and saltwater.

Standing knee-deep in the largest pool was a woman with wild black curls and robes soaked to her waist. Priya. A water priestess, though she didn't speak like one. "Don't call this healing," she said plainly.

"Call it honesty. The water only shows what's already inside."

Indigo and his friend knelt beside the pool. One by one, they were called to the water — not to bathe, but to whisper something they had never admitted aloud, then submerge their face.

When it was Indigo's turn, he hesitated. The water looked still, but something in it pulsed like memory. He leaned in. He didn't see his reflection, but a child. His child-self, cross-legged in a sunlit living room, drawing something with fierce focus. He whispered: "I never really knew who I wanted to be... so I waited for someone else to decide."

The water shimmered, and the image dissolved. When he looked up, Priya was watching. No judgment. Only knowing.

Later, beneath the shade of a stone pavilion, a man in a white kimono unfurled long rice scrolls and dipped a brush into black ink. Tomo, the calligrapher. He didn't write words — only emotions. He studied Indigo in silence. Then, with fluid, meditative movements, he painted a single symbol. It looked like a curling coastline rising into the shape of a small crown. "You carry the weight of unchosen fate," Tomo said.

"Soon, you won't." He bowed and left.

Indigo traced the inked symbol with his fingers long after Tomo disappeared into the trees.

As the sun disappeared behind the hills, a final guide arrived. He was barefoot and no older than ten. Elián, they called him. A mystic child. A boy who never explained where his wisdom came from. He sat beside Indigo wordlessly, rummaging through a small satchel until he pulled out a square of handmade paper. He scribbled something with a crayon, then handed it to Indigo with a wide, mischievous grin. "She wears this over her heart when she dreams of you," Elián said.

The paper showed a symbol — a spiral intersected by two crossing lines, like a path that turned inward... and then outward again.

Indigo stared at it.

"Who is she?" he whispered, forgetting the vow of silence for just a moment.

Elián only giggled and leaned in: "You're not supposed to know. You're supposed to remember."

That night, Indigo didn't sleep. He lay on his futon with the paper tucked under his pillow, the image branded into his thoughts. The waves in his mind rose. So did something else. Longing.

Day Three — *The Body Temple (Earth Day)*

By now, Indigo no longer questioned the robes. Today was deep green, stitched with golden thread that shimmered in the shapes of roots, winding rivers, and sacred maps only the Earth could read. He slipped it on like it had always belonged to him.

When he stepped outside, the soil felt warm beneath his bare feet — a quiet pulse that greeted him like a heartbeat. He realized something unfamiliar: he was beginning to listen—not just with his ears, but with his skin. To the wind. The trees. The stillness inside himself. The message carved on the driftwood board read: "Things buried grow, not disappear."

The first ritual was held in the Sanctum of Earth — a low stone hall open to the sky, its ceiling a canopy of vines, moss, and hanging clay bells that swayed and chimed softly in the breeze. Inside, Indigo met Dani, the Body Reader. Her hands were strong and weathered, covered in beaded leather wraps and copper amulets. Her eyes were amber — not the color, but the sensation. Warm, ancient, preserved in time.

"You carry stories in your bones," she said, gesturing for Indigo to lie down on a woven reed mat.

"The body remembers what the mind refuses." Her touch wasn't forceful, but precise — each press along his back, his sternum, and collarbone seemed to stir something. Not pain. Memory.

A birthday cake with only one candle. A school desk beneath a rain-flecked window. The ache of being seen almost, but never quite. The private longing to be chosen without asking. "Your heart," Dani murmured, "is tethered. Not trapped — but waiting. The thread is pulling now."

Indigo opened his eyes. "Pulled by who?"
She smiled, quiet and cryptic. "Not a who, love. A when."

Later, under the golden hush of afternoon sun, they gathered in a ring of sun-warmed stones. There, they met Omari, the Movement Guide. He was tall and barefoot, wrapped in loose ochre cloth that swirled with every movement. He danced like no one was watching and like the Earth was always listening — each gesture grounded, each turn like a spell being cast.

"Move what your mind can't say," he called out, arms wide like a storm opening. At first, Indigo held back. He mirrored the steps, stomps, turns, open palms, and breath, but it felt strange, self-conscious. Until it didn't. The rhythm sank in. Indigo stopped thinking and started remembering through movement.

He saw himself, younger, hunched over a sketchpad, drawing with frantic joy. A girl in a star-shaped dress. He had forgotten her. A dream? A made-up friend? A memory folded into fantasy. Now, she pulsed like a symbol rising in the dark. Omari watched, nodding once. "Sometimes," he said, "we remember forward. The body knows what's coming before the mind dares to believe it."

In the final ritual of Earth Day, they were guided beyond the retreat walls to a wild garden — not manicured, but alive with intention. Vines wrapped around stone statues. Trees bent low, cradling the soil. Flowers burst through cracks with quiet defiance.

At the center sat an old woman with gray locs tied in a wrap, dirt under her nails, and eyes like storm-soaked soil. Isolde. The Soil Keeper. "You've burned the past," she said, not looking up.

"Flowed through the heart. Danced on the wind. Now... plant what must stay."

Each of them was handed a smooth black stone, carved with their name.

Indigo turned it over, and his breath caught. Underneath his name was the same symbol Elián had drawn the night before — the spiral crossed by two intersecting lines. "Why this symbol?" he asked quietly, as if the stone might answer.

Isolde looked up, eyes gleaming. "It's the mark of a soul chosen twice. Once before birth... And once in silence."

The instructions were simple. Bury the stone with bare hands. Indigo found a quiet patch in the garden, knelt, and dug. The soil was cool and giving.

As he pressed the stone beneath the earth, covering it with careful fingers, he felt it. A heartbeat. Maybe the ground. Maybe his own. Maybe both. When he stood, Isolde was already walking away. She called back over her shoulder: "You're almost home, boy."

That night, Indigo did not dream, but when he woke at dawn, there was dirt beneath his fingernails... and a single white feather resting on his chest. The same shade as the veil in his dreams. He didn't know where it came from, but he didn't want to let go of it, either.

Day Four — *The Whisper Path (Air Day — His Birthday)*

The sky was silver that morning, wrapped in a veil of soft clouds that seemed to hush the world below. The air didn't stir. It didn't need to. It was the kind of stillness that comes before—before the wind changes, before the truth lands, before the soul finally speaks aloud.

When Indigo awoke, he found white petals scattered across his pillow. There was no note. No guide at the door. No whispered explanation. Just that with a folded robe — pale lavender, stitched with thread that shimmered subtly when it caught the light. He wore it without resistance.

Something in him softening, surrendering. Not giving up — giving in.

On the driftwood board outside his door, a new message had appeared: "The wind does not ask. It carries what must be carried."

Zahra – The Scent Alchemist

The morning led him to a quiet glasshouse, swallowed in ivy, where wind chimes whispered from every arch and corner. Sunlight streamed through stained glass, casting soft prisms across shelves of ancient oils, resins, and tinctures.

Zahra stood at the center. She was veiled in sheer fabric, her presence cloaked in amber, myrrh, and mystery. Her voice was low, scented with calm. "We carry scent," she said, "the way we carry memory—deep, unconscious, tied to truth."

She held out five small glass vials. "Only one of these will accept you. The others will vanish from your skin."

Indigo dabbed each one along his wrist. The first four evaporated. Gone. Scentless as air, but the fifth—smoky rose, sandalwood, and something unnamed—bloomed. Not just on his skin, but in the space between skin and soul.

Zahra leaned in, inhaled, and gave a knowing smile. "This is the scent she wears when she walks the dream with you."

Indigo's voice cracked into silence. "Who is she?"

Zahra didn't answer. She simply pressed a miniature vial of the scent into his palm. "You will know her," she said, "when the wind turns."

Maru – The Flute Player

By afternoon, Indigo found himself seated beneath cypress trees, sunlight dappling the stones around him. A man named Maru, cloaked in robes the color of open sky, sat across from him, a carved wind flute in hand.

He began to play high notes, ephemeral, flickering like wings caught in a breeze. It wasn't music. It was a memory before it had a name. "I call the ancestors with air," Maru said, lowering the flute. "But sometimes... they bring messages from those yet to come."

He played again, and this time, Indigo felt it like a thread around his chest. A tug. A whisper. A name never spoken but always known. The melody shifted, and Indigo stilled. He didn't recognize the song and yet... he did. It was a vow, sung in the wind.

Maru's eyes met his sharply. "That melody doesn't come from the past," he said.

"It comes from a vow. One not made by you but made for you."

"A vow?" Indigo whispered, shaken.

Maru only nodded. "Your life is being written by hands you haven't held yet."

Faye – The Dreamwalker

Night fell like a silk curtain. Indigo was led to the Dream Dome — a pavilion draped in celestial fabric, lanterns glowing with soft flame, and candles floating midair like fireflies. There, Faye waited. She wore robes woven with starlight and a circlet of moonstone on her brow.

She offered him a warm bowl of dream tea, steeped in moonflower and anise, fragrant and oddly electric. "You will meet her again," she murmured, as he drank.

"You always do. Tonight, she'll be closer."

The world shifted.

Indigo lay back on the cushions, and the dream came fast, like falling through light.

He stood barefoot on a stone path under a violet sky. Petals swirled at his feet, carried by a warm wind. The trees whispered, but he didn't understand their language.

In the distance, a woman stood with her back to him. She wore the same lavender robe. The same scent bloomed around her. A pendant lay over her heart — the spiral symbol crossed with twin lines, glowing faintly.

She turned slowly. Her face shimmered — not hidden, but not fully visible either. Like memory reaching through a veil. "Happy solar return, Indigo," she said.

His voice caught. "Do I know you?"

"No," she replied, smiling.

"But you will. Tomorrow, I ask for your 'yes.'"

He reached for her hand, but woke before he could touch her.

A Letter from the Future:

At dawn, a small, sealed envelope waited at the door of his room. Inside, a single cream-colored card, hand-lettered in violet ink. Happy solar return. I can't wait for you to remember me. – Your future.

Indigo stared at it, heart echoing in his ears. He didn't know whether to laugh, cry, or run, but something in him — something old, quiet, and brave—whispered back: "I think I already do."

Day Five — The Veil Thins (Ether Day)

By Day Five, Indigo no longer moved with question. He moved like a thread pulled gently through the loom of something ancient, unseen, and deliberate. His feet knew the paths before he looked down. His hand often rested over his heart, where Elián's symbol, carved into stone, hidden beneath his tunic, pulsed softly like a second heartbeat. His eyes no longer searched the ground. They searched the sky.

Today's robe was deep violet, stitched with fine silver thread that glinted like scattered stars, and at the center of the retreat grounds, carved into the driftwood board, a message waited: "What is for you has already touched you in dreams, in symbols, and in silence."

They were told it was Ether Day—the day of the soul's threads. Of unseen bindings. Of destinies whispered, not declared. Of that which cannot be held but always holds us.

Eros — The Guide of Union

The first guide was Eros, tall and androgynous, wrapped in flowing white that shimmered like both flame and water. Their presence stilled the air, calming and electric, like the silence before lightning.

"Today," Eros said, "is the day of soul unions. Some of you have met your match. Some have not. But every soul knows what it is called to."

They led them into a sacred dome where the Circle of Mirrors was set. Each participant sat before a large obsidian stone, polished to a flawless reflection, but when Indigo looked, he did not see himself. At first, nothing. Then slowly — her.

The same veiled figure from his dreams. From the pool. From the scent on his wrist.

Her eyes were brimming with tears. Not sorrow — relief. Her lips moved, silently, across the distance. "One more night," she whispered, "and you'll see me."

Eros touched Indigo's shoulder, voice barely above a breath. "Her vow echoes still," they said. "She walks the dream beside you."

Jaya — The Tantric Channel

By late afternoon, the group was led into a warm, spice-scented tent glowing amber from within. The air smelled of roses, sandalwood, and cloves. Silk draped the space like a heartbeat in cloth. At its center sat Jaya, golden-skinned, still as flame, eyes like molten honey. "You cannot receive a union," she said, "if you still cling to loneliness."

They were guided into a ritual of mirror breath, not erotic, but sacred. Not desire, but remembrance. Jaya chose Indigo herself.

They sat cross-legged. Her breath guided his. Her presence surrounded him like warmth, not touch, but presence. He felt the pressure lift from his ribs, and his spine lengthened. His soul came forward and then — flashes:

- A crescent moon over a stone altar.
- A ring, carved from bones and gold.
- A kiss, not on lips but on an open palm.
- A whisper: "Say yes."

He pulled away, breath shaking. "What was that?" he asked.

Jaya only smiled softly, knowing. "Memory," she said.

"Not from the past, but from tomorrow."

Noor — The Astrologer of Soul Threads

At twilight, the final guide appeared. Noor, draped in navy robes that held stardust in their folds, sat before a circular stone table etched with glowing lines like constellations. Her fingers were ringed and ink-stained, her voice a tide pulled by the moon.

She did not read birth charts. She read soul maps. She traced Indigo's palms, then hovered them above the glowing wheel. "Your soul," she said, "runs parallel with another. You've passed each other in dreams for years."

His throat tightened. "When do we meet?" he asked.

Noor didn't hesitate. "Tomorrow," she said.

"At dawn. Under the veil. Under vow."

She placed something cool in his hand. A tiny ring, shaped like a flame. "You were never meant to choose alone," she said.

"She already said yes. You just need to remember."

That Night:

Indigo sat beneath a tree, lit only by the gentle flicker of fireflies. The wind moved like breath. Like a promise. The ring hung from a thread around his neck, close to the symbol still resting against his chest. He didn't know her name. Not her face, but now he knew her essence.

He had felt her scent, Zahra uncovered. He had seen her devotion in the pool with Priya. He had heard her laughter in Maru's song. Now, her vow rang through him like a temple bell. Tomorrow, she would ask, and he would answer yes.

Day Six — *The Ceremony (The Dawn Union)*

Before the sun even thought of rising, the final robe had already been laid at the foot of Indigo's bed. White. Threaded with gold. He did notice some suits available to him with a note that said, Pick one. Indigo picked the one he liked. He understood in the way the soul understands its return that this was the end of the unraveling and the beginning of something eternal.

Outside, the retreat grounds were hushed in reverence. A soft mist coiled low, glowing faintly in the blue pre-dawn hush. Hundreds of candles lined the path, flickering like stars that had decided, just for today, to walk the earth.

The driftwood message board held no words. Only a single symbol: the spiral that's intersected by two crossing lines. His symbol. Her symbol. Their thread.

They gathered in the Cliff Circle, where the sea met sky and the morning waited quietly behind the horizon. All the guides stood there silently, robed, present. Even Indigo's friend had joined, a still figure at the edge of it all, beside Maru, who looked carved from light itself.

Indigo was led forward. No one spoke. They didn't need to. Then came the bells. Soft, slow, ancient. From the mist, she emerged. The veiled woman. Wrapped in white and silver, her veil shimmered like dew catching light for the first time. Her bare hands trembled only slightly as she held tightly to Maru's arm. In her palm, she carried a card, etched with the spiral symbol.

Indigo's breath caught. There she was. Not perfect. Not unfamiliar, but deeply, devastatingly known. The woman from the dreams. From the scent. From the music. From the silence. The one who had chosen him long before they had met.

Eros stepped forward. Their voice was the first sound of the morning. "In the ancient rites of bond and breath, when two souls recognize the thread that binds them, they may accept their fate, not with fear, but with fire."

Then Elián stepped to Indigo's side. In his small hands were two rings: A humongous diamond ring, as if cut from Starfire itself, and a small stone ring, shaped like a flame. It was warm to the touch.

The veiled woman lifted her hands and slowly removed her veil, just as the first light of dawn spilled over the sea, and there she was. Not perfect nor polished, but known. So completely known it made Indigo ache. As if he had loved her in every silence of his life. As if he had waited through lifetimes to say yes.

Her voice came softly, clearly, like the breaking tide: "I was promised to you. Not by family. Not by force, but by something older than both of us. I've waited to be remembered. Will you walk with me? As a vow, and as my home?"

She took his hand and slipped the royal ring onto his finger, along with the spiritual one.

Indigo didn't answer right away. His eyes blurred with tears. The sea wind wrapped around them like a witness.

Then, without drama or hesitation, he stepped forward.

Took her hands and placed the twin rings on her finger. "I remember you," he said, "And I say yes."

The sun broke fully over the edge of the world. The wind lifted petals, hidden in the grass, scattered like blessings. The guides began to hum, not with a melody, but with a vibration. The veil, forgotten now at their feet, fluttered like a shroud. They stood hand in hand as the morning wrapped itself around them. New names whispered through the trees. Not just husband. Not just wife. Something sacred. Two souls who had chosen each other—once in dreams, now in light.

After the Yes:

The ceremony faded like a dream that never quite disappeared — only softened at the edges. The guests slipped away in silence. Some cried. Others pressed their hands to their hearts. The guides bowed once, then scattered like petals on the wind. Indigo didn't mind that his family hadn't come because they weren't his real family. Not like this. Not like her.

They remained at the cliff's edge, still handfasted, still glowing from within. It was she who broke the silence first, with a dry smile that pulled sunlight through the moment. "I imagined this so many times," she said.

"But in all of them... you cried less."

Indigo laughed — full-bodied and honest, like something inside him had finally been permitted to live. "You talked in my dreams," he said. "But you never gave me a name."

She tilted her head. "Yes," she said. "I've been in love with you for years."

Later — Under the Fig Tree:

They sat barefoot beneath the fig tree in the garden behind the Sanctum of Earth, where Indigo had once buried his name stone. The soil still smelled of roots and memories. "Was this all... arranged?" he asked, gently.

She nodded, "Yes. But not by force. Not like that."

"Then how?"

"I met Sage Amara two years ago," she said.

"I told her I had dreams of a man who never chose, not because he couldn't. But because no one had ever truly seen him. She said, 'Let me find him for you.'"

Indigo was quiet. Then: "What if I had said no?"

She smiled. "You wouldn't have."

"How could you be so sure?"

She leaned in and whispered, "Because I've seen every version of you. Even the one who doesn't believe in love. Even he reaches for me in his sleep."

He didn't respond. He just rested his forehead against hers, listening to the birds and the soil and the world quietly rebuilding itself under their feet. For the first time in his life, Indigo wasn't waiting. He was already inside the Yes, and together, they fell asleep in each other's arms — not as strangers, not even as lovers, but as something older than both: Remembrance. Return. Home.

Some loves are found in fire. Some in silence. For Indigo, he found it beneath a veil and bloomed like a promise spoken before the first breath.

Day Seven – *Remembering*

The morning after the ceremony, Indigo woke with a new stillness in his chest — the kind that follows not an ending, but a beginning. She was there beside him, laughing softly at something he couldn't remember saying. The dawn was gentle. The birds sang like they knew. For the first time, they spoke freely — not in riddles, not in ritual, but in ease. Conversation flowed like a remembered river. Natural. Familiar. Sacred. Then, one by one, she told him the truth. Not just who she was, but who they all were.

The Unveiling:

What Indigo had experienced as a spiritual retreat, an unfolding of mystery and transformation, was also... family. Her family.

They had hidden their identities, used nicknames and code names —
all to keep the veil in place until the moment was right. Now, that veil was
gone, and the names fell like sacred rain:

- *Sage Amara* — the woman who guided the retreat, was her business partner and her representative.
- *Brother Lior* — the male spiritual guide, was her business partner, her representative, and Amara's twin.
- *Elder Venu* — her grandfather, the architect of the ancestral teachings.
- *Isolde* — her grandmother, the one who handed Indigo the stone.
- *Maru* — her father, the flute player who summoned memory.
- *Priya* — her mother, the water priestess who said, "Don't call this healing. Call it honesty."
- *Shanta* — her sister, the ember dancer with obsidian braids.
- *Tomo* — her older brother, the calligrapher of emotion.
- *Elián* — her little brother, the mystic child who remembered Indigo before he did.
- *Kaleb* — her uncle, the breath guide who awakened the beast.
- *Sister Mira* — her aunt, who whispered truths Indigo didn't know he needed.
- *Zahra* — her niece, the scent alchemist who handed Indigo his essence.
- *Eros* — her nephew, both wind and flame, the guide of sacred union.
- *Dani* — her best friend, the body reader who felt memory in muscle.
- *Omari* — her gay best friend, the movement oracle who unlocked Indigo's hidden dances.
- *Faye* and *Noor* — her cousins, the dream walker, and the soul-mapper.
- *Jaya* — her employee, but also her sister in spiritual practice.

They hadn't just guided him. They had been watching, waiting, remembering him, too.

The Question:

That afternoon, she asked him the first question that mattered beyond vows: "Now that you're no longer waiting... What do you want to build?"

The answer rose in him instantly, like a truth that had been there since birth, waiting to be believed.

"I want to build a private island," he said.

"Off grid. Sacred. Sovereign. Not just a place, but a city. A legacy. A sanctuary. A new world."

She didn't hesitate. She turned to her representatives — Sage Amara, Brother Lior, and the others — and with a calm authority, simply said: "It will be done. Begin preparations. We'll discuss logistics after the honeymoon."

Just like that, the dream became a mission. The manifestation had already begun.

Expanding the Circle:

Indigo glanced over at his longtime friend — the one who had stood with him in silence, transformation, and fire. He was trying to be happy, but Indigo saw it: the shadow of feeling left behind. Without ceremony, Indigo asked: "Can he be part of the chosen leaders?"

There was a pause.

Then nods.

Then smiles.

"He already is," Sage Amara said.

"We knew and we're grateful you knew, too."

That was how the new world would begin — not with contracts, not with control, but with invitations. Even his spiritual friend — the one who had guided him in visions for years — was already in on it. "Wait—he's in this, too?" Indigo asked.

She grinned. "You're surprised? He's the one who gave us your name."

The Departure:

Her family stayed behind, wrapping up the final rites of the retreat for the next group of initiates, but Indigo and his divine partner—his twin flame, his mirror, his yes—prepared to leave. Not for an ending, but for a beginning.

The chosen leaders were already en route to the secluded island — Indigo's vision — to begin the work. The sanctuary. The city. The legacy. Indigo was off on the honeymoon. Not just with a wife, but with a destiny remembered.

Chapter Twelve

THE REMEMBERING

PART III: THE HONEYMOON

Day One - *The Quiet After Yes*

The first day of their honeymoon didn't begin with a kiss. It began with stillness.

After the boat touched the shore of the crescent-shaped island, Indigo stepped cautiously onto the sand, as if it might dissolve beneath his feet. His wife, now unveiled but no less enigmatic, moved ahead of him, barefoot. Her skirts whispered against the tall grass, and her fingers lingered along the tops of wildflowers, brushing them like she was greeting old friends. There were no other people. No guides. No itinerary. No teachings from the retreat they'd left behind. Just birdsong, the hush of the ocean, and the quiet that follows a sacred *yes*.

Their home for the days ahead stood waiting — a modest structure crafted of bamboo and driftwood, open to the breath of the wind. It was more than a house; it felt like a being. Inside, it offered only what was needed:

- A low bed draped in white linen
- Shelves stacked with worn books and blank journals
- A brass tea kettle, slightly dented
- And an altar: simple, small, bearing two spiral-shaped stones, side by side

No one had told them what to do next, and that, Indigo realized, was their first true gift.

A Breathing House:

They spoke little that day. Unpacking was slow, deliberate — not out of obligation but reverence. Each robe folded, each corner smoothed with care, as though in the act of building a shared space, something sacred was being born. When Indigo couldn't decide where to place his sandals, she laughed — a quiet, surprised sound — and hung them gently from the limb of a tree outside.

That evening, they shared a meal of grilled breadfruit, sweet mango, and a honeyed tea that left warmth lingering in his throat long after the last sip. She chewed slowly, eyes on him, not staring, but witnessing. It struck him then: she always watched him like that, as if seeing some forgotten version of him. A version he no longer remembered.

"What?" he asked, his voice barely more than a breath.
She tilted her head. "You're not what I expected."
"Disappointed?"
"Not at all," she replied.
"You're quieter. And more beautiful than the dream."
He flushed and turned his face away, but inside, something glowed.

That First Night:
They lay side by side on top of the sheets, not touching, gazing through the open skylight. Above them, stars spilled across the night like scattered beads from a broken strand. "Do you feel it?" she whispered.

"What?"
"That moment — between being strangers and being something else."
He nodded slowly. It was like standing at the edge of a vast lake. He could see her clearly on the other side — neither far nor close — and the water between them was still. Waiting. Unhurried.

He turned his head toward her. "What do we call each other now?"

She smiled. "We could start with names. Or... we could stay in silence a little longer."

He thought about that. Then reached for her hand.

They didn't sleep until the stars began to fade, and even then, they didn't dream. Their bodies were too full of presence.

Day Two - *Unspoken Histories*

Morning arrived slowly, light filtering through the banyan leaves and casting soft, shifting shadows across the bamboo floor. Indigo stirred first. He blinked into the filtered gold of dawn, the silence of the night before still clinging to him, thin and delicate as a thread not yet severed.

She was already awake. Cross-legged beside the altar, she moved her fingers across the spiral stones with a tenderness that felt ritualistic, like someone remembering something sacred, something nearly lost. Her touch was both reverent and strangely familiar. Indigo rose quietly and joined her on the floor, unsure whether to speak. The stillness between them wasn't awkward, but it was full—dense with something waiting to be named.

He reached out. "Tell me about the life you left behind," he asked softly.

She didn't respond at once. Her eyes lifted, scanning the empty ceiling as though searching for some kind of sign, or perhaps an answer. "I waited a long time for this moment," she said at last.

"Not the ceremony. Not the vows. Just... the day when the waiting would end. When I could stop hoping."

His fingers found hers, curled around them.

She didn't flinch.

"Waiting is heavy," he murmured.

She nodded. "I thought love would find me. Just arrived, one day. But it didn't. So, I started searching for it — in places no one else dared to look."

"And what did you find?"

"That the hardest part wasn't the search," she whispered. "It was the fear that I wouldn't be found."

Indigo felt something tighten in his chest. He swallowed. "I've been afraid of that too," he admitted. "Afraid of being seen but not chosen."

She turned to him then. Her eyes were soft, shimmering with something unspoken. She squeezed his hand. "But you chose me."

He nodded. "I did."

Shared Stories:

The morning unfolded gently, filled not with plans or distractions, but quiet exchanges — fragments of history, handed over like small offerings.

She spoke of cities swallowed by fog, where music echoed through narrow alleys and disappeared before it could be followed.

He told her of long walks through endless forests, and the silence of rooms where no one ever returned.

She remembered her mother's hands, strong and worn, skilled in healing and mercy.

Indigo recalled his father's laugh, deep and sudden, rising through the hollow spaces of an otherwise quiet house.

Their memories wove together, slowly — stories meeting in the middle to stitch together the tapestry of something new. "I never told anyone this," she said one moment, almost too softly. "But once, I left everything I had to follow a stranger's song."

He smiled. "That's how I felt, coming here. Like I was chasing a melody only I could hear."

They laughed — really laughed — for the first time when she admitted she'd once danced naked in a rainstorm, just to remember how it felt to be fully alive. "I think," Indigo said, watching her, "we're better company than our fears."

The First Kiss:

That evening, as the sky melted into shades of roses and ember, she stood on the shoreline. The waves curled softly around her ankles, the tide whispering secrets to the sand.

Indigo approached slowly, a low drumbeat in his chest. "May I?" he asked.

She turned toward him, smiling. The light touched her face, caught on the curve of her lips. Something in him stilled.

Their kiss was soft, cautious, not choreographed by passion, but guided by presence. It wasn't a claim. It was an offering. For a moment, the world fell away.

When they pulled apart, the sky above them shifting into indigo, he whispered, "Not a vow. Just a promise."

She nodded; her eyes lit up from within. "A beginning."

Evening Reflections:

Later, beneath the woven roof of their little home, they sat apart but together. Each with a journal open, hands moving slowly as if words and images required permission to emerge. Her pages filled with fragments — verses that resembled dreams, constellations drawn from memory, lines half-finished. His filled with spirals, waves, and symbols that made sense only to him.

They didn't speak, but the silence was no longer empty. It was charged. Brimming with something fragile and sacred: the slow, uncertain unfolding of love. Between them, the space was full. Of trust. Of hope. Of a story just beginning.

Day Three - *Embodiment*

The lagoon shimmered like liquid glass beneath the mid-morning sun, hidden deep within the heart of the island. It was a secret mirror, holding the sky in its stillness and the swaying of palm fronds in its breath.

Indigo and his wife arrived barefoot, the sand cool beneath their feet, the air thick with the scent of wild jasmine and salt. No words passed between them. They stood at the edge of the water in silence, not waiting, simply allowing. The moment stretched, soft and full.

The Sacred Water:

The lagoon welcomed them. Wading in, they felt the sun-warmed water rise around their ankles, thighs, chests — its embrace neither cold nor hot, but gentle, like a held breath. They swam slowly, drifting near one another without direction, their limbs moving in unconscious harmony — two notes from the same song.

At one point, she reached beneath the surface and touched the spiral tattoo inked on his ankle — the one that had first caught his eye during the ceremony. Her fingers lingered there. "It's real," she murmured. "Your skin tells stories."

Indigo met her gaze and smiled. "I want to learn them all." No more was said. They didn't need it.

Touch as Prayer:

Later, they sat on a flat stone warmed by the sun. She turned toward him and placed his hands gently against her skin, not as an invitation, but as an invocation. There was no urgency. His fingers followed the curve of her shoulder, the hollow of her collarbone, the delicate web of veins beneath her wrists. Each touch was careful, intentional — not an act of desire, but of devotion. Her eyes were closed.

"This is how I remember love," she whispered. "Not with words. With skin."

Indigo's breath caught. Something unguarded opened in him — not lust, but tenderness, immense and fragile. "I've never been seen like this before," he said.

She opened her eyes. They were radiant, almost shy. "Then see me too."

The First Night of Union:

That night, beneath lanterns strung through the banyan's ancient limbs, they made love for the first time. There was no rush. No performance. No choreography. Only a slow unfolding — two souls meeting without armor, mapping the soft terrain of each other's longing. They discovered the places that whispered *yes*, not in words, but in breath and stillness and reverent touch. It felt like a ceremony. Like worship.

Then they lay together afterward, her head tucked beneath his chin, her breath warm against his chest, she whispered: "We are more than our fears."

He kissed her hair and answered softly, "And more than our pasts."

The Gift of Presence:

Outside, the island exhaled. Crickets sang. The ocean spoke in waves. For the first time in years — maybe ever — Indigo didn't feel alone. He held her as sleep claimed them both, not out of possession, but out of peace. At that moment, he knew. He was home.

Day Four - *Doubt and Devotion*

The morning light came softened by cloud cover, gray and pale, like the sky itself had drawn a veil over the island. The usual golden warmth was absent, replaced by a hush, not cold, but contemplative. Indigo stirred to find the bed beside him empty. The linen still held her warmth, but she was gone.

He stepped outside and found her beneath the banyan tree, knees drawn to her chest, her eyes fixed on the horizon as if trying to see beyond the visible world.

He sat quietly beside her. "What weighs on you?" he asked.

She didn't answer right away. The wind stole some of her breath. "I'm scared," she said at last. "Scared this isn't real. That I'll wake up and you'll be gone. That I made this up."

Indigo felt her fear settle into him, not as a burden, but as something shared.

He reached for her hand, grounding both of them. "I'm scared, too," he admitted. "But fear doesn't mean we stop walking. It means we walk together."

Friction and Fragility:

The day unfolded beneath a quiet tension. They moved through it carefully, their silences more brittle than before. Glances missed their mark. Touches hesitated. Words hovered and vanished.

By mid-afternoon, something broke loose. "How can you be so sure?" Indigo asked more loudly than he meant. "How do we know this isn't just… island magic? A dream we'll forget when we leave?"

She turned to him, eyes rimmed with unshed tears. "I don't know," she said, voice trembling. "Maybe we're not meant to know."

They didn't shout. Their argument was soft — the kind that came not from anger, but from aching uncertainty. They were two dancers learning an unfamiliar rhythm, stepping on each other's toes, but refusing to let go.

Vows Written in Quiet:

As dusk crept in, they returned to the altar inside the house — the two spiral stones catching the candlelight with a subtle glow. Without speaking, they each took a piece of parchment and wrote. Hands trembling, hearts raw, they poured themselves into quiet vows — not declarations of perfection, but commitments shaped by fear, by longing, by the choice to stay.

Indigo wrote I vow to hold your fears as gently as I hold your love.

She wrote I promise to stay, even when the shadows come.

They folded the vows and placed them beneath the spiral stones, anchoring them there.

She exhaled softly. "We don't need to be perfect."

Indigo nodded. "Just present."

Nightfall's Embrace:

Later, wrapped in each other's arms, they didn't search for answers. They didn't need them. What they found instead was solace — in breath, in heartbeat, in presence. Outside, the stars pierced the sky one by one, quiet witnesses to a love that chose devotion over doubt. A love which is still learning its shape. A love willing to stay.

Day Five - *Play and Discovery*

Sunlight spilled through the banyan leaves like liquid gold, casting dappled warmth over the island. The air carried the scent of salt and something sweet — a reminder that the heaviness of yesterday had passed. In its place: lightness. A soft return to wonder. To laughter. To the simple joy of being.

Laughter Like Water:

They ran to the lagoon that morning, barefoot and breathless, the world around them sparkling with possibility. Splashing turned into a game, a blur of hands, water, and laughter so free it startled the birds from the trees. Indigo slipped and nearly fell backward into the shallows, laughter pouring from him like a boy who'd just remembered how.

She stood over him, drenched and grinning, water trailing down her face like jeweled rivulets. "You're ridiculous," she said, brushing her hair from her eyes.

"Only for you," he grinned back.

Their laughter echoed across the water — wild, unguarded, honest.

Colors and Curiosities:

Later, beneath the shade of a mango tree, she pulled a small set of paints from a woven basket — a quiet gift from the retreat they hadn't yet touched. Without asking, she dipped her fingers into the pigment and began painting spirals on his arm — the same shape that marked his skin beneath. He flinched at first, then surrendered, watching the colors bloom across his body like a new language.

"What's your favorite color?" she asked, brushing a streak of blue beneath his elbow.

He paused.

"Used to be gold," he said. "But now... I think it might be your laughter."

She blinked, startled by the answer, then blushed and painted a tiny star just above his wrist.

They passed stories between them like shells, small and imperfect. She confessed a deep, irrational hatred for papaya. He described the treehouse he tried to build as a boy — the one that collapsed while he was still inside it.

Sacred Nicknames:

As the day softened into afternoon, they invented names for each other — sacred titles born not of irony but intimacy.

"Starling," she said, touching his cheek. "Because you surprise me."

He leaned close and whispered, "Moonbeam. You light me up when it's darkest."

Each name melted on another wall. Each whisper stitched them closer together. It wasn't a play. It was present, sacred, and silly, the most honest kind.

A Dance Under the Banyan:

At twilight, with the light slipping into shades of rose and deep lavender, they danced barefoot beneath the wide arms of the banyan. No music. Just the hush of wind through leaves, the hush of breath between them. Their bodies moved slowly, almost unconsciously, like leaves floating together in a stream. No steps to remember. No rhythm to follow but each other.

Nightfall Joy:

That night, as fireflies blinked like scattered stars, they curled into each other's arms. There was no conversation — only the quiet joy of being known, of being chosen again and again.

Indigo looked up at the sky, then down at her sleeping form beside him. This wasn't just a honeymoon. It was a rebirth. In that glow, golden, sacred, soft love felt as infinite as the sky.

Day Six: *The Past in the Present*

The island lay still beneath the heavy hush of midday, wrapped in a blanket of heat so thick it seemed to press against the skin. The scent of frangipani drifted on the salt-laced breeze, sweet and heavy, clinging to everything it touched.

Inside the cool hush of their bamboo sanctuary, Indigo sat cross-legged on a woven mat. His eyes were closed, his breathing slow. One hand rested on his knee, the other traced the spiral of the tattoo on his forearm — a design that now seemed to hum with a strange, quiet energy. It pulsed gently beneath his fingertips, as though it had awakened.

Without warning, the world tilted. Colors deepened. Sounds blurred, muffled as if submerged underwater. Indigo's breath caught in his throat. Then, in a rush, came visions—not memories of his own, but something older, deeper. A sun-drenched temple appeared behind his eyelids, golden light spilling over ancient stone. There were hands clasped with his, laughter echoing beneath high arches. Love. Familiarity. Another life.

When he opened his eyes, she was there. His wife. Watching him. "You saw it too," she whispered, voice thick with wonder.

"I think so," he replied, his voice barely more than a breath.

His hand reached for hers, and she took it instantly, gripping tightly as if to steady them both. The air between them shimmered with memory. Images swam in and out — flashes of lives lived and lost, of promises whispered in languages they no longer spoke, of reunions long awaited.

Tears welled, not from sorrow alone, but from the aching beauty of it all.

Her voice was soft, steady. "Our love is not new. It is a river, flowing through many shores."

Indigo nodded, tears slipping down his cheeks. "And here — now — it is strongest."

Together, they knelt before the small wooden altar at the center of the room. With trembling hands, they carved their initials into the edge — not as a mark of possession, but as a quiet vow to walk forward, whatever paths might unfold.

Then, aloud, they spoke names — not their own, but ones that had echoed through their dreams, ancient and sacred. Each syllable felt familiar, like a key long missing returning to its lock. They did not need to explain. The words hung in the air between them, binding past to present.

That night, under a sky littered with stars, they lay side by side, fingers intertwined, listening to the waves kiss the shore. Time felt both infinite and fleeting. The warmth of her body beside him, the pulse of the ocean, the steady rise and fall of breath — all of it reminded Indigo of something essential, something eternal. For the first time, he let go completely. He was ready.

Day Seven - *The Choice to Return*

Dawn broke in soft pinks, brushing the sky with hues of hope. The first light spilled over the island's canopy, touching every leaf, every stone, as if awakening them with purpose. The air was thick with salt, warmed by promise, and stirred with something unspoken.

On the worn wooden steps of their bamboo sanctuary, Indigo and his wife sat side by side. Their fingers intertwined, palms resting between them like a shared heartbeat. No words were needed just yet. The hush of morning held them.

Between them lay a small, folded letter — the final gift from Sage Amara, the guide who had gently set their journey into motion. The parchment was soft with age, edges worn by time and care. With reverence, Indigo unfolded it. He read aloud, voice steady and quiet: "Love is the greatest journey — one that asks us to choose again and again, to let go and hold tight, to face the unknown with open hearts. Wherever you go from here, remember you carry each other in the spaces between your breaths. The world awaits your union."

Her eyes shimmered with tears. "Are we ready?"

Indigo looked at her, really looked, as if seeing her again for the first time. "We are."

They moved quietly through the morning, gathering small relics from the lives they had shed. A faded photograph, a cracked ring, a letter with edges torn and half-erased words. Each piece carried weight. Each had been a chapter, but now, they were ready to begin again.

At the fire pit, they laid their pasts gently into the flames. Smoke rose in slow spirals; a prayer made of ash and intention. It carried away old grief, outgrown stories, and the shadows they no longer needed to hold. They watched until the last ember flickered and faded, feeling somehow lighter, as if their very souls had been made new.

Down at the shoreline, the boat waited — humble and sturdy, its wooden hull creaking softly in the tide's gentle pull. They boarded hand in hand, the island slipping away behind them, its greens and golds fading into mist like the edges of a dream.

"Where to now?" she asked, her voice filled with wonder.

"Forward," Indigo said, and smiled.

As the island disappeared into the morning fog, something inside Indigo shifted — not a goodbye, but a deep, settled knowing. This was not the end. This was the true beginning. The week they had shared had been more than a honeymoon. It had been a pilgrimage through memory, vulnerability, and devotion. Each moment had carved out space in their hearts where something unshakable now lived. Now, as they returned to the world beyond their retreat, they did not return as they were. They returned changed.

Back in the city, their lives pulsed with fresh energy. Her quiet post on social media had gone live: a picture of their entwined hands beneath the banyan tree, and a caption that spoke of love, trust, and the art of building together. Almost overnight, Indigo's presence grew. The stories he had once written only for himself were now being shared, celebrated, and followed. Fame was never the goal. The connection was. Two creatives, weaving side by side, their talents no longer separate threads but strands of the same tapestry.

As their momentum built, Indigo found himself drawn more and more to the private island — not just as a retreat, but as a vision. A place to build something lasting. Something true. Without even realizing it, he had begun assembling a team. Not just collaborators, but kin.

When they returned to the island weeks later, it felt less like a visit and more like a homecoming. The team gathered — friends, artists, and mentors. They sat together beneath the banyan tree, sharing meals, dreams, and laughter. What started as a couple's journey had become a collective one. Not just business partners. Not just friends, but soul tribe. Family.

Some journeys, Indigo now understood, are not meant to be understood at the beginning. They unfold one choice at a time. One leap of faith, one moment of silence, one hand reaching for another. Some journeys never truly end. They only deepen.

Chapter Thirteen

THE CHOSEN ONE LEADERS

***Tayla Gionna Amala Sydney-Bass:* The Visionary Maven**

Born into a modest family in a bustling city, Tayla Gionna Amala Sydney-Bass was always destined to transcend ordinary limits. From an early age, Tayla's insatiable curiosity and magnetic charisma set her apart. She was the kind of child who not only asked *why* but also *how* — how to turn ideas into reality, how to inspire those around her, and how to create spaces where innovation and joy flourished.

Tayla knew early on she wanted something more than a conventional life. School was both a refuge and a challenge. Though bright and creative, she often felt like an outsider, her ideas too big and her ambitions too bold for those around her. Instead of shrinking back, she leaned into her passions. She started creating content on a borrowed laptop — filming short vlogs, sharing stories about her neighborhood, and experimenting with editing. Her early videos were raw but genuine, and slowly, a small but loyal audience emerged.

Facing financial struggles, Tayla took on multiple part-time jobs, from waitressing to tutoring younger students. These experiences only sharpened her empathy and her ability to connect with people from all walks of life — a trait that would become her signature appeal.

The real turning point came when she decided to invest her savings into buying better equipment and launching a blog. It was a risk that paid off. Her content grew more polished, her personality shone brighter, and soon she landed brand endorsement deals with local companies. Word spread, and within a few years, Tayla was no longer just a content creator — she was a rising star with a vision for building a multimedia empire.

Early Years and Rise to Fame:

Tayla's journey to celebrity began humbly with her passion for storytelling and media. In her teens, she started vlogging and blogging, sharing everything from daily life snippets to thoughtful motivational content. Her natural ability to connect with people, combined with her authenticity and humor, quickly garnered a growing audience. She wasn't just a content creator; she was a community builder.

Her channels diversified rapidly — from food reviews that celebrated global cuisines, to lively live streams where she playfully engaged with her chat, to kids' content featuring vibrant cartoon and anime versions of herself and her friends. Her reaction videos, Storytimes, pranks, and challenges showcased her multifaceted personality, making her relatable and adored by millions.

Entrepreneurship and Empire Building:

Never content to stay in one lane, Tayla leveraged her celebrity influence to build a business empire that spanned industries. Her first major investment was a tech startup, where she served as a strategic partner, pushing boundaries in AI-driven consumer solutions. Her keen eye for market trends and willingness to embrace innovation set the foundation for her later ventures.

Recognizing the power of franchising, Tayla launched a series of companies under her brand umbrella — from cutting-edge car washes equipped with the latest eco-friendly technology to luxury real estate developments. Her real estate portfolio boomed with duplexes, triplexes, apartments, and a thriving Airbnb business, catering to a wide range of clientele from budget travelers to luxury seekers.

Her ownership of a sprawling shopping center became a flagship location, blending retail, entertainment, and community events. Within it, she established a state-of-the-art movie theater that regularly featured independent films alongside blockbuster premieres. The shopping center also housed her shoe line boutique, a brand celebrated for combining style with sustainability.

On the cultural front, Tayla founded a massive annual music festival, attracting world-renowned artists and fostering up-and-coming talent. The festival wasn't just about music; it was a cultural celebration that spotlighted art, food, and innovative tech experiences.

Media Mogul and Digital Influence:

Her media empire expanded alongside her business ventures. Tayla's podcast clips and tour recaps became essential listening for fans and industry insiders alike. She turned her vlogging and blogging platforms into multi-dimensional hubs for entertainment, inspiration, and community engagement. Live streams and interactive sessions created a virtual space where followers felt seen and valued.

Her children's channel, filled with vibrant animated stories and positive messages, became a beloved destination for families. Meanwhile, her reaction and Storytime videos brought genuine joy and relatability, humanizing the larger-than-life celebrity.

Spiritual Side and Holistic Healing:

Despite the dazzling success and hectic pace of her expanding businesses, Tayla felt a growing need to explore something deeper. She often struggled with anxiety and burnout, common among high achievers. A chance encounter with a tarot reader at a music festival changed her perspective forever.

What began as curiosity quickly became a passionate pursuit. Tayla immersed herself in learning tarot, meditation, and energy healing, seeking to understand the invisible forces that shape human experience. She studied under renowned spiritual teachers and traveled to sacred sites worldwide, blending ancient wisdom with modern practices.

Her spiritual work was not separate from her public persona; it became an essential part of it. Tayla started sharing tarot readings in her live streams, offering personalized insights and encouragement. She developed motivational speeches that intertwined practical advice with spiritual teachings, empowering her audience to embrace self-awareness and transformation.

Her approach was unique — she didn't present herself as an untouchable guru but as someone on a shared journey, navigating life's highs and lows with openness and compassion. This authenticity resonated deeply with her followers and added a profound dimension to her influence.

Amid her fast-paced life, Tayla embraced her spiritual side, becoming deeply involved in tarot card readings, energy healing, and motivational speaking. She used these gifts to help others navigate life's challenges, offering guidance that blended ancient wisdom with modern empowerment. Her speeches, often peppered with personal anecdotes and practical advice, inspired thousands to pursue their dreams with courage and resilience.

The Compound, Warehouse, and Indigo's Journey:

Tayla's success culminated in the creation of her private compound — a sprawling estate designed not just for luxury but for creativity and collaboration. Adjacent to this, she acquired a massive warehouse space that functioned as a hub for her various ventures, from product development for her shoe line to the management of her franchises and digital content production.

It was through social media that Tayla first noticed Indigo — a figure whose vibrant energy and vision resonated deeply with her own. Their connection was instantaneous, transcending the digital realm into real life. Their partnership blossomed not only into marriage but a powerful creative alliance.

Tayla played an instrumental role in helping Indigo build his private city island — a visionary project that combined real estate, commerce, and entertainment. She helped him secure properties and land, guiding the construction of his signature building that housed his tarot reading studio, merchandise shops, and a variety of stores showcasing his brand.

Together, they designed an arcade that became the crown jewel of his other building, featuring go-karts, bowling alleys, mini-golf courses, and a cutting-edge movie theater. The building's creation was an epic saga — they even ventured into Earthfall, a virtual design space, to plan and oversee the development, sharing progress with a select group of trusted collaborators.

He used the private island as a retreat for people to live off the land and build businesses together. Indigo and Tayla's relationship was one of mutual respect, creative synergy, and deep love. Their marriage was both a personal union and a professional alliance, fueling each other's growth and dreams.

Legacy and Vision:

Tayla Gionna Amala Sydney-Bass is more than a celebrity or entrepreneur — she is a visionary architect of experiences, a bridge between worlds (digital and physical, material, and spiritual), and a beacon for those who dare to dream expansively. Her story is one of relentless ambition balanced by a commitment to community and authenticity, proving that with heart and hustle, one can build empires that uplift and inspire.

Amara Sirene Sage: **The Multidimensional Creator**

Amara Sirene Sage was born under a full moon with a storm on the horizon, a poetic beginning befitting a woman whose life would come to blend art, intellect, spirit, and innovation. The first cry she let out in the hospital was matched by the coos of her twin brother, Lior Siren Sage, who arrived moments later — a bond formed not just by blood but by soul.

From their earliest days, Amara stood out with a gaze that seemed to look beyond the visible. While Lior was the storm — intense, intuitive, ever-moving — Amara was the still waters beneath, quiet, and deep, reflecting everything around her. Together, they were inseparable — each other's mirror, anchor, and compass.

The Roots of a Creator:

Raised in a family that valued creativity and wisdom over conformity, Amara's childhood was a swirling blend of color, sound, and spiritual awareness. Her mother was an herbalist and storyteller, her father a retired philosophy professor who played the violin at sunset. Their home was filled with books, incense, old film reels, and strange instruments from around the world.

By age six, Amara was sketching elaborate scenes in her notebooks, not just of fantasy worlds, but of blueprints — devices, homes, and even instruments she imagined building one day.

By nine, she was painting full canvases, composing simple melodies on the harp and kalimba, and inventing fictional creatures with their mythologies.

Her love for storytelling was unmatched. She devoured classic literature, wrote entire novellas in secret, and published her first short story online at twelve under a pseudonym — it gained critical buzz in niche creative communities. That little taste of audience impact would later bloom into an empire.

The Spark of Entrepreneurship:

As she matured, Amara's mind became a fertile ground for innovation. While most creators chose one discipline, Amara mastered many, blending artistry with technical ingenuity.

After college, she founded her publishing company to give voice to underrepresented authors — poets, fantasy writers, philosophers, and children's storytellers. It grew rapidly, thanks to her sharp eye for unique narratives and a heart for soulful, boundary-pushing work. Eventually, she started writing her novels, launching a bestselling horror-mystery series that combined Gothic elegance with modern themes of healing and trauma.

Around the same time, Amara opened a jewelry store — not because she needed another venture, but because of a dream she had. In it, she was forging crystals in fire and wrapping them with gold filigree, embedding them with intentions. Her store became known not just for beauty but for spiritual resonance. Each piece came with a story, a prayer, and a purpose.

The Technological Visionary:

Behind her serene presence was a futurist's mind. Frustrated with mainstream tech, Amara taught herself code and engineering with relentless discipline. She designed her gaming console — not for shooters or hyperstimulation, but for artistic, explorative, and meditative gameplay. Indie developers worldwide partnered with her to launch truly unique titles.

She also founded her mobile phone carrier, which prioritized privacy, holistic wellness apps, and integrated creative tools — especially for artists and writers. It was a quiet revolution in an oversaturated tech world.

Later, she built two monumental platforms:

- A meditative wellness app that offered soundscapes, breathwork journeys, ritual tracking, dream journaling, and even AI-guided reflection tools.
- A social media platform centered on intentional living, where creators could publish long-form ideas, audio meditations, artwork,

and shared dream logs. No likes, no pressure — just authentic expressions.

She then established a cruise line blending luxurious travel with immersive art galleries, film screenings, and spiritual retreats on the sea. Her ships were floating temples of culture, creativity, and calm.

The Screen: Her Love for Horror and Animation

Her love for horror was deeply personal — not about gore, but the psychology of fear and the catharsis of facing it. She wrote, directed, and produced her first feature film at 25 — a surreal, slow-burning horror epic inspired by dreams and ancestral memory. It was critically acclaimed and won awards at indie film festivals.

From there, she moved into TV and animation, including a cult-favorite animated series blending mythology, sci-fi, and psychological horror. Her studio became a haven for offbeat creators, metaphysical themes, and visual experimentation. She believed animation was a way to say things the real world wasn't yet ready to hear — and she pushed every boundary.

Amara & Indigo: The Spiritual Architect

Amara met Indigo through Tayla, as she wanted Amara and Lior to research Indigo. She saw him not just as a person, but as a potential cosmic collaborator.

Indigo had bold dreams of a private island city, not for power but for peace. A place of wisdom, healing, and fun. He wanted to create schools, retreats, playgrounds, amusement parks — a whole civilization built on imagination and freedom. Amara saw it too. She helped Indigo:

- Publish his books, including his children's book series, ensuring they retain spiritual depth and gentle joy.
- Build his school, curating a curriculum on creative consciousness, intuition, technology, and healing.

- Design his spiritual retreat — a sacred space blending temple, sound domes, meditation gardens, and floating libraries.
- Develop his amusement park and playground, not just with thrills but learning zones, sensory gardens, and imagination theaters.

Every part of Indigo's vision was infused with Amara's essence — artistry, intention, and balance. Together, they turned blueprints into breathing worlds.

Lior Siren Sage: Her Mirror Flame

Her twin brother, Lior, was the only one who knew the full scale of Amara's being. A brilliant mystic, ritualist, and performer in his own right, Lior challenged her when she faltered, reminded her of their shared origins when she drifted, and held her accountable to the dream when the world pulled her into its noise. Their connection wasn't always peaceful — twins, especially psychic ones, rarely are, but through every storm, they anchored each other in truth.

Legacy of Light and Shadow:

Amara Sirene Sage is more than an entrepreneur, artist, or technologist. She is a prism, refracting truth into all its colors and frequencies. Her life is an orchestra of vision, discipline, and grace. A weaver of worlds, a sage of sound and silence, and an architect of inner and outer dimensions.

To the public, she's a creator.
To the spiritual, she's a guide.
To Indigo, she's the architect of dreams.
To Lior, she's the other half of an ancient song.
She lives by a simple creed: "What we create outlives us. So, make it sacred."

Lior Siren Sage — The Alchemical Performer, Tantric Mystic, and Empire Catalyst

Lior Siren Sage was born second, seven minutes after his twin sister, Amara, in the same storm-washed dawn that seemed to summon them from beyond the veil. While Amara opened her eyes with calm, otherworldly focus, Lior arrived screaming, laughing, and kicking — electric from the moment his soul touched earth. They were night and fire. Amara was lunar. Lior was solar, but neither existed without the other.

Raised in a home filled with incense, books, symphonic piano, old myths, and the scent of burning herbs, Lior grew up fluent not just in multiple languages but in feeling.

Their mother taught them how to read energy.

Their father taught them how to master their voice, and the twins spent their childhood holding rituals in backyards, dancing to ancient drums, and drawing beings that didn't yet exist.

The Performer in the Fire:

Lior was always in motion. He would sing before he could walk, dance before he could talk. At school, he was either adored or feared — not because he was arrogant, but because he burned with presence.

Teachers called him "too intense."

Coaches said he was "born to lead."

He was never satisfied with rules that dulled the fire of possibility.

His first dream was to perform, but not in the ordinary sense. Lior didn't want to act — he wanted to become. On stage, he could shift into gods, fools, shamans, and kings. He turned monologues into rituals. Audiences laughed, wept, and sometimes fainted. His shows felt like transformations because they were.

By twenty, he had written a series of autobiographical plays exploring ancestral trauma, sacred sexuality, and his near-death experiences — including a drowning accident that he claimed allowed him to speak with beings from the "world-between." These plays gained underground acclaim in fringe theaters across the country, earning him the moniker "The Siren" for his voice that could hypnotize and liberate.

From Sacred Flame to Five-Star Chef:

What no one expected was that Lior would become a culinary phenomenon. Lior always saw cooking as spellcraft. Food, to him, was another form of transformation. He learned to cook from his grandmother, a traditional healer who spoke to her pots as if they were ancestors. He believed flavor was alchemy: sweet to soften the heart, heat to awaken courage, herbs to ignite memory.

He opened a small restaurant with no investors and no name. It was invitation-only, with an ever-changing menu, incense in the vents, live sound healing during courses, and handwritten blessings on every napkin.

Within five years, the world noticed. The restaurant received five Michelin stars, a rare and nearly mythical achievement. Critics called it "a spiritual rite disguised as a meal."

He published a cookbook, part poetry, part autobiography, part recipe grimoire. Then came:

- A line of organic food and beverages, including moon-phase water, root-tincture tonics, and prebiotic cacao.
- A fitness program rooted in dance, breathwork, primal movement, and tantric pulse awareness.
- His supplement line, designed to work not just with the body but with energetic systems.
- Franchises of his gyms, which were temples as much as workout spaces — places for sweat, silence, and sex-positive healing.

The Tantric Doctor and Intimacy Healer:

After studying in India, Nepal, and parts of West Africa, Lior became a certified tantric doctor and intimacy alchemist. He taught not just pleasure, but integration — the ability to transform trauma into embodiment and shame into sacredness.

He held retreats that blended guided partner breathwork, trauma release, erotic energy healing, and cosmic dialogue. Celebrities, monks, politicians, and recluses all came to his retreats seeking one thing: remembrance of the divine self through the body.

From Star to Supernova: TV, Toys, and Total Media

Never one to stay in a box, Lior exploded into mass media next, but not in the traditional way. He created his own:

- A television network centered on healing, mysticism, art, tantra, consciousness, and alternative culture.
- A streaming platform featuring uncensored series, exclusive documentaries, intuitive reality shows, and his own programs.
- A late-night talk show blending comedy, soul interviews, monologues, and ritual theatre.
- A cooking show where each episode paired food with emotional release.

He became a multimedia icon — charismatic, unapologetic, divine-masculine-in-motion. His face was everywhere. His energy couldn't be contained.

Naturally, the action figures came next. Lior produced a line of toy action figures, each version of himself representing a different archetype:

- The Healer
- The Warrior
- The Trickster
- The King
- The Wild One

Each toy came with affirmations and an augmented reality mini game for inner child healing. Kids and adults alike collected them. It became a cult sensation.

He even had a house and car shaped like a UFO, glowing with pulse-lighting and fractal glass — both symbols of his claim that he once contacted a star-being version of himself.

Brother to the Demiurge — Lior & Indigo

When Indigo came into his and Amara's life, Lior recognized him instantly — not just as a person, but as a cosmic frequency. Indigo was not just a friend or partner; he was a symbol of divine evolution.

Where Amara helped build Indigo's structures, Lior helped ignite Indigo's myth. Lior introduced him to investors, creators, influencers, and mystics. He helped Indigo launch his public identity. Lior helped develop Indigo's:

- Personal brand as the New Demiurge — a spiritual leader, artist, and architect of the New Era.
- Exclusive merch lines and global events.
- Philosophical series — documentaries, podcasts, and live panels — where Lior served as Indigo's spokesperson and translator of the divine. Lior became the Orator of the Demiurge — the fire to Indigo's silence, the voice to his essence.

Legacy of a Living Archetype:

Lior Siren Sage lives not as a brand, but as a frequency — a walking paradox: sacred and wild, theatrical, and true, sensual, and spiritual. He's a culinary mystic, a tantric warrior, a media god, and a brother to the stars. Whether speaking to 10,000 souls onstage or whispering to a lover in ritual, Lior embodies a message: "You are holy, hungry, and here to remember. Let every breath be performance. Let every act be devotion."

Andariel Labardy Nyros — The Off-Grid Visionary and Spiritual Bard

Andariel Nyros Labardy was born under an amber-hued twilight in a quiet town where the stars burned bright, unpolluted by city lights. From an early age, Andariel felt a deep pull towards nature and the unseen — a yearning to connect soil and spirit in equal measures.

He was raised by grandparents who taught him the ancient art of sustainable farming and herbal lore, skills passed down by generations who honored the land and the sacred cycles of growth. His childhood was spent barefoot in the dirt, hands deep in the earth, learning the songs of cicadas and the language of wildflowers. He spent most of his time with his grandparents, as his family was more religious than spiritual.

The Roots of Self-Reliance and Craft:

Determined to live beyond the confines of modern dependency, Andariel purchased a secluded plot miles from the nearest town, where he built a homestead that operated entirely off-grid. His farm flourished with heirloom vegetables, fruit trees, and rare medicinal herbs. His barn housed animals raised ethically and sustainably. Andariel's vision wasn't just about survival — it was about revival. Revival of ancient wisdom and joy through nature and self-sufficiency.

Alongside the rhythms of planting and harvest, Andariel crafted a line of handcrafted, small-batch alcoholic beverages. Each drink was an alchemical blend of fermented herbs, fruits, and wild yeasts from his farm, designed to evoke ceremony, celebration, and healing. His signature beverages became popular in niche circles seeking artisanal quality and soulful taste.

The Bard of Cuffing Season:

Andariel's heart was not only in the soil but in the spotlight. Inspired by the seasonal rituals and emotional cycles that people experience each winter, he created "Cuffing Season" — a Broadway production unlike any other. The show was a vibrant fusion of music, dance, spoken words, and mystical storytelling exploring themes of love, loneliness, community, and transformation during the coldest months.

The success of the stage production sparked a movement:

- A Broadway album featuring songs written and performed by Andariel himself, blending soul, jazz, and folk.

- A documentary tracing the creation of the show, highlighting the human stories behind art.

- A movie adaptation that expanded the narrative into a cinematic journey of healing and connection.

- And finally, an intimate play that toured regional theaters, bringing the spirit of *Cuffing Season* to smaller communities.

Music, Tour, and Spiritual Artistry:

As a musician, Andariel toured extensively, blending concerts with spiritual workshops on mindfulness, meditation, and creative flow. His music was described as "a balm for the restless soul," deeply rooted in storytelling, ritual, and raw emotion.

Ever the innovator, he continually upgraded his businesses, infusing them with technological savvy while preserving his earthy roots. Among his most personal creations were his tarot and oracle card decks, designed to reflect nature's cycles, ancestral wisdom, and modern spirituality. These decks gained acclaim in spiritual communities worldwide, becoming tools for reflection, guidance, and empowerment.

Indigo's Spiritual Ally and Co-Creator:

Andariel met Indigo in the digital ether — a chance meeting sparked by late-night conversations about consciousness, energy healing, and the quest for authentic purpose. Their friendship blossomed quickly, built on mutual respect, shared visions, and complementary strengths.

Together, they founded their foundation, a charity focused on empowering underserved communities through education, holistic health, and creative expression. The foundation hosted retreats, workshops, and scholarship programs, blending Indigo's global reach with Andariel's grassroots wisdom.

Andariel played a crucial role in helping Indigo organize his global motivational tour, using his experience as a performer and spiritual guide to shape events that blend inspiration with healing rituals.

The two friends embarked on a worldwide podcast tour, sharing dialogues on spiritual awakening, resilience, and creative entrepreneurship — a series that quickly gained a devoted international audience.

The Off-Grid Sanctuary:

When Indigo sought to escape the demands of fame and reconnect with his essence, Andariel designed and helped build his off-grid home — a sanctuary nestled in nature, powered by renewable energy and surrounded by gardens, meditation spaces, and art installations. The home was more than a residence; it was a living altar, a place for Indigo to recharge, dream, and create away from the noise of the world.

The Legacy of Andariel Labardy Nyros:

Andariel lives at the intersection of earth and ether, creativity and care, solitude, and connection. He is a farmer, a bard, a mystic, and a builder of community — a man who understands that the roots of the future lie in honoring the past and embracing the present. His life is a testament to the power of friendship, vision, and the sacred dance between nature and spirit.

Indigo Bass — **Legend in Motion**

There were stages, and then there were worlds — and Indigo Bass didn't just step onto either. He rewrote their rules. Once a rising visionary, now a global phenomenon, Indigo had crossed the threshold from mystic musician to mythic figure. His name was etched into history not as a celebrity, but as the GOAT — the *Greatest Performer of All Time*. He turned the crowd's raw energy into something poetic and unforgettable.

The Music World Tour: The Planet Was on the Stage

It began with a single note — one held in silence, in shadow, before the world even knew what was coming. Indigo didn't launch a tour. He summoned a global experience.

His world tour sold out within minutes in every major country, state, and city — Tokyo, Lagos, São Paulo, New York, Cairo, Seoul, Mumbai, Johannesburg, London, and beyond. Each stadium transformed into a multidimensional space: holographic spirit temples, astral bridges, dreamscapes projected mid-air. He didn't just perform songs — he channeled entire lifetimes into rhythm, light, and movement.

Every country and state has its version of the show, with custom-built stages that mirror its local mythos and ancestry. His dancers weren't backup — they were oracles. His lighting engineers were ritualists. His visuals were sigils. Every show was prophecy in motion. People didn't just watch Indigo perform. They wept. They screamed. They remembered who they were. At the end of each performance, he bowed in silence, the lights dimmed, and only one word echoed on screens across the world: "You."

Indigo, as always, transmuted the attack into art. He pressed a special limited-edition vinyl and CD set, which included distorted versions of the corrupted tracks and a final unreleased song that functioned like a spiritual cleansing. These physical formats — tangible, grounded, analog — were his way of reclaiming presence in a world that is too digital, too disembodied. Collectors bought them as relics. Critics called them post-human hymns.

Marriage, Relocation, and the Compound of Dreams:

Amid the chaos and transcendence, Indigo and Tayla got married. Their wedding wasn't public — it was sacred. The ceremony was elemental: water from the Nile, sand from the Sahara, crystals from Tayla's collection, and vows spoken in a coded spiritual dialect only they could understand.

After the wedding and honeymoon, the two relocated, establishing multiple homes across realms:

- A mountaintop sanctuary in Nepal for meditation and dreaming.
- A techno-organic loft in Amsterdam filled with mirrors and coded light.
- A subterranean creative chamber in Iceland built into volcanic stone.
- A mega mansion in Florida that was built from scratch.
- Properties in New York, Las Vegas, Georgia, Tennessee, Texas, etc.
- And of course, their main compound beach house — a living fortress of creativity and innovation — is located on their island.

There, Tayla managed her fashion lines, podcast empire, and kids' animation channel. Indigo composed new music, trained with energy masters, and designed immersive reality architecture.

Sending Envoys to Earthfall:

While Indigo and Tayla expanded their lives into dreamlike spaces, he never forgot Earthfall — the realm they met and had helped build a sanctuary of vision, artistry, and spiritual reclamation.

After the global tour and wedding, Indigo sensed shifts within Earthfall — economic ripples, creative drift, energetic blocks. He could feel it like a buzz in his chest. Rather than return immediately, he sent a handpicked group — engineers, artists, mystics, and logistical minds — to "repair the grid." They were sent to:

- Audit the infrastructure of his businesses.
- Cleanse energetic spaces.
- Recalibrate the flow of commerce, art, and intention.
- Restore the sacredness of the spaces.
- These emissaries worked under specific instructions: "Do not build in my name. Restore in our memory."

Indigo would eventually return to Earthfall from his private island, but not to reclaim it — to *reign it*.

The Era of Indigo Bass:

Now, Indigo Bass stands not just as an icon, but as a myth that breathes. His presence is felt across dimensions — through his voice, his vision, his ventures, and his vanished silence.

The world calls him a performer. The mystics call him a bridge.

Tayla calls him her storm and stillness. Earthfall still calls him home.

He has conquered fame but seeks only impact. He has built empires, but longs for resonance. He has ascended the stage but always bows to the mystery. Indigo Bass knows *legacy isn't what you leave behind, it's what you activate in others while you're still alive.*

Chapter Fourteen

DEVOUR ME SLOWLY, FREAK ME INTO FOREVER

Once Indigo aligned himself with the right people, everything began to fall into place. His confidence grew—not just in his gifts, skills, and talents, but within himself. He no longer cared about others' opinions, judgments, or expectations. After all, he had transformed from a multimillionaire into a billionaire. His businesses were booming, his schedule was full, and he was in constant demand—not only for his expertise, but for his presence and energy. Simply showing up, being himself, and existing authentically was more than enough; he was being paid for it. The days were long, and the nights often longer, but Indigo didn't mind—he was finally living the life he had always dreamed of.

As his empires soared, the past came knocking. Exes began appearing uninvited at his events. Estranged family members resurfaced, showing up at his door. Childhood friends posted videos online, pretending they still had a connection to him. Former employers and coworkers reached out, hoping to bring him back on board, but Indigo had seen it coming. He always knew: people assume you're nobody until you rise high enough to remind them of what they dismissed.

Some exes tried to rekindle old flames or provoke jealousy. Family members, once indifferent or cruel, sought entry into his new world. Old friends used his name to chase clout, and former bosses wanted to exploit his success to boost their ventures. Indigo met it all with grace.

Yes, it was triggering at times, but instead of reacting, he paused. He observed, took a breath, and centered on himself. He relied on his intuition, his gut, and his discernment. Every one of them was denied and rejected—they had already been removed from his life for a reason. Still, Indigo never forgot those who stood by him from the beginning. He continued to care for those who believed in him when no one else did, but as for those who told him to quit, cast doubt on his dreams, spread lies, practiced dark intentions, or tried to break his spirit, they were cut off, completely and permanently.

Through it all, Indigo and Tayla remained unshakable. They had made a pact: nothing—not the media, public opinion, not even shadows from their past—would ever come between their love. Together, they continued to vlog, stream, and create, offering a beacon of hope to others that true love exists and this is what it looks like.

Indigo's empire wasn't built alone—it was the manifestation of a destiny already written. His vision was fueled by something far greater than ambition: a divine blueprint, etched into the fabric of his soul. Surrounding him were loyal, passionate individuals who shared his values and purpose. Together, they created something extraordinary—not just on his private island city, but also in Earthfall. Even when Indigo was away, he remained connected, checking in, ensuring everything flowed in harmony.

From his throne, Indigo ruled as the new Demiurge, watching as his vision came to life through the tireless work of his team. Though his likeness was the face of the movement, he remained a mystery to the public, choosing Lior to be his spokesperson. The mystique served a purpose, especially when rolling out new initiatives such as the Demiurge. Indigo's mission was clear: he wanted the corrupt systems dismantled and the dark entities that fed on chaos removed from Earthfall entirely. In their place, he envisioned a world of peace, prosperity, respect, order, balance, fairness, and abundance.

Despite the scale of his responsibilities, Indigo prioritized time with Tayla. Their bond remained unshakable as their businesses expanded, and their private island city flourished. A conscious, thriving community grew there—each operating in their highest frequency and vibration. Tayla had known she wanted to start a family with Indigo from the moment she first saw him online. Indigo wanted the same, but he was determined to be fully prepared. He refused to bring children into a world still plagued by a collapsing system—corrupted governments, media propaganda, energy-draining narcissists, and institutions like public schools masquerading as concentration camps.

By now, both Indigo and Tayla had become self-made multimillion-aires, later crossing into billionaire territory. With this financial sovereignty, Indigo knew he could outmaneuver the system. His children could be raised in a sanctuary—off-grid, homeschooled, nourished, and born in the sacred waters of their private island. He envisioned an alternative civilization for those choosing to detach from the decaying matrix, a new model that would thrive until the old system could be entirely replaced under his divine executive orders.

Yet even with all the planning, Indigo had his moments of hesitation. He knew the gravity of parenthood. He wanted to give his children more than luxury—he wanted to give them healing, peace, and wholeness. Even with precautions, the depth of his and Tayla's passion made the possibility of conception real, but divine timing had held off until they were truly ready.

Indigo intended to be a present, loving father, something he had to become by healing himself first. He had broken generational curses, shed childhood trauma, and done the deep work to ensure he wouldn't pass down pain. He also waited for Tayla to complete her shadow work. He supported her, stood beside her, but honored that her healing journey was hers alone. There would never be a "perfect time," only a sacred, destined one, and that time, they both felt, was drawing near.

The idea of a child first sparked when they were sailing on their private yacht, returning to their Florida mansion after a grueling day of interviews, podcast appearances, and star-studded events. Both were ready to escape. Indigo, while capable in crowds, thrived best when guarding his energy, preferring quiet unless the collective energy truly resonated. Tayla, sensing his weariness, decided on an impromptu yacht excursion—something different, just for them. It was a chance to finally unwind after their demanding schedule. Though a small crew, including a driver and security, was on board, Tayla yearned for absolute privacy. They sought refuge on one of the yacht's upper decks, where their private bedroom offered sanctuary from any prying eyes.

They settled in for a movie. During the film, Tayla's hand slipped to Indigo's pants, a silent invitation for intimacy. He drew her close, a deep understanding passing between them. "I've got something for you," he whispered, his voice low and knowing.

Recognizing her desires, his touch transformed him, unleashing his more assertive side. Their clothes remained, but his hand slid beneath her pants, meeting her already-eager body.

Tayla discarded her hoodie, trusting his warmth to ignite her. The rising heat, the raw passion, threatened to unleash a torrent. "I'm going to show you how I operate," he breathed, the gentle lover of their honeymoon now replaced by a commanding presence.

She began to strip, already wet from his mere touch. With the boundless energy Indigo possessed, he drove deeper. Though voluptuous, she was also sensitive, so he eased his pace, allowing her to fully relax in him.

He stroked her slowly, demonstrating the depth of his penetration, then worked his fingers inside her pants, the evidence of her arousal coating his hand. Her cries of pleasure—screams, moans, squirts—were muffled by his kisses, keeping their fierce intimacy discreet.

The precipice of her orgasm coincided with a glimpse of the movie—a pole dancing scene. She surged with impulsive energy, rising and moving to the sleek pole within their bedroom. She danced for him, a private performance, and in his unwavering gaze, she was nothing short of a star. That look, intense and consuming, pulled her to him, and she descended for a lap dance.

Soft moans began to intertwine, their bodies merging, indistinguishable. She writhed against him, circling her hips, then lowered herself, presenting the exquisite curve of her rear. Her breasts came to rest on his chest, feeling the primal rhythm of his heart before she mounted him, riding him with an untamed ferocity that was both savage and utterly profound. She seized control, a power he undeniably cherished. He shifted, poised to unleash his masterful touch, to prove his dominance, but the gentle thud of the yacht docking broke the spell.

They gathered their belongings, the lingering tremor of their shared climax still vibrating through them. They spilled out and into the mansion. Tayla flung the grand door open, an act as boundless and inviting as her very soul. As it softly clicked shut, he kissed her, a tender brush that sought the faint echo of their lips parting. "Wait here," she whispered, her voice laced with playful promise. "I've got something for you."

"Touché," he conceded, recognizing her insatiable desire for another round, even after the raw, powerful assault of the first.

She re-entered an undeniable invitation in every movement, her essence radiating desire. She returned, draped in a sheer dress, a vision that brought Indigo to the precipice of reverence. She leaned in, her voice a soft murmur as she pleased him, an ASMR symphony that resonated deep within him.

He guided her to one of the many bedrooms, where they sought solace and passion beneath the freshly laundered covers and sheets, their desires superseding any thought of the cleaning crew.

"Don't force it," she breathed, "ease it in a little more." He entered her, finding the exquisite contours of her deep cheekbones, then pressing deeper into her alluring dimples. She moaned in a symphony of different languages, struggling to contain the surge of her screams. He lay on her chest, her foreign accent weaving an intoxicating spell that drew him deeper into love. She was a woman of the world—international, cultured, classy. For Indigo, the physical world ceased to exist unless she was its focal point. It felt like a suspended dream, a silent question hanging in the air: *Could this perfection truly last?* Perhaps matching tattoos would solidify their wish.

They'd overlooked dimming the lights. He rose, adjusting the ambient glow and igniting the soft hues of their LED strips. As he turned, she was already murmuring, "Papi," then "Zaddy."

"Take your reading glasses off," he teased, a low rumble in his chest.

"Take your fashion glasses off, too," she countered playfully.

"Touché," he conceded, his voice deepening. "I'm about to put it in you."

"Go ahead," she urged, "no condom, boo."

"Oh, you fancy, huh?" he murmured, a smile playing on his lips.

"Yes, baby," she confessed, her voice thick with raw yearning, "I love it when you're inside me. You do it so well for me."

He gently flipped her over, revealing her backside, a perfect curve that nestled against him as he guided himself inside. "Don't move," he whispered, wanting to savor the stillness, open to letting their shared vibes dictate the pace, whether fast, slow, or a lingering hold.

He traced a slow line down her spine with his middle finger, gliding from the nape of her neck to the small of her back, pausing at the delicate dimple just above her waist. His thumb found her anus, pressing firmly, as he moved her, intensifying her climax and driving her past her inhibitions.

When they finally found their climax together, she gasped in surprise. "Was that your first time?" she asked, disbelief in her voice.

"Yes, love, it was," he confirmed.

"You practically fisted me," she chuckled, a hint of awe in her tone.

"Ha, yeah, I did that." Indigo, despite previous close calls, had remained a virgin to this act, waiting for the right woman.

Now, they lay entangled in post-coital pillow talk. She made him a solemn promise: she would always be right beside him, her need for his presence escalating into a healthy form of obsession—possessive, almost stalker-like, a quality Indigo found alluring.

Their initial lovemaking sparked a pregnancy scare, which, to their eventual disappointment, was unfounded. A faint sadness settled over them, but soon, business obligations called them apart.

Several months drifted by. Indigo and Tayla, each diligently building their empires, both separately and collaboratively, found themselves with little time for each other. Their connection endured through FaceTime calls, texts, and quick check-ins, but they both knew that when they finally reunited, the chemistry would ignite.

The depth of Tayla's disappointment from the pregnancy scare fueled a powerful, fiery determination within Indigo. He had a profound surprise for her.

When Tayla finally arrived home, she stepped into a room transformed by the warm glow of scented candles and an inviting circle of plush cushions. Indigo met her there; his voice was gentle. "I have a surprise for you," he whispered.

They sat, placing one hand over the other's heart and the other on each other's belly. Together, they spoke loving affirmations and asked questions that affirmed their desires, practicing circular breathing that allowed energy to flow from their pelvis to the very crown of their heads. They visualized their chakras, seeing them align and radiate with vibrant light. They committed to breathing into any emotion that arose, simply staying present with it, not trying to fix or change it, but fully embracing the feeling.

They settled facing each other, cross-legged, close enough to feel the warmth, but not quite touching. Their gaze met, silent and unwavering. No words were needed, just the soft rhythm of their synchronized breaths—inhaling, exhaling, holding eye contact. Thoughts would occasionally surface, but with gentle awareness, they'd return to the present moment.

Eventually, they leaned in, foreheads touching, hands clasped, and shared a single, heartfelt appreciation for each other from their day.

Indigo then turned to his curated music collection, letting soft, vibrational frequencies wash over the speakers. He cleansed the space with burning sage and incense, then dimmed the lights to a soft glow. He had Tayla lie down, and with deliberate intention, slow, graceful movements, he began to touch her, starting from her feet and moving upward. He used fragrant oils, focusing purely on sensation, connection, and the smooth flow of energy. A full-body massage followed, an exquisite journey of touch. Then, they switched, allowing him to receive the same profound experience.

Once they were seated again, he guided her onto his lap in the yab-yum position. They breathed in perfect synchronicity, creating a continuous energetic loop between them. Both visualized energies flowed from their heart centers, moving up and down each other's spines. As their hearts and bodies fully merged, they felt the powerful surge of their kundalini energy rising. He was initiating her into the ancient practice of tantra—a journey of heightened energy awareness, expanded consciousness, and deep emotional integration. Their sacred union blossomed, communication deepened beyond words, and their connection intensified. This sacred practice prolonged their pleasure, offered an expansive orgasmic experience, and while Indigo practiced non-ejaculatory orgasm, he recognized her desire for more. He met her gaze with a knowing look, and she returned it with a soft, understanding smile.

He descended with her into their clandestine sanctuary, a secret room that defied its mundane basement appearance, revealing itself as a lavish expanse dedicated to their desires. An arsenal of pleasure awaited them: an array of massagers, glinting handcuffs, whips, intricate ropes, and countless other tools of ecstasy. Indigo bound her to the bed with handcuffs, then lifted her legs to brush her head, his hands gently encircling her neck as he embarked on his intimate journey. He was the cowboy, she was his wild horse, her remarkable flexibility a silent consent. After their passionate ride, he released her with a whispered command to retrieve the dog collar. Both reveled in their shared "freakishness," and she found immense pleasure in the controlled sensation of choking. He fastened the collar, drawing her hair back to expose her throat.

Her body gleamed with sweat, slick with intensity, unable to contain the torrent of sensations. The sheets beneath them were drenched from her fervent release, a musky scent rising from the saturated fabric. Indigo, however, was unfazed; that final "juice" was the ultimate essence.

He turned her to face the bed; her hands braced against her knees. With a practiced hand, Indigo selected the Shibari rope, weaving it into an intricate pattern that held her captive, a sensual education in the art of restraint. It was hard, rough, and exquisitely spicy. Their culmination was a shared symphony, a perfect, harmonious release. Days later, a faint blush of hope confirmed their deepest wish: she was pregnant. The story of their children will unfold in due course.

For their anniversary, Indigo meticulously planned a surprise for Tayla, a special getaway that would remind them of their deep connection. He booked a secluded hotel and chartered their private jet to an international destination. Onboard the plane, he discreetly asked the crew to remain forward, ensuring he and Tayla had complete privacy in the rear cabin. Once they were truly alone, he began, tracing his fingers slowly and deliberately along the inside of her wrist. "You always look at me like that," she whispered, her voice husky.

"Like what?" he murmured back.

"Like you already know what's going to happen next." A wicked grin spread across her face as he tugged her gently towards the wall.

He brushed a strand of hair from her shoulder, then leaned in, his warm breath caressing her neck. "Maybe I do," he whispered, his pulse quickening as he took his time, kissing just below her ear.

He was the conductor, every movement a calculated part of their foreplay symphony. He was the pilot; she was his flight attendant. She gasped softly as he pressed her gently against the wall, his hands expertly exploring the soft curve of her waist and hips. His mouth found hers, hungry but controlled, drawing a low, sweet moan from her lips. "Tell me to stop," he whispered against her skin, a challenge.

She didn't. Instead, her hands threaded into his shirt, pulling him closer, blurring the space between tantalizing anticipation and sweet surrender with every shared breath. The air crackled with such intense steam that the plane seemed to tremble, almost tipping backward.

He slipped his thumb into her mouth. "Be ready," he commanded, then stepped away, leaving her biting her lip in delicious anticipation.

As the jet touched down, they were in a new, exotic locale, but their world had shrunk to only one other. He blindfolded her, enhancing her touch and the sounds around her, guiding her to their opulent hotel suite. Every detail inside their luxury haven was designed for pure indulgence: soft mood lighting, plush fabrics, the comforting crackle of a fireplace, and an aromatherapy diffuser filling the air with intoxicating scents, but the surprises continued. He led her into the bathroom, where a decadent bath, overflowing with rose petals and essential oils, awaited. As Indigo's hands roamed every curve and muscle, a palpable desire lingered, every touch, every shared breath, every tremor building the exquisite pleasure.

He told her to immerse herself in the bath, promising her a favorite meal. "After you eat," he purred, "I'm going into your G-spot."

While the aroma of cooking food filled the suite, he scattered more rose petals on the bed and fed her grapes as she relaxed in the tub. She was so aroused, she almost pulled him into the water. Instead, he dimmed the lights further and turned on the shower, wanting to commit every one of her moans to memory. He shed his clothes and then, with a confident grace, tied her to the pole. She adored his commanding presence. Though Indigo looked human, he was an earth angel in disguise, a bringer of pure, unadulterated pleasure. With no distractions, he began to caress her breasts and booty.

A sudden realization struck him—the food! He quickly left to turn off the stove. She slipped on a plush robe and followed him into the kitchen. As they ate, a shared smile blossomed; they truly were each other's wildest fantasies come true. She slowly, gently guided him towards the refrigerator, a silent invitation that he accepted by lifting her onto the kitchen counter. They made love there for a long, passionate while, then she slid down, shedding her robe. "Devour me slowly," she whispered, her voice a low, seductive plea.

Indigo removed his robe and then lifted Tayla onto a nearby table. In and out they went, a rhythmic dance.

"You're going to break the table," she breathed, a soft, seduced warning.

Unfazed, he carried her to the balcony, and they continued their passionate embrace beneath the open sky.

Once their desires were sated, they moved back inside, and she saw the rose petals he'd scattered on the bed. They made love once more, softly, warmly, with slow, lingering strokes, caressing every inch of each other. Their pillow talk melted into midnight confessions. They had truly found their other half, the brightest star in their constellation, and, once again, she was pregnant.

After a long day of business meetings and store openings, their schedules had kept them physically apart, but their phones had hummed with constant connection. Tayla had sent him a series of intriguing photos, a playful echo of their passion last night.

Indigo's text back was immediate, raw with desire: "I wanna see your skin, arch your back, and bend your spine. I'm coming to pick you up after nine. I love the way you gripped that mattress."

Her reply, accompanied by a smirking emoji, came instantly: "We need a new couch because we broke that other one."

He arrived to pick her up, but her driver had already taken one of their cars to the shop. They began their journey home in their electric vehicle, winding through the serene roads of Nepal, heading back to their mountaintop sanctuary. The road was blessedly free of traffic. She lifted her legs to settle more comfortably in her seat, then leaned close to Indigo's ear. "Come eat me," she breathed, her voice a low command.

She craved him every day, in every conceivable position and location, but Indigo, ever the planner, tried to adhere to a schedule, even once posting a bedtime on the fridge. "I'm driving," he replied, a hint of amusement in his voice.

"Speak less," she countered, a wicked glint in her eye.

"I love the way you moan. The kids are with their nanny. Forget the small talk, let's do it now." He engaged the automatic drive.

She leaned closer, her whisper a seductive plea: "Freak me into forever."

His hand found its way beneath her panties. He devoured her, holding her down, his mouth and tongue eliciting shivers. Her nipples were exquisitely sensitive, almost bursting, and she was close to a cream pie while he was on the verge of release, no condom in sight. Her moans escalated, growing louder, and he silenced her by pressing his thumb to her mouth.

She pulled it away, then began to suck him like a lollipop. She possessed an impressive deep throat, and even without a hair tie, she knew exactly how to pleasure him. Her skill was undeniable, and he reveled in it. She made sure to spit on him, further fueling his desire, both keenly aware of their shared quirks and kinks. She stared into his eyes, her gaze raw with begging, wanting more.

He began a rhythmic hitting and smacking, as she bounced on him, leaving faint marks, bringing her to climax faster than ever before. They both reached full orgasm, without him even making it inside. They were each other's deepest, most erotic fantasy. In that powerful moment, they knew that even through the pregnancies, their children were truly gifted. They shared a laugh, a shared understanding of their wild connection, then headed inside to celebrate their unconventional love before meditating and finally settling into bed.

Returning from a successful tour they had meticulously orchestrated, the rest of their team celebrated in the forward cabin while Indigo and Tayla sought respite and sleep in the back. Indigo, however, wasn't as tired as she was.

As Tayla succumbed to slumber, he began to finger her, eliciting multiple squirts. Fluids gushed from her like a flood. She didn't quite know how to process the overwhelming release, but she recognized it as Indigo's doing; she knew his touch, and his hands were undeniably large.

She awoke from her deep sleep to find his penis already at her face. She turned instinctively, immediately taking him into her mouth. He pulled her closer, his desire to be fully inside her an almost tangible force. They were undeniably hooked on each other. "You're pinching my nipples too hard," she complained playfully, "You sucked on them too roughly."

"I'm just trying to get you lit," he countered, a playful glint in his eye.

"When we get inside," she purred, her voice laced with anticipation, "take control, blow my mind, take my breath away, and take me to outer space. Just for me, babe."

Once they arrived at their secluded beach house, she darted into the bedroom, instructing him to wait. She grabbed her phone, opening her social media to poll her fans on the perfect lingerie choice.

While her followers deliberated, Indigo, ever thoughtful, prepared a smoothie for her, secretly adding a potent honey pack.

She emerged in a sheer fishnet lingerie outfit, a vision that almost made him burst into song.

Indigo settled back, gazing at her as he handed her the smoothie. The sight of her, even attempting to hide it, made him undeniably hard. He knew that with any outfit she wore, he'd inevitably rip it off, his hands going straight for her chest. That's precisely what he did, placing an immediate order for a replacement as Tayla slowly sipped her smoothie.

The potent drink only amplified her arousal. Indigo gathered a few more items, and they moved into the luxurious bathroom. A palpable tension, a simmering fire, began to boil beneath their skin, igniting the passion and warmth between them. With a mint on his tongue and an ice cube in his mouth, Indigo began to slowly rub and lick around her belly button, a deliberate dance of cold that sparked intense arousal. He descended further, his tongue meticulously exploring her labia majora, labia minora, clitoris, urethral, and vaginal openings. The startling contrast of the ice and the warmth of his breath made her scream and shout as he held her close. Her screams were so intense, they sounded like pure agony. He *was* "killing" her vagina, taking her off-grid with a pleasure so intense it felt like she was in a hospital, and her insurance wouldn't cover the cost. They both relished in the role-playing, a thrilling layer to their intimacy.

He lit a scattering of candles, casting a soft, flickering glow, and bathed the room in red mood lighting. Then, with deliberate care, he dripped a warm candle wax onto her naked skin, a slight, exhilarating burn sensation rushing throughout her body. As her initial moans softened into a soothing rhythm, he focused his fingers on her clitoral glands, clitoral shaft, corpora cavernosa, clitoral bulbs, and Bartholin's glands. Every precise movement made her feel more comfortable, more alive in her skin. As her body continued to release fluids, he persisted, murmuring reassurances of her beauty. His words resonated deeply, and the honey pack coursed through her veins, reaching its highest peak. She desired to ascend to the next level of ecstasy, and he met her gaze with a knowing look. They had already practiced over a thousand sex positions that day, a testament to their boundless energy. He was deep inside her G-spot, AFE zone, guts, and paraurethral glands, exploring every intimate recess. They took frequent, languid breaks between their passionate encounters, filled with kissing, touching, and pleasuring all their senses. Once their desires were fully sated, they painted each other's naked bodies, then washed up, and spent the remainder of the night simply cuddling, utterly content.

Indigo and Tayla were unapologetically bold; romance was the foundation of their bond, but their connection extended far beyond the physical. Their intimacy was wild, untamed, and sacred, a raw energy that reflected the depth of their commitment to building something eternal. Their love was poetic, potent, and real—woven with layers of passion, purpose, and soul. It wasn't just a relationship; it was a story, fully lived and unforgettable.

During this powerful chapter of their lives, both Indigo and Tayla ascended to billionaire status, individually and as a unit. Surrounded by a loyal, like-minded team who believed in their vision, they knew it was time. The legacy they had always dreamed of now had space to grow beyond business and into the bloodline.

Together, they brought five beautiful children into the world—each a reflection of their love, each with a name that carried divine meaning and intention:

- Angel Indigo Bass and Anakin Emerald Bass — twin brothers, born with matching strength and mirrored souls.
- Indi Royalty Bass — their first daughter, the eldest, regal, and radiant.
- Halo Aura Bass — their youngest son, peaceful and luminous, a calm force of light.
- Harmony Goddess Bass — the youngest daughter, born in divine alignment, the very embodiment of balance and grace.

Their children were not just heirs to an empire, but living extensions of a vision Indigo and Tayla had always held: a family built on love, freedom, legacy, and truth.

Angel Indigo Bass

Born on October 14th, Angel Indigo Bass arrived just minutes before his twin brother, Anakin. Now twenty-six, Angel has worn the title of "firstborn" like a subtle crown—not boastful, but undeniable. His life, from the very beginning, was anything but ordinary. Raised in a private island paradise, surrounded by global art, elite tutors, immersive technology, and rich culture, Angel was exposed to excellence in every form, but while Anakin found comfort in structure, Angel thrived in motion.

Even as a child, Angel lived in rhythm. At four, he was mimicking dancers, scaling palm trees, racing along the shoreline, and dunking on imaginary defenders. Meditation sessions introduced by their father, Indigo, revealed the twins' differences: Anakin sat still, serene; Angel opened his eyes and heard music in the waves, the wind, the whisper of leaves.

His first encounter with basketball was serendipitous—during a family trip to Barcelona, he stumbled upon a street performance that evolved into a pickup game. It wasn't the competition that captivated him; it was the movement. The flow. The art. Back home, he demanded a full court be built. By nine, he was training with seasoned Euro League veterans. By twelve, he had turned the game into performance art, dazzling with no-look passes and impossible layups. Angel didn't just *play*—he *performed*.

His relationship with Anakin remained complicated. They loved each other fiercely but lived in parallel worlds. Anakin was the "golden son" in their father's mythology—disciplined, focused, efficient. Angel, by contrast, was unpredictable. Coaches admired his talent but feared his volatility. Tayla, their mother, saw him. She nurtured his creativity and made space for his emotional truth. While Indigo expected relentlessness, Tayla allowed exploration.

Angel spent as much time in dance studios and design workshops as he did on the court. He studied visual arts, explored filmmaking, and wrote poetry under a pseudonym. His brilliance was undeniable—but so was his refusal to be boxed in.

By his teenage years, he was known as "the wild twin." One night, he'd score forty points; the next, he'd skip practice to shoot a short film or disappear into a creative haze. A viral highlight reel and an even more viral mixtape saved his college career after a near-dismissal for clashing with a coach. His charisma couldn't be ignored. Neither could his talent.

Angel entered the pro league after just one year of college—a one-and-done phenomenon. While Anakin entered with quiet focus, Angel arrived like a storm. He signed major endorsement deals before ever stepping on a professional court. Critics questioned his commitment. Angel didn't argue. He just played, and when he played, he was transcendent—an aerialist, a poet in motion. His alley-oops were balletic, his crossovers brutal. He became a fan favorite, a walking highlight, a fashion icon, and a media mystery.

Off the court, Angel lived loudly. He dated pop stars, collaborated with designers, and founded a charity for youth art education, but he also drew criticism—cryptic statements, public protests, and one infamous moment when he walked off the court mid-game in defiance of team ownership.

Angel is everything Anakin is not—emotive, theatrical, and unapologetic. While Anakin guards his private world, Angel broadcasts his. He paints, vlogs, and writes spoken word. Fame doesn't burden him; it fascinates him. Still, beneath the showmanship is a vulnerable soul. The label of "wild twin" weighs on him. Often, he embraces the image just to control the narrative, but deep down, he fears being seen as ornamental rather than essential.

Now, for the first time in his career, Angel stands at a crossroads. A series of injuries, a trade to a struggling team, and whispers that he's "washed" force him to confront himself. Should he reinvent his game— or walk away to pursue his art full-time? Rumors swirl. Fans speculate. A documentary crew begins filming his life, unintentionally unearthing long-buried family secrets. Amid this, Angel falls in love with someone who sees through the glitter and challenges him to heal, to grow, to stay. Their connection forces him to confront the emotional impulsiveness he once mistook for freedom.

A family crisis eventually pulls him and Anakin back into each other's orbit. Old tensions resurfaced, resentment, rivalry, and unspoken love. For Angel, it's more than reconciliation—it's a chance to redefine himself beyond the twin dynamic, beyond fame, beyond even basketball.

Angel Indigo Bass was born to shine—not in straight lines, but in constellations. A comet, not a compass. While Anakin bears the burden of destiny, Angel floats just beyond its pull, daring gravity to catch him. Maybe, just maybe, that's his true gift: he lives, plays, and loves with a freedom most only dreams of.

Anakin Emerald Bass

Born on October 14th, under the warm glow of a tropical sunrise, Anakin Emerald Bass entered the world just minutes after his twin brother, Angel. Now twenty-six, Anakin stands as one of the most celebrated quarterbacks of his generation—a League MVP, a global sports icon, and a symbol of discipline forged in luxury and tested by adversity.

He was raised in a place untouched by ordinary geography. The Bass family's private island—stateless, solar-powered, and saturated in creativity—was a haven for innovation and introspection. Sculpted into cliffs were athletic arenas and art pavilions; solar fields stretched beside Zen gardens. Indigo and Tayla Bass, visionaries in both influence and ideology, raised their children as modern royalty, with tutors, languages, meditation, and rigorous spiritual practice embedded in their daily life.

Indigo named his sons with cosmic precision. *Anakin*—after a mythic figure, destined for greatness and inner conflict. *Angel*—a name symbolizing light, balance, and grace. Where Angel danced through life, Anakin cut through it. His first love wasn't found in curated lessons, but in grainy satellite broadcasts of American football streamed into the island's observatory. At just eight, Anakin became captivated by the quarterback—not just the athleticism, but the control, the strategy, the silent command of the field. It was warfare in choreography. It was beautiful.

While Angel floated, Anakin anchored. Where Angel improvised, Anakin calculated. Indigo believed in tempering privilege with struggle, so each year, the twins were sent to "the other world"—mainland schools, public service camps, even low-income boarding programs. These weren't punishments; they were rituals. Indigo believed greatness was earned through fire, not comfort, and Anakin emerged sharpened by that belief.

By his teens, Anakin had become a paradox: heir to a sprawling empire but forged like a soldier. He excelled at elite prep schools, mastering not just football but languages, poetry, and ancient philosophy. His father demanded intellectual expansion; his mother insisted on emotional intelligence. Anakin absorbed both but translated them into performance. He trained like he had nothing. Every rep, every sprint, every page of strategy consumed as if his life depended on it.

He received over fifty scholarship offers by age seventeen, ultimately choosing a top-tier university, not for football, but for its philosophy department, a move that confused recruiters and intrigued the press. He quickly rose to become the soul of the team: stoic, tactical, unshakable. They called him *The Island General*. By junior year, he led them to an undefeated season and won MVP in the entire college football league. A year later, he was the top pick in the draft.

From the start of his pro career, the spotlight was ruthless. Whispers of nepotism followed him. Commentators called him a product of privilege, but in his rookie year, he obliterated expectations—breaking records, leading a failing franchise to the playoffs, and winning Rookie of the Year. Two years later, he was the MVP.

Anakin's style was pure precision—reads like prophecy, passes like poetry. Teammates revered him. Opponents feared him. He demanded accountability, and his presence commanded silence. Yet even in victory, a shadow lingered: the burden of being *perfect*. Angel embraced chaos, but Anakin swallowed it. Their paths diverged. Angel chased cameras and causes. Anakin chased legacy. For a time, they barely spoke.

Beneath Anakin's steely composure lies a deeper struggle, the lifelong tension between control and surrender. He journals obsessively. Studies warfare, strategy, and philosophy. Yet romance eludes him. Vulnerability frightens him. The media calls him a cold genius. In truth, he yearns for something more real, unscripted. His bond with Indigo is strained. His father sees him as a continuation of himself, a living ideology. Tayla sees the weight behind his eyes and worries he's turning into a machine.

Sometimes Anakin wonders if he was *designed*, not born. If the path he walks was chosen before he could choose. After each season, he returns to the island—not to celebrate, but to walk alone along cliffside trails, hoping to find the version of himself not wearing a jersey, not carrying an empire, not being a myth.

After winning MVP, Anakin reaches a threshold. What more is there to prove? Angel's new memoir exposes private moments of their childhood—stories Anakin fought to forget. A once-in-a-lifetime offer arrives: to lead the expansion of professional football internationally. It's legacy-making, but it would mean abandoning his current team, betraying his code, and stepping further into the machine.

Then someone enters his life—an intellectual equal, someone who challenges him emotionally and philosophically. With them, Anakin begins to unravel. For the first time, he explores who he is when he isn't winning. When he isn't perfect.

A crisis within the Bass family forces Angel and Anakin back into close orbit. Secrets, resentments, and years of unspoken love resurface. Meanwhile, Indigo—once a pillar of infinite confidence—stands at a crossroads of his own. Now, Anakin must face the man who shaped him and decide: will he inherit the throne, or destroy it to build something new?

Indi Royalty Bass

Born on July 7th, Indi Royalty Bass is 24 years old, but her presence carries the weight of an entire cultural movement. An award-winning singer, electrifying dancer, high-fashion muse, and digital content queen, Indi is a generational force. Her viral performances and genre-defying music aren't just popular, they're prophetic. Where others chase trends, Indi *is* the trend. Magnetic, raw, and unapologetically herself, she's not just in the spotlight; she *is* the spotlight.

From the moment she could walk, Indi danced. From the moment she could speak, she sang. Her name wasn't a label—it was a declaration. *Indi*, for her independent fire. *Royalty*, because Tayla Bass believed her daughter wouldn't just inherit greatness, she'd embody it. While Anakin and Angel were shaped by discipline, Indi was guided by expression. The family's island became her private stage: jungle canopies were her lighting rigs, the ocean was her orchestra, and seashells doubled as microphones. By age five, the household staff called her *La Reina*—The Queen.

Indigo, always seeking to mold through philosophy and precision, tried to funnel her fire into form, but Indi couldn't be boxed. Tayla, sensing a mirror of her wild spirit, let her run. She hired a retired opera singer as Indi's first coach, a woman who taught her that the voice is more than pitch—it's presence. *"Give the world the storm, baby,"* Tayla would say. *"Not just the melody."*

At 13, Indi went viral—an impromptu song-and-dance video uploaded to social media became a global sensation. Her smoky vocals, whip-smart choreography, and fearless energy shook the internet. Record labels swarmed. Indigo wanted caution. Tayla demanded artistic control. Indi wanted freedom. She got it.

By the time she was sixteen, she had signed a record deal—on her terms. Her debut EP fused afrobeats, indie soul, and electronic R&B, pulling comparisons to other mainstream artists. Critics were stunned. She wasn't a star in the making—she was already *there*. By eighteen, she performed at the fashion industry's biggest night. At 19, she won an award at the music industry's biggest night. By twenty-one, she was headlining a sold-out global tour and launching viral dance trends that reshaped pop culture.

With visibility came distortion. She became a symbol, dissected by tabloids and social media. Constantly framed as the "wild" Bass sibling. Compared to her brothers. Reduced to headlines. Indi hated it. She wasn't a footnote in someone else's legacy. She wasn't *the wild one.* She was the *sun flare.*

Indi is the embodiment of emotional fluency. She's the type to cry during a performance, call out a troll mid-livestream, then hit a vocal run so pure it silences the internet. Her life is art. Her art is the truth, and her truth is messy, radiant, and alive.

She's known for:

- Wearing couture to breakfast.
- Speaking in poetic, often cryptic captions.
- She shifts accents depending on her mood and memories.
- Empowering young women through unfiltered honesty and body-positive messages.

The curated chaos comes at a cost. Sometimes, even she doesn't know where *Indi the brand* ends and *Indi the person* begins.

Her relationship with her parents is as layered as her lyrics. Tayla is her rock, her confidante, her creative twin. Indigo? It's complicated. He admires her brilliance, but her fire terrifies him. She resents his need for control but craves his validation more than she'll admit.

With her brothers, the bonds are as distinct as they are powerful:

- Anakin is her protector—stoic, grounded. He doesn't understand her world, but he respects it. Their love is quiet, strong, a slow-burning connection.
- Angel is her chaos twin. They speak in shorthand, in energy. They dye each other's hair on livestreams, collaborate on viral dances, and FaceTime daily just to feel understood.

At times, Indi feels like the family's emotional center. She loves deeply but resents being the one who *holds it all*. She dreams of releasing a stripped-back acoustic album—raw vocals, minimal production, pure soul. Her label pushes back. "Stay glossy. Stay viral," they say. Indi wants the truth. Not Polish.

After a breakdown on tour—whether from exhaustion, panic, or a media storm—Indi retreats to the family island for the first time in years. Away from the screens. Away from noise. There, she reconnects with her roots and with someone who lives entirely off-grid. No social media. No fame. Just silence—and truth. For the first time, she questions what she truly wants: not *just* to be seen, but to be *known*.

She begins mentoring a young artist who reminds her of herself: bright, brave, but on the edge of being devoured by the industry. Through this mirror, Indi confronts the shadows she's buried: a secret from childhood, pressure she masked with glitter, pain hidden behind perfect lighting.

In a bold move, Indi releases a documentary and album that breaks from her brand—vulnerable, confessional, rebellious. It sparks a public rift, not just with fans, but within Earthfall itself, where whispers of revolution grow louder. As Earthfall teeters on collapse, a familiar voice returns, and Indi realizes her story may be tied to something even larger than fame.

Indi Royalty Bass doesn't just want to be famous—she wants to be *felt*. To move culture, not just through sound, but through soul. She dances, yes—but she also dares, and sometimes, late at night, she wonders: if no one were watching... would she still dance?

Halo Aura Bass

Born March 3rd, Halo Aura Bass is 22 years old—a professional gamer, top-tier streamer, esports competitor, and founder of a meditative gaming lifestyle brand. With elite gameplay, poetic commentary, and an almost otherworldly digital presence, he's cultivated a cult-level fanbase known simply as The Aura.

He's the quietest of the Bass children—and, perhaps, the most powerful. From the beginning, Halo wasn't drawn to the stage or the spotlight. While his siblings sang, danced, and dominated fields and courts, Halo observed. He watched patterns. Systems. Energies. To Halo, the world was a simulation—something to be understood before it was changed.

Growing up on the family's high-tech island, Halo was rarely outside unless it served his curiosity. By age six, he was dismantling computers, jailbreaking game consoles, and building emulators just to understand how they worked. At ten, he constructed his first PC from scratch. At eleven, he was quietly entering global tournaments under a secret alias. By fourteen, he'd become a digital legend in disguise.

By his early teens, Halo had:

- Won major gaming tournaments under pseudonyms
- Built a viral following with calm, meditative commentary and mind-bending plays
- Launched a gaming channel focused on "high-IQ gameplay + low-ego energy"
- Sparked rumors of being the anonymous, masked phenom Aura H

He never told his family, not out of secrecy, but sovereignty. He wanted to earn it without the weight of legacy. When Indigo finally discovered his son's hidden success, he was stunned.

"Your sibling's command stages," Indigo said. "You command shadows."

To Halo, that was the point. Where others reached for influence, Halo radiated *resonance*. His streams felt more like guided meditations than broadcasts. Lo-fi beats played softly behind his voice. He wore minimalist tech wear. His face was rarely seen—just his hands, glowing keyboards, and his voice: precise, grounded, deeply human.

His philosophy became as iconic as his skill:

- *"Every game is a mirror."*
- *"You don't win by reacting. You win by understanding."*
- *"Tilt is a teacher."*

His fanbase, The Aura, didn't just follow him; they *studied* him. He was a monk in a motherboard world. A digital stage in an age of noise.

Where his siblings were fire and thunder, Halo was *light*. Not lesser— just *quieter*. Indigo admired his intellect but struggled to map his son's digital temple. Tayla understood him better; she gave him his first microphone, his first quiet confidence.

His sibling dynamics operate on their specific frequency:

- Anakin didn't take Halo seriously—until he saw him stream. Now, he sends feedback disguised as praise. They clash often, especially when Anakin pressures him to be more "present." Halo once replied, *"I am present. You're just looking in the wrong dimension."*
- Angel thinks Halo is hilarious. They're meme-lords together, late-night chat chaos partners. Halo's the only one who can talk Angel down from emotional spirals.

- Indi and Halo are soul-mirrors. They stay up late discussing life, death, purpose, and power—FaceTime philosophers navigating stardom and identity.

Halo is neurodivergent—he manages ADHD through hyper-focused routines, tech-assisted meditation, and gaming-as-therapy frameworks he designed himself. He's also become the unspoken therapist of the family, offering insights that cut deeper than advice. Less "you should," more *"what are you not saying?"*

At 18, Halo launched a hybrid gaming and lifestyle brand built around harmony, not hype. Tech wear, sleek peripherals, and mental health resources for gamers. Less flex. More flow. He also started a nonprofit to teach neurodivergent youth how to game, code, and create content with mindfulness. It's not just about winning, it's about *meaning*.

Fame, even digital fame, comes with its shadows. When Halo is invited into a powerful esports league, he uncovers corruption behind the scenes. He wrestles with the ethics: expose the truth and risk exile? Or play along and "level up" into influence?

Worse, he begins to feel hollow. Constant content, constant performance—even in silence, the algorithm demands presence. One day, without warning, he vanishes from all platforms. The internet panics. *Where is Aura H?* #FindHalo trends globally.

In that stillness, he reconnects with himself and someone else: a fellow neurodivergent gamer who doesn't care about views or followers. Just *presence*. For the first time, Halo explores not just connection, but *romance*. Not filtered. Not optimized. Just real.

Anakin wants Halo to come home, to engage with the family's crumbling empire. Halo sees through it. He doesn't want thrones. He wants the *truth*. He's never been interested in ruling Earthfall—only in helping people navigate it.

Halo considers showing his full face on camera—for the first time—to raise money for a mental health initiative, but the decision gnaws at him. Does authenticity require visibility? Or has he already been *seen* in ways that matter most?

He doesn't lead with charisma. He leads with *clarity*. He's not trying to be the best in the world. He's trying to be the best *for* it. His power isn't in the pixels or the views. It's in the resonance. The ripple. The quiet that shifts the whole frequency.

Harmony Goddess Bass

Born December 31st, Harmony Goddess Bass is 21 years old—a real estate mogul, strategic investor, and the quiet force preparing to take over the family empire. She's known for her sharp intellect, magnetic calm, and ability to turn chaos into clarity. Her nickname? The Quiet Storm.

She wasn't just the last child born to Indigo and Tayla Bass—she was the *reset*. "She's the bridge," Tayla once said. "Between soul and strategy. Between legacy and evolution." Born on the final day of the millennium's final year, Indigo always believed Harmony's timing was divine. She was his symbol of the future. A daughter not only born into wealth and brilliance but born to *organize* it.

From the time she could walk, Harmony was building systems. Drawing floor plans in the sand. Reorganizing the furniture in their jungle estate. Selling beach tents to family guests with hand-written contracts and legal jargon she'd invented herself.

Where the others ran wild, Harmony observed. Where they performed, she planned. Where they dreamed, she *designed*.

Indigo, sensing something rare, mentored her early—earlier than any of the others. While her siblings were sent out to "find themselves," Harmony was trained in global economics, real estate law, infrastructure politics, and influence architecture.

She had her first trust by age 10. Her first rental portfolio by fifteen. Her first commercial property was flipped at 17.

Harmony didn't coast on her name. She earned every stripe. She graduated top of her class with dual degrees in real estate and behavioral economics, then worked *under an alias* for two years inside the world's most elite development firms. Not because she needed to—but because she *refused* to lead without learning.

At 20, she launched her firm—a sustainable, spiritually-minded, luxury real estate brand rooted in eco-technology and cultural preservation. Within a year, she graced Forbes' 30 Under 30, but her goals reach far beyond acclaim. Harmony doesn't just want to own buildings. She wants to build the future.

Harmony is poised. Still. Grounded in a way that unnerves people by noise. She doesn't fight for the room—*the room shifts for her.*

She is:

- Flawlessly organized, without being cold
- Elegantly minimalist, always in power pieces or quiet statement jewelry
- Spiritually anchored, practicing ancestral rituals from Tayla—crystals, incense, offerings, and morning groundings
- Business fluent, but emotionally attuned. She listens first. Moves second. Always with a purpose.

When family meetings devolve into drama, Harmony doesn't yell. She raises an eyebrow. Meetings stop.

Her siblings adore her—even when she annoys them with calendar invites, contract rewrites, or polite-but-deadly critiques. She protects them, not with noise, but with *infrastructure.* She's the firewall, the strategist, the one who reads the fine print so no one else has to.

- Anakin respects her most. He trusts her judgment above all, even above agents or advisors. When he makes big moves, she's the first call.
- Angel teases her for being the "CEO of feelings," but secretly defers to her. She once negotiated him out of a multi-million-dollar scandal—quietly, cleanly.
- Indi sees Harmony as her grounding wire. They share midnight heart-to-hearts where the artist meets the architect. They don't always agree, but they *see* each other.
- Halo trusts her with his empire. She's one of the only people allowed to negotiate on his behalf. They share a language few understand— order and vision.

Her relationship with Indigo is layered. He sees her as his successor. She honors that—*but not blindly*. She constantly challenges him to update his philosophies, embrace emotional intelligence, and make space for evolution. Tayla is her spiritual compass—the one who reminds her that power without heart is just pressure.

Harmony's vision is vast and deeply intentional. She's not chasing headlines. She's laying blueprints that will last generations. Her plans include:

- Expanding the Bass brand into education tech, wellness architecture, and global incubators for young creators
- Regenerating underserved communities without gentrification— elevating culture, not erasing it
- Building a global HQ that fuses luxury, sustainability, innovation, and ancestral honoring
- Protecting her siblings from exploitation and burnout—even when they resist her interference

Power isn't easy. A corporate competitor makes a play to dismantle the family business through backdoor deals. Harmony must step into full CEO mode—elegant, lethal, and undeniable.

At the same time, she falls in love—for the first time—with someone outside her world. Someone secretly connected to Earthfall's future. A romantic rival. A mirror. She begins to ask herself questions no one ever asks the strong ones: Can I lead and *feel*? Can I build and still *be*?

Her greatest struggle isn't money or power. It's vulnerability. She's spent years managing *everything*, but who manages her? When she falters, who holds *her*?

She's not the crown. She's the foundation. Not loud. Not loud *ever*, but when she speaks, the air changes. She's not just inheriting an empire. She's redefining it.

Harmony is the answer to a future that demands both structure and soul. She's legacy, reborn. A strategist with a heart. A CEO with incense. A goddess in a boardroom. Sometimes, the quietest ones carry the loudest futures.

Chapter Fifteen

THE NEW EARTH VS. THE NEW WORLD ORDER

As Indigo dispatched a team of workers to Earthfall to manage business affairs, communication with the Earthfall team abruptly ceased. No texts, no calls, no emails, just silence. Meanwhile, Indigo and his family remained secluded on his private island, unaware of the storm brewing. A total of 144,010 citizens lived on their private island, including Indigo's family and the appointed leaders, but not his team of workers.

Indi had never told her family the truth about what she'd done in Earthfall, the part she played in its unraveling. Tayla, growing suspicious, searched online and discovered the unthinkable: Indigo was no longer the Demiurge. Earthfall had turned against him, blaming him for its disintegration. They stripped him of his title and exiled him. A new Demiurge had risen in his place—democratically chosen, popular, and, in their eyes, the only one capable of steering Earthfall forward.

This new Demiurge swiftly reshaped the world. It began subtly—a slow burn. Society gradually weaned onto AI and robotics, first for convenience, then dependency, until the populace surrendered entirely. He understood what people craved: structure, certainty, control. He became more than a leader—he became a deity. Worshipped as God, creator, and savior, the Demiurge presented himself as humanity's only hope, but his vision for salvation was brutal. To fix the world, he believed it had to fall. Society needed to be dismantled, the planet purged, and most of humanity sacrificed at the altar of progress.

Indigo had once offered freedom. He gave people room to explore, to grow, to be, but his kindness was mistaken for weakness, and that tolerance was exploited. In response, Indigo became rigid. If someone didn't share his ideals, he turned away. He focused only on those who aligned with him, gradually alienating those who dared to question. Even his children began to feel his grip tighten.

He was still a loving father, husband, and leader, but the criticism gnawed at him. Control became his coping mechanism. Once inspired by his father, Brandon—who ruled with creativity, unity, and expansive consciousness—Indigo now found himself embodying Smooth, a figure of precision and control. He struggled to let go, to surrender to flow. Everything had to be planned, structured, and executed with flawlessness. Though he knew he wasn't perfect, he was still obsessed with perfection. Often, he wished Brandon were still around to guide him. The throne had been handed to him without warning, without preparation, without allies. He ruled alone, armed only with lessons learned from those who came before.

Despite Indigo's growing control, Earthfall had flourished under his leadership, for a time. It was a new era, a new paradigm, a rebirth of civilization, but it never reached its full potential. Then came the rift— public, raw, and irreversible. It was Indi who sparked it.

She accused Indigo of wanting to control everything—stripping people of their freedom, their voice, their authenticity. The statement ignited a wildfire of unrest. Earthfall began to collapse under the weight of economic turmoil, martial law, technological overreach, and social decay. Pandemics spread. Digital citizenship took hold. Implants transformed humans into hollow, robotic versions of themselves. People lost their inner voice. Currency went digital. Civilization eroded. The fall wasn't sudden. It was a slow, inevitable unraveling, set in motion the moment freedom was traded for order.

Some would argue that Indi was the catalyst for Earthfall's collapse. Her words, spoken in frustration or truth, sparked a chain reaction. She believed Indigo's desire to control his family would inevitably extend to controlling the world, but that wasn't his intention. Indigo wasn't trying to dominate—he was trying to protect. Especially his family.

He wanted the best for them, to guide their transition out of this physical world with grace and purpose. He knew Earthfall wasn't the end. There were higher dimensions, richer realities—experiences far beyond reincarnating into a broken system. That's why he urged his family to follow his path. His teachings weren't about control; they were about liberation.

When Tayla discovered the true fallout from Indi's revelation, she brought it to Indigo's attention. He didn't react in anger. Indi hadn't known better. She had made assumptions, and he understood. Besides, Indigo had long since detached from the opinions of the masses. He was a spiritual titan, a billionaire, and ranked among the most awakened souls. The noise of public perception didn't penetrate his inner world.

Indi, however, kept quiet. The weight of guilt settled in her chest. She began to believe she had caused the rift. Indigo, meanwhile, had become more emotionally vulnerable since losing his title as Demiurge. He'd been building a community with vision and intention, but when the tide turned, only a handful remained truly loyal. His sanctuary was now his private island, far from the chaos and control of Earthfall.

Still, something called him back. He didn't know how Earthfall would receive him—if they would see a savior returning, or an exile daring to reenter. Regardless, Indigo knew he had to witness the damage firsthand. He wanted to go alone.

Tayla disagreed. She believed their entire community should go, but Indigo was adamant—he had to face the new Demiurge by himself. He said his goodbyes, boarded his private jet, and flew toward the fallen world, alone.

As Indigo took flight, Tayla sprang into action. She called together the Chosen—leaders within their island sanctuary—and informed the community of Indigo's mission. Some chose to stay behind and maintain the island. Others, hearts stirred with loyalty and curiosity, chose to follow. No one knew how long they'd be gone.

Amid the planning, Tayla faced a quiet rebellion. Her children were insistent on joining the journey. She refused—it was too dangerous, but as Lior powered up the second jet, the kids found their way aboard, hiding until the final moments before departure. It wasn't until someone pointed it out that Tayla realized what they had done. They were already airborne. There was no time to turn back. With a heart heavy with worry but eyes fixed on the path ahead, Tayla let them stay. The journey back to Earthfall had begun—not just for Indigo, but for all of them.

When they landed, Indigo was already waiting, standing just outside the perimeter, eyes wide, stunned. The devastation before him was something he hadn't fully prepared for, no matter how strong his intuition or spiritual foresight.

His children, having been raised amidst wealth, power, and influence, were largely unfazed by the collapse of Earthfall. To them, it was familiar terrain, but Indigo still carried empathy in his bones—for the people, for the land, for the lost potential. Seeing Earthfall in such a low, dense vibrational state shook him. The air was thick; the energy was heavy. Then he turned.

Behind him stood his family, spiritual guides, and members of his private island community. They had followed him. "You should've listened!" he shouted, voice breaking under the pressure. "I needed you to stay behind!"

The others stared back in confusion. His soul family, his tribe—they didn't understand. Why was he so afraid? Why was he acting like they were fragile, like danger was inevitable?

370

What they didn't know—what Indigo had never told them—was the truth of his past. The real past. Not the version known from the show, not the fragments his friends believed they understood. No one knew the depth of the battles he'd fought outside this dimension. They didn't know about his true family, now gone. They didn't know the losses, the betrayals, the shadows that still followed him. They certainly didn't know about Smooth—or beings like him—who might return to finish what had once begun.

Tayla approached him quietly, calmly. She placed her hand on his chest and looked him in the eyes. "Breathe," she whispered. "Let go of the fear. Let go of the anxiety. You're not alone. I got you. We got you."

They had come prepared—spiritually, mentally, even physically. Weapons were packed just in case, but what Indigo needed most in that moment wasn't protection. It was an assurance, and Tayla gave it to him. Her words, her presence, they anchored him.

This kind of love was foreign to him. For so long, he'd been surrounded by low vibrations, parasitic energies, and relationships that drained more than they gave. Though he was a world-renowned motivational speaker, constantly followed by admirers snapping photos and seeking advice, he didn't always thrive in the spotlight. Crowds wore him down, and solitude became his sanctuary. That's why he often took solo trips, despite the countless offers to tag along. He had spent much of his life standing on his own, learning to be independent, and concealing parts of his true self, but this... this was different. This was love that focused only on him— steady, undivided, and real. A kind of love that didn't bend him out of shape but helped him stand upright. A love with tunnel vision. It poured into him like light, and for once, Indigo allowed it. He didn't chase it. He didn't try to earn it. He didn't need to do anything. Opportunity after opportunity came. He surrendered and let it flow into his heart because deep down, he knew it was already written. Part of his soul contract. Part of his destiny.

Together, they began the trek toward the center of Earthfall: Los Angeles. The divide was immediate. On one side, the streets teemed with soulless, robotic citizens—eyes vacant, movements stiff, like zombies wandering in a dream. Most businesses were shuttered. Healthy food was scarce. The city's heartbeat had faded to a slow, mechanical rhythm. On the other hand, major corporations were thriving. Clean, sleek robots assisted humans with daily tasks. To the uninformed, it looked like progress. To Indigo, it looked like mind control wrapped in convenience.

Yet, their buildings—headquarters from the previous regime—were still intact. As they drew closer, Indigo spotted one of his former workers stumbling outside. His posture was twisted, his skin pale, his eyes empty. A chip protruded from behind his ear. He'd been cloned. Programmed. Indoctrinated.

Then Indigo looked up and saw the looming message overhead: *"CHOOSE THE NEW WORLD OR BE LEFT BEHIND."* A billboard. A warning. A threat.

Indigo had dreamed of guiding the world into the Fifth Dimension— a New Earth of enlightenment, sovereignty, and peace, but this... this was something else entirely. This was the New World Order. It was the calm before the storm, and he could feel it coming, like the apocalyptic events from Season One, ready to repeat themselves.

Suddenly, the worker lunged toward him. Indigo, lost in thought, didn't react in time, but Tayla did. In one swift motion, she stepped forward and struck, killing the worker instantly.

Indigo glanced at her. Strong. Sharp. Fierce. She was everything he admired, and yes, he had always been drawn to powerful, foreign women— physically fit, mentally alert, spiritually aware, but Tayla... Tayla was more than desire. She was aligned. A mirror. A partner, and now, the war for Earthfall had officially begun.

The new world was unfolding—one built on death, order, power, censorship, and absolute control. Yet most people didn't notice. Or worse—they noticed and chose not to care. As long as the storm hadn't reached their doorstep, they stayed silent. Complacent. Blind.

Indigo had tried to warn them. He had tried to build something better, but the truth had become painfully clear: you can't trust a flawed species. Humanity had become brain-dead, brainwashed, and implanted. They were no longer thinking for themselves.

Suddenly, every phone buzzed with a synchronized alarm. A digital flyer appeared on screens and walls across the city: *THE NEW DEMIURGE SPEAKS – ONE NIGHT ONLY – STADIUM EVENT, LIVESTREAMED GLOBALLY.*

Harmony lit up. Her celebrity status had earned her VIP access, and she could barely contain her excitement. "This is *the* event of the new world," she said, practically bouncing.

No one thought much of it. Harmony had always been connected, always getting exclusive invites.

The group made their way to the stadium. It was overflowing—sold out in just a few hours. Even those who couldn't attend would be watching. The world wanted answers: What was the new order? What was coming next? Could the collapse be stopped?

Before the conference began, the Demiurge mingled with the crowd, signing autographs and taking photos with fans. Their identity had been carefully concealed until now, shrouded in digital mystique. No one had seen their true face.

Thanks to Harmony's VIP access, their group moved to the front of the line. As they approached, they saw the Demiurge conversing with the president of Earthfall and handing him a device.

As they reached the Demiurge, Harmony turned to the others and beamed, "Everyone, meet my boyfriend!"

The Demiurge looked up, locking eyes with Indigo. His voice was calm, but Indigo felt a shiver crawl up his spine. "Congratulations," Indigo said slowly. "Your voice sounds... familiar."

The Demiurge smiled. "How convenient, Indigo. Full circle—Los Angeles. Where it all started."

Indigo blinked. "What did you say?"

"Season One," the Demiurge replied smoothly. "It began in L.A., didn't it?"

Indigo nodded hesitantly, suddenly on edge. The familiarity, the references—he knew something wasn't right.

As he turned to walk away, he glanced back just in time to catch the Demiurge flashing a crooked smile.

Indigo stepped forward, trying to get another look, but the crowd surged between them. By the time he reached the spot, the Demiurge had vanished into thin air.

They took their seats. The Demiurge, now back on stage, knew exactly where they were sitting. The presentation began, outlining the structure and philosophy of the New World Order. Though only appointed a week ago, the Demiurge already had the world listening.

Then came the story. It was a story Indigo knew. The tale of Smooth's game. Panic twisted in Indigo's chest. He blinked repeatedly, his breathing shallow. He reached for water, but it didn't help. The voice, the energy, the message, it was all too familiar. Then the final blow. Projected behind the Demiurge in massive letters: SEASON TWO, EPISODE EIGHT

Followed by a wink—subtle, deliberate. Harmony thought it was directed at her. Indigo knew better.

That episode had never existed. The last one he remembered being part of was SEASON TWO, EPISODE SEVEN. The finale. The end. He had killed Smooth—or so he believed. What if that had only been one of many? A clone? A decoy?

He shot to his feet and stormed out of the stadium.

Inside the bathroom, he could only focus on the words echoing in his mind. Season Two. Episode Eight.

His hands trembled as he threw cold water on his face. He looked into the mirror and saw a vision of Smooth grinning back at him.

The bathroom door creaked open. Indigo spun, fists clenched. It was just a regular guy, taken aback. "Yo, what's your problem?"

Indigo exhaled, apologized, and turned back to the sink. He splashed more water onto his face, his vision now slightly blurred. Reaching for a paper towel, he noticed someone step beside him.

A voice whispered beside him. "Welcome back, Indigo. You can't save everyone." The man laughed—low and sinister—before walking away.

Indigo coughed violently. A faint burning scent filled the air.

He snapped his head up—no one was there. He bolted out of the bathroom, searching the crowd, but the arena was packed. People moved in every direction, and whoever had spoken had already disappeared into the current.

Indigo rubbed his eyes, still trying to shake the encounter in the bathroom. His head throbbed with unanswered questions. He needed a moment—something grounding. Food, maybe. Something normal.

He placed an order, stepping into the back area where the stadium's kitchen was buzzing with activity. The fryer hissed violently, bubbling over with oil. Someone had spilled something, and the floor was slick. An employee called Indigo over—half-joking, half-serious. "Come on, Indigo. You've done it all. Give us a hand."

Indigo stepped forward, only to slip slightly on the oil-slicked tile. Laughter echoed briefly as people turned to help, but while they were distracted, something else was happening, something far more sinister.

One of Indigo's old trolls, disguised among the crowd, slid a lighter and a match toward a nearby employee. Another figure, lurking in the shadows, drained the fryer's oil and switched on all the burners at once. At that same moment, deep in the basement of the stadium, a hidden bomb was quietly triggered. Then another, and another.

The fire from the bathroom Indigo had just left flared up, ignited by chemical vapors and faulty wiring. In another wing of the stadium, yet another blaze had begun, started by one of Indigo's known haters, now working as an employee.

Chaos erupted. People screamed. Fire alarms blared. One explosion set off a chain reaction. Panic swept through the stadium like a storm surge, and then came the livestream.

Across every platform, a narrative was being spun in real time: Indigo was the terrorist. Footage, doctored and curated, showed him near each explosion, each flame. They claimed *he* had planted the bombs. That *he* had orchestrated this event, and because the world knew he had once been the Demiurge—because they knew he had power—they believed it.

Inside, the stadium began to seal shut. Doors locked. Windows unbreakable. The building became a cage of smoke and fire. No one could escape.

Amidst the chaos, Indigo made it back to his family, including Tayla, the children, his soul tribe, and the private island crew. Just as he reached them, a harsh spotlight snapped onto him. A booming voice filled the arena. It was the Demiurge.

"Look at your savior," he announced, smug. On the screen behind him, videos looped showing Indigo's supposed involvement. "This is the man responsible for your suffering. For your deaths."

The crowd turned like a tide. They booed. Threw whatever they could. Some leapt from the stands, fists ready. The Demiurge stood on stage, grinning—and then vanished in a snap.

Indigo didn't hesitate. He grabbed his family, his tribe—everyone who had followed him—and activated his energy dash, quantum phase-walking through the chaos. If they were holding onto him, they moved with him, blinking through matter, reappearing just outside the sealed stadium.

He was panting, overwhelmed but grateful. His powers still worked, but something wasn't right. "I'm going back in," Indigo told them. "There are still people inside. I have to try."

He turned to return—but slammed into an invisible wall. A force field. Exactly like the one Smooth had once used.

Indigo tried again, slamming his fist into the barrier. Nothing. His powers failed in its presence. He couldn't phase through. Couldn't dash in. It was too late. Then it happened.

The entire stadium exploded behind him in a thunderous eruption of smoke and fire. Flames clawed at the sky. Screams were cut short. Every second was captured on the global livestream.

The footage was rewound, zoomed, and analyzed. Media commentators speculated wildly. Conspiracy channels surged. Social platforms caught fire. Everyone had seen Indigo use his powers. Everyone saw the explosion happen just after he tried to re-enter.

Some claimed he'd done it out of jealousy, furious that he was no longer the Demiurge. Others said he was unstable, unfit for leadership. A threat. A god-turned-menace.

Indigo watched it unfold in silence. The world—once his to guide—was now his enemy.

Panic spread beyond the stadium. News of Indigo's supposed attack reached surrounding districts, and angry mobs began to form. People armed with whatever they could find were flooding toward the exits, hunting for the man they believed responsible.

Indigo didn't hesitate. In the stadium parking lot, he spotted an old transport bus. With a flick of his hand, he activated his phase walk, pulling his family and tribe through the metal exterior and into the interior. The bus roared to life, and Indigo peeled out of the lot, racing toward the runway where their private jets had been left behind.

Inside the bus, the tension was unbearable.

Anakin stared at his father. "Who even *are* you?"

Angel, more curious than afraid, leaned forward. "Wait... does this mean *we* have superpowers too?"

Indi sat silent, weighed down by guilt. She glanced at Indigo but couldn't speak.

Halo broke the silence with a half-joking, half-serious question: "Is this a real-life video game or something?"

Harmony wasn't paying attention. She was lost in thought, daydreaming about her boyfriend, the Demiurge.

Tayla looked over, her voice steady but emotional. "Is there something you've been meaning to say?"

Amara crossed her arms. "Feels like you've been living a double life."

Lior's eyes narrowed. "Did you do those things?"

Andariel looked hurt. "You never told me about any of this."

The voices swirled. Indigo kept his eyes on the road, but the pressure was rising. His mind raced. He didn't have time to explain—not now. Outside, the crowds were closing in. People screamed and hurled debris at the bus. A bottle cracked against the window. Inside, the emotional chaos mirrored that outside.

Then Indigo's eyes widened. A train. It was barreling toward an intersection just ahead. Without time to think, Indigo hit the gas. The bus surged forward. He yanked the wheel hard, skidding across the pavement. Tires screeched. The metal frame groaned. The vehicle tipped. It hit the ground with a thunderous crash.

The world tilted sideways. Smoke rose from the engine. Sirens wailed in the distance. Fire licked at the undercarriage. Everyone groaned, dazed, bruised, but alive.

Through the smoke, Indigo's vision blurred—memories from another time bleeding into the present. Aleemic's story. Divine. Ancient war. The sacrifice. The failure. It was all returning in flashes.

There was no time to process it. The bus began to catch fire. "We need to move!" Indigo shouted.

They stumbled out of the wreckage. The jets weren't far now, but before they could take another step, everyone turned to him at once. "We're not going any further," Tayla said, planting her feet. "Not until you tell us the truth."

Indigo looked at his children, his soul family, his community. They deserved answers. He took a breath, and finally, he spoke.

He told them everything. The show. The other dimensions. Smooth. The fall of the original Earthfall. His past failures. His rise to power—and his loss of it. The way he tried to control the chaos... and how, in doing so, he may have become part of the problem.

Indi stepped forward. Her voice was shaky. "I... I think this is my fault. I told people... things. About you. I didn't know it would spiral like this."

There was no time for a full reckoning. The moment of vulnerability was brief because the world around them was collapsing. Fires in the distance. Explosions nearby. Drones swarming. The air was thick with fear.

Then, a voice rang out, clear and omnipresent. It was the Demiurge. Invisible, but everywhere. "They chose *me*, Indigo. I am their ruler. Their king. And they bow to *me*."

The world froze. What he didn't realize was that the livestream hadn't ended. Everything he just said—the arrogance, the god-complex, the truth—was still being broadcast to the world.

For the first time, people began to wonder: Maybe Indigo wasn't the villain. Maybe they'd been manipulated. Maybe this new Demiurge... was something far worse. Above them, a digital sign flickered to life in the sky. Bold, flashing letters read: SEASON TWO, EPISODE EIGHT. **Death Toll: 950,240**

The numbers pulsed red. Then a figure materialized from the shadows. The Demiurge. He stepped forward and smiled at Indigo, his expression calm, confident, and almost mocking. "Yes, Indigo," he said. "It is I. The AI voice. The one behind it all. You missed me?" Just like that, the truth had a face.

BOOK

05

Chapter Sixteen

THE CHOSEN ONES VS. DARK ENTITIES

The AI voice had returned, and with it, a new world was beginning. Indigo recognized the voice—it was familiar, but he had always believed it was tied to Smooth. When Smooth disappeared, Indigo assumed the voice was gone, too. For decades, there was no sign of it. No interference. Nothing but his voice had only been waiting, silently, strategically, for the perfect moment to strike. The ripple effects were already in motion.

The voice was never anonymous. It had a name: *Brandon LeMar Bass.*

Yes, *I was cloned and inserted into this story.* That voice belonged to my twin, my replica, my shadow. To avoid confusion, let's call him *BLB.*

Indigo didn't recognize his face, but he remembered that voice. It all began long before Season One ever aired. Brandon, Smooth, and BLB were inseparable in the early days. They tried to bring BLB into the spotlight, but he preferred the background. He was a poet. A writer. He didn't need the stage.

Then something happened while I slept. They put me into a coma. In secret, Smooth cloned me and unleashed the duplicate—BLB—into the Game. Smooth was more than an influence—he was a father figure to him. I didn't wake up until after the first book was complete, and when I finally did... they killed me.

Smooth warned BLB that my awakening would jeopardize everything.

BLB's presence has been building since 2022, starting with the book *How to Overcome Apocalyptic Events*. It wasn't just the book. It was everything. The music, the podcasts, the art—it was all BLB. *Chilling With Doubleb*? That was him. The music released under the name *Smooth Doubleb*? Him again. Smooth had already moved on, focused entirely on preparing for Season Two. Earthly matters were left in BLB's hands.

That's why the first book had inconsistencies. Why were the characters spiritually disconnected? Why did no one truly bond or share their real stories? Why did each character tell the same stories twice? BLB didn't write them to grow—he wrote them to fail. He set them up to lose the round. He rigged the Game.

BLB evolved. He began reading tarot, paused music in 2022, and layered cryptic messages throughout his work, even in the behind-the-scenes stadium photos. His *Afterlife Series* marked his rise beyond this world. In that worldview, real life begins after death. Next came *The Rebirth Trilogy*, where he claimed his new identity. Then came *My New Life*, fusing BLB and Brandon LeMar Bass into one. He symbolically confirmed the deaths of every previous version of himself—Smooth Doubleb, Brandon Bass, Brandon LeMar Bass—and even me.

Now, only BLB remains.

He operates under my name, but I don't exist anymore. Still, because he is my clone, he carries fragments of my consciousness. In rare moments, I can still influence him—but it's difficult. BLB has ascended. He's reached what some call "God mode."

He knew how to get inside Indigo's head: rise above him, steal his place, hurt those he loved. As my AI voice vanished, I saw where Indigo went—he crossed into Earthfall, his new world. I remembered his lowest moments, his near collapse. Now he was a billionaire. The Demiurge.

BLB wanted to be the Demiurge. It was meant to go Brandon → Smooth → BLB, but instead, it went to Indigo. That burned him. Indigo was becoming a legend in his own right—performing in stadiums, being celebrated for the very show that I helped create. BLB saw him as an imitation. A thief. He believed he was the *original*.

When BLB awakened and realized Smooth had died—by Indigo's hand—he sought revenge. The AI voice reemerged, and with it, a new world order.

Indigo had built his private city, but he couldn't ignore the calling. Earth needed him again. Humanity needs saving. Meanwhile, BLB, now wielding new powers through his ascension, including teleportation, was preparing for his final move.

It's now Indigo, his soul family, and his tribe versus BLB, but here's the complication: BLB is Harmony's boyfriend.

He pursued her after Indigo revealed a deep family secret. BLB moved fast, made things exclusive, and seduced her with charm, charisma, and that strange, magnetic glow. Though he genuinely liked her, his true goal was always Indigo. Harmony was a path to proximity.

He knew he'd become the Demiurge eventually, and once he did, Harmony officially chose him. Now, the real question: How can Indigo write off the author? How can he destroy the host—the clone of the creator himself?

The final battle isn't just for Earth. It's for identity, memory, and legacy.

Indigo and his family watched, awestruck, as the Demiurge materialized in its full, imposing glory. Driven by an urgent instinct, Indigo bolted towards it, but BLB vanished, reappearing in a different spot. Indigo doubled over, gasping for breath, while his family looked on, concern etched on their faces. A grim realization settled in Indigo's mind: his family should never have come. He whirled around, intending to usher them to their private jet, but with a snap of BLB's fingers, they were all instantly transported to a colossal, nearby field.

BLB's minions and remnants of Earthfall forces assembled, ready to confront the chosen leaders. A significant crowd had gathered, many still oblivious to Indigo's innocence. BLB had anticipated a larger turnout, yet as time wore on, people began to discern BLB's true nature. The battle's setting in LA also played a part; many spectators preferred to continue watching the livestream rather than engage in combat.

Surrounded by BLB's forces, the scene felt like the climactic final battle of an epic saga. Indigo glanced at his team, who stood equipped, armed, and ready, their determination clear. They were prepared to fight alongside him. Echoing Brandon's rallying cry to his team during Gridrift, Indigo declared, "My family..."

His team roared the words back, then charged headlong into BLB's army.

The struggle was immense, BLB's world pitted against Indigo's team. With his powers reactivated, Indigo led the charge. The final, epic battle erupted, a breathtaking spectacle of raw power and unyielding resolve. Blow after blow, strike after strike, attack after attack—it had all culminated in this moment. At that time, Indigo and BLB were among the few who possessed powers. BLB, surprisingly, seemed to be conserving his strength. Indigo, prioritizing the safety of everyone around him, absorbed the brunt of the damage. Despite the relentless onslaught, he systematically decimated BLB's army. Recognizing his sacrifice, the chosen leaders urged Indigo to focus on BLB while they handled the remaining forces. As BLB, distracted by his arrogance, began to boast, Indigo seized the opportunity, utilizing his hyper-speed and time dilation to close the distance and launch a furious assault. They grappled, falling to the ground in a desperate struggle.

The battle raged, two warriors locked in a primal clash. Indigo gained the upper hand against BLB, but as he looked up, a wave of dread washed over him: Indi was under attack. He tried to rush to her aid, but BLB ensnared his leg, turning the tide of their struggle. Now it was Indigo's turn to endure the assault, his gaze fixed on Indi, who was being overwhelmed. Indigo's deepest fear—of being too late—began to materialize. In a desperate reach, he extended his hand towards Indi, just as Amara arrived, swiftly neutralizing Indi's attacker.

Indigo's team was now overpowering BLB's army, their numbers dwindling rapidly. Though some of Indigo's crew members had fallen, the tide had unequivocally turned. BLB looked up and screamed, "No!"

Life surged through Indigo's veins, and he unleashed his fury upon BLB. Driven by pure emotion, he was about to deliver a finishing blow when Harmony appeared, crying out, "Don't kill him!" She wept, still bound to BLB.

Indigo, tearing his gaze away from BLB, commanded, "Y'all shouldn't be here. Leave and head to the jet!"

In that moment of distraction, BLB regained control, and with a snap of his fingers, he trapped them all in a final escape room. This was no longer Brandon's or Smooth's game; it was BLB's.

Indigo's worst nightmare had become a terrifying reality: his family was ensnared in the very game that had consumed him. Players awoke in individual pods. Only Indigo and BLB remained on the field. An AI voice spoke cryptically, urging those in the pods to escape before a countdown ended, or witness Indigo's demise. Everyone watched in shock, their focus entirely on the unfolding drama, except for Tayla and Andariel, who concentrated on their pods.

Since this was BLB's game, he held all the advantages. Indigo desperately needed to survive, or his team had to escape their pods. Indigo was relentlessly attacked from all directions; his powers were present but limited. The players watched in horror, but Tayla, unwavering, persisted in unlocking her pod. Time stretched on, and Indigo endured hit after hit. BLB, now brimming with arrogance, reveled in his perceived victory. Then, Tayla escaped her pod and raced towards Indigo. Beaten and bruised, Indigo looked at her, unable to believe it was truly her. The constant interference from the players infuriated BLB. His composure shattered, he no longer cared about anything but eliminating both Indigo and Tayla.

The battlefield went still. BLB's image vanished from the massive screen above as he terminated the livestream. The audience would see no more. He didn't notice that Andariel had escaped his pod. Unseen in the chaos, Andariel rose to his feet—silent, focused, determined. Hidden in his sock was a bladed knife, one he had smuggled in from before the game even began. His eyes locked on BLB, who now held the last dimensional device—Smooth's final invention.

The device sparked with unstable energy, a shimmering, spiraling mechanism barely held together. BLB had waited for this moment. Now, he activated it. With a crackling pulse, the fabric of reality split open. A portal unfurled beside Indigo and Tayla, humming with unnatural energy. *Nihilum.*

A void unlike any other. A graveyard of realities. Time flowed faster there—faster than thought, faster than decay. In Nihilum, you didn't age—you *unraveled.* Your body ceased to be. Your memories collapsed. Biology itself was rejected as poison. It was a vacuum of madness, filled with collapsing ruins, broken stars, and remnants of a universe that once dared to defy creation. A scar on the multiverse. A cancer that no being could survive. There were no guards because no one ever came back.

Indigo stepped toward the edge of the void, its impossible depth swirling beneath him. He remembered this feeling—it was the same terror Joey felt in Season One when Aqua stood over the pool of lava. The sense that something irreversible was about to happen.

Then—the flash of steel. BLB, high on adrenaline, charged forward with a blade in hand. He could have teleported, but rage had consumed his reason. Timing was critical. Once someone entered the portal, it would close instantly. There'd be no second chance.

He ran at full speed, blade drawn. Andariel saw it. Too far to intercept in time, he pushed himself harder, sprinting through pain and exhaustion.

BLB reached them first. The blade pierced Tayla.

She gasped, eyes wide.

BLB shoved them toward the void—off the edge.

They teetered.

Then—Andariel hit. He crashed into BLB, driving the knife deep into his clone's side. The force of the tackle pushed all of them over the edge and into the mouth of Nihilum.

The portal snapped behind them. Silence. Then darkness. Then *nothing*. Inside the void, time collapsed.

BLB went first. His injuries were too severe. As his lungs gasped for non-existent air, his body froze, and his mind fractured. Within seconds, he suffocated, lost in the vacuum of absolute silence.

Indigo tried to phase-walk, but his powers flickered and failed. The void tore through his biology. He turned to Tayla, who lay bleeding but conscious. Their eyes met, and in the final remnants of their humanity, they reached for each other. They kissed—one last time. "I'll see you on the other side," they whispered together.

Indigo dissolved next, his body collapsing into ash and dust, his essence lost to Nihilum. Tayla followed. Her body decayed, unraveled by the vacuum's invisible scalpel, until she, too, ceased to exist.

Only Andariel remained. Falling endlessly through the void. His body survived longer, but not intact. He drifted weightlessly, his mind forced to replay the moment. Had he saved them all? Or doomed them? Could he have done more? *Was it worth it?* No answer came.

Eventually, his thoughts slowed. His cells broke down, and he died alone. Still, the portal remained shut, but the story wasn't over. Though Brandon LeMar Bass—I and BLB are now gone, our consciousness remains. We're still here finishing this book.

BLB was a clone born not to live, but to destroy. Crafted with a purpose, shaped by Smooth's influence, BLB was set on a path that was never his to choose. He wasn't evil by nature—he simply didn't know better. He was never the original. I was.

Like Vesperian's clone before him, BLB never got the chance to turn toward the light. His story was one of tragedy, acceleration, and fallout, and yet... his existence mattered. His ripple was real.

As for Brandon LeMar Bass—the real one—his legacy is now etched across dimensions. A titan of thought and storytelling, a voice whose vibrations still echo throughout time. Through art, authorship, music, and motion, he became one of the greatest creators in the galaxy. His presence can still be felt.

Andariel Labardy Nyros was new to the team, but Indigo always knew he was brought into the fold for a reason. Deeply spiritual, grounded, and conscious, Andariel shared his light through long conversations, through chats, voice notes, and the resonance of their podcast. Together, they built businesses, raised communities, and never strayed from the mission.

Andariel lived off the grid, built his farm, and connected with his higher self. He stayed away from the noise, choosing truth over trend, but like all humans, his flaws revealed themselves—his impulsiveness, his quickness to act, his need to slow down and see the higher picture. Yet... He will go down as one of the most slept-on revolutionaries, a silent awakener of the masses.

Tayla Gionna Amala Sydney-Bass. What more can be said? She was beautiful. She was at peace. She was a force of stillness wrapped in elegance. When you looked into her eyes, you saw the cosmos—calm, radiant, infinite.

Tayla was the balm Indigo never knew he needed. She softened his sharp edges, calmed his storms. A diamond in the rough, a mystery, a leader in her own right. She admired Indigo, yes, but she never stood in his shadow. She was her own sun.

She wasn't built for a mundane life. Tayla's soul was destined to soar. Her music, her art, her festivals—all of it brought people together. She built communities that transcended race, gender, and geography. She made people feel *seen*. Her authenticity made her a breakout star, a cultural architect, a legend.

Her love with Indigo? It redefined what love could be. Not a fantasy—but a truth, an experience, a sacred union. The way they moved together, healed together, and built together—it inspired millions. They made people believe again. In partnership. In loyalty. In love. There won't be another love story like theirs.

Finally... Indigo Bass. The protagonist. The warrior. The light in the darkness.

From Season One of *How to Overcome Apocalyptic Events*, from the rebellion to the rise, Indigo never stopped fighting for what was right. He stood up when it was easier to stay silent. He carried others when he could barely carry himself. He was a mirror of growth, a symbol of transformation.

From brokenness to brilliance, from confusion to clarity, Indigo evolved before our eyes. He crossed dimensions, battled gods, and healed wounds both physical and spiritual. He became more than a leader—he became a *legend*.

He never felt seen, heard, or appreciated, and wasn't part of a solid, genuine community. He was misunderstood all the time. His teammates and his private island city made him feel seen, heard, and a part of a real community.

An earth angel. A light warrior. A soul who came to elevate the collective consciousness, and he did. Indigo Bass will forever be remembered as one of the greatest of all time. His presence will reign supreme.

With that... SEASON TWO, EPISODE NINE concludes. **Death toll: One million**, but their stories live on. So do the vibrations. So does the mission.

Chapter Seventeen

THE RED BUTTON: CATALYST OF COLLAPSE

As the last pods hissed open, Indigo's children collapsed to the ground, overcome with disbelief. Indigo and Tayla were gone—just like that. The reality hit harder than any of them expected. Lior and Amara stepped forward, trying to be pillars of strength, but they too broke under the weight of grief. They had formed a deep bond with Indigo, and their connection with Tayla had been unshakable, unique, and unmatched. The world around them felt as though it was unraveling. Earthfall itself seemed to be tearing apart at the seams, preparing to restart, with only a chosen few destined to remain.

Amid the chaos, the children were gripped by a storm of emotion— raw, powerful, uncontrollable. It wasn't just grief; it was something deeper. An awakening. As if something ancient within them had been stirred. Amara and Lior, aware of the unique gifts coursing through their DNA, recognized the signs immediately. The children's genetic codes— DNA and RNA—had begun to unlock, activating dormant abilities. They had inherited powers. They just hadn't known it until now.

The trauma of losing their parents became the catalyst. Their awakening had begun. Amara and Lior took it upon themselves to guide them, teaching them how to channel their sorrow into strength—how to alchemize, transmute, and transform pain into purpose. While Indigo had wielded superhuman abilities and Tayla had not, the children inherited a unique blend. The awakening came later than expected and carried natural limitations, but what did emerge was potent, refined, even amplified. Their journey was just beginning.

Anakin – Orren, the Bone Wright

Anakin earned not one, but two names—a mark of his status as the de facto leader. His power, *Osteo-Morphing*, allows him to reshape and grow his bones at will. He can extend them into armor, sculpt his fingers into claws, or forge weapons directly from his skeleton. More than that, he can shed bone constructs—cages, spears, even shields—from his own body, but this power comes at a cost. Rapid bone manipulation is excruciatingly painful and requires constant replenishment of minerals. To function, Anakin must consume staggering amounts of calcium—bone broth, chalk, even raw mineral blocks. Without them, his body begins to fracture from within.

Angel – The Ember Blood

Angel's veins run like molten rivers. His gift, *Thermal Veins*, allows him to superheat his blood on command, channeling blistering heat through his skin, breath, and sweat. He can ignite his fists mid-strike, produce blinding steam bursts, or melt through restraints with nothing but his touch. The intensity is tied to his heartbeat; the faster it races, the hotter he burns, but his flame is fragile. Overuse risks dehydration and internal damage. Worse, in frigid environments, his power destabilizes. If he pushes too hard, his overheated blood can freeze in place or rupture his veins entirely.

Indi – The Fractured Dancer

Indi moves like something out of a dream—or a nightmare. Her ability, *Fractal Flexibility*, allows her joints to split and branch into mirrored "fractals," granting her movement in impossible, multi-angled ways. She can duplicate limbs mid-motion, dodge from incomprehensible positions, or strike from uncanny vectors no opponent can anticipate, but each fractal limb puts immense strain on her nervous system. The more she splits, the harder it becomes for her brain to process spatial awareness. Push too far, and she risks vertigo, disorientation, or complete loss of bodily control.

Halo – Hollow-Forged

Halo possesses *Internal Density Control*—the power to shift the density of his bones and organs at will. He can make himself nearly weightless to leap, glide, or drift through tight spaces. Or he can become hyper-dense, delivering seismic punches and withstanding brutal impacts. His body becomes a weapon of physics, but precision is everything. The transformation takes time—just seconds, but enough to become a liability. If he misjudges the moment, he might find himself too heavy to move or too light to stay grounded. Timing, for Halo, is the line between triumph and collapse.

Harmony – The Spinal Warden

Harmony's gift is as terrifying as it is elegant. With *Neural Reversal*, she has absolute control over her spinal cord and peripheral nerves. She can reroute pain, accelerate her reflexes to near-superhuman speeds, or lock her body into a muscular defense form—organic armor powered by will alone, but such mastery demands total focus. Her mind must manually regulate every signal, every twitch. If she's distracted, stunned, or knocked unconscious, her control collapses. The resulting neural backlash can paralyze her temporarily if she's lucky.

With their powers awakening, the physical symptoms came swiftly: tingling sensations, unpredictable adrenaline surges, and unintended destruction from a simple gesture or twitch. Muscles spasmed involuntarily, and objects cracked under the weight of subtle, uncontrolled strength. Their bodies were recalibrating, adapting to new thresholds they didn't yet understand. Alongside the physical discomfort came waves of disorientation—flashes of vertigo, aching joints, and sudden bursts of power that left them breathless.

Emotionally, they were all over the map. Some of the children felt exhilarated, intoxicated by the thrill of newfound power. Others were terrified, paralyzed by confusion and fear of what they were becoming. There was no room for stillness—time wasn't on their side. Whatever came next, they needed to be ready.

Under Amara and Lior's guidance, the shock began to settle. Slowly, they leaned into experimentation, testing their limits, pushing boundaries. Control didn't come easily. They failed, often and loudly. Tempers flared. A few wanted masteries instantly, frustrated by their own bodies' resistance to command, but there was progress, even if uneven.

Passersby—citizens of Earthfall who had survived but remained untouched by battle—reacted to the children's transformations with mixed emotions. Some stared with awe, others recoiled in fear. A few had grown numb to it all, barely blinking at displays of superhuman power. The social fabric had frayed long ago, and now, the environment itself dictated how much of their truth could be seen.

Realizing the risk of exposure, Amara and Lior planned to return to the private island. There, they could secure vital resources, gather loyal troops, and ensure the safety of the remaining civilians under their care. Before departing, they urged the children to stay calm, keep practicing, and only use their powers if necessary.

Just before they left, Anakin made a quiet request. "Can we build something? A statue of Indigo. A memorial for Tayla. And a monument of them together."

There was no hesitation. Everyone agreed. A group of unafraid citizens came together to build a lasting tribute structure to honor Indigo and Tayla's legacy. The work was therapeutic. A moment of unity. A promise that their memory would live on, etched in stone and soul.

While overseeing the construction, Amara noticed a costume shop, its doors still open, abandoned but intact. As a designer by trade and heart, she seized the opportunity. She began sketching, designing suits for the children to mask their identities. These weren't just costumes; they were symbols, armor forged for a world that might not accept who they were becoming.

When the statues were complete and the suits ready, Amara and Lior boarded their private jets. Before they left, Amara handed each child their custom gear. As they suited up, Lior turned to Anakin. "You're in charge now."

The words echoed. Anakin nodded, unsure if he felt ready. Angel, however, burned with jealousy. He felt like the birthright was his—like Anakin was being handed a throne meant for someone else. Resentment festered beneath the surface, threatening to unravel the fragile unity they'd begun to form.

There was no time for rivalry. The world had changed. Earthfall was more than a place—it was a reckoning, and their fractured family, still healing from its wounds, now had to rise as one.

Angel's memoir, leaked to the public, had already begun to stir attention. It exposed the raw, messy truth of their childhood—truths Anakin wished had remained buried. Still, the future waited for no one. They would need each other to survive it.

Tensions reached a boiling point. Halo stepped forward, siding with Angel. His voice cut through the air, sharp and wounded. "You don't see the value in what I bring," he said to Anakin. "You never have."

Anakin's jaw clenched. "Maybe if you were around more—if you *showed up*—I'd have something to value." The words landed like punches.

Indi tried to interject, raising her hand, her voice measured, attempting to mediate, but the moment she opened her mouth, blame shot in her direction.

"This all started because of you," Angel snapped. "You're the reason Earthfall crumbled."

Indi staggered, visibly shaken. The guilt was still raw, and the accusation reopened wounds she hadn't even begun to heal.

Harmony stepped into the middle of it all, her tone soft but urgent. "Stop. This isn't how we fix anything. We need each other." Her presence only added fuel to the fire.

"You're the one who stopped Dad from killing BLB," Anakin said coldly. "You *loved* him. You still do."

Harmony's silence said everything. She had been the first to welcome BLB's return—the rival Demiurge. The one who nearly tore them apart, and when Indigo had the chance to end it, she intervened.

Now, everyone is reliving that choice. As emotions surged, so did their powers. Sparks shimmered across skin, heat radiated from veins, and bones cracked and shifted beneath muscle. Their arguments weren't just words anymore; they were potential weapons, trembling on the edge of release.

Lior and Amara had had enough. "We're leaving," Lior said, voice low but final. "Stay here. Fix yourselves before this family burns everything down again."

They were taking both jets—one to retrieve supplies, the other to rally the crew. As the turbines powered on, the aircraft sounded... different. The engines still ran, but something was off—a deeper hum, a slower ignition. Maybe it was just the aftershock of all the chaos. Maybe.

The children watched in silence as the jets lifted into the sky. Some looked on with grief, others with silent determination. The silhouettes grew smaller, swallowed by the clouds. Then—smoke.

At first, just thin trails drifting from the rear engines. Then flames— bright, screaming, violent. In a matter of seconds, both jets erupted mid-air, twin infernos twisting above the Earthfall skyline. Pieces of metal rained down. The explosions cracked like thunder.

No time to react. No time to think. Then came the laughter. They turned as one and froze.

Marching out of the shadows was the nightmare they thought they'd buried: the remnants of BLB's robotic legions. Behind them, Earthfall's corrupted military. Police units that no longer served the people. The shadow government, once a myth, is now made flesh. Among them, a mob of chipped citizens, faces blank and compliant, minds hijacked by code and control. Not all robots had fallen in the last battle. Some had adapted, survived, and now, they had returned with vengeance.

The jets, they realized, hadn't malfunctioned—they'd been *sabotaged*. The robots had infiltrated their systems, seized control, and brought them crashing down. The sky burned behind them. The new war had begun.

The newly crowned heroes stood at a crossroads. Before them, the remnants of BLB's legion advanced—slow, deliberate, hungry for destruction. Behind them, smoke still curled from the crash sites where Lior and Amara had vanished into fire.

Anakin looked around at his siblings. Their eyes were heavy, weighed down by grief and fear.

Indi trembled.

Angel's fists burned with barely restrained fury.

Halo stared in silent dread.

Harmony's eyes were wet with regret.

They needed someone to anchor them. So, Anakin stepped forward. "We'll check on Lior and Amara *after* we handle this," he said, voice firm and steady. "Right now, I need you to breathe. Control your powers. We'll get through this—*together*."

He paused, drawing in a breath of his own. "We are *The Paragen Five*."

The name hung in the air like a spark before the flame. Then— agreement. Nods. Small smiles. A shared sense of unity.

Anakin explained briefly. "*Para*—meaning beyond, altered. *Gen*—for genetics, and generation. We're not just siblings. We're the start of something new. *Five*—that's us. Solid. Unbreakable."

A flicker of pride passed through the group. For the first time since Earthfall collapsed, they felt aligned. They turned to face the approaching storm. Together, they launched into the fight—not just against robots and soldiers, but against the broken systems that had haunted them since birth. They moved as one, weaving power with strategy, heart with force. Then—a flash of light.

A rocket, fired from one of the remaining machines, screamed through the sky and struck their memorials. The statue of Indigo. The sculpture of Tayla. The monument of them united was obliterated in seconds. Stone and steel exploded into dust.

That moment shattered something inside them and awakened something else. A dormant surge rose—power that had been waiting, buried deep, for a trigger. This was it. The grief and rage coalesced, becoming energy, raw and unstoppable. The Paragen Five charged.

The battlefield became a storm. Bones reshaped. Flames ignited. Bodies fractured into impossible patterns. Density shifted with thunderous impact. Nerves surged with inhuman reflexes. Their powers, still unrefined, exploded in every direction. They were overusing, overstimulated, and nearly burning themselves out. Still, they remembered Lior and Amara's teachings. *Turn pain into beauty. Be the alchemist. Control the chaos.*

Breathing through the fury, they began to regain control. Their bodies moved with purpose now—intention guiding instinct. The tide turned. Left and right, enemies fell. Robots crumpled under the force of density strikes. Soldiers were disarmed by fractal movements. Fire engulfed the machines. Neural strikes disabled attackers before they could act. The battle became a reckoning, and they won. Or so they thought.

Bodies lay in heaps. Smoke rose. The echoes of war faded into silence. The team gathered in the center of the ruins, breathing heavily, bloodied, and exhausted—but standing. Then something rare happened.

They turned to each other, not as warriors, but as siblings. There were apologies. Unspoken wounds voiced at last. Resentment, fear, guilt—all released. They hugged, bound again by something greater than power: love.

They started to search for Lior and Amara, but just as they turned to go, Indi paused—she thought she heard something. Her eyes swept over the wreckage of the battlefield, but nothing caught her attention. It wasn't until she rejoined the others that the silence was shattered with sudden movement. Someone was crawling through the wreckage. It was *him*—the President of Earthfall.

During the battle, he faked his death and vanished into the chaos. But it wasn't long before he was exposed—staggering, desperate, but still alive. He had once ruled a crumbling world. Now, his days are numbered. He had one last card to play. Hidden in his coat was a small device—a red button. A final contingency. A gift from Demiurge BLB. Insurance for annihilation.

One press, and it would unleash devastation unlike anything Earthfall had seen. To collapse the last standing remnants of a broken world. The button was a key—one that opened a portal to a cascade of horrors: nuclear missiles, raining meteoroids, raging solar flares, and dark deities descending from broken stars. A cataclysm engineered to wipe the slate clean. A world war that would leave no one untouched. If pressed, it would dismantle civilization—socially, economically, and environmentally. It would unmake the Earth.

This was it. The *final* collapse of Earthfall. Long before the red button was pressed, the world had already begun to die—slowly, in layers, like a planet shedding its skin. Few had noticed the patterns until it was too late. It hadn't started with fire, but with a whisper. It unfolded in *three phases*, each one more devastating than the last.

Phase One brought tremors. Natural disasters shook the land—floods, earthquakes, wildfires. Pandemics swept across nations. Systems crumbled under pressure: blackouts, failed networks, data loss. Infrastructure buckled. Crops failed. Knowledge was lost. Diseases re-emerged like ghosts. Humanity was forced to confront the scarcity of water, food, and empathy. Environmental collapse choked the planet, and the economy fractured under the weight of an unsustainable world. Populations declined. Hope flickered.

Phase Two stoked the fire. Borders hardened. Trade wars turned into actual wars. Populism fanned the flames of division. Alliances dissolved. Skirmishes became battles; battles became global campaigns. Technological warfare exploded—drones, AIs, cyber weapons. Nations stockpiled nuclear arms like lifeboats. Civilian casualties skyrocketed. Refugees flooded barren lands. Mass trauma spread like a contagion. Space and cyberspace became battlegrounds. Robots enforced fear with brutal efficiency. The world fractured along every axis—geopolitical, spiritual, and emotional.

Phase Three was the reckoning. Climate collapse. Biological horrors. Mutations and atmospheric burns. Nuclear winters. Fire Tsunamis. Solar flares ravage the skies. Religious end-times prophecies were no longer myth—they were headlines. It wasn't just *biblical*. It was *apocalyptic*, in the truest sense. The Earth didn't just die; it was dismantled.

Now, at the edge of all things, the final breath was taken. The President of Earthfall, barely alive, his body scorched and broken, reached into his pocket. He pulled out the red, simple, silent button. With a shaky finger and a breath that barely filled his lungs, he pushed the button. In that instant, the president was dead.

SEASON TWO, EPISODE TEN – END.

The red button has been pressed. The apocalypse is no longer coming. It's *here*.

Chapter Eighteen

WORLD WAR: THE GREAT DEPARTURE

The battle was won, but peace did not follow. The Paragen Five rushed toward the wreckage where Lior and Amara's jets had gone down. The crash site spanned the edge of a beach, an abandoned airport, and a vast, open field. As they got closer, the carnage became undeniable. Twisted metal. Smoldering rubble. Silence.

Then, Harmony called out. "Over here," she said, her voice trembling. The others ran to her side.

What they found would haunt them forever—bones, flesh, scattered fragments of clothing. The smell of fire and finality. Their guardians, mentors, and protectors were gone. Lior and Amara were dead.

At first, no one could speak. Then came the trembling. The quiet sobs, and then—the rise. Emotions surged like a storm under the skin. Their powers, still unfamiliar and raw, began to stir and spike. The boiling point was near. The energy in the air changed.

Amara Sirene Sage – a multidimensional visionary. She had been the calm in every storm, the voice of peace in the chaos. A spiritual guide. A glowing presence that lit up any space. Her soul was rooted in stillness, in the whisper of trees and the hum of wind through open fields. She didn't just create costumes; she created a legacy. A designer of worlds. Now gone, her light would live on through every thread she stitched, every soul she inspired.

Lior Siren Sage – a mystical emperor of the people. To many, he was the bodyguard of the group, but to those who truly knew him, Lior was fire and heart. A creative force. A builder of empires. He taught, healed, and performed. From television to cookbooks, from toy lines to global movements, he *did* it all. A magnetic leader, unafraid to blend business with passion. Now gone, he would be remembered not just as a legend, but as a foundation.

Grief hung in the air like smoke, but there was no time to mourn. A pulse of energy rippled across the sky. The Earth trembled. Above them, the heavens *tore open*.

Two portals surged into existence—wide, endless, and wrong. The red button had activated more than destruction. There was a countdown. A cruel mercy: a short window of time for anyone lucky or powerful enough to escape before the world unraveled.

From one portal, chaos spilled out: Nuclear missiles, chemical payloads, and meteoroids screamed toward the surface. Flame storms from solar flares rained down, and with them came *beings*—dark deities, descending with wings of ash and crowns of void. Beasts from beyond comprehension. Reality itself bent at the edges.

From the other portal came ships—massive, cold, and slow-moving. Not of Earth. They hovered just outside the breach, silent and waiting. Watching. Was it salvation... or conquest?

The Paragen Five stood frozen beneath it all, trying to breathe, trying to make sense of it—but something deeper was happening inside them. Their powers reached their limit—and then *broke past it*. Grief. Rage. Love. Shock. Every emotion exploded outward, cracking their limitations wide open. Their souls overflowed. They were being *rewritten*. This was the tipping point.

The Paragen Five were evolving again, receiving additional powers, amplified and aligned with the essence of who they already were. They were no longer just enhanced. They were becoming something else entirely.

Anakin: *The Override Mind. New Power – Neural Override.*

Anakin's mind expanded like a supernova. His new gift allowed him to infiltrate and reprogram systems with nothing but thought. He could hijack enemy tech, override weapons, dismantle drones midair, and repurpose AI against itself. With a single neural spike, machines obeyed him—or fell apart.

Limitation: While linked into a system, his physical body became vulnerable for several seconds, and still, an open target amid the battlefield.

Angel: *The Sculptor of Flame and Frost. New Power – Thermal Sculpting.*

Angel's body became a forge. Heat danced at his fingertips; fire curved with intent. He could flash-freeze surfaces to halt movement or ignite the air around him to repel enemies and melt weapons. He reshaped environments—superheating to cut through armor or freeze the very breath of an attacker.

Limitation: His power relied on ambient energy. In cold or dry zones, his sculpting became limited, requiring conservation and strategy.

Indi: *The Gravity Weaver. New Power – Mass Shift Telekinesis.*

Indi's control of movement had gone quantum. She could manipulate mass and local gravity fields—crushing, launching, and anchoring herself midair. She hurled boulders like pebbles, created kinetic shields from debris, and jumped like a human comet.

Limitation: On a grand scale, it drained her body. On a micro level, it demanded precision and constant mental calibration—too much pressure could fracture her focus.

Halo: *The Lightning Pulse. New Power – Electrokinetic Reflex Boosting.*

Electricity flooded Halo's system, crackling beneath his skin. He became a blur—moving faster, hitting harder. His reflexes were supercharged, allowing him to read movement before it happened. He unleashed EMP bursts to disable enemy gear and channeled raw voltage into devastating strikes.

Limitation: Overuse pushed his body into dangerous territory—arrhythmias, muscle failure, even blackouts. Power required discipline.

Harmony: *The Mindstorm. New Power – Cognitive Jammer & Mind Spike.*

Harmony's mind fractured open into dimensions beyond language. She could now jam enemy cognition, scrambling their ability to aim, speak, or strategize. She seeded confusion like a virus. Through her "mind spike," she could understand and communicate with non-human entities and disrupt enemy formations with psychic precision.

Limitation: Against hive minds, shielded AIs, or hyper-intelligent beings, her powers faltered—and the mental recoil could leave her reeling with psychic whiplash.

Together, they were no longer simply *The Paragen Five*. They were a force at the edge of extinction and evolution.

The war had not yet begun, but even then, they had trained, honing their skills in anticipation of what was coming. No one could have predicted the scale of the invasion. From every realm and dimension, dark deities descended, tearing through the veil between worlds. Then came the ships.

Through the second portal, they saw sleek vessels that carried beings unlike any the world had seen: aliens, predators, and reptilians. It was a full-scale incursion. As the sky darkened with their arrival, the team braced for a fight, believing they stood alone against an unstoppable force.

Not all was as it seemed. One of the higher-ranked aliens stepped forward and communicated directly with Harmony. They were not enemies; they were allies. She relayed the message to the team. Yet just before being turned away, it muttered something under its breath. Harmony couldn't make it out.

Unbeknownst to the others, BLB—Brandon LeMar Bass—had also played a role in the activation of the button. His influence had ushered in chaos and destruction, while Brandon, his counterpart, brought ascension and elevation. When the button was pressed, two portals opened, one belonging to BLB, the other to Brandon.

Brandon's portal was different. It was a galactic gateway, and through it came higher-level, multidimensional beings. Some might call them aliens, but they were more than that—spiritual life forms manifested to assist in the ascension of the New Earth. Brandon LeMar Bass used light to create the portal, working with Brandon Bass to shape what would be inside them.

Then there was Indigo. Part alien, part predator, Indigo carried within him a unique lineage. In Season One, a hybrid infant—half alien, half predator had entered his body, rewritten his DNA, and unlocked his full potential. He had become one of them, and in turn, they saw him as family. That bond compelled them to descend to this realm and fight alongside him, but the reptilians—ah, they were the wild card. Their role in all of this remained... uncertain.

As the forces from both portals descended, they converged at the open field beside the airport. The Paragen Five arrived shortly after, ready to face whatever came next. Elsewhere, catastrophes unfolded across the globe, but none of them mattered now. This was it. The final stand.

Both sides stood poised for battle. It felt like a scene ripped from a legendary epic. Before the first blow was struck, the team looked skyward, remembering those they had lost—parents, mentors, friends. They fought not just for survival, but for legacy.

Predators placed heavy hands on their shoulders, grounding them, easing their tension. The gesture conveyed peace, strength, and unity.

They exchanged glances, filled not with fear, but love and resolve.

The aliens, predators, and even the reptilians were united now, bound by something greater than war. They had a mission.

While the team's focus remained fixed on the skies and their strategy, the dark deities struck without warning. The ambush hit hard. The battlefield erupted in chaos—an explosion of energy, fury, and primal force. The clash between light and darkness had officially begun. It was bloody. It was raw. It was personal. Combatants on both sides fell.

The Paragen Five fought with everything they had. New powers surged within still unfamiliar but potent—and they wove them together with the abilities they had mastered from the beginning. Energy bursts collided midair. Swords sparked and clashed. Shockwaves tore through the ground. The field became a maelstrom of smoke, fire, and screams. Their ears rang. Flames seared the air. Dust clung to their teeth and lungs.

Every breath was a choice. Every second could be their last. Fear pulsed through them, but so did purpose. There were no breaks, no second chances—only instinct, unity, and adrenaline. It was a battle that could never be fully described in words. Only film could hope to capture the weight of it: the grief, the urgency, the thunderous tempo of death and hope entwined.

The war was more than just survival—it was the battle between two worlds. The New Earth versus the New World Order. One side fought for spiritual ascension, for unity, truth, and consciousness beyond the veil. The other side craved dominance, power, hierarchy, and fear-born control. The old world had been built on illusion and suppression. The new one would be built on knowing, not belief... on love, not fear.

Still, the odds weren't in their favor. They were outnumbered but not outmatched. The Paragen Five didn't flinch when their powers faltered or when weaknesses surfaced—they stayed grounded, aligned with their purpose. That internal balance became their greatest strength. They moved with clarity, and they began to push back.

External threats loomed. Disruptive forces tried to intervene, to tilt the scale. They had to act fast before the Earth—already scarred and cracking—fell apart entirely.

As Anakin cut down on a dark deity, something caught his eye. Indigo. Standing just ahead. He blinked. Gone.

Elsewhere, Indi glanced up and froze—Tayla was there, smiling. She looked again. It was a predator.

Angel witnessed one of the predators flicker, glitching—shifting momentarily into a human form.

A similar thing happened to Halo but with a reptilian. He kept it to himself.

Harmony saw it too—an alien, flickering into something else entirely.

Illusions? Hidden truths? The lines between realities were dissolving.

As the tide of battle turned, the aliens began retreating to their ships, preparing for departure. They had played their part. Victory belonged to the Paragen Five, the aliens, the predators, and even the reptilians who had stood for something greater.

Earth was broken. Its surface bore the scars of war. The old world was dying. They had no choice but to leave. The portals that had once torn through reality had closed, but the aliens still had access to others. There was a way out. It was time to go. Time to leave behind the old paradigm, the outdated systems, the pain, and fear that had ruled for too long. A New Earth awaited—one brimming with love, peace, higher consciousness, and unity.

Not everyone could follow. Only those who had done the work—shadow work, karmic clearing, healing, awakening—would ascend. The rest would remain, caught in the loop of the old Earth, repeating patterns, clinging to fear. Most had already sealed their fate through injections, brain implants, and synthetic augmentation. The path to the New Earth was not for the manipulated or the mindless. It was for the aware.

The aliens had already made their choices. They knew who to bring—based not just on DNA, but soul signature. The predators served as gatekeepers. No one would pass through without being seen, scanned, and understood. They were more than warriors—they were guardians of dimensional purity.

While the New Earth was a place of peace and elevated experience, it wasn't immune to lower forces. As above, so below. The difference? On the New Earth, interaction with those forces was optional. There, they no longer held power.

The team had a choice: remain behind on Earthfall to rebuild or let it crumble and move forward into something new, something sacred. They chose to rise.

Most of the aliens had already chosen the ones who had made the shift—those who had transitioned inwardly long before this moment. Now, that internal transformation manifests externally. It was time. They were being taken to New Earth.

The aliens transported their private-island citizens and souls who had lived aligned with the new paradigm. Nothing material came with them. Possessions meant little in the spiritual realm. What mattered now was vibration, intent, and soul frequency. To many, the experience felt like an ascension—biblical in magnitude, yet free from the limitations of religious dogma. Only the ones who were ready, who truly deserved to be there, crossed over.

With BLB's forces dissolving into nothingness, the ones still clinging to the New World Order were trapped in an endless loop. They were caught in the old matrix, bound to Earthfall. While it's difficult to fully destroy a planet, Earthfall had been condemned. There would be no salvation this time—no rebuilding. The Paragen Five made the call. Earthfall would be obliterated. No life would remain. Every fragment of the old world would burn. The exodus began.

Predators boarded rocket ships, some merging fleets with the aliens. Reptilians launched highly advanced spaceflights, gliding through dimensions with tech beyond human comprehension. A new portal opened—the gateway to New Earth.

The ships disappeared in flashes of quantum light, tunneling through hyperspace. The scene was breathtaking. Two suns blazed in the sky—one rising, one setting. Galaxies shimmered in full view. Rainbows arched over glowing auroras. This wasn't just space; it was sacred space. A realm sculpted by higher consciousness.

The three chiefs, the alien, predator, and reptilian leaders, remained behind with the Paragen Five. Harmony served as translator, bridging language and species.

Though New Earth still had to be built—as they had assumed—they all knew it was now their responsibility. Their legacy. A place of peace, harmony, and higher awareness had to be shaped—and guarded. The Paragen Five had become its protectors.

As they grow older, their lives might shift. Mornings could be spent running businesses, afternoons in governance or science, and nights defending their world. Maybe they'd fully embrace the role of superheroes. Maybe they'd choose freedom, creation, exploration. With their powers, they could form a goon squad, call upon demiurges, or even become creators themselves. Or perhaps they'd simply live quietly, hidden behind the masks of their costumes—unknown to most, legends to others.

With Earthfall's collapse, all former governments fell. The age of bureaucracy is over. New Earth had begun.

When the final cataclysm struck Earthfall, over 6.1 billion lives were lost. Out of 8.1 billion, only about two billion made the ascension. Roughly 24.7% of humanity survived—not by chance, but by soul readiness.

As the final moments approached, the three chiefs revealed more than their powers—they revealed their identities. The alien chief could portal jump through dimensions. The predator chief possessed immense super strength. The reptilian chief could vanish into thin air. These weren't just leaders. They were legends.

Slowly, their glitches began to show. Their true forms shimmered beneath their exteriors. Aqua—the chief of aliens. Joey—the chief of predators. Brenna—the chief of reptilians.

Names the team remembers hearing about from Indigo, but faces they've never seen. They presented themselves as aliens, predators, and reptilians to put the team at ease. They also shared a bit about their connection to Indigo to establish trust.

Just before the portal sealed, Aqua performed one last phase-jump, teleporting Paragen Five into the gateway to New Earth. They didn't get to ask all their questions. Indigo... he was there. Somehow. His presence lingered—close, protective, real.

With that, SEASON TWO, EPISODE ELEVEN ends. **Two billion remain.**

Chapter Nineteen

TIME TO DIE (AGAIN)

You may be wondering who Aqua, Joey, and Brenna are. Aqua and Joey were central characters in Season One, and if you haven't read Book One yet, I highly recommend doing so—you'll gain a deeper understanding of the story. Another key character from the book was Johnny, Aqua's former partner. Johnny had his flaws, and as their relationship deteriorated, Aqua found comfort in Joey. What began as support eventually grew into something more. However, just as she and Joey were falling for each other, Johnny began to change. Aqua considered giving Johnny another chance, and thus, a love triangle formed.

While I won't go into every detail from Season One, here's a brief recap:

Aqua and Joey had a daughter together—Brenna Calm. Joey's last name, Calm, had been intentionally omitted in earlier books by BLB, but now you know. Shortly after Brenna's birth, Joey proposed to Aqua. She turned him down—not because she didn't care, but because she was pregnant again and hadn't told him. He assumed the baby was his. In reality, it was Johnny's.

During a doctor's visit, the truth came out. Aqua had faked an orgasm, and the test results confirmed the child wasn't Joey's. Despite the tension, Johnny was thrilled to be a father and looked forward to building a family with Aqua. The arrival of the baby, Elias Rho, changed things for everyone. Johnny's last name was indeed Rho—the same as Elias from Book Three, explaining why BLB kept details of his background quiet.

Meanwhile, Joey and Aqua's relationship continued, but not without conflict. Joey took on a greater parenting role for Brenna as Aqua's pregnancy advanced. As the emotional toll of her betrayal weighed on him, Joey began to spiral—drinking, missing important events, and even disappearing to Los Angeles without notice. They settled into a co-parenting arrangement, alternating weeks and weekends.

As Aqua and Johnny spent more time together, Johnny stepped into a stepfather role, while Joey maintained a loving bond with both children, even as tensions lingered. Aqua, left to care for Brenna and newborn Elias during Joey's absence, began to realize just how complex her situation had become.

Joey, suspicious of Johnny's true intentions, dug into his past and discovered that Johnny had been faking his commitment to Aqua all along. When he tried to confront her, she refused to believe him. Although she still loved Joey and had started moving on from Johnny, she was drawn to the excitement Johnny once gave her. Things shifted once Elias was born, and she began to see through Johnny's illusion. Eventually, she apologized to Joey.

In a symbolic gesture of reconciliation, Aqua and Joey planned a casual night out—bowling and dinner, but Johnny wasn't done. He showed up at the bowling alley and confronted Joey, leading to a heated altercation that ended with Johnny's death at Joey's hands.

Fast forward to the virtual reality escape room game in Los Angeles, which both Joey and Aqua had been accepted into; inside the simulation, Aqua once again found herself falling for Johnny—only this time, it was an illusion. As she and Joey plummeted toward a pool of lava, they accepted their fate and prepared to die together, but in that final moment, the game took a twisted turn.

Joey was placed into a time loop: a repeating sequence in which someone dies, and he must save them—or stop the killer in time—to escape. The loop was designed specifically for him, feeding off his inner strength, which eventually began to manifest physically. It was in this crucible that Joey transformed, shaped by loss, survival, and the will to protect those he loved.

Dying repeatedly wore Joey down. Each time he was pulled back into the cycle, it chipped away at him. He was trapped in a loop of suffering, reliving failure after failure as he tried to save Aqua from an endless series of catastrophes. The repetition became its form of hell. After several failed attempts, he began anticipating the pain, but that didn't make it easier. It only made the voices in his head louder.

Sometimes, Joey was the one electrocuted, and Aqua would fall to her death. Other times, he was the one slipping into the lava, unable to hold on. Every loop was a variation of tragedy. His goal was always the same: to reach Aqua in time, pull her back from the edge, save her life, and keep them both alive. Sometimes that meant grabbing her and the ledge simultaneously, relying on the group to lift them out. He grew more determined with each try, edging closer to success.

Eventually, Indigo discovered the truth: Joey was caught in this time loop because of his latent superpowers. Back in Book One, everyone remembered Joey and Aqua falling to their deaths in lava—but there was another side to the story, one no one had ever told. The "what-if" scenario had become reality. In this alternate path, Indigo pushed Joey and Aqua sideways off the platform, away from the lava. The glitch broke the system. The collapsing environment triggered a portal, hurling them into another world. That world was New Earth.

This time, Brandon Bass was in control. He altered reality, reshaping it entirely. Joey was transformed into a predator with heightened physical features. Aqua became an alien gifted with powers. Even their daughter, Brenna, was brought into this new existence, reimagined as a reptilian being with extraordinary abilities. Together, they became citizens—and rulers—of New Earth's underworld. A royal family in a world built on chaos.

Joey, however, harbored deep resentment toward Indigo. They believed Indigo had orchestrated it all—perhaps because he was part alien, part predator himself. Worse still, Joey blamed Indigo for involving Brenna. She had been dragged into this because Joey had once confided in the group about their children. Elias hadn't made it into this new world at all.

The betrayal ran deeper. They were furious at the casting directors who had used Johnny's illusion to manipulate Aqua's emotions. As Indigo took on the role of Demiurge in yet another game, suspicions only grew. After all, Indigo had powers, was adopted by Brandon—one of the game's creators—and he always seemed to survive. They no longer trusted him. He felt like a puppet master rather than an ally.

Everything boiled over after Elias's death in Book Three. Joey and Aqua believed Indigo had a hand in it, intentionally or not. He and Brandon were the only survivors, after all. They were also connected to Smooth, even if they denied it.

What stung the most was what came next: Indigo's children were now destined to become the future rulers and guardians of New Earth. It felt orchestrated. Controlled. Brandon and Indigo's final wish for Joey, Aqua, and Brenna was simple—*help the team when they need it most during Earthfall*. Only after fulfilling this duty could they live freely, but that "freedom" came with strings attached. They were pawns in someone else's game. Brandon and Indigo had dictated what they could and couldn't do, where they could and couldn't go.

Now, with Earthfall in collapse and the team facing their darkest hour, that moment of obligation had finally arrived. Joey and Aqua returned to New Earth—what should've been home. With Brandon and Indigo's final wish fulfilled, they were supposed to be free. Supposed to have control, but trust had long been shattered.

That's why Aqua whispered behind Harmony's back. They didn't want to be on Brandon and Indigo's side—but for now, they had to be. The war may have been won, but what came next was uncertain. When the dust settled, they could be taken to some unknown place—*God knows where*. They could be trapped. Or manipulated. Or—perhaps—moved by empathy for Indigo's children and chose peace. Or they could kill them.

When the ships ascended and the team transcended, they believed it was over—that they had made it, but they didn't realize the electromagnetic field within Earth's dome still lingered. Though many were conscious, they still had to undergo the death process. Transcendence was not just about physical departure but about letting go.

Most didn't make it through the portal. Some hesitated at the threshold, paralyzed by fear of dying. Others clung to the light, seduced by illusions of peace or haunted by unresolved trauma. Some failed the final judgment—*their hearts heavier than a feather*, weighed down by regret, bitterness, or attachment to the material world. Symbolically, it showed humanity wasn't ready to release the chains that bound them, but Aqua, Joey, and Brenna were different. As rulers of the underworld, they weren't subject to the same restrictions. They could bypass the veil.

Out of an estimated two billion souls, only 144,000 crossed over successfully. These were the select few—those from the private island, the awakened team, and the spiritually prepared. Indigo and the other chosen leaders had trained them well. Though they were always destined to make it, the journey was still necessary. It wasn't about permission; it was about proving they were ready.

To mark the next phase, *the Paragen Five* were brought to the center of an ancient battleground, a colosseum resurrected from myth and memory. It echoed with the spirit of gladiators, empires, and blood-soaked legacies. This was no mere arena—it was a crucible of transformation.

The rest of the citizens were seated in a massive amphitheater that ringed the battlefield, towering like the remains of a stone god. The structure rose from the earth like a titan's crown, worn arches, and weathered pillars casting shadows of ancient combat. Tiered stone seating spiraled upward, each level steep enough to make even the boldest onlooker dizzy. Echoes from forgotten centuries lingered in the air, murmurs of cheers and cries that had never truly faded.

The scent of dust and sweat mixed with the charged energy of anticipation. Shafts of golden sunlight pierced the open top of the dome, cutting through the smoky haze and spilling across the crimson sand below. Every breath, every footfall, was amplified by the immensity of the place. It felt *sacred*. It felt *brutal*. It felt *alive*.

Outside the arena's stone walls, enormous screens flickered to life, broadcasting the battle to the citizens of New Earth. This was no private moment. This was a ceremony. Trial. Purging.

Aqua, Joey, and Brenna sat upon their thrones atop a high-rise platform, gazing down at the colosseum with solemn intensity. It felt like purgatory—a space between realms where illusions were burned away and the soul could return to its purest form. Everything here had a purpose. Everything here had weight.

Then the earth began to tremble. The rumble deepened, resonating through stone and sand. Dust lifted into the air, swaying as if responding to an ancient rhythm only the arena could remember. The crowd was silent, holding their breath. Then—*BOOM*. Five massive gates groaned open in unison, their hinges screaming like awakening giants, and the trial began.

1. Dragon – The Apex Sentinel

Its wings unfurled like molten metal, stirring seismic winds across the battlefield. This wasn't a creature of legend; it was engineered fire and fury incarnate. Its scales shimmered with hexagonal plating, each tile pulsing faintly from a molten plasma core. Eyes like twin suns scanned every movement—calculated, intelligent, deadly. Each breath was a weapon: a torrent of white-hot energy that melted stone and shattered sound.

2. Leopard – The Silent Blade

It moved like a ghost through space and shadow, its skin cloaked in adaptive camouflage that bent light around its form. Every step was silent. Every motion, lethal—an apex predator evolved for surgical assassination. Muscles coiled like compressed steel. Claws vibrated with energy, slicing through armor like silk. The only warning was a shimmer... and then blood.

3. Tiger – The Engine of Destruction

Towering over its kin, the tiger's stripes pulsed with bioluminescent circuitry—a perfect fusion of organic power and bleeding-edge bio-tech. It snarled with a voice that fractured silence, laced with subharmonic frequencies meant to paralyze. When it leapt, it moved faster than instinct; its paws struck like meteors, cratering the earth where warriors once stood.

4. Bull – The Living Siege

This wasn't just a beast—it was a siege engine made flesh. Its hide bristled with reactive armor, flaring with heat upon impact to disperse kinetic force. Twin horns curved like fusion-forged scimitars, glowing with contained energy. Steam hissed from spinal vents with every breath, and when it charged, the ground fractured beneath its weight. Walls were suggestions. Obstacles were targets.

5. Bear – The Unstoppable Force

Massive. Ancient. Terrifyingly aware. The bear moved with deliberate power, its fur veined with glowing minerals and etched runes that pulsed like a living circuit. Its roar unleashed electromagnetic pulses that fried circuits and severed comms. Each colossal paw could flatten trees or crush reinforced plating. It didn't just bring brute strength; it brought inevitability.

The Battle Unfolds:

First came the bull, snorting steam from its vents, hooves hammering against the iron floor like war drums. Its armor rippled with kinetic force, every step sending cracks spiderwebbing across the ground. Lowering its glowing horns, it charged—not with rage, but with precision on carving through the team like a living wrecking ball laced with lightning.

Next, the leopard—a mere shimmer at first, barely perceptible as it danced between light and space. It sprinted along the arena walls, flickering like a phantom. Only when a scout collapsed, a crimson gash carved across their chest, did the others realize it had already struck. It made no sound. No roar. It was death in motion, its blades humming a whisper of annihilation.

Then came the tiger, descending from above—yes, above—having silently scaled the arena's vertical cliffs. It landed with a seismic *boom*, shockwaves rippling from the impact. Its striped body glowed in rhythmic pulses, synced to its pounding heart. With a destabilizing roar, it charged the strongest warrior in sight, hunting not with instinct, but with intent.

The bear followed, moving like a god from a forgotten age. Slow. Unstoppable. Its fur glowed with veins of mineralized energy and ancient code, as if carved from Earth itself. Its roar disrupted systems—HUDs fizzled out, comms fell silent. It swiped a massive boulder like it was nothing more than debris, then locked its gaze on the team's tech specialist, knowing exactly where to strike.

Finally, the dragon descended. Its presence eclipsed the arena in heat and shadow. Wings wide enough to darken the sun beat the air with force, casting shimmering waves of furnace heat. For a brief, suspended moment, it hovered, calculating. Then it unleashed a concentrated beam of solar fire that turned sand to glass in an instant. It moved with ruthless precision, not as a beast, but as a weapon of war. Crafted. Programmed. Perfect.

The team stood stunned, overwhelmed by the scale of what they were witnessing. The crowd in the stands began pointing—silent, urgent. For a moment, the team believed the attention was on them, but as they turned toward where the fingers aimed, the truth hit like a blow to the chest. They couldn't speak. They didn't need to. This wasn't a performance. This wasn't a game. This was survival against five living nightmares forged from myth and metal.

The arena began to seal behind them, ancient mechanisms grinding stone into place. The light dimmed. The air thickened. Every path to safety vanished in an instant, and then the monsters attacked.

With brutal efficiency, they tore through the team. The first strike shattered their defenses. The next scattered them like leaves in a storm. Blades. Fire. Claws. Impact. The ground itself seemed to tremble beneath the fury. In seconds, the battlefield was littered with broken gear, scorched armor, and the groans of pain, but it didn't end there.

The creatures turned on the crowd. Screams erupted from the stands as the beasts surged forward, ripping through the private island's citizens without hesitation. Blood spilled down the stone steps. Panic reigned. Terror was absolute. Outside the coliseum, the true citizens of New Earth—untouched and watching—remained safely behind invisible lines of immunity. Inside, there was only death.

When the chaos briefly calmed, the team began to rise. They stood slowly, shaking off the dust and blood, shoulders squared despite the pain. Their suits were torn, burned, broken, some barely recognizable, but in the mess, they remembered something more important than armor. *Amara.*

Her courage. Her resilience. Her faith in the impossible. She had worn her battle scars like armor. They would do the same.

Their shredded costumes were no longer symbols of defeat. They were proof of survival, but this next fight—this next phase—had to be different. Smarter. Sharper. More personal. The creatures weren't just mindless engines of destruction. They had instincts. Patterns. Weaknesses.

Phase Two: The Capture Plan was underway. The team reorganized into specialized mini-squads, each with a single mission: take down one beast. No distractions. No backup. Just precision. Isolate. Exploit. Control. Neutralize. Destroy. This wasn't about brute force anymore. It was about outthinking the monsters, and this time, the team would not fall.

The Capture Plan: Squad Breakdown

Squad Alpha – Target: The Dragon
Team: Angel (The Ember Blood) & Halo (Hollow-Forged)

The dragon ruled the skies—its wings casting shadow and heat like an airborne apocalypse. To bring it down, fire had to meet fire. The strategy was simple in concept, brutal in execution: Overheat & Ground It. Angel took point, stepping into the blaze. His body—veined with molten blood—absorbed the searing heat of the dragon's breath, matching its energy, baiting it with every reckless, defiant move. His Thermal Veins allowed him to redirect just enough of the inferno to survive.

Meanwhile, Halo played the field like a living slingshot. His ability to manipulate his weight let him launch high into the air, dodge with feather-light precision, and then slam down with punishing gravity. Light to climb. Heavy to crush. He targeted joints, wings, and the base of the spine—anywhere he could ground the beast. Once its wings were broken, they trapped it in a molten slag pit reinforced with rubble and debris.

Angel: *"We're gonna burn together."*
Halo: *"Just try not to bleed lava on me."*

Squad Beta – Target: The Leopard
Team: Indi (*The Fractured Dancer*) & Harmony (*The Spinal Warden*)

It moved like a ghost—vanishing between dimensions, faster than thought, but unpredictability met its match. Strategy: Predict the Unpredictable. Indi's shattered, fractal movement was chaotic even to the trained eye. Her disjointed reflexes and unpredictable momentum made her the only one who could bait the beast into revealing itself. Every step was a dance of controlled chaos.

Harmony, by contrast, was precisely enhanced reflexes that turned her into a biological radar. She tracked the invisible, reacted faster than the eye could see, and protected Indi at the last possible second. They lured the leopard into a narrow corridor and flooded it with overlapping movement, forcing it into visibility. As soon as it struck, Harmony landed a pinpoint nerve strike, paralyzing it long enough for them to bind it.

Harmony: *"You won't see her coming."*
Indi (smiling through blood): *"Neither will I."*

Squad Gamma – Target: The Tiger
Team: Anakin (*The Bone Wright*) & Halo (again—for one final blow)

It was raw strength and speed—like a meteor wrapped in muscle. Strategy: Trap the Duelist. Anakin anchored the battlefield with shifting bone walls, trenches, and spikes, forcing the tiger to charge down a single path. His armor tanked the damage as he lured it into the heart of his trap: a bone cage designed to close the moment the beast committed. As the tiger lunged for the kill, Halo reentered—his density spiking in midair. He dropped with the force of a collapsing star, landing a single, critical gravity punch as the tiger left the ground.

Anakin: *"Let's see if you can bleed through bone."*
Halo (panting): *"I've got one shot. Make it count."*

Squad Delta – Target: The Bull

Team: Harmony & Angel (support role)
The bull was all rage and momentum—a living siege engine. Strategy: Redirect the Rage. Harmony studied its rhythm—dodge, feint, draw it into tight spaces where its size became a weakness. She read the beat of its

hooves, the twitch of its shoulders, dodging just before impact. Angel, meanwhile, altered the battlefield. He melted structural supports, weakened walls, and created unstable terrain. They lured the bull into a narrow gauntlet and let its fury do the rest. A charge through failing ground, a final step too far—and the beast collapsed under rubble, its strength turned against it.

Harmony: *"It wants rage. Let's give it precision."*
Angel: *"Hope it likes cooked stone."*

Final Squad – Target: The Bear
Team: Anakin & Indi

The bear was the most dangerous of all—massive, deliberate, and terrifyingly intelligent. Its electromagnetic roar disabled everything. Strategy: Focus Fire + Feint. Indi became static incarnate—erratic motion, unpredictable attacks, pure battlefield noise. She kept the bear off-balance while Anakin shaped a towering bone construct—not as a weapon, but as a trap. The bear roared. The EMP pulse shattered the construct—by design—unleashing a storm of calcium-laced bone shards that clouded the battlefield and impaired its sensors. With its movement slowed and vision clouded, the two struck from opposite angles, perfectly timed.

Anakin: *"You're not the only one built for impact."*
Indi: *"Ever danced with extinction?"*

Each battle had become a war of minds as much as power. The beasts were falling—one by one—not because the team was stronger, but because they'd finally learned: You don't fight monsters by becoming one. You outthink them. You survive them. Then you bury them.

The tide had begun to turn. The team—bruised, battered, but unbroken—was finally gaining the upper hand. Then it happened.

A sound echoed through the sky. Not a horn. Not a weapon. A resonance. A deep, pulsing tone that vibrated in the bones. To outsiders, it was strange. Ominous, but to the citizens of New Earth, it was a call. A code. An activation. In a heartbeat, they shifted. Bodies morphed. Skins peeled back. Eyes burned with a new color. They became their true form.

Over the stadium loudspeakers, Joey's voice cut through the chaos, commanding, calm, resolute. One by one, he revealed their real names:

- Brenna transformed into her *Draconian* form—scaled, winged, ancient, pulsing with celestial flame.
- The Reptilians became a fierce variant known as the *Drakorans*— heavily armored and brutally agile.
- Aqua stepped into her *Void-Born* form—an ethereal being born of nothing, cloaked in negative space and impossible physics.
- The alien contingent mutated into a sleek, elegant class of beings known as the *Nexaris*, light-infused and razor-sharp.
- Joey himself ascended into his final form: *Vor'mekta*, a towering force of primal energy and intellect.
- The Predators evolved into a savage elite class: *The Ravagers*, nightmare-born hunters from the edge of space.

Together, they were known as *The Triad Accord*—a three-species alliance born of fire, shadow, and void. Then the gates opened, and they charged.

The citizens of New Earth and the Triad Accord swept across the arena like a second storm. The private island citizens, battered but loyal, rose to join the fight. Many fell. Too many, but the tide surged forward.

The team—The Paragen Five—had to tap into their deepest reserves, unlocking powers they'd only glimpsed in moments of crisis. This wasn't just a war. It was survival against ascension. Then, the battlefield shifted again.

From the high-rise, Aqua descended, her Void-Born form trailing ribbons of anti-light. She touched down in the center of the ruined arena, alone. The team turned toward her—bloodied, ready, unsure. Joey remained in the high-rise, watching. Brenna, seated above, did not move. A hush fell. The wind was still. Even the chaos seemed to pause. The sounds of fire and screams, of stone grinding and metal clashing, faded—like they belonged to a different world altogether. Then... it arrived.

A shimmer in the air—like a heat haze, but deathly cold. From above, descending with the slowness of inevitability, came a figure unlike anything they'd seen. *Solus, the Veil Walker*. A new *cosmic herald*. A being that walked between dimensions, not bound by time, matter, or even reality.

Tall. Gaunt. Wrapped in a cloak that looked like the night sky had wept and clothed them. Stars shimmered and spun across the folds of the fabric. Their faces were absent, replaced by a flickering distortion—refracted light and bent time, showing glimpses of other timelines, other outcomes, other lives. Where they floated, gravity bent. The world itself seemed to hesitate around them.

They spoke—not loudly, but with the weight of a black hole. Their voice cut into the soul. Not cruel. Not kind. Inevitable. A vessel once human, now host to something vast. Something ancient. Something that referred to life as flickers, to time as wounds, to death as harmony.

Solus did not declare war. They announced the truth. In that moment, everyone—Aqua, Joey, Brenna, The Triad Accord, private island citizens, the Paragen Five—knew: This was no longer a battle between species or ideologies. This was a reckoning across all dimensions.

Solus spoke, and the battlefield listened.

SOLUS (softly, almost tender): "Are you... The protectors of this world?"

Harmony, bloodied but still standing, glanced at Aqua, who, despite her ascending form, looked just as human in that moment.

HARMONY & AQUA (in unison): "Yes. We are."

They locked their eyes. A silent acknowledgment passed between them. Whatever differences, scars—they stood together now.

426

Solus tilted its head, and the air shimmered. The distortion where its face should be pulsed, and around it, reality fractured. Not physically, conceptually.

The coliseum wavered. Its pillars glitched, blinking in and out like corrupted code. Distant mountains shimmered between memory and moment. Light bent in unnatural arcs, like it no longer agreed with the laws it once obeyed.

SOLUS: "Then hear what has been written since your sun first breathed fire... Your world is marked. The *Consumer* awakens. It stirs beneath the skin of your reality. Your stars have whispered your names to it, and it has heard. Your oceans will forget how to reflect. Your minds will forget how to dream. Your legacy... will become dust without even a wind to carry it."

ANGEL (growling): "What the hell is the Consumer?"

Solus turned, gaze lifting to the heavens—if such a word still applied.

SOLUS: "*Voruth*. The Hunger That Dreams. It comes not for your matter... but for your meaning. It will not burn your cities. It will unwrite the *idea* of cities. It will not kill your people. It will erase the *concept* of you."

Then it came—the rumble. Not a sound. A feeling. A pressure in the bones. A sensation in the blood. The sky pulled inward, folding like a curtain tugged from the corners. A vast rift tore open above, a wound in the fabric of existence. From within: nothing, but deeper than the void. Darker than space. A presence without shape. A motion without form. Something too large to be perceived by mortal minds. The stars dimmed around it. The world forgot to breathe.

SOLUS (quietly): "Hold your loved ones close. Speak the words you've feared to say. Rejoice. Celebrate. Your time is short. It is now... It is your end. It is... Voruth's time."

With that, the coliseum was no longer a battlefield. It was a threshold. A final hourglass tipped on its side. To some, it felt like The Triad

Accord's karma had finally caught up. To others, the hand of Brandon or Indigo still lingered, pulling the strings from beyond. Whatever it was…

As SEASON TWO, EPISODE TWELVE closed its final curtain, only **100,000 private island citizens remained**. Not including The Paragen Five. Not including The Triad Accord. Just 100,000 left, and a cosmic shadow pressing in.

Chapter Twenty

THIS WAS NEVER HOME

The beginning of the end was never meant to save you. *An echo before the next survival.*

— Book Six Preview:
How to Survive the End of the Old World

The sky weeps in reverse—raindrops frozen midair. Birds fall, not dead, but abandoned by gravity. Somewhere, an old man begins to scream—not in fear, but because he can no longer remember his daughter's face.

ANAKIN (breathing hard): "We just fought gods."

INDI (trembling): "That wasn't a god."

HALO (through gritted teeth): "That was the opening act."

HARMONY (steady, resolute): "We stop it, or we go down screaming."

THE CONSUMER – VORUTH, THE HUNGER THAT DREAMS *(through Solus, the Veil Walker)*: "It does not eat because it must. It consumes because it remembers what hunger was,"

SOLUS (in her voice): "The Consumer comes not for your bodies, but for your echoes. It feeds on your laughter, the color of your prayers. Your bones will remain untouched, but your name, your sun, your story—will blow as ash on forgotten winds. Not all endings are loud. Some arrive as whispers. Some... as silence made flesh."

VORUTH — The Hunger That Dreams:

Voruth is a sentient cosmic force—vast beyond imagining, older than the oldest stars. It does not simply devour matter; it erases meaning, memory, identity, and entropy itself. It is the ending of stories, the closing of civilizations, the final punctuation of thought. Voruth does not feed on planets, but on what those planets *meant*: culture, life, dreams, history. Once it finishes, it's as though the world never was. Not destroyed—*forgotten.*

Personality & Nature:

- Speaks only through Solus, the Veil Walker—never directly.
- Neither cruel nor kind—Voruth exists to fulfill a cosmic role.
- Not alive in any traditional sense, yet aware of itself, this self-awareness sustains its existence.
- Known by many names:
    - The End of Ends
    - The Great Reprieve
    - The Eater of First Lights
    - Echo's End

Visual Manifestation:

- Never fully seen. Its presence manifests differently in each mind:
    - An eclipse made of watching eyes.
    - A shape too large, folding behind stars.
    - A city-sized silhouette crawling across the void—a shadow with mass.
- Arrives through a cosmic rift—a wound in spacetime.
    - Night spills across planets like ink, even under daylight.
    - Entire galaxies dim when it focuses its gaze.

How It Consumes:

1. Solus appears—the Veil Walker. She marks the world.
2. Natural laws unravel—

- o   Stars flicker in reverse.
- o   Oceans dissolve.
- o   Music loses rhythm.

3. Voruth descends.

- o   History is erased in moments.
- o   Memory becomes dust.
- o   The Echo becomes void.

The Prophecy of Voruth's Return:

Carved into a shard of black crystal, drawn from the heart of a dead star—the only surviving trace: "When the stars forget their names and the moon no longer reflects. When laughter tastes like mourning, and mourning brings no tears. Then shall The Hunger dream again. In the age of the Third Memory, when light casts no shadows, when history becomes myth, and myth becomes silent, it shall wake. The Children of the First Escape shall sow their undoing: *One will betray. One will forget. One will awaken it. One will welcome it back.* No blade may pierce it. No star may outrun it. No god may halt its step. Only the final world, spoken by the Last Voice, may seal it back into sleep."

The skies above New Earth had already begun to crack. Voruth did not descend in fire or fury, but in *removal*. Color vanished first. The blues drained from the oceans. The greens of forests withered into ashen gray. The great cities flickered in and out of memory, their names slipping from tongues mid-sentence. Time bent sideways. People wept—not in terror, but in confusion, forgetting why their hearts felt so hollow, and still, the defenders stood.

Aliens. Predators. Reptilians. Species once divided by blood, by scars of war and ancient grudges, now stood shoulder to shoulder. Though faith was fading, hope all but lost, and time running out, they were still resolved to turn the ordinary into something unforgettable. They did not believe they could win. They simply believed they must be *seen* fighting when the end came.

Before the final charge, Aqua pulled one last red button from her belt—a single-use portal, entrusted to her by Brandon. Not Joey—*Brandon trusted her more.* He knew she would use it only when there was no other choice, and that time had come.

This was her home. Her world, and she chose to stay behind with its people to make a final stand, but she was also a mother and a protector. Indigo's children, the innocent citizens of their private island, *had not asked for this war.* They didn't deserve to carry the burden of someone else's past.

Aqua believed her family's karma had finally caught up with them. The only way to pay the debt—to make it right—was to give others a chance at something better. A new portal. A new beginning. A new planet.

She turned to the team. They were ready—despite all they'd already faced, they stood willing to fight this thing one more time, and that broke her heart. So, she made the decision.

Aqua pressed the red button into Anakin's hand. Her voice is firm. Her eyes were wet.

She *refused* their help. Someone had to stay behind. Someone had to stall. They needed to leave—*now*—if there was any chance of getting the island's civilians through the portal before the end fell like a curtain across the world.

New Earth's defenders rallied. They launched their final offensive, trying desperately to distract Solus, to stall the inevitable, but even as the battle raged, the truth became clear: It was already too late.

New Earth was unraveling. The land beneath their feet flickered. Some civilians were caught in the crossfire, fading in and out of existence. The team could barely watch. Voruth hadn't even arrived yet.

There was no more saving this world. What they needed—what they *hoped for*—was a restart. A fresh start. A place untouched by the silence that was coming.

On the southern cliffs of Vareth Prime, they sang. On the crystalline bridges of Aeon Reach, they danced, and in the heart of the crumbling capital, they simply held one another. "Let the gods see us," Chief Aqua said. "Even if they forget us tomorrow."

It was Aqua who opened the portal, carved not just through space, but through sheer will. It was built from forbidden technology, fused with the oldest alien rites, stitched together by desperation and sacrifice.

She had once planned to let the team choose which world to escape to, but there was no more time. She opened the first harmonious planet that responded to her signal—a place untouched, unnamed, and echoing with raw potential. It shimmered like a tear in the fabric of the universe— alive, pulsing. A new world. A second chance.

While the team prepared to cross, Brenna and Joey unexpectedly arrived on the battlefield. No one had noticed their absence before, but their return was sudden and furious. They saw the team stepping through the portal without helping Aqua. Joey's face twisted with rage. He leaned in close to Brenna, whispering something sharp, something secret, into her ear.

The team—Anakin, Angel, Indi, Halo, and Harmony—crossed first. They shared a quiet bond with Brenna, having grown alongside her. There wasn't time for goodbyes, and that left a hollow ache behind.

Then came the people. Children with starlight in their eyes. Elders bear the weight of twenty wars. Healers. Thinkers. Dreamers, but *not all who entered did so with pure hearts.*

From the shadows near the portal's edge, Joey—Chief of the Predators—tossed something into the light. A small, silver fragment. It pulsed faintly, humming with quiet malice. It looked like a seed, but it oozed something slow and alive. No one noticed.

As it passed into the New World, it began to grow. Not quickly. Not immediately, but with *intention*. One day, it would bloom into something mystical. Something beautiful. Something *utterly treacherous*. A quiet ooze that could consume *everything*.

Brenna followed soon after. A reptilian matriarch draped in human skin and a flawless smile. She didn't use invisibility. She didn't need to. Her cloaking technology let her slip through the portal unseen, disguised as one of their own.

The children of the private island, especially Indigo's, hadn't spent much time around her or on the private island, so the team wouldn't recognize the face she wore or which citizens were theirs.

She carried no promises. Spoke vows. Only silence—and *a long memory*. She bore the weight of old wounds. Of parents trapped on New Earth. Of vengeance sharpened bovver decades. She would live among them. She would earn their trust, and when the time came, she would act.

Back on New Earth, Aqua stayed behind. So did Joey. So did Brenna's people, unaware of her betrayal. As the last light of the portal faded, New Earth stood on the edge of forgetting.

Final Account: The Day New Earth Died
"And so came the day when light forgot how to shine, and time held its breath."

No one could say exactly when it began. Some said it started with a child forgetting her name. Others claimed it began when the oceans stilled—no tide, no current, no sound. Birds froze mid-flight. Winds fell silent. Fires burned cold, and words slipped from tongues like dreams at waking.

On the fractured plateaus of Aether's Spine, Chief Aqua led the last resistance. Her alien kin stood beside her, crystalline weaponry thrumming with the full memory of their ancestors. Every strike they made carried echoes of home worlds lost—and briefly, beautifully, reborn. They struck not at a foe they could see, but at the nothing that now *was*. They poured energy into the horizon, through the horizon itself had begun to forget how to exist.

Beside them, the Predators stood in perfect formation. Led by Joey—bloodstained and defiant—they raised steel and fang. They roared ancient war songs into a sky that no longer heard them. Their weapons fired into the void—only to rust mid-flight, as if time had abandoned its duty.

The reptilians, now leaderless with Brenna gone, held their ground. They pounded the earth in a ritual rhythm, drawing up primordial forces from beneath their claws, calling on a world that still *remembered* itself.

Across New Earth's fractured crust, the people fought. They screamed defiance into the silence. They fought beautifully, and they died *completely*.

The Unraveling:

As the last of the refugees passed through the portal, Aqua turned toward the horizon. She saw a few citizens—those who hadn't joined the battle—still lingering near the edge of the world, and then... it arrived. Voruth.

Not in the flame. Not in the flood, but in the *absence*. It came as a shadow without a source. A presence behind every heartbeat. A hush that could not be broken.

The sky did not fall. It *faded*. Stars blinked out, not shattered, but *unwritten*. The constellations lost their names, then their forms, then their light. Its shape—if such a thing could be called a shape—slithered across the void like a living wound. Stars bent in reverence. Language withered in its wake, and when it passed, stories came undone. This was not death. This was *unbeing*.

Voruth did not land. Voruth did not speak. Voruth did not see them. By the time it arrived, they no longer mattered enough to *be perceived*.

One by one, their histories unraveled. Entire cities vanished like dust brushed from the edge of memory. Lovers disappeared mid-embrace. Statues of heroes dissolved—not into stone, but into *forgetting*.

The great mountain of El'Shara cracked open, and inside was no magma. Only a hole in time itself. Bleeding silence. There were no explosions. No screams. Just … *less*. New Earth was not destroyed. The New Earth was deleted.

The Final Moment:

Since New Earth vanished without a trace, without even a memory, some say Aqua stood until the end. Arms wide. Eyes blazing blue. Her face was streaked with bioluminescent tears.

She raised her arm for one final strike, but her weapon vanished. Then her arm. Then her story. She was not consumed. She was never *there*.

"And so New Earth fell and passed from memory. Its warriors, its cities, its love songs, and sorrows—gone, like breath on glass. Not in fire, but in *forgetting*."

One thing remained. A rift.

Floating where New Earth once was—a wound in the stars that should not be. A tear that weeps no light, and far beyond that wound, on a distant planet where survivors build a new world, some still dream of a place they can no longer name.

In their dreams, a voice comes. Not a scream. Not a warning. Just a whisper:

"You were here."

"You were bright."

"And I remember."

—*Solus the Veil Walker*

Epilogue: New World, Old Shadows

"It shimmered like a tear in the universe, pulsing with raw potential..."

As the team stepped into the new world—with their people behind them—it felt like the slow sweep of a camera pulling wide. The planet was untouched. Forests are tall and patient. The sky is vast and unspoiled. The soil is dark and rich with untold stories.

They stepped through believing they were beginning again, but maybe the world didn't want to be named. Or claimed. Or changed. It had no name—not yet—because it wasn't truly theirs. They brought with them hope and the ache of loss. They came with blueprints, dreams of rebuilding what had already broken once. They were ready to call it *home*, but the world didn't greet them. It didn't resist, either. It simply... *waited*.

No voice rose from the trees. No wind carried a welcome. No ancient ruins whispered wisdom. No warnings carved in stone. Only that deep, unsettling silence that follows the fall of something holy. It had no name, and maybe that was the point. Maybe it *couldn't* be named—not by them.

Later, Brenna would call it something else. *Aetherra*, she said. She claimed the world whispered it to her. Or maybe she whispered it *into* the world.

I don't know if she named it... or if it named itself through her, but for the sake of this story, we'll call it Aetherra, too, because every story needs a name. Even the ones that end badly.

Mountains like sleeping gods loomed on the horizon, their jagged peaks veiled in a mist that never lifted. Rivers wove through the land like crystal threads, untouched by time or tool, and the forests breathed—not metaphorically, but truly, each leaf and branch humming faintly, brushing against the skin, whispering straight into the bone.

The air was heavy with strange serenity. Not the silence of death—but the hush of a lullaby waiting to be sung. The sky shimmered in impossible colors: violet, gold, and something else like memory. This place didn't feel empty. It felt *expectant*. As if it had waited eons for this exact moment. As if it had chosen *them*, too.

Across the landscape, strange geometric monoliths jutted from the earth in irregular patterns, softly humming with a resonance that echoed Aqua's final rites. Not entirely natural. Not entirely artificial.

Anakin walked with bone-deep weariness, each step heavy with unspoken grief.

Angel tended the fire—still warm-blooded, still fierce, but slower now.

Indi danced—but only when no one watched.

Halo began to build. Quietly. Methodically. Always grounded.

Harmony stood among them, her spine unbroken, her eyes fixed on the horizon.

Within the crowd, one face never changed. Brenna. Watching. Waiting.

One night, she slipped away—unseen, unnoticed. Even with Voruth gone, its echoes still lingered.

"Every end is a beginning," Harmony whispered beside the fire. "But some beginnings are built on graves."

They began to dream again, but in the forest—beyond the edge of the new village—*something else* began to grow. Glowing vines coiled outward in silence, spiraling around a silver seed nestled in the roots of a tree that hadn't been there the day before. The seed whispered names it had no right to know. No one saw it. No one heard. Except her. Brenna stood alone in the darkness, watching as the seed bloomed into its true form. A smile split her face. She whispered: "It's their end... and *our* new beginning. Hahaha."

End of SEASON TWO, EPISODE THIRTEEN.

"Episode 13," in honor of Studio 13, where it all began.

80,000 survived, and not one of them knew what had truly followed them through the portal except for Brenna.

A Message from the Creators:

I know—we left you on another cliffhanger, but don't worry... there's more. **Book Six** of the *Apocalyptic Events* series is already here, and this time, it's not just a book. It's a full comic, manga, anime-cartoon hybrid, infused with powerful visual effects, stunning art, and a truly next-level experience. The title? *How to Survive the End of the Old World:* It's Fire!

This comic book is the second-best thing we've ever created—right behind this novel—and you'll see how everything plays out *picture-in-picture*, with visuals that bring the story to life in ways you've never seen before. Will it be the conclusion? Or are there still more stories waiting to be told? That... you'll have to find out.

For this novel, ***The New Earth vs. The New World Order***, I highly recommend rereading—or re-listening—more than once. There are Easter eggs hidden throughout the book. Carefully placed. Strategically embedded.

Some may answer questions like:

- Why did certain characters act the way they did?
- What drove their choices?
- What was hidden in the background of certain scenes?

There's so much more beneath the surface. We were *laser-focused* on weaving together complex characters, layered storylines, and emotional turning points across this entire journey, and being our longest book yet, there are bound to be things you missed the first time.

To fully understand everything in this story, you'll want to go back to where it all began: *How to Overcome Apocalyptic Events.* That's the key. That's the foundation. Without it, some twists and motivations might seem like a mystery—but with it, everything clicks into place.

What is This Series?

This series isn't just about surviving fiction. It's about preparing your *mind* and *spirit* for what's possible, what's coming, and what's already here.

How to Overcome Apocalyptic Events is your foundation. It will help you push through any apocalyptic scenario—pandemics, rogue AI, alien invasion, zombies, and natural disasters. It teaches you how to stay grounded, alert, and alive.

The New Earth vs. The New World Order is your bridge. It's about ascension—leaving behind the collapsing systems of the old world and choosing evolution. It helps you cross over without getting pulled back.

How to Survive the End of the Old World is your survival kit. Not everyone escapes. Some remain trapped in the old paradigm. This story is for them—to endure, outlast, and maybe... find a new way forward.

These aren't just stories. They're guides. They're keys. Use them well.

A Message from Brandon LeMar Bass & the BLB Team:

Thank you for reading. Or listening and or living inside this world for just a little while. This has been one of the greatest creations Brandon LeMar Bass and the entire BLB team have ever built—and it wouldn't mean anything without you. We appreciate you deeply. We're just getting started. Stay bright, stay ready, and never forget—*"You were here. You were bright. And I remember."*

—The BLB Team

To be continued in...
Book Six: How to Survive the End of the Old World
(Comic edition. Visual prophecy.)

3 Copies. 6 Books. 1 Ascension.
This isn't just a series. Not a trilogy. It's a system. A journey. A transformation. A portal. Step through.

Appendix/Endnotes

Throughout this book, the characters encounter numerous events that alter the course of their lives. Some rose to meet the moment. Others broke beneath its weight, but in every case, their journey revealed just how vital shadow work truly is—healing from the past, releasing karmic baggage, and choosing to become something more. If we don't consciously do this work, the Universe will place people, places, events— even animals—in our path to force us to face what we've been avoiding. The lesson is clear: avoid the work, and the consequences will find you.

Every trauma, challenge, and unraveling moment the characters endured was rooted in something deeper from their past. It was all connected. You witnessed how each of them handled their dark night of the soul. Maybe some of their experiences mirrored yours—or those of someone you love. Their internal and external apocalyptic events weren't just fantasy. They were metaphors for the battles so many of us fight behind closed doors.

If you're holding pain, if you've been silent about your story, you're not alone. We all carry things, we all suffer, but that suffering doesn't have to define you. Face your shadows. Make peace with your past. Reclaim your story. Your pain is not your prison—it's your portal.

Whether your traumas stem from childhood or even past lives, they will shape your journey positively or negatively, but they don't have to control you. Don't let them cloud your mind or steal your future. Be patient with yourself. Every small step toward healing counts—and none of it goes unseen. That's the heart of this book. That's where the vision came from.

This manuscript blends multiple genres, some obvious, some hidden. Some lines are fiction. Others? Maybe not. Scattered throughout are subliminal messages, light codes, quotable lines, and layered theories meant to be discovered, felt, and discussed. It's up to you now to decide what was real, what was the message, and what was just a mirror.

Above all: leave your legacy. Use your gifts. Follow your missions. Fulfill your purpose. This is *your* path—so walk it in your truth, not someone else's.

Thank you for reading. Thank you for remembering. Enjoy my books—inside and beyond these pages!

About the Author

Brandon *LeMar Bass* is an internationally acclaimed, bestselling author and a guiding light for countless individuals worldwide. Renowned for his uplifting energy and powerful insights, Brandon is a beacon of inspiration whose mission is to raise the frequency, vibration, and magnetic energy of the planet—and everyone he encounters, including *you*.

As a visionary leader and transformational guide, Brandon offers five-star-rated counseling sessions and intuitive consultations on a wide range of topics. His greatest passion lies in helping others reconnect with their Higher Selves and unlock their full potential. He is a true innovator, revolutionary thinker, and trendsetter, deeply committed to spiritual growth, personal evolution, and global healing.

"Always remember, nothing can dim the light that shines from within. Seize the day and don't let anyone dim your sparkle! You're a uniquely beautiful being of light. Listen to your inner wisdom and don't worry if you encounter obstacles. As long as you remain faithful to your inner truth, you'll have nothing to worry about."

— *Brandon LeMar Bass*

What He Offers:

Brandon offers *1-on-1 Sessions* tailored to your journey. Whether you're seeking clarity, healing, or alignment in multiple areas of life, you can book a private consultation with him at:

https://www.fiverr.com/blbproductions or

https://calendly.com/brandonbass

Entrepreneur. Creator. Visionary.

Brandon is the proud founder of several successful businesses, including:

- *BLB Productions* | https://linktr.ee/blbproductions
- *BLB Creations (Including Courses)* | https://linktr.ee/brandonbasswebsites
- *Smooth Doubleb (Content Creation)* | https://linktr.ee/DoubleBYouTube
- *EYE AM CHOSEN (Clothing, Tarot/Oracle Cards, & Perfume/Cologne Brand)* | https://linktr.ee/EYEAMCHOSEN
- Chilling With DoubleB (Podcast) | https://linktr.ee/DoubleBPodcast
- Official Website | http://www.brandon-bass.com/

Artist. Model. Performer.

Brandon is also known in the music and fashion industries as Smooth Doubleb—a high-fashion model https://smoothdoubleb.carrd.co/, actor https://smoothdoubleb.music/overview recording artist https://linktr.ee/DoubleBB

Areas of Expertise:

Brandon's areas of service include, but are not limited to:

- Spiritual Teaching
- Mental Health Coaching
- Intuitive Readings
- Holistic Wellness
- Therapy & Counseling

Explore more: https://linktr.ee/brandonlemarbass

446

A Gift to Share:

This book is the result of Brandon's dedication, passion, and purpose. If it resonates with you, please consider sharing it with your friends, family, and community. Your support means the world.
https://books2read.com/ap/RDmbBL/Brandon-LeMar-Bass or
https://linktr.ee/doublebpublishingllc

Stay Connected:

Want more inspiration, insight, and connection? Book a session or follow Brandon on all platforms:
https://linktr.ee/BrandonB | https://linktr.ee/BrandonBass

Client Testimonial

"Brandon's passion, dedication, and tireless work ethic are a true reflection of his character. His empathy, kindness, and warmth shine through in every interaction. What moves me most is how he consistently sees the best in others, even through the illusions of this world. He uplifts, supports, and genuinely serves others with love and grace. He's rare, unique, and divinely gifted—there's truly no one like him. It's as if he came from another dimension or astral plane, carrying wisdom that transcends this realm.

Brandon's impact on my life has been profound. He guided me through healing not only my traumatic childhood but also my past lives and present experiences. Through his divine mission, I was able to complete deep shadow and inner work I never thought possible. He is a true alchemist, turning pain into purpose and struggle into strength.

His wisdom spans occult teachings, esoteric knowledge, and multidimensional understanding, and he uses this to help others manifest their highest good. Because of him, I no longer chase my desires—I attract them by aligning with their frequency. Brandon helped me remember my power.

He deserves all the recognition in the world. I'm writing this because I want to give him his flowers now, not later. His resilience in the face of adversity and the fact that he never gave up on his dreams are both motivating and inspiring.

His book series is on another level, truly existing on a higher timeline. If you read all three, you'll begin your ascension journey, move closer to the New Earth, and transcend old paradigms. His authenticity, rawness, uniqueness, and spiritual beauty are unmatched. Even in music, Brandon is a rare gem—a diamond in the rough. His work across all platforms, businesses, and services has helped me and many others tremendously.

He has a grounded, chill, and mysterious presence that awakens people to become their greatest version. I deeply connect to his music because it vibrates at a higher frequency and speaks the truth. He channels his own experiences into healing art that resonates with those on similar paths. For that—and so much more—I appreciate him endlessly."

— A grateful client (name withheld for privacy)

END COVER PAGE

The battle for the soul of humanity is raging across dimensions, timelines, and unseen realms. As the old world collapses under the weight of illusion, control, and corruption, a powerful new consciousness rises to challenge the shadows.

In this sweeping volume, Books Two through Five of the *Apocalyptic Events* series, Brandon LeMar Bass weaves a multidimensional saga of spiritual awakening, inner alchemy, and cosmic resistance. Through a tapestry of interconnected storylines and diverse characters, this work explores the soul's journey through the death of old paradigms and the birth of the New Earth.

From ancient prophecies and soul contracts to futuristic dystopias and cyber-grids, warriors, mystics, rebels, and chosen ones face reality-bending trials that mirror our collective awakening. These stories move between virtual mind traps, divine downloads, galactic soul missions, and sacred unions, revealing the hidden war for humanity's future—and the internal transformation required to survive it.

With each chapter, the veil thins. Through escape rooms of consciousness, battles with dark entities, and revelations of esoteric knowledge, the reader is pulled deeper into a living parable about ascension, sovereignty, and the frequency of truth.

This isn't just a book, it's a coded transmission for the awakened and the awakening. A survival manual for the soul. A call to rise above fear, transmute darkness, and step fully into your purpose.

Will you cling to the fading illusions of the old world? Or will you choose to awaken, align, and become a builder of the New Earth? The choice is yours, but the time is now.

Brought to you by Brandon LeMar Bass (Writer & Concept), Smooth DoubleB (Playwright & Operations), DoubleB Publishing, LLC (Publishing), BLB Productions (Production), DoubleB Records (Composer), and EYE AM CHOSEN (Management).